The day Elvis met Nixon, December 21, 1970.

Author's Note

This book is a novel, a work of fiction. References to real people, events, films, songs, establishments, organizations, or locales are intended only to provide a sense of authenticity and are used fictitiously. The characters, dialogue, incidents and events are either the product of the author's imagination or are used fictitiously and are not construed to be real. Any resemblance to actual events or persons, living or dead, is entirely fictitious or coincidental.

Any patents or trademarks referred to in this novel are the sole property of their respective patent and trademark holders.

Cover design by Joe Burke, Joanne Blunt and Jess Kensington.

www.howhollywoodkilledjfk.com

"There are three things in life which are real -
God, human folly, and laughter.
Since the first two are beyond our comprehension,
We must do what we can with the third."
-John F. Kennedy

"The goddam movies. They can ruin you. I'm not kidding."
-<u>The Catcher In The Rye</u>

"<u>Hooray for Hollywood!</u>"
-songwriter Johnny Mercer, 1937

HOW HOLLYWOOD KILLED JFK©™

STARRING ELVIS PRESLEY

JOHN WAYNE AND FRANK SINATRA

A Twisted, Tinseltown Tale of Power, Greed & Revenge

Joe Burke

For the last American originals,
who made entertainment history,
Mr. Moresco, who made history entertaining,
& for "Fitzy."

FORWARD

At 12:30 PM on the hot afternoon of November 22, 1963, President John Fitzgerald Kennedy was shot and killed while sitting in the back seat of a midnight blue, suicide-door, custom-made, 1961 Lincoln Continental convertible during a parade in Dallas, Texas.

And yet, the same question has plagued us for generations ...

Who killed JFK?

Today, the answer to that question lies before you.

After having exhaustively and painstakingly researched the details of the assassination of President John F. Kennedy for over thirty years, and after having met and gotten to know "Fitzy," I have come to the following conclusion ... Hollywood Killed JFK.

The facts of the tale, indeed, take us west ... to the land where dreams come true - Hollywood, California ...

- Joseph Burke, November 2, 2010

THE TIMELINE

Late January- Early March, 1958   Elvis Presley films and records the song soundtrack for his fourth motion picture, *King Creole*, about a young, talented singer who is blackmailed by his evil, plotting manager.

March 24, 1958   Elvis Presley is inducted into the U.S. Army at the Memphis Draft Board and is assigned serial number 53310761.

March 28, 1958   Private Elvis Presley arrives at Fort Hood, Texas for basic training and is stationed there for six months.

June 10, 1958   While on military leave, Elvis holds a recording session, his last until 1960.

July 2, 1958   *King Creole* opens nationally and the reviews are the best Elvis will ever have for his acting. It becomes a top film at the box office. The movie, originally intended for the late James Dean, is set in New Orleans and is based upon the Harold Robbins novel, *A Stone for Danny Fisher*. It will come to be regarded as Elvis' finest film, his greatest acting performance, and proof positive of his potential to become a respected serious actor.[1]

August 8, 1958   Gladys Presley, Elvis' beloved mother, is hospitalized with acute hepatitis. Threatening to go AWOL if not given leave immediately, Elvis is granted emergency leave and arrives in Memphis on the afternoon of August 12th. She dies in the early hours of August 14 at age 46. Her body lies in state at the Presley home, Graceland, for four days. Elvis is devastated.

September 19, 1958   Elvis sails to Germany, arriving on October 1.

He will be stationed in Friedberg for 18 months, eventually maintaining an off-base residence in Bad Nauheim, Germany, shared with his father and grandmother, and some friends from Memphis.

March 3, 1960 Elvis returns home to the United States, officially completing his Army military service.

October 24, 1960 John Wayne's *The Alamo* is released in theaters.

November 8, 1960 JFK narrowly defeats Richard Milhous Nixon in presidential race.

October 24, 1962 Frank Sinatra's *The Manchurian Candidate* is released in theaters.

November 22, 1963 President John F. Kennedy is assassinated in Dallas, Texas.

THE PLAYERS

Elvis Aron Presley – American singer-actor, born to Vernon and Gladys Love Presley. Served in US Army 1958-1960

Colonel Tom Parker – Born Andreas Cornelis van Kuijk in Holland before illegally immigrating to the United States, dishonorably discharged from US Army, later became Elvis Presley's manager

Francis Albert 'Frank' Sinatra – American singer-actor

Joseph P. Kennedy Sr. – American businessman, diplomat, and father of American President John Fitzgerald Kennedy

John 'Duke' Wayne – American actor, best known for war films and westerns

Richard Milhous Nixon – World War II veteran, Congressman and Senator from California, 37th President of the United States

Ian Fleming – Former British intelligence officer, Author of the 'James Bond' novels

John Fitzgerald Kennedy – Son of Joseph P. Kennedy, World War II veteran, Congressman and Senator from Massachusetts, 35th President of the United States

Bebe Rebozo – Florida banker of Cuban decent, confidante of Richard Milhous Nixon

James "Jimmy" Stewart – American actor, World War II veteran, Brigadier General in the United States Army

Ed Sullivan – Newspaper gossip columnist and television variety show emcee

Ann-Margret – Swedish-born American actress-singer-dancer

Howard Robard Hughes – American aviator-inventor-billionaire-recluse

The late **Marilyn Monroe** – American model-actress-singer

And a cast of thousands …

Elvis Presley, December 21, 1970.

DECEMBER 19, 1970

"It's me," Elvis said.

"Where are you," asked Fitzy, who was house-sitting Elvis' place back in Hollywood.

"Love Field airport in Dallas, Texas," Elvis answered, nervous, paranoid, his fingers tapping his hip.

"Now, tell me, is there anyone with you, Elvis?" asked Fitzy, in his thick Irish brogue.

"Nobody," said The King, adding that he was on his way to Los Angeles and wanted Fitzy to pick him up at LAX.

Now, Elvis never did anything alone. He always wanted at least five guys around him just to watch a football game on TV. So Fitzy was understandably concerned, and all the more so when Elvis told him his own flight number and arrival time, which for Elvis was like the President driving his own car.

"What happened," asked Fitzy.

Elvis told Fitzy how he had been home at Graceland and that his wife and father and The Colonel were yelling at him and cussing him out over how he spent his money.

"So I just up and left, man. I'm just tired of it. And then I landed here in Dallas on a layover. Got me to thinkin' about Kennedy. 'Bout what happened. I wanna tell you all about it when I see you. Just meet me at the airport."

Fitzy raced to LAX airport and waited for Elvis to arrive.

Inside Fitzy's car, a 1966 powder blue Ford Mustang, with no bags in hand, and continuing even after they got back to Elvis' place, Elvis told Fitzy the story. The whole story. Most of which Fitzy already secretly knew. When Elvis finished, he said that he was leaving for Washington, D.C. in the morning to go see President Nixon. Before he left the house, Elvis took his commemorative World War II Colt 45 revolver off the wall, bullets included, and stowed it in his bag.

When he left, Elvis was wearing tight-fitting dark purple velvet pants, a white silky shirt with a very high collar, his chest exposed, a dark purple velvet cape, a gold chain and medallion, and heavy silver-plated amber-tinted designer sunglasses with his initials "EP" built into the nose bridge. Around his waist was a heavy metal belt with a huge four-inch by six-inch gold buckle.

As Fitzy bade him farewell and wished him luck, he remained concerned for his friend, but he wasn't surprised. Not much surprised Fitzy. Not anymore, anyway. He had learned that men, people, had to do what they had to do. Live their own life. So he just waved him off, silently, with a silent prayer that he would be okay.

Once airborne, Elvis asked the stewardess for some stationery, which she got for him. He then met some men who were returning home from Vietnam, to whom he gave every penny of his pocket money. Five hundred dollars in cash. Then Elvis, who had only written maybe three letters in his entire life, all while stationed with the Army in Germany, started to write his fourth to the 37th President of the United States, Richard Milhous Nixon ...

Dear Mr. President,

First I would like to introduce myself. I am Elvis Presley ...

When he finished the letter, as the plane's engines hummed, as he leaned back in his seat, still thinking about The Colonel and Love

Field and Kennedy and Nixon and his whole crazy life and career and his time in the Army in Germany, and his mother, Gladys Love Presley, his best friend. The thirty-four year-old Elvis Presley looked out his airplane window, and again remembered one of the worst days of his life …

I made a deal that day with the devil himself … Daddy never stood up for me that day … Daddy. Daddy, Daddy … how will I ever be free? It's like I'm in prison …

Granted Emergency Leave from the Army to attend his dear mother's funeral, Elvis had been so distraught that he had thrown himself atop the coffin as it was being lowered into the ground. It had taken four of his friends to physically recover him and restrain him afterwards. He had been inconsolable. Weeping. Overcome with grief that was so deep and unrelenting it came out of him in currents.

His father, Vernon, was drunk as usual. Not too drunk but just enough to be numb. Just stupid. The rest of the Presley cousins and other relatives, had been stone drunk. Dead dunk. Night and day, the whole week.

The Colonel had been doing his best to both falsely console and manipulate the two of them at the same time. He had the new representation and percentage contracts right there in his back pocket, the same place he hoped to have the Presley's within the next few moments, now that Gladys was out of the picture.

Within a few minutes, all three were seated at the kitchen table, the place where The Colonel always closed the deals. Get 'em into the kitchen, he always knew. Then ask politely, 'Ma'am, may I trouble you for a glass of water?' People feel comfortable at their own kitchen table, knew The Colonel, makes them feel like they're in charge a little.

He placed the contracts face up at Vernon and put a ballpoint pen on top. And he waited. The Colonel knew another thing too: The man who talks first loses every time. Vernon talked. "Son, this is all happening too fast." He rubbed his faced hard with his wrist. Elvis braced his thighs and looked down at the contracts, then at his daddy, then at the contracts again. He hadn't read them. It didn't even occur to him to. Mama had always done that for him. Now it was finally up to Vernon to come through for him, for the family, and do the right thing, and act like a man, for once.

"You better give me something, Dad. You better give me something," pleaded Elvis quietly. Vernon Presley had fear in his eyes. He was babbling, "Son who's gonna take care of us? Who's gonna pick us some greens? Who's gonna feed them chickens ..."

The Colonel waited an appropriate length of time.

And then a little more.

Now.

"Mr. Presley, Sir," began The Colonel, softly at first, "This is the opportunity of a lifetime." He turned to Elvis and rested his hand on the bare forearm, just below the edge of Elvis' Sunday-best short-sleeved shirt. "Son, with the plans I have for you, why, you and your daddy'll be able to take care of your whole family, in high style, for the rest of your days, aunts, uncles, cousins, cats, dogs ... long after I'm dead and gone, that's for sure." There was one trace of honesty in the words too, as The Colonel had already had the first heart-attack, he knew his next one would probably be the last.

A minute passed. Vernon's eyes were vacant, lost.

Even though Elvis was legally an adult, he always deferred any matters of business, or 'numbers,' to his elders. "Daddy ... answer him," Elvis whispered. "Aren't you gonna stand up for me?" Suddenly Elvis screamed. "Daddy?!" He leapt at Vernon, The Colonel intercepted Elvis atop the table and held him, lowering him into his chair. "Stop it! Boy, now just stop it! What? You wanna kill your own father ..." The Colonel looked at Elvis but played to Vernon. "On the day he's just laid his dear wife to rest ..."

15

Elvis loosened his thin necktie and began to stand, wriggling his long arms loose by their sides. He looked quickly at The Colonel, then Vernon, and moved a few steps towards the door, looking back at them both once more, and then rushed from the house, the screen door hitting the house hard behind him. Vernon sat frozen, passive.

Elvis slowly climbed into one of his four brand new Cadillac's and with every once of energy he turned the ignition. He sat and stared at the custom dashboard radio, and then turned it on. The announcer's voice said, *"... and coming up now another request, one of Mister Jimmy Van Heusen's best featuring The Voice himself ... here's Mister Crooner, Frank Sinatra with - 'The Tender Trap' ..."*

Inside the house, Vernon picked up the ballpoint pen.

Inside the Caddy, Sinatra's voice became increasingly louder and louder with each verse that vibrated through Elvis' custom speakers. Sinatra sang about how it was too late to get out because now you're married and the deed is done and you're trapped forever and ever and ever ...

Elvis looked up at the new big house he called Graceland. The house he bought for mama. She won't be here no more, he thought. Mama isn't here no more. Who's gonna help me fall asleep at night? Mama, she ain't gonna be there no more. Mama, how'm I gonna fall asleep at night?! Mama!! Oh mama! Elvis was in agony, down to his core. His very soul and being. He couldn't describe it this way if he tried, but his loss was truly felt in his bones. He looked at the big house and then remembered the smaller one they had come from.

"That man ruins everything he touches, I can sense it," Elvis could see his mama say. *"He's no good. I know people, and I have a feelin' in my body about that man and it is not a good one!"*

And then quieter, more tenderly, Elvis thought he heard Sinatra sing ...

"... And you're trapped - with - himmmmmm ..."

ACT I
THE BACKSTORY

*A*ccording to history books, at the end of World War II in 1945, defeated Nazi Germany was divided into four zones occupied by the United States, Great Britain, France, and the USSR.

In 1949, the three western zones became West Germany, and the Eastern Zone became East Germany, and Berlin, the former capital, which was divided into East Berlin and West Berlin. Eventually, the political 'Iron Curtain' dividing the former Germany was physically divided by barbed wire and concrete by the Soviets, as they built the Berlin Wall.

Although it was technically 'peacetime' in the late 1940's and throughout the 1950's, the 'Cold War' between the United States and the Soviet Union was at this time tense. And the steadily growing antagonism in the area ensured that a continuing American military presence in West Germany was deemed to be vital and necessary.

This was the climate, political and otherwise, when newly discharged and recently promoted 'Sergeant' Elvis Presley returned home from Germany to the United States after serving his country for two years in the United States Army.

MARCH, 1960.

A band played 'Auld Lang Syne' in the midst of a late winter northeast blizzard as Elvis exited the Fort Dix, New Jersey barracks paymasters office with his final government-issued check in hand, smiling handsomely. He walked towards the throngs of newsmen, newsreel photographers and popping flashbulbs and fireworks, as the heavy, cold snow pelted his Class-A uniform dress blues. Overhead, a huge hand-painted sign read 'Welcome Home Elvis!' Elvis smiled and greeted the crowd. He was finally back home on American soil.

"Man, it sure feels good to be …" he sighed softly, as if to himself, looking around and shaking his head as if it were all a dream.

Movie star handsome, lean and chiseled, Elvis appeared happy for the early morning fans and cameras, but privately, he was nervous and a bit afraid. Some onlookers even noticed a trace of sadness. His beloved mother Gladys gone, it was a different, empty home he had returned to in a rapidly changing, and aging, America. He had no one to turn to for guidance, and he knew that from this point onward he was wholly dependent upon his manager, The Colonel, like it or not. And he knew that The Colonel knew it too.

Just then, out from behind a color guard carrying a huge American flag, like a clown out of a cannon emerged Elvis' portly, obnoxious, controlling manager, Colonel Tom Parker, dressed informally in an open short-sleeved tan sports shirt (like an oversized bowling shirt), and an old pair of brown shoes. The fat man may as well have been wearing track shoes though, considering the speed with which he rushed to get beside 'his boy.'

"… And don't forget my commission," growled Colonel Parker, loud enough for all to hear. An embarrassed Elvis smiled broadly and dutifully handed over the $109.54 government check. The Colonel briefly inspected the pair of marksmanship medals that hung

18

over Elvis' breast pocket, as he folded the commission check twice, and tucked it deep into his front pants pocket, under his keys.

Elvis noticed a handful of military brass saluting The Colonel. The Colonel, without removing his customary white, ten-gallon cowboy hat, returned the salute, as if he were a veteran himself. In fact, nothing could have been further from the truth. Parker, few knew, after illegally entering the United States from Holland at the age of twenty, had as a young man quickly become a wide-eyed and willing protégé of renowned circus mogul P.T. Barnum. From Barnum, Parker learned everything about promotion: How to build a product image and how to maintain it, selling it over and over again to the solvent and unsuspecting masses. At the root of Parker's drive and ambition was one primal want: Money. If there was money to be made, Parker would make it. All he needed was the right product. Back in 1955, he had found that salable product. A young, talented, mama's boy by the name of Elvis Aron Presley.[2]

A newsman extended a microphone to Elvis, "Welcome home, Elvis. How do you feel?"

"Tired," Elvis replied. The newsman laughed and shook Elvis' hand. *What I really feel like is a cartoon character, with this here circus around me. Shoot, I feel like Captain Marvel.*

Army MP's closed ranks as six teenage girls attempted to break through the tumultuous, cheering crowd. Elvis noticed them and smiled as he stopped to say hello, reaching into his carrying case and pulling out six autographed photos, one for each girl. "Say cheeeeese," prodded the Colonel, as the cameramen clicked away. Elvis shot them his best lazy, lopsided grin.

With Elvis closely in tow, The Colonel's bulk then created a

---

[2] Soon after his arrival in the U.S., van Kuijk changed his name to Tom Parker and entered the U.S. Army. Shortly into his second tour of duty, Pfc. Parker deserted his unit, suffered a nervous breakdown, spent four months in Walter Reed Army Hospital, and was discharged for reasons of 'Psychosis, Psychogenic Depression, acute, on basis of Constitutional Psychopathic State, Emotional Instability.'

broad path past six Military Police officers as he hustled Elvis into a black chauffeur-driven limousine just off the tarmac. Holding the door open from inside, The Colonel put his other arm around his 'boy' to allow the photographers a few parting shots. A well-known photographer for *Life* magazine and his assistant positioned themselves to take a quick photo of Elvis for an upcoming *Life* cover. The Colonel recognized the photographer and moved quickly, and as his bulk barred Elvis from their view, he said loudly, "You don't think I'm gonna let you put my boy on the cover without us getting paid for it, do you?!"

"For *Life* magazine … $25,000!!!" bellowed The Colonel as he squeezed into the back seat behind Elvis and pulled the door shut as the limo pulled away.

"Okay, you can take off your hat now, son," said The Colonel without looking at him.

Two years since leaving civilian life, seventeen months since he was last on American soil – while on special emergency leave to attend his mother's funeral - twenty-five year-old Elvis removed his dress hat and leaned back in his seat, casting a backward glance at the forty-car motorcade of reporters, photographers, and fans that fell in behind them on the snow-covered highway. In a way he felt like a foreigner now, like he didn't belong.

Elvis drummed his fingers nervously against the limo's velvet upholstery. All he wanted to do is go back to Graceland and sleep. See his daddy. And go to the cemetery to see his mama. As the parade of cars moved along, The Colonel and his sole client sat quietly, awkwardly.

"Hello, son. How are ya feelin'?" tried The Colonel. "You ready to get back to work?"

"I just wanna get home, Colonel. No more parades. No more three-ring circuses for a while, okay?" Checking the throng of cameras slowly disappearing behind them in the side-view mirror, The Colonel said under his breath, "Right, boy, right."

The Colonel was thoughtfully conniving. "Son, we've been busy these last few months. I can't tell you ..." Elvis thought quickly about his daddy, wondering why he wasn't here too. *Prob'ly back home in his sittin' chair with a glass of hootch in his hand, he decided, sadly.* He looked out the car window vaguely at nothing in particular. "Two years ..." he sighed. "Haven't sang on stage in two years. Two years wasted, gone ..."

"What is the matter with you, boy?" snapped The Colonel. "I've gone to a good deal of trouble to arrange the parade for you and so forth, more motion pitchas ..."

Elvis threw his head back against the seat cushion. "Colonel, I just got back ... a parade?!"

The Colonel paused and added with bullshit feeling, "Elvis, son, just because your parents ... your daddy, and the entire country for that matter, happen to be proud of you ... and your dearly departed momma, rest her saintly soul. Why I bet she's awful proud of you too, up there in ..."

Elvis glared at The Colonel and quietly but forcefully interrupted, "Colonel, I'm tired. Just get me home to Graceland ..."

"Tired?" He paused. "I take care of everything while you're gone. For two years I've been planning this. Keep your name in the magazines. Keep the fan clubs happy. You know I want nothing for myself, you know that my entire life is devoted to helping you ... and your pappy." Elvis waved the back of his hand at him, motioning for him to stop the nonsense. "Colonel ..."

"... your whole family ..." said The Colonel, looking away.

Elvis rolled his eyes and whispered, "Colonel. Same 'ol Colonel ..."

The Colonel turned back, agitated. "You'll do as I say, son. You'll do it for your mother and your father and your country and you'll do it for me. Because since I've been in this country I learned one thing. My job is to keep him happy. And by him I mean The Man.

21

The more He's happy the less He bothers me and the better I run My business! And My business is You. Everything is going according to plan, just like I promised you it would. So stick to the plan! Remember, you're the clean-cut All-American boy now. So act like it! You do your job, and I'll do mine."

The Colonel waited for an answer. None came.

"So we know where we stand, don't we, son?"

Elvis didn't move. He was feigning sleep. Silence.

"Well," said The Colonel, "Sleep now 'cause first thing tomorrow it's back to business." He fanned his fingers and began counting. "The train's takin' us from New York – then to Washington … where some of my friends in government got some honors for you, military honors … then we got some recordin' to do for the boys at RCA in Memphis, you can rest up overnight, see your pappy … then the train'll be takin' us to Florida, Miami Florida, for The Frank Sinatra Show. At Mi-am-i Beach!"

The Colonel thought about patting his boy on the knee for encouragement, but then thought better of it. Enough already. Instead settling for a simple yet insincere, "Welcome home, son. I'm proud of you. The whole country's proud of you."

Elvis vaguely remembered the scheduled recording sessions. He was looking forward to recording some ballads, like the Dean Martin and Mario Lanza records he had listened to over and over again overseas. He liked their style. He thought about his next film, a musical comedy about a soldier based in Germany titled *G.I. Blues*.

Man, what an original story, he thought.

King Creole and Jailhouse Rock seemed like distant memories now. So much for getting those serious, dramatic roles The Colonel had promised. Elvis yearned to be a serious dramatic actor, in the footsteps of method actor James Dean, who had been killed in a car crash in 1955.

Elvis sank deeper into the seat and started to fall to sleep, seeming to visibly melt under his manager's very presence. As he slipped out of consciousness, his eyes flickered and his face glistened with sweat. He fidgeted and talked, muttering in his sleep. He was frightened and scared, and he had a right to be. A lot had happened while he was in Germany. Jerry Lee Lewis married his thirteen year-old cousin and had been publicly disgraced. Little Richard had gone into the seminary. Bill Haley and the Comets were a one hit wonder. Buddy Holly died in a plane crash. And the rest, Fabian, Frankie Avalon, and Ricky Nelson, even the talented Bobby Darin, seemed to be all Elvis imitators.

As if on purpose, Rock and Roll, as Elvis remembered it, was over.

As the long, black limousine rolled along, The Colonel forgave Elvis' somewhat rude manners. He knew that his 'boy,' now stateside and finally under his sole absolute control, would have to be re-conditioned. But for the time being, they were off to Miami to tape "Frank Sinatra's Welcome Home Party for Elvis Presley," Elvis' first public appearance in two years.

That is, after Elvis went to visit his mother's grave in Memphis, for the very first time.

The 'Welcome Home' show was sponsored by 'Timex' watches and taped at Miami's Fontainbleau Hotel, the famous Florida stopover for celebrities, politicians, mobsters, and the like, where Sinatra was closing out a three-week engagement, as he juggled recording sessions, film commitments and his various other new business ventures.

During the train ride to Miami Beach, Elvis and The Colonel stood on the train's rear platform, waving to fans and signing autographs during stops. It was like a whistle-stop campaign, as if Elvis was running for office.

"Man, look at 'em all!!" Elvis said to his entourage of friends, as he stood on the back end of the caboose, waving and tossing mementos to the masses. At one point Elvis saw an 'Elvis For President' sign pass by.

"President?" he laughed. "The fan clubs, they must all be a little crazy, man."

But as Elvis had triumphed in 1956 and 1957, Frank Sinatra had watched, listened, and brooded. By 1960, as he awaited Elvis' Miami arrival, he was nervous. Sinatra, 'The Voice' who had made the bobby-soxers 'swoon' back in the day, honestly sensed that the jazz and swing era might be coming to an end, and he was not happy with the rock and roll alternative.

"There's no beat," said Sinatra, waiting for Elvis to arrive. He thumbed his silver-plated cigarette lighter and touched the flame to the tip of a non-filtered Camel.

"It just doesn't swing."

"Sign of the times, Frank," said Jimmy Van Heusen, who Sinatra called 'Chester,' and who made up one-half of the cream of

Sinatra's songwriting crop (along with Sammy Cahn).

"Sign of the times. I'm tellin' ya, one of these days we'll all be out of business. Jukeboxes are just the beginning. Pretty soon, they'll be pipin' the music in."

Sinatra nodded faintly almost in agreement as he hoped and prayed for the best. *But Jesus Christ, how many Gershwin and Cole Porter versions can I do?* He pushed up the bill of his golf cap and exhaled a billowy white cloud of smoke.

"World's changing, baby. There's no stoppin' it, either."

Sinatra tapped the piano impatiently.

"Hey Suntan Charlie," Sinatra said to Bill Miller, his ultra-pale complexioned pianist, "Gimme a 'C' here, will ya. We got a show to do."

But seriously Frank, tell us how you really feel ...

Back in 1957 Sinatra said, "My only deep sorrow is the unrelenting insistence of recording and motion picture companies upon purveying the most brutal, ugly, desperate, vicious form of expression it has been my misfortune to hear and naturally I'm referring to the bulk of rock and roll. It fosters almost totally negative and destructive reactions in young people. It smells phony and false. It is sung, played, and written for the most part by cretinous goons and by means of its most imbecilic reiterations and sly, lewd – in plain fact – dirty lyrics, it manages to be the martial music of every side-burned delinquent on the face of the earth."

What a week it had been, Sinatra was lucky to have any musicians at all. On Friday, his eighteen year-old daughter had gone up to Fort Dix, New Jersey to meet Elvis after he was discharged. On Saturday the Film Actors Guild (F.A.G.) went on strike for the first time in history. Christ, they hardly had any time to rehearse. And they had a show to do. (A big 'shew,' as Mr. Ed Sullivan would say).

This was Sinatra's fourth and final Timex Special. The previous broadcast, a Valentine's Day tribute featuring actress-singer-dancer Juliet Prowse, Sinatra's then girlfriend, (soon rumored to be romantically linked to Elvis), had been just 'average' in terms of audience response. Fearing cancellation, Sinatra needed desperately to better his ratings, so he grudgingly agreed to pay The Colonel an unprecedented $125,000, outbidding television pioneer and old drinking buddy Jackie Gleason and even Ed Sullivan himself for Elvis to do just two songs for six minutes work, more money than any other performer had ever been paid in television's brief history.

Despite Sinatra's legendary generosity, he made it no secret he was infuriated by The Colonel's demands.[3]

"Hey, I am no cheapskate. Bob Hope I am not," Sinatra said off-the-record. "I sprinkle it around better than anyone. But this guy's insultin' my intelligence here a little bit I should say."

Sinatra's daughter Nancy was on hand too, gushing over Elvis, to whom she had earlier delivered two silk tuxedo shirts, as both a gift and a hint on behalf of her father that this show - his show - is to be a black tie affair. There would be no glittery gold lame suits for this event.[4]

"Hey, kitten!" Sinatra called out his daughter, who had escorted Elvis into Frank's dressing room, "Your boyfriend cleans up nice, don't he?! Man, dig the pompadour … he looks just like Tony Curtis!!"

Sinatra pumped Elvis' hand gladly, like a politician, while he grabbed his shoulder. Elvis was much taller than he'd expected. At least six-feet, anyway, Sinatra figured. And the new, piled up hairdo made him seem even taller. Sinatra thought about his shoe lifts. His height had never really bothered him. Five-seven, five-eight. *Whatever.* He just didn't want to look too short by comparison on TV.

---

[3] Friends since the 1940's, Jackie Gleason claimed that Elvis should have 'comeback' on his show on principle, since it was his show that had introduced Elvis to America even before the historic Sullivan shows in 1956 (in reality though, it was Sinatra's former boss, Tommy Dorsey, and his brother Jimmy, who had introduced Elvis back in 1954 on episodes of their *Stage Show* program).

[4] Nancy Sinatra later co-starred with Elvis in his 1968 film *Speedway.*

He shrugged to himself and tilted his golf cap at an angle, drawing his forefinger along the brim.

It's attitude that matters, baby.

Over Sinatra's shoulder, Elvis noticed a red, white and blue poster with a smiling photo of one of the presidential candidates on it. 'John F. Kennedy' it said. 'Leadership For The '60's.' Sinatra jerked his thumb at the poster and beamed, "That's my buddy there. Just won the New Hampshire primary. You know what they say," Sinatra said, showing off his newly acquired political smarts, "As goes New Hampshire, so goes the country!"[5]

Sinatra gave Elvis, who had never heard of Kennedy, a happy 'good to see ya' once over. "Will ya look at this guy, kitten," he said to his daughter, "He's like the jolly green giant!" The two singers chitchatted and got to know each other a little bit. Sinatra was clearly in a good mood. Everything was clicking. "Okay, kid," he said to Elvis. "You ready to swing?" His daughter laughed, embarrassed a little. She adored her dad but next to Elvis, she hated to even think it, he seemed a little 'square.'

"Now ... whaddaya say we try this?" said Sinatra more like an order than a question, sheet music already in hand. "There aren't too many of your numbers that I can do, but I know you can do some of mine. You do ballads real nice. So let's try this. I do 'Love Me Tender' ... and you pick one of my numbers, okay. Whatever you feel comfortable with ..."

Elvis looked down and then over at Sinatra's daughter and laughed a little, his eyes opening wide as he tossed his eyebrows and smiled. "How about 'Witchcraft,'" the girl chimed, in her cute little red dress, sitting nearby with her knees together, her face smiling. "Elvis could imitate you Daddy. It'll be a hoot! They'll love it." Sinatra liked the idea, mostly because it made his daughter happy.

---

[5] At JFK's personal request at a Hollywood party one night, Sinatra songwriter Sammy Cahn reworked the lyrics of 'High Hopes,' from the ironically titled Sinatra film, *A Hole In the Head*, into a campaign theme song that Sinatra recorded for Kennedy.

"Okay kitten." he said, before he added, kidding, "But ... I am not imitating *him*!"

Grinning, having some fun, he then jerked a thumb at Elvis. "Okay, let's get started with some rehearsin' here today. Like my friend Jackie Gleason says ... gimme a little travelin' music ..." Sinatra made a Jimmy Durante-like Gleason move towards the piano, motioning Elvis to join him.

"Now I don't know what other singers feel when they articulate lyrics," began Frank, showing Elvis his own personal margin notes on the sheet music, "But being an 18-karat manic-depressive and having lived a life of violent emotional contradictions, I have as you may know an over-acute capacity for sadness as well as elation. I know what the cat who wrote the song is trying to say ... I've been there, and back, jack ... now this little number here ..."

Elvis listened close.

Why is Mr. Sinatra telling me this? Showing me his music notes? That's none of my business. That's personal.

But Elvis was never ever one to judge, having never walked in that man's shoes.

Sinatra's daughter just rolled her eyes matter-of-factly.

Yup, that's my daddy.

After rehearsals, Colonel Parker gave Sinatra his creepy, phony two-fingered handshake and cornered him into a private closed-door one-on-one. Sensing instinctively and immediately that The Colonel was a world-class bull-shitter, incapable of telling the truth, Sinatra at first held his own, telling The Colonel, "Don't ever tell me what to do. Suggest. But don't ever tell me."

The Colonel persisted, and Sinatra, ever impatient, responded, "Look, pal, enough of the scam, is this going to be an ocean cruise or a quick sail around the harbor? I got things to do here, places to go, people to see ..."

To everyone's surprise and amazement, after the brief, private meeting with Colonel Parker, Sinatra did a 180-degree turnaround and even issued a positive press release …

"The kid's been away for two years and I get the feeling he really believes what he's doing," Sinatra said to the press with flat affect, eyes glazed.

Three years ago you couldn't have gotten them in the same room, onlookers and Sinatra's core musicians whispered. Now the two superstars were rehearsing a duet with Sinatra smiling and Elvis in formal wear.

The next day, just before showtime, Sinatra silently observed that Elvis was a little jittery. Sinatra had been in the business a long time. He knew the score. He took Elvis by the arm, gently. "Listen … easy with the bennies, kid. I tried those when I was with Dorsey." Sinatra tossed his eyes and lolled his head, "Aye-aye-aye. Buddy Rich ate 'em like candy, the gorilla." He slapped Elvis' shoulder. "Bennies. Not my bag. But, hey, I'm for anything that gets you through the night, kid, be it prayer, tranquilizers or a bottle of Jack Daniel's. Okay, kid. Just go easy. Don't beat yourself up. To be a hero? Why? For what?" Elvis nodded but his mind was elsewhere. [6]

"Mr. Sinatra. How do you think I should I do it?" asked Elvis before the intro.

"What kid? Do what?" answered Sinatra, anxious, the curtains just about to open up.

"Imitate you. Interpret … your song …"

"Kid, no-no-no … wait a minute here," Sinatra began, reaching up to drape his lanky arm around Elvis.

"Y'ever study method acting, kid, they ever teach you that stuff in acting school?"

---

[6] 'Bennies' is slang for Benzedrine, an amphetamine.

29

"Uh, I never been to acting school, sir. Not really, anyway. Colonel said no. Said it would hurt my performance. Kill my natural … instincts, they said."

Sinatra smiled. *Instincts. Listen to this. Kitten was right, this kid's okay.*

"Well, maybe they're right," said Sinatra. "I was never much for school either. It takes a lot of concentration. I can sing and talk, but I got no patience to write. I haven't the talent for it. That's why they call me 'One-Take Charlie.' My first take is my best. 'Cause that's where my energy is. And that's all I got. It's all used up after that first take. Lights, cameras, all that mutha jazz has gotta get moved again. Drives me nuts. I don't buy this take and retake stuff."

Sinatra paused and secretly inhaled through the side of his mouth quickly before continuing. A little 'breath control' trick he learned from his days with trombonist and trumpet player Tommy Dorsey. "The key to good acting on screen is spontaneity, because there's something you lose a little with each take. You know what I mean? Plus, it's five in the morning so they can get the sun in the shot and all that crap, and if I'm up at five in the morning, that means I haven't even been home yet, capiche? So I'm just gettin' in, you see? I'm already fractured, man. Gonzo."

The Dorsey Deal

In 1939, an unknown but talented crooner named Francis Albert Sinatra left Hoboken, New Jersey and signed an exclusive performance agreement with the popular Tommy Dorsey Band. Under the terms of the contract, which was written by Dorsey himself, the bandleader reportedly took an incredible 33% of all of Sinatra's earnings, for *life*! Dorsey's manager took an additional 10%, and Sinatra's own agent took another 10%. In all, 53% of the young man's earnings were gone before taxes and expenses. Union memberships took another 30%. It was so bad that Sinatra had to borrow money to buy a suit for his stage appearances. As his popularity grew, Sinatra spent thousands of dollars on legal fees to break the deal, but Dorsey had twice Sinatra's money and twice the legal muscle. Although accounts differ as to exactly how the deal was actually brokered, Sinatra and Dorsey eventually went their separate ways.

Elvis listened attentively, knowingly. He had heard that Mr. Sinatra liked his bourbon.

Sinatra laughed. "We're all night owls, man. It's show business, baby. Accept it." He held up his index finger and continued, "But that's for actors. Remember, we're singers. When you sing a song, you really get into it. You really know when you nailed it, right? You just know."

"Uh, huh. Yes, sir," said Elvis quietly.

"Co-Rect. That's because you're a singer, and you know singing best. You feel it in your gut. Deeper. That's how real actors, trained actors, New York actors ... that's why, that's how ... method actors, guys like Mumbles Brando, like poor Monty Clift, that's how they feel ... they feel scenes. Same way we feel songs." Elvis listened attentively, trying to understand it all.[7]

Sinatra plucked a single strand of lint from the left shoulder of his tuxedo jacket. "Once you're on that record singing, it's you and you alone. . . . With a film it's never like that - there are producers and scriptwriters, and hundreds of men in offices and the thing is taken right out of your hands. With a record, you're it!" Elvis brightened up and nodded. Like he finally understood.

"So just feel it, kid. Know the words and feel it. If you want to get an audience with you, there's only one way. You have to reach out to them with total honesty and humility. Go with your gut. Because first and foremost we are singers. It's ... it's ... Method Singing. Ha ha, get this, listen to me, One-Take-Charlie here ..." Sinatra laughed at his thought. "That's it! We're .. Method ... Singers." He gave Elvis a playful sideways whack on the arm.

"Okay ... Method-Singing ..." Elvis whispered to himself, deep in thought, as if he were trying to dedicate the concept to memory.

---

[7] Method actor Montgomery Clift was a four-time Academy Award nominee and starred with Sinatra in 1953's *From Here To Eternity*.

"C'mon, focus, kid, focus," jabbed Sinatra. "Just focus. C'mon. Concentrate. One thing at a time." Sinatra turned to offer Elvis one last bit of advice. "And remember, kid, an audience is like a broad. If you're indifferent to them, it's Endsville, baby."

Then bandleader Nelson Riddle, whom Sinatra called 'Admiral,' raised his arms, and the curtains parted. "And now it's … show-time! Let's go out there and murder this mutha!" Sinatra braced Elvis' chest and turned to stride onstage alone and into the lights to introduce his show, and to personally introduce Elvis Presley to an American television audience (of millions) for the first time in two years.

The show was a success. Sinatra swung through a few bars of 'Love Me Tender' while Elvis, in his fitted tux, swaggered through his own finger-snapping Dean Martin-ized version of the classic Sinatra standard *Witchcraft*. Elvis was unusually subdued, but ever so suggestive and polished on stage. "He's still got it," they all said. "He's still got it!"

In the end, Sinatra had been smart enough to admit Elvis' appeal, and despite being $125,000 lighter in his money clip, ratings for the show, broadcast over a month later, showed a 67.7 percent audience share. His temporarily hurt pride notwithstanding, Sinatra could not have been more pleased. "Well, Elvis," Sinatra declared good-naturedly after their duet at the show's end, "All you seem to have lost is your sideburns."

The Welcome Home Special had been a test, to see if Elvis could still 'knock 'em dead,' And he had proved to everyone that he could. His talent and skill hadn't gone away in Germany, despite his lack of practice.

As for Sinatra, when the curtains closed, he tossed his other ball back into the air.

Sinatra had a President to elect. And he was going to win.

Sinatra felt it in his gut.

With its simple, formulaic plot and ever-present musical numbers, *G.I. Blues* may as well have been a documentary about Elvis' Army days in Germany, Although location backdrop scenes had been shot in Germany prior to Elvis' release, the rest of the film was shot at the paramount lot in Hollywood.

GI Blues, like many of Elvis' movies, was a Hal Wallis Production, and it was his third Presley picture to date. Wallis had been a key Hollywood player for decades, producing some of the biggest films in history. *Sergeant York* starring Gary Cooper. *The Maltese Falcon* and *Casablanca* with Humphrey Bogart. *Yankee Doodle Dandy* starring James Cagney. *Gunfight At the OK Corral*, with Burt Lancaster and Kirk Douglas. John Wayne's *Rio Bravo*, and Lancaster's *The Rainmaker*, the last two in which Presley, before being drafted, had been considered to appear. While planning *Rio Bravo* with John Wayne, Wallis was quoted as saying that his dream film was a western starring Wayne and Presley, which due to The Colonel's demand for top billing for Elvis in *Rio Bravo*, never came to pass. Presley had performed a screen test for *The Rainmaker*. In 1960, Wallis was quoted as saying that "An Elvis Presley film is the only sure thing in Hollywood."

Elvis' co-star, Juliet Prowse, had been dating Sinatra ever since they filmed *Can-Can* together in 1959, and rumor had it they were even engaged, but on the set of *G.I. Blues*, she and Elvis were really hitting it off. "Man, those legs of hers just go on forever and ever and ever," Elvis was overheard bragging to friends about the dancer. "She does this thing where she reaches down and grabs her ankles and ..." Elvis nodded once and grinned, "Whew!"[8]

---

[8] *Can-Can* had given Prowse international stardom, especially after Soviet leader Nikita Khrushchev proclaimed her saucy can-can dance 'immoral,' giving her and the film worldwide publicity and notoriety. The film co-starred Shirley MacLaine.

On their way back from the Paramount lot to The Beverly Wiltshire Hotel one night, after filming a few scenes with Elvis driving an Army tank, the same job Elvis had in the service, one of the boys asked, "Hey, E, anything for *us* back at the house tonight?"

"Yeah!" Elvis said. "Blondes Brunettes Redheads, all kinds!!" *Man this movie life is like being on tour. Everywhere it's girls girls girls!!!* Back at the hotel, the boys had drinks flowing. Elvis changed out of his costume government-issued dress khakis, and changed into a silk black sports shirt, white slacks, and just cleaned white bucks, piling his hair up real high, like Tony Curtis, just like Sinatra had said. He looked handsomer than *ten* movie stars.

Elvis grabbed a Pepsi and sat down at the piano. He'd been going four nights straight. He was beat.

He played a few gospel songs, songs his mama used to sing. *Mama had a fine voice ... a fine voice.* Then his random, photographic mind wandered back to his dressing room conversation with The Colonel that day ...

"Colonel, Where's my advance money?" he had innocently asked back at the Paramount lot. *"The hundred thousand. Like we agreed on ..."*

"I'm broke," lied The Colonel. *"And keep your voice down, not in front of the shoeshine boy here."* They walked over a few yards, away from the stand.

"Yeah," Elvis said firmly. *"I wish I was broke like you. I want my share by the end of the day."*

"We're partners son. You get yours when I get mine."

"Yeah, but I ain't partners with your crap tables," Elvis demanded. *"So you pay me, then you pay them. My share. Like the contract says. I know that much ..."*

The Colonel held his index finger up and shushed him. "Not so loud so's the boy can hear ... now listen to me, son, I'll settle it with your daddy tonight, I'll work on it ..."

Daddy. Elvis rolled his eyes. *Way to go, daddy, thought Elvis. If only mama had been there, things might have been diff ...*

Elvis snapped out of it, realizing he was sitting at the piano in the hotel room. He glanced up at his friends, embarrassed, and then closed his eyes and started to sing the gospel song, *Take My Hand, Precious Lord.* Some girls and a few of the guys gathered in close. Elvis loved that song. So had mama. He looked at the girls all dressed up and thought about how much mama liked pretty things but would never wear them. Elvis sang and tried to imitate country singer 'Gentleman' Jim Reeves. Mama liked his version best. [9]

When he finished that song he went on to another, as if in a trance. Elvis then began to sing 'Amazing Grace,' softly, gently, easily accompanying himself on piano, as those gathered grew silent ...

> *Amazing Grace, how sweet the sound*
> *That saved a wretch like me -*
> *I once was lost but now am found*
> *Was blind, but now I see ...*

His close friends applauded quietly, but the hangers-on had some trouble reconciling Elvis the Pelvis singing gospel music so honestly and beautifully. But to all present Elvis smiled humbly in acknowledgement. Yet The Colonel wouldn't leave his thoughts.

A deal with the devil himself ... Daddy never stood up for me that day ... Daddy. Daddy, Daddy ...

Lost in the crowd, still playing the piano softly, Elvis' mind slipped away again, back to the day it all happened, the day they had buried his mother.

---

[9] 'Take My Hand, Precious Lord' was written by 'Georgia' Tom Dorsey, known as the 'father of black gospel music.' No relation to the famed trombonist and Big Band-leader Tommy Dorsey.

"That man ruins everything he touches, I can sense it," Elvis could see his mama say. *"He's no good. I know people, and I have a feelin' in my body about that man and it is not a good one!"*

And then quieter, more tenderly, Elvis thought he heard Sinatra sing ...

"... And you're trapped - with - himmmmmm ..."

One of the boys handed him a Pepsi. He snapped out of it, back to the present.

Damn, how long was I away this time?

He shook his head and looked. Except for his friends, everyone was gone. He started to consciously play the piano again, but mindlessly, just messing with chords. After a few minutes of playing and singing some harmony with the boys, it was like he and the boys were all alone. He always cherished this time. Singing with friends at the piano. Worries all washed away. And for a stretch, everything was okay.

He was able to forget about those other things, even if just for a little while.

Sinatra's TV Special variety show was cancelled immediately after the Timex 'Welcome Home Elvis' special, the victim of poor 'overall' ratings. Sinatra had hoped that the Elvis special would help save him, which is why he even considered entertaining The Colonel's exorbitant sum, but even before the show's great ratings could be announced, ABC had already made their decision. Despite it all though, Sinatra's take was still a cool $3 million.

Shrewdly, trying to be smart, trying to get ahead of the game, still working to make up for the bad years when he couldn't even pay his bar bill, Sinatra had arranged for his payment to be staggered over several years for tax purposes. But ABC had a clause in the contract stating that Sinatra would receive his payment in one lump sum if the series got cancelled. And since the series existed only during a single tax year, the IRS demanded full payment, penalties, and interest totaling over $1 million.

To Sinatra, the tax hit was like another punch in the gut. Even to him, here in 1960, seemingly at the zenith of his professional career, one million clams was a lot of jingle. *Keep moving, keep moving*, he always said to himself. It was the only way he thought he'd ever catch up from the bad days. The pre-*From Here To Eternity* 'Best-Supporting Actor for his portrayal of Maggio' days. The days when his bar tab with Gleason at Toot's Shor's had exceeded his income. So at JFK's urging, Sinatra went to Old Man Joe Kennedy for help. "Frank, why don't you call Dad?" After all, business was Dad's territory. JFK never even carried money, let alone knew how to manage it.

As it was, Old Man Kennedy just so happened to be in town, staying at The Fontainbleu on 'business' the week after the 'Welcome Home Elvis' taping. Sinatra had known the Old Man for a few years, and respected him for his 'take no prisoners,' 'screw them before they screw you' philosophy. "He hates the same way I do," thought Sinatra as he made his way up to the Old Man's plush suite that day.

When Sinatra entered the room, Old Man Kennedy was on the phone. Upon seeing Sinatra he immediately and at once shooed his young, barely legal secretary away into the adjoining suite.

I'd bet ten to one the training bra can't even type. Sinatra helped himself to a glass of Jack Daniels from the service bar. Three ice cubes. Plunk-plunk-plunk. *Nice.*

"… and Teddy, now listen to me now, can you hear me?" sniped Old Man Kennedy in his whiny, tinny voice. "Teddy, get the wax out of your ear … there's a briefcase in the basement, near the water heater. That's right, near my riding boots and saddle. Get it today and put it in my study, there's a storm coming tomorrow … good, put the boat away too … the briefcase, yes, I need that out of there in case the basement floods again … my study. Right. Okay then, I'll call you tomorrow … love you too, son, right-o, bye for now …"

Sinatra laughed to himself. *Riding boots and saddle? On Cape Cod?* Out the window, Sinatra saw some kids playing on the beach outside and he thought about his three kids, how much he missed seeing them every night.

Life's a bitch.

Old Man Kennedy hung up the phone and pushed the bridge of his round tortoise shell eyeglasses against the top of his straight pink nose. "Damn Atlantic ocean!" Kennedy sneered as he took his seat. "Frank, I like to launder my money, but not with salt water …" He greeted Sinatra while seated with a quick and careless handshake.

So Sinatra thinks he wants to get into the political game. May as well, all my boys think they can sing.

"Frank, pour me a ginger ale, will you?" said Old Joe. "I prefer to wait until five for my daiquiri, giving Sinatra a little dig for imbibing during the day." *I'll get you your little ginger ale*, thought Sinatra as he glanced across Kennedy's thinning white hair and stained yellow teeth, all six hundred of them.

Cripes, the Kennedy dentist must make a fortune.

Old Man Kennedy rarely drank, and never to excess, he had seen too many men lose their wits and make poor decisions under its influence, usually to his advantage. The Irish Curse, they called it. But he did enjoy the quick pre-dinner cocktail, as did his oldest surviving son, Jack, who loved his late afternoon banana daiquiri, usually after a 'quickie.' Kennedy sipped his ginger ale and bit an ice cube and said, "So … Frank … I hear that you and Jack are having the time of your lives together out West."

Sinatra stirred his three cubes in his golden glass of bourbon and grinned slyly.

Old Man Joe knew that his son's fondness for Sinatra was simply based on the fact that Sinatra was Hollywood, and JFK loved everything Hollywood, especially Hollywood starlets. The gossip. The romances. And he loved being a part of it. And now here he was running for President. Even his father had to smile at the irony of it all.

The Old Man waved a dismissive hand. "Now that's all well and good. That's what women are for. You boys deserve to have a little fun … as do *all* of us," he winked. "But there are forty-eight other states in the country besides Malibu Beach and The Sands you know … so please, try to keep Jack on the straight and narrow, Frank, will you. At least until November. We have a campaign to run here, and all the tail and all the ass will still be there after the election." *Sinatra watching Jack, Christ, we may as well give the keys to the convicts*, thought the Old Man.

"Sure, Joe. Sure thing," Sinatra impatiently nodded, he looked over Kennedy's shoulder and out the window at the turquoise surf. What a far cry from the Hudson, he thought. And that was from the Jersey side.

Kennedy wasn't accustomed to being ignored. "You have to be somewhere, Frank. You have a date?"

"No, I'm here …"

"Tell me, Frank," inquired Kennedy, playing to Sinatra's ego,

39

"How are we doing in California? What do you hear?"

Sinatra's mouth got crooked. "Now, I'm no clairvoyant …" He paused to see if his use of the big word registered with Kennedy. It didn't. "But I think this thing we cannot miss. Book it we should, I say. A hundred to one. Why I'd even lay a million to one. Jack's a sure thing. It's in the bag, Joe, I'm tellin' ya!"

"And Frank, tell me, on what do you base this vast political knowledge?" Kennedy said the word 'vast' like it was never going to end.

"It's all over town, LA, New York, why … even the cabbies and shoe-shine boys are on board. You know just the other day this Irish kid says to me …"

"Just as I thought. That's what I was afraid of," said the Old Man. "What the hell do they know? If taxi drivers and shoe shine boys think they know the political game, we can't take any chances."

Sinatra wasn't insulted at being one-upped. He was impressed. *Shit the Old Man really knows his stuff. I can learn a lot from him.*

Kennedy sensed Sinatra's sudden humbling. "Now, Frank. How can I help you. Because if you recall, *you* asked to see *me*. Remember?"

"Mmmm. Yes. That's right, Joe. I'm in a little bit of a jam with the feds, and I could use a little, um, assistance." Sinatra had wanted to say 'favor,' but didn't. And Sinatra rarely stammered or said words like 'um,' but Kennedy was one of the very few men who made him nervous. The other two were Eleanor Roosevelt and his mother.

Sinatra explained the tax issue at hand.

Kennedy already knew all about Sinatra's problem, but he took it all in and acted like he gave it some thought, turning at one point to gaze out at the Miami ocean skyline himself. *Miami cannot even begin to compare with the French Riviera. Hell, it's not even in the same league as Nantucket Sound …*

40

Kennedy turned his head and considered Sinatra for a moment. *He can sing. Almost as good as Bing Crosby. He can act. Not bad, for a singer. But as far as television goes, however, he is a complete disaster.*

"So we have a little tax problem, do we?" the Old Man crowed. "Business is a bitch, isn't it Frank? Hell, I don't have to tell you, you own your own record company now, don't you?" Old Man Kennedy asked, his cold, blue, steely eyes smiling as he motioned Sinatra to refill his extended glass.

"What is it … Reprise Records ..?" Kennedy pronounced it incorrectly as 'Ree-prise' instead of 'Rih-preeze' on purpose, just to break Sinatra's balls. He already knew the name and correct pronunciation of the record label. Joe Kennedy never asked anyone a question he didn't know the answer to.

"Yeah, you got it right," Sinatra was surprised the Old Man knew the name, but then again, he always made it his business to know. The mispronunciation didn't faze Sinatra, lots of people got it wrong. Sinatra answered, "Reprise Records. President and Chairman of the Board. Finally, my own boss. My own tapes." Sinatra beamed proudly, as he privately worried over faltering sales.[10]

Then Sinatra decided to brag, fan his feathers and crow a little bit, show the Old Man that he knew a thing or two. "I've discovered," he began, "And you can see it in other entertainers … when they don't reach out to the audience, nothing happens. You can be the most artistically perfect performer in the world, but an audience is like a broad … if you're indifferent, it's Endsville. That goes for any kind of human contact … a politician on television, an actor in the movies, or a guy and a gal. It's as true in life as it is in art."

Kennedy wouldn't give him the satisfaction. "But *business* isn't easy, is it?"

---

[10] Sinatra sold Reprise to Warner Brothers in 1963, but he remained on the label for life.

Sinatra just nodded. *Gimme a break. This joker must be kidding. Show business?! Show business makes the stock market and politics look like a fuckin' shoeshine stand. No, scratch that, a lemonade stand.*

"It ain't bad," Sinatra finally said out loud. "Beats waitin' tables." He had wanted to say 'beats cleanin' up college guy's puke off barroom floors, like he did in Hoboken, but thought better of it. He was pretty sure the Old Man was a college guy.

Then he saw the Old Man winding up for the pitch. *Here it comes*, he thought. Sinatra had heard the whole Old Man Kennedy story before. But he sat patiently and listened to it again. He had to. He had no choice.

"Before conquering the stock market," Joe Kennedy began as he pontificated in the third person, "Joe Kennedy had made his first millions as a Hollywood producer from way back in the 1920's, long before he became a ... became involved in the 'distilled spirits' trade, and even longer before he had barely even given a thought to national politics.

"Look at the bunch of pants pressers (Jews) in Hollywood making themselves millionaires, Kennedy had said before going West in 1926. I could take the whole business away from them.

"And he almost did," he said. "Back in the days of Charlie Chaplain and Babe Ruth and Harry Houdini and the 'Roaring Twenties' ... you remember Houdini, don't you, Frank? He could get out of *any* jam ... Anyway, back in the day, the younger, but by no means less ambitious version of the man you see before you today had effectively infiltrated the incestuous world of Hollywood, setting his template for the machinations of profit (or more accurately, the unlucky ones knew, 'profiting at the expense of others'), and returned back East to the stock market and his growing young and handsome family, with a veritable fortune."[11]

---

[11] Paramount's 1953 film *Houdini*, a biographical film about the renowned magician and escape artist, starred Tony Curtis and Janet Leigh.

Sinatra sighed and wished all of his own audiences were as captive as he was at this very moment.

Joe Kennedy's Hollywood Years

In 1926, Kennedy led a group that acquired Film Booking Offices of America (FBO) an American movie studio of the silent era, and producer and distributor of mostly low-budget films. The studio, whose core market was America's small towns, also put out many romantic melodramas, non-Western action pictures, and comedic film shorts. In 1928, using RCA Photophone technology, FBO became only the second Hollywood studio to release a 'talkie.' one of the major studios of Hollywood's Golden Age. And a controlling portion of stock from The Keith-Albee-Orpheum Corporation, the owner of a chain of motion picture and vaudeville theatres, was sold to Kennedy from whom it was purchased earlier by RCA as part of the deal, along with FBO), that created RKO. After the establishment of RKO, motion pictures, not vaudeville, became the primary focus of theatre entertainment.

"Bottom line was ..." Joe Kennedy said, "Joe Kennedy knew Hollywood. And he knew *what* sold. And *why*. He understood, and he understands, marketing. And Kennedy knows now, instinctively, that the crucial deciding difference between his son and the other candidates, is his son's - your friend's - Hollywood celebrity status, sex appeal, and confidence and ease in front of a camera. And he knows today, that the country and its politics are on the verge of a new era, an era where the intrusive immediacy of television will make politics entertainment, and where style will win over substance, perhaps forever!" Kennedy expelled his last breath of hot air before sucking in some more.

"Yes! Joe Kennedy's second born son is good in person, that goes without debate, but on film, on camera, he is a movie star!"

Sinatra silently agreed. He had already given it considerable thought. JFK was a little like Cary Grant except with a different, but similar, aristocratic accent. Not Boston. Not Irish. Not even Harvard. Just different. *But Jesus, will somebody please pass me the fucking popcorn already ...*

Kennedy forged on. "Frank, Joe Kennedy knows he is going to buy the election. It is already in the works, and has been for a while. But dammit! Joe Kennedy is NOT going to pay for a landslide! ... Joe Kennedy needs a guarantee! ...

"Frank," said Kennedy, his pulse slowing, "You and I are cut from the same cloth. We both worked our way up to where we are today. Very much the same way. 'If it is to be - it's up to me!' Right?! And we both know the same people, and you know the people I mean ..."

Sinatra listened. He knew. He had heard how the Old Man had screwed over the studios back in the twenties, how he ruined careers. How little he cared for actors. One deal he made had almost put the old Western 'eight-day' serial shorts out of business, almost costing a lot of early cowboy actors their careers, including an ambitious, strapping young actor named John Wayne.[12]

There was no way the Old Man could go back and ask Hollywood for a favor. It'd be like walking into a crossfire, for crissakes.

Kennedy said, "You see, Frank, they can help us win. But I can't go to those 'Hollywood' people. It might come back at Jack. But you can."

He paused and considered Sinatra for a moment, playing to his blind ego had paid off. He knew it already. Kennedy knew that Sinatra knew, it's not how you begin, it's how you finish. How you get there doesn't matter. Just win.

"And maybe ..." Kennedy added. "... you could persuade your friends in the entertainment business to do the same ..."

---

[12] In 1928, cowboy silent film legend Tom Mix, a fan of Wayne's football exploits at USC, got him a $35 a week job working as a prop man at Fox studios. Director John Ford saw Wayne loading furniture onto a Fox truck one day, gave him some bit parts to play, and the rest is history. In 1929, Joe Kennedy hired Mix, but when he merged his studio with RKO, Mix's career ended.

"Sure Joe," said Sinatra. "I get your drift. I'll do anything for a friend, you know that."

Kennedy inhaled impatiently, "Now Frank, the best thing you can do – for Jack – for you, is to ask for their help as a personal favor. A favor to *you*. Keep Jack, and myself, out of it."

Sinatra immediately saw himself as the kingmaker, and saw the Kennedys as his chance to go legitimate and get the upper-class respect he so craved. "Sure, Joe. It's a couple of phone calls."

"Good," said Kennedy, standing, ready to dismiss Sinatra. "So we have an understanding. Quid pro quo," added Kennedy.[13]

Sinatra nodded yes. They shook on it.

"And while we're at it, let's see if we can relieve some of those Hollywood heebies of a few million of their *quid* in the process, right?!"

Sinatra hated bigotry, but didn't show it. Not this time. "Sure thing, Joe. I'm your guy."

The Academy Award winning actor-singer gratefully reached for the door, relieved that his tax problem would be addressed and that he was about to become King Shit of Hollywood Democratic politics. *This is the big time, baby. This'll show 'em all.*

"Oh yes, and Frank ..." Old Man Kennedy added.

"Yes ... what's that Joe..."

"Fix yourself ... one for the road. After all ... it is Saint Patrick's Day ... and tell that Cockney actor my daughter married to lay off the call girls a little, at least until the campaign is over." Kennedy tapped his ear and smiled as if to say, 'I hear everything.'

---

[13] Quid pro quo is Latin, meaning, "something for something."

45

Brother-in-Lawford, the poor bastard. He was hopeless. What a putz. Sinatra's eyes danced as he felt the tax burden slide off his shoulders. He bit his lower lip in triumph and opened the suite door. Old Man Kennedy waved him off and reached for his phone. Sinatra closed the door, certain that Little Susie Cupcake would be on her way back any minute now.

So Old Man Joe 'arranged' through his vast Washington contacts (for he was a contributor to all the key Washington players, not just Kennedys), for Sinatra to have his tax burden reduced to just $65,000. And Old Man Kennedy was happy to do it. Sinatra would just owe him a favor, that being, to fully use his Hollywood and 'entertainment business' contacts in the coming months for Jack's election.

Quid pro quo.

'The New Frontier,' JFK's 1960 campaign slogan which became the label for his administration's foreign and domestic programs, may well have been former Hollywood producer-bootlegger-Ambassador Old Man Joe Kennedy's most famous and profitable production of all. Joe Kennedy relished in his own genius. 'The New Frontier.' It was a Romantic Comedy, Film Noir, High Drama and a Western all rolled into one.

With his financing and under his skilled direction, his self-assured, confident second-born son, like a Hollywood leading man, would project the movie star qualities of charm, sex appeal, humor, optimism, and the appearance of wholesome decency. It was a role JFK was very comfortable playing. He knew the script by heart. And he had successfully played the role his entire life - in sickness, in World War II as a hero aboard PT-109, and in politics. Joe Kennedy knew that it was a very compelling story.

'New Frontier' Trivia
John Wayne appeared in the 1935 film *The New Frontier*, not to be confused with his 1939 film, simply titled, *New Frontier*, both produced by Republic Pictures. Additionally, In 1956 The 'New Frontier' resort and casino had the distinction of hosting Elvis Presley in his first Vegas appearance. Howard Hughes purchased the Vegas resort in 1967 and shortened the name to 'The Frontier.'

"I'm going to sell Jack like corn flakes," Old Man Joe Kennedy said to himself, as little Susie Cupcake serviced him under the desk. He knew it was all about product and, er, positioning. Give them what they want. The bigger the story, the more they'll buy it. After all, he knew, it's all just a movie, anyway.

Instead of being shown in movie theatres, Old Man Kennedy envisioned 'The New Frontier' to be shown on miniature movie screens in living rooms all over America. Premiering nationwide, from state to state, and in every city and town across the country. On the *new* movie screen. Television.

JFK and PT-109

In 1942, JFK (now "Ensign Kennedy") was working for Naval Intelligence in Washington, and sleeping with a Danish beauty named Inga Arvad, a columnist for a Washington newspaper. An exotic, well-traveled woman, Inga had connections to Adolf Hitler and other Nazi leaders, a circumstance which eventually got JFK in trouble with his superior officers., who feared 'Inga Binga' to be a Nazi spy. The young ensign was reassigned to a bureaucratic post in South Carolina, and his romance with the Danish beauty fizzled. Bored, JFK begged his father to pull strings to get him assigned to sea duty. Joseph Kennedy, Sr. obliged, and in late 1942, JFK was given an assignment on a Motor Torpedo Boat, or 'PT boat,' as it was informally known. After six months of training, he and his crewmates shipped out from San Francisco, bound for the South Pacific and combat with the Japanese. Promoted to lieutenant early in 1943, he was given command of a boat designated PT 109, and was the skipper of this boat on the night of August 2, 1943, when it was rammed by the Japanese destroyer *Amigari.* Two of JFK's crew were killed outright, while the others tried to stay afloat amid the wreckage. Under the young lieutenant's leadership, eleven men, several badly wounded, managed to hang on to the half of the PT boat that was still afloat and wait for help. None came, and after nearly fifteen hours, JFK led the men on a grueling swim to a nearby island. From there, he and a subordinate made various forays through the coral islands, searching for help. It was days before they found a group of natives who carried a message to a British base, some thirty-eight miles away. Finally, on August 7, JFK and the other survivors were rescued by a party of British scouts and carried to safety. The ordeal made JFK a war hero. He received the Purple Heart, as well as the Navy and Marine Corps Medal. After the PT-109 incident, however, JFK's chronically frail health gave way. He contracted malaria, and his back problems returned. He was rotated back to duty in the U.S., and by spring of 1944, he was diagnosed with chronic lower back disease. JFK soon found himself the focus of his father's thwarted ambitions. Joseph Kennedy, Sr. had seen his eldest son, Joe Jr., die in a war that he himself had opposed, so he channeled all of his energies and ambitions into a political career for his second-born son. "It was like being drafted," JFK later described it. "My father wanted his oldest son in politics. 'Wanted' isn't the right word. He demanded it."

The New Frontier, starring John Fitzgerald Kennedy, coming to a living room near you. Enjoy a three-year plot of dramatic conflict and crises, humorous and passionate speeches and press conferences, as America's vigorous, handsome young President takes on a new decade of challenges and makes the world safe from evil and oppression, winning security, democracy and justice for all.

'Live theatre,' on television screens worldwide. With Jack as the star. And with Frank Sinatra's help, it now had a soundtrack too.

... It's all just a movie, thought the Old Man from behind his closed office door. If they all only knew, it's all just a movie ...

Susie Cupcake was finished, and Kennedy was relieved (but not nearly as relieved as was she was).

He patted her on the ass.

Right-O! Good! Now get back to work!

Juliet Prowse had been 'stood up.' Frank Sinatra had broken their date. "I'm not used to men breaking their date with me," she told Elvis, furious.

"Did he say why?" asked Elvis, in earnest but also expecting a load of Sinatra bullshit.

"He said he has a cold. Frank Sinatra has a cold. You should hear him, you would think he had cancer. He is such a … how shall I put it? A hy-po-chon-dri-ac."

Elvis laughed to himself. *Bullshit. He's no hypochondriac. More like a bullshit artist. A cold? You mean a bourbon cold. A Kentucky cold. The same one all my relatives always get. Man, if I had a nickel for every time I've heard that one.* He looked at her legs and followed them up to her head. *Man is she a long one. Must be close to six feet tall.* His eyes went down to her legs again. He thought again about that ankle thing she did.

Enough Sinatra already.

"Will you be my date?" asked Elvis, still in his army costume from filming that day.

"You know I'm Frank's girl, sweetie. We're practically engaged." The word 'engaged,' and the thought of it, kind of scared Juliet. She liked Frank but he was controlling and complicated and difficult to deal with when he was drinking, which it seemed was most of the time.

"Engaged!" Elvis laughed to himself. In the script's final scene he proposes to Juliet. But seriously? Engaged? Sinatra? Bullshit. Elvis knew the drill. Sinatra asked practically every girl he meets to marry him. He's engaged to get married to a new chic almost every month.

The joke was, Sinatra's had longer engagements at The Sands. What a load of shit.

"You don't need me," said Juliet, pretending to be shy. "A rich American like you should have no problem finding a date. I see the way they look at you. I have eyes. Natalie Wood, all the others …"[14]

Elvis stayed on message though, continuing to deliver his absurd, unbelievable lines as convincingly as he could, "C'mon baby. I'm lonely." Inside, he was laughing out loud. Despite his fame and the women throwing themselves at him, Elvis never took himself too seriously.

"I'd appreciate it if you didn't call me 'baby'. You overestimate your attraction, soldier." Juliet was having some fun with him now.

"Okay …….. baby …" grinned Elvis.

Juliet smiled and gave Elvis a long, sideways look as they passed the shoeshine stand on the Paramount lot.

"Let's get out of here," she whispered. "Let's go somewhere else, okay."

"Okay, ma'am," he said.

"I don't like 'ma'am' either."

"Good. Neither do I," Elvis answered quickly. "Where are we going?"

"Food," she said, rubbing her tummy, making a sad little girl's face. "I need a sandwich. Come. I'll feed you." *Just don't fall in love with me, okay. Please, just promise me that, she said to herself.*

---

[14] Both Elvis and Sinatra had been romantically linked to actress Natalie Wood, who costarred in *Rebel Without A Cause* and *West Side Story*, among many other films, including John Wayne's *The Searchers*.

51

"Danke Skoen," said Elvis. "It's German for 'thank you," he said, playful and proud all at once. Juliet laughed. Elvis was like a little boy sometimes.

Juliet rolled her eyes. "I know, Elvis. I know what it means." She took his arm. But he *is* charming, she thought. "Here." She stopped him in front of the deli. "Let's get some coffee … and some strudel." Elvis liked the way she said 'sta-rew-dahl.' *Boy, this is just like in the movies. And with real movie stars!* He felt like he was seven years old, like a kid in a candy store.

He opened and held the door for her and in they went.

Inside Juliet's dressing room trailer after a long day of shooting, Elvis was eating a leftover piece of strudel and pacing the tight floor of her dressing room trailer.

"I'm sick of this shit," Elvis cursed. "I'm gonna fire that bastard. I never liked him and neither does my daddy. I'm gonna go right out there and fire his ass right now."

"Then go do it." Said Juliet, slowly massaging moisturizer up and down her legs.

But Elvis stayed put. He couldn't. Something held him back. It always did. He sat down and bit into a piece of strudel. Juliet remembered what she had heard from some dancers she knew, that Elvis had been considered for the lead in *West Side Story*. But she decided not to bring it up. She wasn't sure if he knew.[15]

"I'm gonna fire him tonight. Tonight," said Elvis, as his eyes pitched downward to Juliet's rear end. "Well … aw, shoot, never mind. I'll fire his ass tomorrow."

Elvis stood up and embraced Juliet from behind. They were two healthy young people, and had a definite sexual attraction, if not much else. Elvis undid his belt. Juliet peeled off her panties, spread her long, lithe legs wide, arched her back, and reached down and grabbed both her ankles. As a dancer she was pretty damn limber.

---

[15] Director Robert Wise originally wanted Elvis to play Tony in the landmark musical *West Side Story*. The Colonel, as usual, interfered, saying the lead role wasn't right for his Elvis. The producers then auditioned Warren Beatty, Tab Hunter, Anthony Perkins, Burt Reynolds, Troy Donahue, Bobby Darin, Richard Chamberlain, and Gary Lockwood before settling on Richard Beymer for the male lead.

"Hurry, baby. Hurry. I never know when Frank is going to come."

Elvis giggled at her choice of words. *What did they call that? A double entrée? A double enten ...*

Aww, who cares ...

"Hurry, baby, he has a temper. Worse than you ..." said Juliet, remembering to omit Frank's name on purpose this time so as not to make Elvis jealous.

Elvis grinned his way through the hurried act. Smiling to himself.

Outside, Sinatra pulled his 1958 Cadillac El Dorado into the Paramount lot. He cared but he didn't care. Juliet was a broad just like all the other broads. But she was *his* broad. There's a code, see. Don't touch my woman. Don't even look at her. Some guys don't understand the code. He wondered what nationality Elvis was. *Where were his people from? Was the kid Italian? Irish? A fuckin' Cherokee? What the hell kind of name was 'Elvis' and 'Presley' anyway?*

Sinatra parked his El Dorado, leaving the keys in the ignition. "Hey Irish," he called out to the startled shoeshine boy. "Keep an eye on the wheels, okay buddy boy. I'll just be a minute." The shoeshine boy nodded that he would. He knew nobody would dare touch Sinatra's car anyway.

Inside the trailer, Elvis smiled. "Ya vol fraulein." They kissed. "Will I see you again tomorrow? Today?" asked Elvis. He frowned, "Is it day or night? I lose track." [16]

"Yes," said Juliet. "It is daytime. I will see you again tomorrow. I have a dancing scene to rehearse."

"Yeah, Me and the boys got some songs to work on too."

---

[16] Translation: German for 'Yes indeed.'

Juliet looked at Elvis' reflection in her cosmetic mirror. *He is so talented. He can sing, he can dance, he can act. With guidance, he could be, how do they say, the 'triple threat,' like Gene Kelly.* Elvis picked up her panties off the floor and held them up to his cheek, his eyes closed. "Elvis dear … take the strudel. But please, leave my panties," said Juliet, taking them from his hand, and with that, Elvis left the dressing room, and the building.

The minute had passed. "Why Frank darling!!! How sweet of you to stop by!!" Sinatra wrinkled his nose like a bloodhound.

Outside Juliet's trailer, on the set, impatient that shooting was being delayed due to 'artistic differences,' The Colonel stepped in front of the director's chair and was overheard ordering around the crew, "Now, in this scene, I want two songs and a fight ..."

During the time of the Second World War, New York theatre actors became obsessed with a new, brooding, sexually neurotic style of self-expression. It was called 'The Method,' and it soon invaded Hollywood.

The Method acting technique was discovered by Russian theatre director Konstantin Stanislavsky (1863-1938) and taught from 1950 onwards at the Actor's Studio in New York, under the directorship of Lee Strasberg, a former pupil of Richard Boleslovsky, who had brought Stanislavsky's ideas to America in the 1920's.

The most important principle of The Method is an actor's total understanding of and identification with his character's motivation. To accomplish this, he or she is encouraged to draw on comparable experiences in his or her own life, including painful ones that have been buried in the subconscious. This 'emotional memory exercise' is intended to produce a greater realism in the actor's subsequent portrayal of the character.

Besieged by the thespian attack, many Hollywood actors too acquiesced to The Method, feeling they had to give in to it, and emulate it, discarding their previously employed sufficient acting manner in favor of this new, irresistible, and destructive form of self discipline that would so surreptitiously and completely devour them. Among The Method's early victims were Montgomery Clift, Marlon Brando, Marilyn Monroe and James Dean.[17]

But not every Hollywood actor became a slave to the Red Menace of The Method. In fact, on the contrary.

---

[17] James Dean idolized Clift and used to call him on the phone 'just to hear his voice.' In 1956 Clift suffered an automobile accident while leaving a party at Elizabeth Taylor's home. The crash left him disfigured and in constant pain, and he became addicted to painkillers and alcohol. His career never recovered. He died in 1966.

There was a group of conservative Hollywood actors and businessmen who were attracted to the acting profession simply because they were good at it. These professionals viewed acting simply as a way to earn a living. They saw it as a business first and a form of self-expression second.

For this group, acting was a journeyman craft to be mastered, like carpentry or stonemasonry.

In short, it was a job. A means to an end.

As time went on, and these Hollywood conservatives began to wield more power and influence within their industry and beyond, they used their craft as an appropriate and viable conduit for the advancement of their deeply held and equally deeply felt conservative causes.

This conservative Hollywood Old Guard resented Hollywood's post-war cultural shift and the new generation of young actors who, in the dawn of rock and roll and Cold War anti-communist paranoia, came to personify what would become the anti-establishment 'generation gap.'

They backed conservative political candidates, and they began to produce motion pictures that worked to advance what they viewed as the proper cause of America, the land that they loved.

These were the same people who also felt that Democrat John F. Kennedy, and the new, popular and lucrative medium called 'television', were their enemy.

And they felt he had to be stopped.

The self-appointed leader of this group was one Marion Mitchell Morrison.

Otherwise known as John Wayne.

The Duke.

John Wayne and his secretary were sitting in his home office in Newport Beach, California, poring over the usual day's mail - bills, charitable requests from hospitals, "Send them all a thousand, double to those hospitals with the cancer kids."

... Easter seals, Christmas seals, The Freemasons, the gas bill, The John Birch Society, the electric bill, dry cleaning bill ...

... Alimony to a couple of Mexican ex-wives ... "We had some good times together," he coughed. "When they weren't trying to kill me!"

He thought about his son and his daughters for a bit, how much he missed them, and then he returned to the mail ... *nothing but window envelopes ... the Bell telephone bill, The Republican National Committee ... The California Republican Committee ...*

"Be nice to find a check here made out to *me* one of these days," said Wayne.

Filming for *The Alamo* had just completed and it would be ready for release later in the Summer of 1960. Wayne was producer, director and star, and it had taken all he had in him financially, mentally and emotionally, and then some, to complete.[18]

Thinking about money and business and then politics, he kindly asked his secretary to pour him a fresh cup of coffee, black, and to get Vice-President Nixon on the line.

---

[18] Wayne had begun scouting locations for *The Alamo* as early as 1954, and had financed the film himself, with some help from investors. One of whom was a Texas oilman said to be the real-life inspiration for Jett Rink, James Dean's character in George Stevens epic film, *Giant*, co-starring Rock Hudson and Elizabeth Taylor.

"Dial up the Vice-President, will you please, honey ..."

Wayne wasn't just worried about the country's political future, he was also worried about his own. All the Hollywood leading men of his generation were starting to pass on. Humphrey Bogart died in 1957. Tyrone Power in 1958. Errol Flynn in 1959. Clark Gable in 1960. And Gary Cooper was on his way. In the last few years Wayne had prayed over a lot of dead men. Then Jimmy Cagney retired. And Cary Grant announced that 1962 would be his final year in films. The only other one left was his friend and fellow Republican Jimmy Stewart.

Wayne knew he couldn't afford to retire or to die, so to make a living and try to recoup his fortune, he had to work. He was too old for the romantic lead. That much he knew. He needed roles that would preserve his image as a wise, mature, and strong man who righted wrongs. But he wasn't confident that character would be accepted by a rapidly changing America, especially with a John Kennedy in the White House.

Wayne's secretary handed him the receiver.

"Hello, Dick, Duke."

"Duke? Dick," answered Nixon, awkwardly, picking suspiciously at his usual breakfast of cottage cheese with black pepper and ketchup, grapefruit, and coffee. His old cocker spaniel, Checkers, waited patiently under the table for scraps. Sadly, they would never come.

"Why, err, hello. Duke, my friend. Why, I was just thinking about you."

Wayne patiently untangled the telephone cord in his lap as he spoke. After a little catching up and some small talk, Wayne asked Nixon if he would help him promote *The Alamo* in theatres.

"It's a helluva picture," Wayne said. "Been in my head for a long time, this one was."

"I know it was, Duke," said Nixon. "You deserve all the accolades for it too. I can only imagine the work involved. And the message is vital to the American people, especially now." Nixon tried to muster up some excitement, "Remember the, Alamo!!" he said, awkwardly.

"Mr. Vice-President, these are perilous times," said Duke. "The eyes of the world are on us. We must sell America to countries threatened with Communist domination. Our picture is also important to Americans who should appreciate the struggle our ancestors made for the precious freedom we enjoy."

"Well, it'll be a great movie," said Nixon. "Movies are important. Good movies. Good versus Evil. Right-versus-Wrong. Us-versus-Them! Not that liberal, eastern intellectual bullshit." Nixon thought about the good old days, when you could destroy reputations and lives without just cause. "Jesus, remember *High Noon*? I still can't believe Gary Cooper agreed to be in that crap! He [unintelligible] used to be one of us, Duke. Remember?"[19]

"That I do," said Wayne, shaking his head in disbelief. Wayne had just visited Cooper in the hospital. *Poor Coop. I'll soon be prayin' over him, too.*

The Motion Picture Alliance for the Preservation of American Ideals allowed Wayne to use his celebrity to further causes he deemed worthy. In the 1950s, Wayne joined Walt Disney[20], Gary Cooper, Clark Gable, and others to assist Nixon and the House Un-American Activities Committee (HUAC) in exposing Communists working in the film industry. Wayne began hand-picking roles and financing the production of certain films, such as the 1952 anti-communist propaganda film, 'Big Jim McLain.'

---

[19] Wayne said *High Noon* was "the most un-American thing I've ever seen in my life." Wayne and director Howard Hawks later made *Rio Bravo* as their pro-America response to the film.

[20] When JFK was shot on November 22, 1963, Walt Disney was in a private plane over Florida, scouting locations for his new Disneyworld theme park.

"But I guess anything's better than television," admitted Nixon. "All those stupid little kids staring at that goddamn boob tube, chewing their goddamn bubble gum ..."

"I agree, Mr. Vice President," said Wayne, conscious of the small screen's growing influence and appeal. "I don't take to it too kindly myself. That dang little screen makes us *all* look bad. It'll be the end of us all someday, mark my words. I'm not happy about it, but as you well know, these are downright scary times we're in."

Ironically, Wayne knew, although Kennedy claimed to have the movie star image and appeal, it was Nixon who was Hollywood's true representative, as he was actually from California and had served as the state's Congressman from 1946 to 1952, and then as Vice-President under Eisenhower until 1960.

"Remember the good 'ol days?" said Wayne. "The Hollywood Ten. We really had 'em on the ropes back then, didn't we, Mr. Vice President? Yes, Sir, we really showed 'em ..."[21]

Nixon pretended to get emotional, "Yes, and, uh, Duke ... how we did it I'll never know, you knew all along exactly how many we'd end up with ... and ... you know, I've trusted your political instincts ever since, my friend."

Wayne looked over at all of his trophy ten-gallon hats hanging on nails across an entire wall of his den. "Yep, ten was the number alright."

"It was a bit of a gamble," said Nixon, using his ever-present poker analogies, "But we won the pot." Nixon loved poker the way some men love women. As a candidate for Congress on the Republican ticket in 1946, Nixon reportedly used $10,000 cash that he

---

[21] In the late 1940s, at the start of the Cold War, Nixon was a vocal member of the House Un-American Activities Committee (HUAC), which pursued alleged communists in government and in Hollywood. Nixon was perhaps the Committee's best-known, most vocal member.

had won playing poker in the Navy during the war to finance his initial foray into politics and, like all gamblers, the burgeoning public servant was always full of blind ambition, always eyeing bigger, more rewarding stakes. For Nixon, of course, the biggest game of all was the Presidency. So Nixon, already anticipating and counting on the Duke's support for the upcoming election, readily agreed to do anything he could to make *The Alamo* a booming success.

Wayne knew he could count on Nixon. He was the one politician that didn't kowtow to the lefty liberals in Hollywood. Although Nixon had grown up in the shadow of Hollywood, he was a family man, and wasn't at all inclined toward its culture or lifestyle. Wayne liked that. *Nixon's a pretty straight shooter, always has been. Even back when he first got elected to Congress back in 1946, when he made front-page news going after all the 'pinkos' in Hollywood. It never went to his head.*

But it was 1960, and if Hollywood was a bellwether for national politics, the Duke had detected a shift in mood. The anti-Communism crusade of the 1950's was losing steam, and Hollywood liberals, even some of the blacklisted Hollywood Ten, had started coming out of exile.

The Hollywood Ten

During the 1947 House Un-American Activities Committee (HUAC) investigations of the Hollywood Motion Picture Industry, ten people refused to answer any questions regarding the alleged political (Communist) affiliations of themselves or others during the hearings. They became known as the Hollywood Ten. They were Alvah Bessie, Herbert Biberman, Lester Cole, Edward Dmytryk, Ring Lardner Jr., John Howard Lawson, Albert Maltz, Samuel Ornitz, Adrian Scott and Dalton Trumbo. The ten claimed that the First Amendment of the United States Constitution gave them the right to refuse to answer questions about their beliefs. HUAC and subsequently the courts disagreed and all ten men were found guilty of contempt of congress. Each was sentenced to between six and twelve months in prison.

To Wayne, Communism remained, in his heart and mind, as evil and malignant as cancer.

"Dick," began Wayne. "I think there may be an eleventh …"

Nixon hushed, relieved that Wayne had brought it up and not himself, "I know. I've suspected it for years. I know." He and Jack Kennedy had entered Congress together in 1946, with offices directly across the hall from each other. They were practically friends.

Wayne figured as much, but he had more, "This Kennedy fellow is one bad actor," Wayne said to Nixon. "And everyone knows it."

"I know," Nixon replied. "Brando. Method. Communist. I heard the same thing. I know." Nixon harkened back to his own, brief stage career in college. "Well, as you know, Duke, I was a bit of a thespian myself, back in the day." Nixon thought back once again, as he often did, to that gloriously fateful day when he had met his beloved wife, Pat.[22]

Boy, did I ever marry up and out of my league. My God, I would do anything for her.

"I remember," mused Wayne, as Nixon shook his jowls back to reality. "But Mr. Vice-President, I'll tell you this much. These stage actors today, I think they're all off their mark. Why this British fellow, Lawrence Harvey, we're down in Texas shootin' the picture and, listen to this one, he makes a play for me. Turns out he's one of those ho-mo-sex-u-als."

---

[22] While in high school, the strikingly pretty Pat Nixon, formerly the Patricia 'Pat' Ryan (born on Saint Patrick's Day), supplemented her income by working as an extra in the film industry. The young redhead appeared as part of a brief walk-on in the 1935 film *Becky Sharp*, as well as the 1936 film *The Great Ziegfeld*. In 1937, while working as a teacher at Whittier College in California, she met a young lawyer, Richard Milhous Nixon, at a theater group when they were cast together in *The Dark Tower*, a mystery drama first produced in 1933 (the play was adapted to film in 1934's *The Man with Two Faces* starring Edward G. Robinson). Nixon asked Pat Ryan to marry him the first night they went out, then courted the redhead he called his "wild Irish Gypsy" for two years, even driving her to and from her dates with other men, as he awaited her answer.

Dirt. Nixon ate this stuff up. The more dirt the better. He preyed on other men's mistakes and 'weaknesses.'

"My God, Duke! What did you do?!"

"Well, as you know, I don't cotton to that notion much. He's a helluva actor, goddammit, but I almost cold-cocked the commie poofter right then and there! But I didn't. Wouldn't have been professional. We had work to do. So I just looked him straight in the eye and told him, 'Sorry pal, but the Duke don't swing that way."

Nixon [expletive deleted] loved it.

Senator John F. Kennedy and his wife Jacqueline were walking in their Georgetown neighborhood in Washington. They bumped into a friend, who was accompanied by a man from Great Britain.

Kennedy extended his hand.

"Kennedy. Jack Kennedy."

Upon being introduced both JFK and his wife gasped and asked the debonair and aristocratic Englishman, "Are you THE Ian Fleming?!"

"Why, yes."

Ian Fleming had served in British Intelligence in the Royal Navy during World War II. From this experience, he learned the workings of the system of spying and the secret service. He started writing his James Bond series in 1951, and had written a new one every year or two, with seven Bond spy thrillers published to date.[23]

Kennedy and his wife eagerly told Fleming he had been introduced to his James Bond series back in 1955, while recovering from near fatal back surgery for injuries that he had sustained during his command of PT 109 during World War II. And he had read *From Russia With Love* when it first came out back in 1957. (In the novel, James Bond has been listed as an enemy of the Soviet state and a death warrant has been issued for him. He is to be not just killed, but 'killed with ignominy,' with his death precipitating a major sex scandal that will be news throughout the world press for months and leave his reputation and that of his entire service in tatters). Kennedy thought

---

[23] In the James Bond novels *Casino Royale* and *Moonraker*, Bond is said to resemble singer-songwriter Hoagy Carmichael, but with a scar down one cheek. Hoagy Carmichael was born on November 22, 1899.

again about the novel and laughed playfully at Fleming's overactive imagination. *Murder and political sex scandals. My God, what a fantastic story.*

So the Senator is a fan, thought Fleming.

Kennedy looked at his watch, a small, square, gold-plated Lord Elgin model displaying only four Roman numerals. XII, III, VI and IX. He gently tugged on the band's alligator strap with his forefinger as he looked up again to address Fleming, who had discreetly noticed a separate, isolated, second hand, located on the lower right quadrant of Kennedy's watch-face.

"Well it seems to me that you'll have to join us for, uh, dinnuh tonight," said JFK. "That is if it's not too much of a, uh, burden for you to bear ..."

"Yes, please, do come," cooed his beautiful, younger wife, Jackie.

Those in attendance later agreed that, even by Georgetown standards, it was one hell of a dinner party.

A record on the Kennedy's stacked turntable played Bobby Darin's newly released, swinging version of 'Bill Bailey, Won't You Please Come Home,' as Fleming was introduced to the dinner guests ...

Won't you come home, Bill Bailey, won't you come home
I've moaned the whole night long
I'll do the cookin', honey, I'll pay the rent
I know I've done you wrong ...

Over dinner and drinks, with the eyes of all guests upon them, Kennedy, anticipating that he would be the Democratic nominee and win the general election against Nixon in November, asked Fleming what his man James Bond might do if he was assigned to get rid of Castro. Fleming had been in British Intelligence, and he was quick to answer the question with flair.

66

The Georgetown table guests, made up of Kennedy intimates, journalists and other Washington insiders, grew quiet and exchanged eyes at the intrigue before them.

Fleming confidently dictated that there were three things that really mattered to the Cubans - money, religion, and sex. Therefore, he suggested a triple whammy. First the United States should send planes to scatter counterfeit Cuban money over Havana. Second, using the Guantanamo base, the United States should conjure some religious manifestation, say, a cross of sorts in the sky which would induce the Cubans to look constantly skyward. And third, the United States should send planes over Cuba dropping pamphlets to the effect that due to American atom bomb tests the atmosphere over the island had become radioactive, and that radioactivity is held longest in the beards, and that radioactivity makes men impotent. As a consequence, the Cubans would shave their beards, and without bearded Cubans there would be no revolution.

Cigarette holder in hand, Fleming stressed that Castro's beard was the key. Without the beard, Castro would look like anyone else. It was his trademark. So, Fleming amusingly suggested that the U.S. should announce that they found that beards attract radioactivity. Any person wearing a beard could become radioactive himself, as well as sterile!

"Then, Castro would immediately shave off his beard and would soon fall from power, when the people see him as an ordinary person." He paused dramatically. "You see, Mr. Kennedy, it's all rather quite obvious," Fleming said finally, grinning.

Kennedy had a good laugh at Fleming's bizarre suggestion. *Don't give up your day job, Ian.* But the intrigue gave him some food for thought and piqued his interest. He'd heard stranger scenarios recently, that was for sure.

The Bay of Pigs
Within six months of Castro's 1959 overthrow of Batista's dictatorship in Cuba, relations between Castro and the US deteriorated and Castro accused the United States of trying to undermine his regime. In January 1961, President Eisenhower, in one of the final acts of his administration, broke diplomatic ties with Cuba (an invasion of Cuba

had been planned by the CIA since May 1960, under Eisenhower). The invasion had been fiercely debated within JFK's new administration before it was finally approved and carried out in April 1961, just three months after JFK took office. The principal invasion took place at the Bay of Pigs on the south-central coast. The invasion force was overcome by Castro's troops, and their last stronghold had been captured, along with more than 1,100 men. Critics charged the CIA with supplying faulty information to the new president. The captured members of the invasion force were imprisoned. The Kennedy administration unofficially backed attempts to ransom the prisoners, but failed to raise the $28,000,000 needed for heavy-construction equipment demanded by Castro as reparations. Castro finally agreed to release the prisoners in exchange for $53,000,000 in food and medicine. [24] Although JFK claimed that the CIA had lied to him, some critics thought that JFK had not been aggressive enough in its support of the Bay of Pigs invasion. The incident was crucial to the development of the Cuban Missile Crisis of October 1962.

Jacqueline Kennedy motioned to her husband as dessert came.

JFK spoke up, "Oh yes … uh, Ian … would you like a, uh, cigah?" asked Kennedy, searching for his lighter.

Judy Garland was singing on the Kennedy's hi-fi record player about 'The Man That Got Away,' whilst Fleming politely waved off Kennedy with one hand. "No no, no thank you my good man, cigarettes have always been my misfortune. I have always smoked and drank and loved too much, and someday, I shall die from having lived too much." Kennedy grinned to himself thoughtfully almost looking at his wife. *Well, there you go, Jackie, two out of three isn't bad.*

Fleming patted his jacket to no avail and added. "And if it weren't for the bloody British income tax I'd be a millionaire!" The wealthy Senator Kennedy appeared mildly embarrassed, then, thinking about his plans for a tax credit if elected, said, "Ian, as of today

---

[24] The anti-Castro, Cuban-born, American WWII veteran, bandleader-actor-businessman Desi Arnaz donated $50,000, through Robert Kennedy, to help finance the release of the captured Freedom Fighters.

considuh yourself an honorary citizen of the, uh, United States."[25]

Fleming bowed with courtesy from his seat and pulled another cigarette from his silver case. Kennedy noticed that the case had a crest on it, a family crest perhaps. Kennedy grinned at his entertaining dinner companion and in one of the pockets of his two-button jacket found the lighter that he had been looking for. He considered Fleming for a moment as he adjusted himself in his seat. Kennedy was always interested in the different directions that the men of his generation took after the war.

Here's Fleming, a career government intelligence offisuh who left and became a writuh because of the war-uh, and here I am a goddamn caree-uh government official who wanted to be a writuh but had to be President because of my fahthuh ...

Ironies always struck Kennedy hard. He flamed his petite Cuban.

"Pardon me," Fleming asked JFK politely, as he affixed his cigarette to it's extended holder. "Do you have a match?"

"I use a lightuh," said Kennedy, puffing away, working to create an ember.

Fleming nodded knowingly, "Better still."

"That is, until they, uh, go wrong," said Kennedy without looking at him, waiting for the tobacco to catch fire, his tall flame dancing.

"Exactly," replied Ian Fleming, thoroughly impressed.

Mrs. Kennedy, sensing the pregnant pause, asked softly, "Oh please do tell us, Mr. Fleming ... what are you working on now? Fleming considered his most attractive dinner hostess for a moment, straightened his dinner napkin in his lap, and said, "Well my dear Mrs.

---

[25] Ian Fleming's father was killed in WWI, just a week before Ian's 9th birthday, May 28, 1917, the day before JFK was born.

Kennedy, there will always be another Bond, as long as I'm alive, of course, but I do have a rather odd twist of an idea, just an idea now, mind you, for a novel ... a children's book really. A rather new, roundabout territory for myself, I should say, isn't it?"

"Oh, how wonderful. Please, Mr. Fleming, do tell us! What is it about!" she cooed, thinking about her children and nieces and nephews and how she was always looking for new books for them.

"The working title is 'Chitty-Chitty Bang-Bang.' It's about a magical car," said Fleming, silver butter knife in one hand, reaching for a crepe, as Kennedy stood awkwardly to light the cigarette Fleming held in his other.

Fleming leaned into Kennedy's seemingly eternal flame and drew on the cigarette gently, but deeply, before he courteously replied to Mrs. Kennedy, "... a car with ... secret powers ... a car that can float and that can sprout wings like an airplane ... and fly away ..."

Then he exhaled, looked at Mrs. Kennedy, smiled, and said, "... it shall be, I hope ... a car that saves the day."[26]

---

[26] In addition to the James Bond series, Ian Fleming also wrote the 1964 children's book for his son, *Chitty-Chitty Bang-Bang*, as the author recuperated from a heart attack. He died on August 12, 1964.

Back in California that same day, John Wayne had publicly criticized Frank Sinatra's decision to hire Albert Maltz, one of the Hollywood Ten, to write a screenplay about Eddie Slovak, the sole American ordered executed for desertion during World War II. [Albert Maltz had also written the lyrics to 'The House I Live In' for Sinatra in 1945. The song was part of a film short that won Sinatra a Special Academy Award. Maltz was later accused of being a communist and named as one of the infamous Hollywood Ten].

Wayne's comments made the papers, and his meddling incensed Sinatra, especially after the negative press and public outcry forced him to fire Maltz. Sinatra went into a slow burn after the incident, and he exploded in anger one night at Hollywood's Moulin Rouge restaurant.

Dozens of Hollywood stars had gathered at the eatery/nightclub for a hundred dollar a plate benefit for mentally handicapped children. The stars came in costume – Wayne in a checkered Western shirt, yellow neckerchief, and white cowboy hat, and Sinatra in an Indian outfit, complete with moccasins, beads, leather shirt and leggings, and a long wig of straight jet black hair, with a headband holding a single upright feather. The restaurant had gone all out for the event, even hiring an extra bartender to work a portable service bar so the stars could have some privacy during the show.

The fundraiser went smoothly and without incident until after the entertainment portion of the evening, when cowboy Wayne sang an off-key verse of the western ballad 'Red River Valley,' and Indian Sinatra crooned his staple standby, 'The Lady is a Tramp.'

Wayne cleared his throat the best he could and hitched his trousers up and went for it, full cowboy, as it were, for the kids.

When the Duke finished, he was greeted with great applause and a standing ovation from the children and their families and caretakers. He took off his big ten-gallon hat and took a sweeping bow, and then waved for Sinatra to take his turn before walking over to the makeshift bar area. Wayne left the stage to enthusiastic applause, but Sinatra, dressed in full Indian garb, was immediately heckled and laughed at. To make it worse there was only a piano player present, not a full band. Perfect accompaniment for Wayne's soft, heartfelt ballad, but not for a tune universally known as a Sinatra showstopper.

But the show had to go on, as they say, so Frank bucked up and sang it from start to finish, in his Native-American Indian costume and long, straight black-haired wig. He was not in 'good voice,' as they say. It was a fine showing for Wayne, no one was expecting much from him musically, but an off-key Sinatra was disappointing, both to the audience and to himself. As a very tiny smattering of applause barely rippled through the room, Sinatra quickly curtsied and then quickly joined Wayne at the bar, snapping his fingers and ordering a Jack and ice.

"Not so easy without Mr. Riddle and his thirty friends, is it Tonto ..." teased Wayne.

Sinatra received his drink in a plastic cup and began picking ice cubes out, flinging them one by one at the young Irish kid tending bar. "What are we, skating here!" Sinatra yelled, as he tossed what was left of the drink into the trash barrel and ordered a fresh one. "Three ice cubes this time, okay buddy boy. Hockey ain't my game, okay chum?!"

Wayne nursed his house whiskey and quietly bit his tongue, embarrassed for the kid he'd asked the restaurant to hire. He'd seen Sinatra in action before. And he was sure he'd see it again after this evening was over, too.

It didn't take long. They almost came to blows after Sinatra kept badgering Duke to "mind his own business" regarding the Maltz affair and the upcoming election. With scores of children crowding all

72

around them, Wayne and Sinatra finally had it out. Friends had to get between the cowboy and the Indian to prevent a fistfight in front of the adoring kids. "Let's take this outside, okay Tonto," said Wayne, giving Sinatra a 'Ladies before Gentlemen' bow.

Wayne started to drape his arm over Sinatra's shoulder as they made their way towards the exit, but Sinatra whacked it away. He held a 'this'll just take a minute, baby' index finger up to fiancé Juliet Prowse, who was sitting at a table alone, and strutted out into the parking lot with Wayne.

"Listen Duke," Sinatra began. "This is complicated here. It ain't all black and white you know ..."

"Well why the hell not?!" demanded the six-foot-four Wayne, even taller in cowboy boots, as he towered over the five-seven or eight inch Sinatra. He started to reach for a smoke but thought better of it, deciding it might be smart to keep his hands free.

"Tell me Frank, y'ever hear of the Domino Theory?" Wayne didn't wait for an answer. "Well you and your commie friend there, Mr. Pro-files In Courage, the lace-curtain arrogant little ... you're just helpin' it roll right on along ..." Wayne made a grand, sweeping gesture with his right arm as he quietly readied to cock his left.

"Whaddaya mean?! He's a Democrat! Doesn't mean he's not American! You voted for Roosevelt once, Y'even told me yourself!!"

"Once," said Wayne. "A lifetime ago. Nineteen Thirty-Six. Everyone voted Roosevelt in '36! Christ! Hitler voted Roosevelt in '36! ... But back then I was a kid, and kids are dumb." Wayne wiped the side of his nose, "And you, Tonto ... ki-mo-sa-be ... are much too ... old to be young ..." Wayne was out of breath and it bothered him.

Sinatra tried to throw his jacket off his shoulder, but the suede, fringed Indian garb costume pullover didn't budge.

Wayne held his hips in his hands. "Profiles In Courage, what a crock of shit! Didn't even write it! Ghostwriters did it for him, the

73

rich, snot-nosed little shit! Was his whoremaster daddy put it on the bestsellers list, not the American people!"

"That's a lie!" yelled Sinatra up at Wayne. Sinatra was out of reach, and off key.

"That's the truth!!" said Wayne.

Wayne kept going. "Little shit can't even keep his dick in his pants - and neither can you, you no good little runt. Why, I was in this town long before you and your commie friend even had your first piece of ass, before you two commies even had hair on those tiny little balls of yours, before your voice even changed, and by that, I mean when it changed - the - first - time! ..."

Sinatra started to swing, not musically, but with his arm.

Wayne caught Sinatra's hand in his fist, held it at his waist in mid air and grinned. Almost a foot below Wayne's line of vision, Sinatra's single feather slid and drooped over his face.

Wayne lowered his voice to Sinatra as a crowd of friends and a few reporters enveloped them. "First *High Noon*, then *Spartacus* ... why I told Coop and Kirk face-to-face they was makin' us all look bad, not to mention their commie screenwriter Dalton Trumbo ... and now you want to put a runaway commie like Eddie Slovak on the screen, and use the other commie, Albert Maltz, to write it ... it's the same as dominos, one after another after another ..."[27]

"Yeah, well ... *Spartacus* was his favorite movie this year," whispered Sinatra to Duke's face. "And you know what else? Very few people know this, but *Red River* is his favorite movie of All-Time ..."

"Whose?"

---

[27] *Spartacus* starred Kirk Douglas, Tony Curtis, Alec Guinness and Lawrence Olivier. It had been suggested that the Roman gladiator film had homosexual undertones. The screenplay was by Dalton Trumbo, a member of the infamous 'Hollywood Ten.'

"Jack's."

"Ja-ack's. Ja-ack's" said Wayne like a schoolgirl, taunting, mocking Sinatra. "Well, it figures …"

Wayne straightened his back and scratched behind his ear.

One more time. He couldn't resist.

"Commie."

Sinatra stepped back in retreat, his driver and beefy, leg-breaker minions feigning his resistance.

"Oughta be ashamed Duke, you big, oversized mug!" he called out from a safe distance. "Votin' against one of your own, an Irishman, and a Catholic to boot!"

"He ain't Irish … he's Hahhhhrvard …" Wayne hated phony, affected accents like Kennedy's. Like Sinatra's. All the 'marvelouses' and 'tremendous' and 'fantastics'.

"He goes to Mass every single Sunday, every single Sunday he goes to Mass," Sinatra demanded.

Wayne roared at that one. "Oh for crissakes Frank will you just stop the bullshit. Sayin' it twice won't make it matter any more! Or make it true! Who the hell do you think you're talking to, the fucking Rotary Club? And I'm Presbyterian, for crissakes!! Have been all my life! Jesus Christ!! … Sunday Catholics! They're the worst goddamn kind. Gives 'em six more days to go fuck it all up again."

"Please," added Wayne. "Frank, spare me the bullshit. If you need to get it off that chest of yours, tell more lies, alleviate more guilt, please, go ahead. But just do me one favor … go tell it to a priest."

The valet brought Sinatra his keys. Sinatra appeared grateful, motioning his driver to duke, err, tip, the valet twenty.

"And as for religion and politics, two different things," said Duke, admiring the white Stetson he now held in his hand. "Church and state, they're like water and oil … ain't that right, dago?" He deliberately rattled the crooner, as he smoothed over his hat's brim.

Sinatra made a weak attempt to break free from his driver, who feigned to restrain him. The only one who called him 'dago' and got away with it was Dean Martin.

"Oh yeah," Sinatra fumed. "You just watch, you'll get yours buddy boy … you wait and see …" Sinatra and his party then exited the Red Mill lot and went off into the night.

Wayne turned and walked back into the event. When he entered and saw the room full of children again, he smiled fondly. *Poor little bastards.*

"Carry on," he waved and said aloud to nobody and everybody at the same time. "Just proves what I've been sayin' all along …"

Wayne pulled a smoke from his cigarette case and felt for his matches.

"Never give whiskey to Indians."

Wayne shook his head and then looked skyward. "Dear God help us," he prayed. "Nixon better goddamn win."

JFK flew to Los Angeles for an intimate $1,000-a-plate Hollywood dinner for a hundred people, including Marlon Brando, Cary Grant, Burt Lancaster, and Gene Kelly, among others. Instead of offering a formal speech, the president table-hopped and socialized, impressing his guests with a wide-ranging knowledge of movies in general and the star's individual careers, specifically. It was a nice, 'no heavy-lifting' event intended to raise a fast $100,000.

As Kennedy chatted with Rock Hudson, the conversation turned, somehow, to Irish ancestry. "You know all the Fitzgerald's are related, right?" JFK seriously kidded, momentarily looking over Hudson's shoulder at the young Irish waiter by the name of Fitzgerald who he could've sworn was the same kid who had shined his shoes earlier that day.

"That's right, sir," Hudson curtly replied to Kennedy. "And I'm sure Ella will be happy to hear about it, too."

"Well, I, uh ..." It was a rare moment to see JFK speechless. He saw the Irish boy smiling, trying to keep a laugh in, which made Kennedy laugh out loud himself.

When desert was served, Kennedy saw the waiter approaching and he tapped the boy's metal nametag and grabbed himself a piece of cheesecake off the tray, saying, "Now, didn't you shine my shoes this morning? And you wait tables, too. Don't you ever stop? Why you'll be wealthier than my father before you're thirty, Fitzy! My God we're everywhere, aren't we. There's just no stopping us Fitzgerald *working* men." JFK winked. The young waiter smiled proudly and then laughed quietly to himself, remembering that when he had shined Kennedy's scuffed old, brown shoes earlier that day, he had told the candidate that his brown shoes would surely earn him the working man's vote. Kennedy must have heard his thought because he immediately said, "There sure as hell aren't any other working men here tonight."

They both laughed and Kennedy moved on, wondering if the young man could secretly build him a lift for his left shoe, to help compensate for his shorter left leg, which combined with his injured back caused him constant muscle spasms and radiating pains which shot down his left leg as he campaigned. Kennedy laughed to himself, imagining the secret shoe lift as a kind of secret gadget, like the ones Commander James Bond always had. JFK's back was so injured and pained that he reportedly couldn't pull on a sock or tie a shoe on his left foot without assistance.

As Kennedy moved on and table-hopped and shook celebrity hands, he finally found himself face to face with Marlon Brando, whom he had never before met. Kennedy extended his hand to the great actor, "How are you, uh, nice to meet you."

Brando, ever the wiseass, replied deadpan, "Man, aren't you bored?"

Kennedy, startled and perhaps a bit offended at Brando's honesty, looked at him and said, "No, I'm, uh, not bored." *But Jesus, these chicken dinners are a goddamn grind, though.*

As Doris Day's version of 'Hooray For Hollywood' played overhead, three tables away, Sinatra seethed when he saw Kennedy conferring with Brando. He was overcome with jealousy. Obsessed, trying to read their lips (impossible with Brando's mumbled elocution and Kennedy's absurd accent), Sinatra nervously ate cheesecake after cheesecake while Brando and Kennedy chatted.

"So, you're not bored?" Brando playfully taunted Kennedy again with a straight poker face, trying to get Kennedy to react, "C'mon, you can't be serious. You've got to be bored." Brando smiled, taking a bite of his own cheesecake. "Otherwise, you are one great actor."

Kennedy briefly considered Brando's smile and forcibly smiled back. He thought Brando was being hostile. Or was it all just an act? JFK was used to some hostility on the campaign trail, but not at a Hollywood event. *Not at a grand a head.* But then he thought about it and admitted to himself that although he didn't consider it a burden, he

78

could never really admit it, it *was* a grind and yes he *was* bored having to do this, going around, night after night, the same conversations, the same chicken and roast beef dinners, for years and years, with everyone gawking at him, muttering. *If I wasn't a politician I would never go out for dinner. I'd rather be home taking a hot bath or reading a book with a bowl of soup and a grilled cheese sandwich or watching a good football game or boxing match. Or in Paris.* Kennedy quickly regained his composure and smiled broadly. "We'll see you soon, Marlon," said Kennedy, moving along. "Look forward to seeing you again."

The young waiter named Fitzgerald was clearing tables and hurried past Kennedy on his way into the kitchen. Kennedy wanted to tip the waiter so he reached into his pants pockets for some cash, but he had no money on him, as usual. So he stepped in front of the waiter, removed his own PT-109 tie clasp from his royal blue and white striped Brooks Brothers tie, dropped it into the waiter's breast pocket, patted him firmly on the shoulder and said, "Here, I only give this to Fitzgerald's." The Irish kid beamed. "Fitzy," added Kennedy, "I think this is the beginning of a beautiful friendship."

The waiter watched, impressed, as JFK strategically made his way toward the exit, so he could bid good evening to each guest as they departed. As he greeted one-by-one each the Hollywood actors and actresses and producers and directors as they passed, giving each his warm, double handshake, with the left hand coming in under the clasp, the six-foot-one inch tall Kennedy couldn't help but laugh to himself. *My God aside from Rock Fitzgerald Hudson they are all so goddamn short and small, like circus midgets. It's like the goddamn 'Wizard of Oz.' Hollywood is like real people Munchkinland. The land of the little people.*

Kennedy saw Brando wave to him as he exited through a side door. He started to wave back but by then Brando was already gone. *Brando, why even he's a giant among men here, Christ, and he can't be more than five-nine. My God, Brando could be the King of Munchkinland.* Kennedy made a mental note to call on Brando at a later date, thinking such an alliance could prove beneficial down the road. He continued smiling and saying goodbye to the last guest, greeting the new guest, and making eye contact with the next guest, doing all three things at once.

Sitting alone at a table after eating his third piece of cheesecake, a jealous Sinatra felt nauseous. When a fourth dish was placed before him, Sinatra threw the plate to the ground, jammed his fork into the table, and screamed aloud, "Fucking New York actors! How much cheesecake do you think I can eat?" He knew that Brando and Kennedy had been talking about acting and politics and women, he just knew it.[28]

Nearby, the Irish waiter laughed to himself. He was about to bring Sinatra one more, final piece of cheesecake.

Compliments of Mr. Marlon Brando.

Brando. Why you hot shit sonofabitch, Kennedy laughed to himself as he shook hands and made small talk. Why you little ball-breaking sonofabitch. I'm going to remember you.

Sinatra discreetly wiped his teeth clean with a napkin.

---

[28] Sinatra called Brando "the world most over-rated actor," and privately claimed to have been initially promised the part of Terry Malloy in 1954's *On the Waterfront*, which won Brando his first Academy Award.

John Wayne, on the set of his next film, *North to Alaska*, after devouring a thick flank steak and killing a bottle of table cabernet, had let several of the cast and crew talk him into a poker game. Fueled by laughter and booze, the game went on well into the next morning.

Wayne talked politics to the boys until dawn.

The Democratic and Republican Conventions were just a week away, and Wayne told the boys how he had just spent $152,000 of his own money on a three-page red, white and blue ad in *Life* magazine, which had appeared in the previous week's Fourth of July edition.

The young card playing crew listened as though captive to Wayne as he ranted and raved about politics - his politics - all night long while they dealt and bluffed and stupidly tried to match The Duke drink for drink.

Feeling as though he was not getting through to the youngsters, Wayne sent one of the crew, the kid in charge of the shoes and boots on loan from Paramount, back to his trailer to grab him another pack of smokes, his reading glasses, and the new July edition of *Life* magazine on his bureau. "The one with the girl who looks like Sophia Loren on the cover!"

When the young man returned with all three items, Wayne lit up a Camel, put on his specs, and then lit into Kennedy, reading his pro-Republican ad to the naïve and captive audience. Holding the magazine at a proper distance, Wayne cleared his throat, set aside an empty bottle of claret and his short glass of tequila, looked down through his cheaters, inhaled, and read …

… To fulfill the … awesome duties of the White House … we need for a man who will put America back on the high road … a man who would say … to hell with friend or foe and that the American softness must be hardened and that there were no ghostwriters at The

Alamo. Only Men." (It had always been widely speculated that JFK's Pulitzer Prize-winning book *Profiles In Courage* was ghostwritten by one of Kennedy's aides).

"Signed," Wayne removed his eye-glasses and looked up at the crew …

"John Wayne."

Wayne stayed on topic all night, talking politics and drinking the boys under the table, taking all their nickels and dimes in the process. At 8:00 a.m. sharp, the fifty-three year old Wayne was on the set, fully costumed, and already made up, but filming was delayed by the red-eyed novices who had missed their wake-up calls. When the stragglers finally made it to the set, Wayne loudly proclaimed, "Well, here come the kids. I had to tuck them in last night."

Then, under his breath, he said, "This country's going soft." Wayne thought about Nixon, "He better win, goddammit."

Aboard JFK's private campaign plane that week, reporters asked Kennedy if he thought the ad was aimed at him. Kennedy, mute from campaign trail laryngitis, dodged the question, and instead scribbled on his notepad to an aide, "How do we cut John Wayne's balls off?" (Wayne later bragged that Republican response to his ad brought in over $5 million to the Nixon campaign).

Kennedy's star power loomed large during the 1960 Democratic National Convention, fortuitously held in Los Angeles, where Sinatra, Janet Leigh, Tony Curtis, Sammy Davis Jr., Nat King Cole, and Judy Garland all took part in high-profile convention-week events that glamorized politics and party.

For the weeklong convention JFK stayed in a small, three-floor, white stucco house owned by Jack Haley, famous for his role as the tin man in *The Wizard Of Oz*. It was a convenient spot, as it was just a short, ten-minute drive to the Biltmore Hotel, which would serve as Kennedy campaign headquarters, and the Los Angeles Sports Arena, where the convention was to be held.

Frank Sinatra spent every waking moment of the week campaigning and fundraising in the Hollywood community (the previous week he had raised over $50,000 alone by taking requests at Tony Curtis' pool, singing from the end of the diving board). The convention opened as Sinatra and other celebrities sang a jazzed up version of the national anthem.

Then Sinatra and Janet Leigh worked the convention floor, tirelessly, like political veterans, strategizing, drumming up support. Always mindful of his appearance, to a point way past vanity, knowing the convention TV cameras were roaming overhead, Sinatra even had his small bald patch covered with black shoe polish that he bought off the Irish shoeshine boy at Paramount.

At the end of the week, on July 15, 1960, JFK won the nomination for President, edging out Colonel Parker's friend, Texas Senator and Majority leader Lyndon Baines Johnson, who then reportedly blackmailed his way onto the Kennedy ticket with sordid and secret details regarding Kennedy's private life and physical health. (Among his many chronic and episodic ailments, Kennedy suffered from a form of Addison's Disease, which if made public along with his affairs would have surely ended his political career at that time.).

Once nominated, Kennedy spoke to those Democrats gathered in the Coliseum as their candidate for President …

… We stand today at the start of a New Frontier …

That night, everyone who was anyone went to Pat and Peter Lawford's Malibu beach house for a celebratory party. Exhausted from the day's events and the non-stop, manic months leading up to them, the party quickly languished, and soon everybody was falling half asleep from the beer, liquor and wine, particularly the local California wine, and the various prescription and nonprescription medications that were so popular with the Hollywood set.

JFK, after quietly slipping away behind closed doors, only to return a few minutes later with a satisfied, ruddy grin on his face, called over his younger brother Ted, already well known as the life of any party, poked him in the chest, and said, "Now, uh, let's get this thing going Teddy, we need to liven things up a bit here! We need you to get up and do your numbers!" ('Do your numbers,' in Kennedy parlance, meant getting up and singing old standards and Irish rebel songs terribly out of key in front of large crowds, friends and strangers. Oftentimes, both).

Teddy, always the dutiful baby of the family, ceremoniously took over the area of the living room that presented itself as 'center stage' and belted out his own tone-deaf yet spirited renditions of Jack's favorite songs, 'Won't You Come Home, Bill Bailey,' and 'Heart Of My Heart,' as well as a few of the old Irish tunes. But the narcoleptic partygoers were a 'tough crowd.' When Teddy finished 'singing,' he said to the captive yet less than entertained houseguests, "Okay then, anybody in the room who thinks they can do better, why don't you come on up here, and give it a try yourself!"

So Frank Sinatra stood up and walked over to the band and called for 'All The Way.'

Then, on the other side of the living room, Nat King Cole, with a voice as smooth as aged Scotch whiskey, got up and sang 'Unforgettable.'

Jack pulled his brother aside and quietly said, "Uh, Teddy, maybe you should have quit while you were, uh, ahead."

Then, for the second climax of the evening, Judy Garland, the star of scores of MGM musicals and the film classic *The Wizard of Oz*, quietly stepped over to the band, all four-foot eleven of her, and sang 'Over The Rainbow,' right there in the living room.

Fitzy, the young Irish bartender, and everyone else present, stood speechless before applauding.

The next night Sinatra was honored to be Kennedy's official guest at an official Democratic Party dinner, seated right beside him on the dais, just as he had been every night that week. By the third course, Kennedy still hadn't arrived. Sinatra grew edgy, and began drinking heavily. He had collected additional cash and checks and as usual, and very much insisted on giving them to JFK personally.

Finally, deep into the roast beef entree, one of Kennedy's toothy sisters stopped by and casually said "Hello, Francis." When Sinatra asked if she had seen her brother, she replied, "Oh, Jack. He went to the movies. But I hear you have some checks for us." Sinatra smiled at her with everything he had. He even batted his eyes. But inside, he was dying.

"I'd like to give them to Jack myself, sister, if that's okay?" Except for Lawford's wife Pat, with whom he was friends', all the Kennedy broads looked the same to him.

The Kennedy sister extended her open hand, right there in front of everyone, and with more teeth than a Great White, kept smiling. The table fell silent. Sinatra gave up and reached into his breast pocket.

"Why thank you Francis. I'll be sure that Jack gets them."

Sinatra boiled.

Seventy million U.S. television viewers tuned in to watch Senator John Kennedy of Massachusetts and Vice President Richard Nixon in the first-ever televised presidential debate. Live from Chicago.

This was television's grand entrance into presidential politics. The first real opportunity for all voters to *see* their candidates, and the visual contrast was dramatic. Nixon had seriously injured his knee recently (after catching it on a car door while campaigning) and had just spent two weeks in the hospital with an infection. By the time of the debate, he was twenty pounds underweight, his shirt didn't fit, and his face was very pale. When Nixon arrived at the TV studio that day, giving Kennedy and everyone else his customary weak, throwaway handshake, he looked like death warmed over. Like a dead fish.

While the TV producer was talking to Nixon, all of a sudden he noticed out of the corner of his eye that Jack Kennedy had arrived. Kennedy looked like a matinee idol. He was tanned, rested and ready. Well-tailored and in command of himself. No one had ever seen a matinee idol-for-president before.

As the television crew prepared, Kennedy was curious, as was his custom. He conferred with the producer, humbly asking his professional opinions and assistance.

"Where do I stand?"
"*Do* I stand?"
"*Should* I stand?"
"Do I sit?"
"*When* should I, uh, sit?"
"Is there a break?"
"*When* is the, uh, break?"
"How much time do I have to ansuh?"
"Can he (Nixon) interrupt?"
"Can I, uh, interrupt Mr. Nixon?"
"Can I have a glass of watuh on the podium?"

Kennedy wanted to know everything. He knew how important this television appearance would be. Nixon wasn't interested in preparations. He had already made one speech that day, at the Chicago Plumbers Union, as if to say 'I have one appearance this afternoon, and I've got another one tonight, and one's just like the other.' Kennedy had had a 'nap' and rested that afternoon, after having helped to stimulate the economy by temporarily employing a member of the world's oldest profession.

The producer said to both of them, "Would you like some makeup?"

"No, thank you, not really," answered Kennedy, who clearly didn't need any.

Nixon, who in addition to being pale and sick had a terminal five-o'clock shadow and very much *did* need makeup, desperately, also said "no." He didn't want history to record that he wore 'makeup' and Kennedy didn't.

When the producer looked at them both on camera, Kennedy looked great. Nixon looked bad. Nixon looked terrible. He looked awful.

But it got worse.

Nixon was wearing a light-colored suit, and Kennedy was wearing a dark suit. Kennedy had already carefully chosen the clothes that he would wear that night, for he knew, from his father, all about color and contrast on film, and on black and white television. So be it face or clothes, Nixon appeared all washed out. The producer, looking at the monitor, called the president of the station and said, "You better look at this." The two of them kind of tapped their fingers and fidgeted a little bit. They called in Nixon's advisor and asked, "Are you satisfied the way your candidate looks?"

"Yeah, sure, we think he looks great!" Nixon's advisor said.

That night, voters *saw* that Kennedy was different from his opponent. He was like Central Casting. He looked the part. He was quick. He had a command of the language. A straight-forward delivery. His obvious charm and seeming shyness had made him an easy guest in America's living room.

But most of all, he didn't sweat.

Right after the program ended, and the cameras were shut off, the producer called over to JFK. "Mr. Kennedy, there's a call for you." It was the pay phone backstage. Kennedy's father was on the line, Old Man Joe, calling from a pay phone on Hollywood's Paramount lot, where he had just gotten a shoeshine (from Fitzy) and met a striking young, aspiring actress. JFK knew immediately who it was. *But how the hell did he get the number of a pay phone in Chicago?*

JFK said 'Hello, Jack Kennedy," to which his father replied, "Did the makeup thing work? It sure looked that way. The paranoid bastard looked like a dead haddock."

"Yes, dad," Kennedy grinned. "He, uh, took the bait all right," Then he added, "… hook, line, and, uh, sinkuh."

Paranoid. I'd be paranoid too if the whole world was against me.

"Great job, son! Now, go get yourself a frappe … on me!"

"Gee, thanks Dad," muttered Kennedy, like a boy. *What am I? Eleven years old? Doesn't he know that I'm running for President of the United States?*

The Frappe.
A frappe is a Boston version of a deliciously thick milkshake made with vanilla ice cream, milk and chocolate syrup. Kennedy virtually survived on them during his early illnesses and hospitalizations, and during his political campaigns.

Nevertheless, Kennedy was better tailored, better looking, and more articulate. Poised, confident and informed. But what few knew was that Kennedy had already had his makeup expertly applied at the hotel before he left for the debate, by an Academy Award-winning Hollywood makeup artist flown in from Hollywood to Chicago, at the express request of his father, Joe Kennedy.

The 70 million viewers who watched the debate on television saw a Nixon who was ill at ease, sickly, and obviously discomforted by Kennedy's smooth delivery and charisma. Those television viewers focused on what they saw, not what they heard. Studies of the audience indicated that, among television viewers, Kennedy was perceived the winner of the debate by a very large margin. It was the night that television and politics fell in love with each other, got engaged, and then got married, perhaps forever.

The following day, nobody watching on TV remembered much either one of them had said, only how they looked.

Sock It To Me …

At the last minute prior to the start of the debate, Kennedy saw that his black socks that were too short, barely covering his ankles, so that when he crossed his legs his bare skin showed between his pants and his socks. Kennedy instinctively knew that this would not 'look good' on television. There was no time for one of Kennedy's men to go back to the hotel to get another pair of socks, so JFK quickly exchanged socks with, and with the help of, one of his aides.

Soviet Premier Nikita Khrushchev was at the United Nations in New York City, where on national television, he took off his shoe and began aggressively banging it on a desk. "We will bury you!" (The United States), he taunted for all to see. "We will bury you!!"

The outrageous pro-communist display was unprecedented. Here was the symbol of Communism taunting America, the leader of the free world, on its own turf! At the height of the Cold War! It was front-page headlines and the top TV news story worldwide. [The Khrushchev shoe-banging incident allegedly occurred during the 902nd Plenary Meeting of the United Nations General Assembly held in New York on 12 October 1960, when the infuriated leader of the Soviet Union was said to have pounded his shoe on his delegate-desk. There is currently no reliable evidence confirming whether the incident actually took place. Witness accounts vary, and there are no credible photographic or video records available. There is at least one fake depiction of the incident, where a shoe was added into an existing photograph].

Personally, Wayne was angered and sickened by the display, but he had to admit, it was great for business. *Free worldwide publicity for 'The Alamo!' You stupid commie bastard!* Wayne's confidence was evident to all as the election-eve patriotic hype became even more fervent. He referred to Khrushchev's UN taunt as his "Russian Christmas gift," coming as it did just in time for Christmas, and the Academy Award ceremony, too. *Yessiree*, Wayne figured he would take home all the Oscar hardware that year. *And to think that at one time the Russians wanted to kill me*, he mused, remembering the story that Khrushchev had told him and Nixon back in 1958. [During Soviet leader Nikita Khrushchev's historic visit to California visit in 1958, the Russian premier had told Wayne and Nixon, through an interpreter, that Joseph Stalin had ordered Wayne to be assassinated by the KGB, but that Stalin had died before his plan could be carried out. Khrushchev said he had personally rescinded the order].

But at Oscar time *The Alamo* lost to *Spartacus*.

It was a disaster. Just like the real Alamo had been. The film didn't win any big awards, and it hardly recouped its investment at the box office. Despite Wayne's superhuman efforts, financing, producing, directing and starring in the epic, Hollywood still didn't take him seriously as a director. In order to survive, he was going to have to continue his cowboy-soldier-action roles for the rest of his career. His financial burdens just wouldn't allow otherwise.

Then on November 5, 1960 his best friend died.

One week after attending *The Alamo* premier in San Antonio, three days before the election, Ward Bond, Wayne's pal and film sidekick in decades of classics, and the star of the TV's *Wagon Train*, suffered a massive heart attack in a Dallas hotel room. Wayne wept uncontrollably for weeks and then went into a profound, quiet depression, refusing food and losing fifteen pounds. First *The Alamo* failure, and now his best friend gone, it was as if someone had cut his heart out.

And *The Alamo* didn't much help Richard Nixon either.

NOVEMBER 8 1960. ELECTION NIGHT
RICHARD NIXON, LOS ANGELES, CALIFORNIA

At midnight, as he watched the election returns from his hotel room at Los Angeles' Ambassador Hotel, Nixon cautiously took calls from key precincts around the country, but particularly Chicago. Privately, Nixon told aides and family that it was over, that Kennedy was going to win.

FRANK SINATRA, LOS ANGELES, CALIFORNIA

Frank Sinatra and Juliet Prowse followed the election returns at the Tony Curtis-Janet Leigh home in L.A., along with the Billy Wilders (Director of *Some Like It Hot*, etc.), the Milton Berles ('Uncle Miltie'-'Mr. Tuesday Night'). The Curtis home took calls from the Peter Lawfords in Hyannis Port. At one point taking a call from one-eyed, negro, Jewish, Sinatra sidekick Sammy Davis Jr., who had stopped his stage act that Tuesday night to get the latest election reports and electoral count. After all, he represented several voting blocks.

Sinatra poured another one and gulped, never turning his eyes away from the TV. "C'mon, concede you sonofabitch!! C'mon!! Concede!!" yelled Sinatra at the TV. But Nixon wouldn't concede, not publicly anyway. Frank was drunk, really drunk. His voice was hoarse, raw. He told Janet Leigh to get him the phone. He called the Ambassador Hotel and tried to get Nixon on the line, eventually reaching a startled campaign volunteer. "Tell the sonofabitch it's over! Tell him to concede! Now!"

JFK, HYANNISPORT, MASSACHUSETTS

A few minutes after 3 a.m., with Kennedy still needing eight electoral votes to declare victory, the TV news team of Chet Huntley and David Brinkley cut to Nixon, his tired trooper-of-a-wife Pat beside him, on the verge of tears.

Kennedy had spent most of his early evening with his father, in the Kennedy's custom-built, basement movie theatre. At first they watched John Wayne's 1948 classic western, *Red River*, yet again, which was JFK's *all-time* favorite movie, co-starring a young Montgomery Clift as one of film's original anti-heroes. (JFK closely identified with Clift's portrayal of the rebellious 'adopted' son who challenges the ultimate paternal authority figure in John Wayne, in what is perhaps Wayne's meanest, most ruthless role). But his father's close proximity, and Wayne's obvious political loyalties, made viewing the film awkward after just a few minutes, so Jack and his father agreed to change reels and watched *Butterfield 8,* starring an especially hot, in her prime, Elizabeth Taylor as a high-priced call-girl, instead.

When Kennedy appeared upstairs after the movie, his anxious press aide urged him to speak to the reporters who were waiting outside, many from around the world. Kennedy calmly made himself a nice turkey sandwich, poured a glass of milk, and pointed a dull knife at the pathetic image of Nixon on the screen and said, "You want me to put on a miserable performance like *that* at this hour of night? Not me. I'm going to bed, and I think, uh, all of you had better do likewise." On television, Nixon said goodnight to his supporters and went off the air without conceding. Kennedy watched and said, "Why in hell should he concede now? If I were him, I certainly wouldn't."

While Kennedy slept, he lost California. But he won Illinois (Chicago), Michigan and Minnesota, and he picked up a few electoral votes in New Mexico, giving him 303 electoral votes to Nixon's 219. The popular vote gave Kennedy a 68,832,818 total, a mere 118,550 more popular votes than his opponent, the slimmest popular vote margin of victory in a presidential election to date.

94

By seven a.m. that morning, a full two hours before JFK even woke up, Secret Service agents were already stationed around the compound.

JOHN WAYNE, NEWPORT BEACH, CALIFORNIA

When Illinois went to Kennedy, Wayne knew it was all over. Election night now reminded Wayne of Oscar night. *The Alamo* lost, and now Nixon.

"Sonofabitch!" Wayne sputtered, half-drunk and watching the late night returns in his den. "Son-of-a-bitch!! After all this work, I thought we'd win something. Anything."

By 4:30 a.m., Wayne had washed down his prime rib and potato with a fifth of his favorite Sauza Commemorativo tequila. He put his feet up on the coffee table before him, watched a snowy 'Test of the Emergency Broadcast System' on television, lit another Camel and began a guttural mumbling of the Ricky Nelson-Dean Martin song from *Rio Bravo ... My Rifle, My Pony, and Me*, laughing at the thought that maybe those were the only three things he had left, aside from his kids, who mostly lived with their mother.

He ended the song with a hacking "Cough! Cough! Cough!" but had held his own through the final stanza. He laughed and thought about Dean Martin. *Ol' Dino must be shitting himself right about now.* Then he lit up, and poured himself a snifter of brandy, just a wee, small taste of the creature, for a nightcap.

He thought about Dean. *Sure be nice to make a picture with Dino again. We had some fun. And that Rick Nelson boy held his own, too. The kid did well.*[29]

.

---

[29] Wayne and Dean Martin teamed up again in 1965's *The Sons Of Katie Elder*.

Wayne looked at the clock on his blue and white RCA clock radio. It was a quarter to three. He thought about Sinatra. *The skinny little commie.*

"But boy, the little big-mouthed son-of a-bitch can sing, I'll say that for 'em."

He laughed to himself again. Then he shut off the TV, and turned on the radio.

It was Sinatra.

"... Every bit of it is myyy-kind-of town – Chi-ca-go is ..."

"Well son-of-a-bitch." Wayne topped off his glass. "Chicago. Now I'll be damned." He lit another one and laughed. "Jesus-H-Christ, that's what I call i-rony ..."

The guy can carry a tune, yessiree. Jesus, just listen to that sonofabitch ...

"In Chicago ...

Chicago ...

Chicago! – My home town!!!"

Wayne cracked himself up again. *I wonder who the hell HE listens to when he's all by himself at four in the morning ... the little chicken-shit commie bastard ...*

He turned up the volume, leaned back and crossed his legs at the ankles, resting his glass on his belly. He stared at the unopened magnum of champagne on top of the TV set, the same spot it had sat since Oscar night, and sighed.

"Chicago. Goddamn Democrats. Country's gone soft ..."

At 10 a.m., the President-elect walked out of his house and saw a group of strange men milling about. A wry smile came over Kennedy's face when a Secret Service agent introduced himself and said that they had set up security around the compound, and that they would be with him from then on in.

"Does this, uh, mean that I won?" Kennedy joked.

"I guess so, Mr. President," said the young, crew-cutted agent, and together they walked towards his father's residence in the compound.

Great. Now I have to deal with all the arrogant assholes and egos who think they deserve a cabinet post or an ambassadorship or a job just because they held a goddamn sign or showed up at a party with free booze. Here we go ...

Old Man Kennedy sensed his son's reluctance and decided to put a fast stop to it. "Now, Jack," said his father, sarcastically, in front of the whole clan. "You don't have to take the job if you don't want it. I'm sure Mr. Nixon wouldn't mind. After all, they're still counting votes in Chicago, you know."

Here we go ...

That afternoon, after Nixon finally conceded, JFK greeted the television cameras, the nation and the world at the Hyannis Armory. The objective members of the press gave him a rousing ovation. He looked at all the cameras. *It was that goddamn TV, more than anything else, that turned the tide.*

In Palm Springs, a very hung-over but quietly jubilant Frank Sinatra, was asked by the Los Angeles press about a rumor that he had won $200,000 in election bets the night before.

"I don't bet on elections," answered Sinatra, straight-faced.

Later in the day, a reporter caught up with John Wayne and put a microphone to his face, as The Duke was getting his shoes shined by Fitzy on the Paramount lot, "Mr. Wayne, what did you think of the election results?" Wayne turned to the scribe, and hiding his annoyance, patriotically said, "I didn't vote for him, but he's our President now. I'm going to support him, and I hope that he does a good job."

Back at his Hollywood office, Colonel Tom Parker was delighted. His close friend Lyndon Baines Johnson, Senator from Texas and fellow 'Snowmen's League' member in good standing, had been elected on the Kennedy ticket as the new Vice-President of the United States of America. The second most powerful man in the country, and perhaps the entire world, was just a heartbeat away from the Presidency. [30]

The Colonel began a letter …

"Dear Mr. Vice-President Johnson,

Congratulations on your election.

If there is anything I can ever do …"

[30] The 'Snowman's League' was an insider's club of The Colonel's own creation which celebrated the art of 'snowing,' which was his slang term for selling and conning, to which he had dedicated his life. He boasted it cost nothing to get into but $10,000 to get out of, and its membership boasted everyone from Frank Sinatra, Bob Hope, Milton Berle and Bing Crosby, to Lyndon Johnson himself. In early 1965, after her father became President, Lynda Bird Johnson visited the set of Elvis' movie, *Girl Happy*.

The eve of JFK's inauguration saw one of the heaviest blizzards ever seen in the history of Washington, D.C. The entire capitol was at a standstill and all traffic was gridlocked. Sinatra's entertainment program, planned at the President's request at the National Armory, had been delayed by the snowstorm.

"Are there any songs that you should like in particular for me to sing, Jack?" Sinatra had asked. "I think *Hail to the Chief* has a nice ring to it," quipped Kennedy.

Sinatra had promised that it would be 'The greatest show on earth' and 'The show to end all shows,' promising that the gate receipts would erase Kennedy's and the entire Democratic Party's 1960 campaign debt "in one night."

But the night was a disaster.

Half the hall was empty. Most of the entertainers were either stuck in traffic or couldn't get a flight into Washington to begin with. Conductor Leonard Bernstein, America's hottest young composer, who had written the music for that year's Broadway hit *West Side Story,* had his car stranded in snow and he arrived two hours late.[31] Calypso singer Harry Belafonte - not a comedian – who had campaigned for Kennedy, ended up telling jokes to the sound of crickets for over two hours. The whole show was like watching a slow-moving train wreck. Towards the end of the program, when an extra exuberant Ethel Merman sang a rousing rendition of 'Let's Call the Whole Thing Off,' the Armory erupted in an impromptu, thunderous applause and ovation.

On the outdoor stage in frigid temperature Sinatra was apologetic to the frozen crowd, "We did not have much time to

---

[31] Leonard Bernstein once called Elvis Presley "the greatest cultural force in the twentieth century."

rehearse because of the weather, but in four years' time we'll really have it in shape."

Like Cinderella, Mrs. Kennedy left the show at midnight, as if she were about to turn into a pumpkin, but the President, not wanting to miss anything, stayed on with his father, Old Man Joe, smoking a long cigar, sipping champagne, and applauding the Hollywood stars in attendance and performers like Nat King Cole, Juliet Prowse, Jimmy Durante, and Ella Fitzgerald.

The next day, Sinatra turned up drunk at the Inauguration ceremony. Paralyzed drunk. Sloppy.

It was ten below zero in the nation's capitol, and he didn't even want to be there in the first place. The Palm Springs desert air this was not. There were supposedly assigned seats for him behind the podium from where Kennedy would give his speech, but apparently there had been an oversight. Frank's name was not on the list.

"But I'm Frank Sinatra," he insisted, "I ..."

"I don't care if you're the Pope," said the cop at the door. "You're not on the list." And the cops threw him out - on his ass. Sinatra had always hated cops, ever since he was a young ruffian in Hoboken, New Jersey, and this episode only cemented it. He retreated to the warmth of his hotel room to watch the speech and festivities on television, with the rest of the country.

Watching Kennedy as he delivered his famous "Ask not what your country can do for you ..." speech, Sinatra responded to the television, "I'd like to ask how come I didn't get a fucking seat at the inauguration, that's what I'd like to fucking ask ..."

Later that evening, at a party at the Washington Hilton, the President disappeared for about a half-hour, leaving Jackie alone in the Presidential Box, as he hurried off to a private party that Sinatra was throwing upstairs for all the invited stars of stage, screen and television. JFK had promised Frank that he would drop in.

When the President called up to the party and asked for the stars to come downstairs to greet him, Sinatra relayed back, "Tell him we're eating." When he finished his meal, Sinatra went downstairs to meet the President, and returned to the party with JFK beside him. Kennedy was apologetic, and star-struck as usual as he eyed the talent ... Juliet Prowse ... Angie Dickinson ...

When the President returned to his seat, and to Jackie, it was with a sheepish grin and a Washington Post under his arm, as if he had just popped out to grab the late edition. Jackie glared at him knowingly.

As JFK's limousine left the last Inaugural Ball of the evening, in the wee, small hours of the morning, without Jackie, who had retired early again, the President spotted Juliet Prowse and Sinatra outside. He didn't want the night to end just yet. He rolled down the window, "Hey Frank!" he asked, his hand playfully slapping the side of the car. "How about giving us a few bars of, uh, Danny Boy!"

Sinatra looked at him oddly, his jaw grinding, but he responded politely.

"Mr. President, I am afraid that tune I do not know."

Disappointed, and a bit perplexed, the President thanked him and the car, accompanied by a discreet team of Secret Service men, pulled away. The President looked back once more, wistfully, knowing that this, his first night in the White House, would in many ways be his last, real night as a completely free man.

The next morning all the Hollywood celebrities met in the hotel lobby to meet the airport shuttle. They had all been invited to fly to Palm Beach to visit the President's father. Frank was not present. Janet Leigh and Tony Curtis went and knocked on his hotel room door. Inside, they found Sinatra still in his suite with Juliet Prowse. They weren't even dressed yet. They weren't even packed. They were just sitting there quietly, eating breakfast.

"We're not going," Sinatra said, with juice, scrambled eggs, sausage links and buttered toast before him. "I have to get back to Hollywood."

So Sinatra and his bewildered cohorts took the 'El Dago,' Sinatra's own $100,000 DC-6 private plane, equipped with an electric piano, sofas, cocktail bar and two restrooms, complete with orange interior, back to California.

[Janet Leigh read Richard Condon's novel *The Manchurian Candidate* on Sinatra's plane 'El Dago' on the way back to Hollywood, the exact same plane later used in one of the opening scenes of *The Manchurian Candidate* film, where Raymond, recently decorated with the Medal of Honor, argues with his mother and step father, played by Angela Lansbury and James Gregory].

Peter Lawford, Tony Curtis and Janet Leigh all later rumored that something had been said after the ball.

Something about a song.

On just the second Friday night of Kennedy's presidency, the President and his brother Bobby, the Attorney General, openly crossed an American Legion picket line outside a movie theater near the White House to attend yet another screening of *Spartacus*, the Roman gladiator film which Kennedy felt exemplified the greatest example of mankind's struggle for freedom. [Concerned that *Spartacus* was yet another sign that Hollywood was falling under the influence of Soviet and communist indoctrinated artists, the American Legion publicly attacked Kirk Douglas, the film's star and executive producer, and Dalton Trumbo, one of the original members of the Hollywood Ten, who had written the *Spartacus* screenplay and was listed in the film's credits].

The American Legion had issued letters to 17,000 veteran posts around the country, advising them not to see the film because of its suspected Communist influence. Furthermore, because of the bloody battle scenes, the skimpy slave and gladiator costumes, and the sexual suggestiveness set in pagan times, the film had difficulty with Hollywood conservatives, who had insisted upon numerous cuts and changes to the film in order to accommodate censorship guidelines.

Kennedy had thought himself invincible within the Hollywood community, but when the conservative Hollywood press got wind of the *Spartacus* picket line story, Kennedy quickly went into damage control mode, and called upon his old House and Senate colleague Richard Nixon for advice.

When Nixon arrived home that afternoon (he had not yet moved back to California, and was still living in Washington at the time), he found a note left by his eldest daughter beside the telephone.

"JFK called. I knew it! It wouldn't be long before he would get into trouble and have to call on you for help."

Nixon dialed the familiar White House phone number, which

he knew by heart. The White House switchboard immediately patched him through to the President. Kennedy sounded tired and tense. He had no time for small talk.

"Dick," he said, "Could you drop by to see me?"

When Nixon arrived, Kennedy was standing at his Oval Office desk talking to Vice-President Johnson. The room was tense. They greeted each other with serious handshakes. This was business, not personal. Bygones were bygones. The Kennedy who Nixon saw that day was a wounded man who was hurting.

When Johnson left the room, Kennedy motioned Nixon to a small sofa near the fireplace. Kennedy sat in his rocking chair. "I had a meeting with some members of the Film Actors Guild (F.A.G.)," he said. "Some of whom had acted, fought, and received screen credit for their work in *Spartacus*. Dalton Trumbo, who wrote the screenplay, and others. Talking to them and seeing their expressions of fear and dismay at the way this film and the way Kirk Douglas and Trumbo are being criticized was one of the worst experiences of my life."

Nixon asked about the actor's morale. Kennedy said, "They have calmed down a bit. Some of them were crying, emotional, in tears. But believe it or not, they are ready to go out and act again if we give them the word and our support."

The show must go on, thought Nixon, remembering his oh-so-brief acting career. *The show must go on.*

Kennedy got up from his chair and began pacing in front of his desk. His anger resurfaced with profanities. He said "shit" at least six times and cursed everyone who had advised him that he could go to the movie successfully and in secret. "I was assured by every sonofabitch I checked with that the plan would succeed."

JFK's Presidency had been going well thus far, he was high in the polls, and the press was treating him favorably, excessively so. But now he was in serious trouble, feeling that he was the innocent movie-going victim of bad advice from men he had trusted. Kennedy continued pacing the floor, his fists clenched, calling the guilty aides every name in the book.

After a few minutes, he sat back down in the rocker. Nixon wondered if Kennedy knew about the secret, clandestine Film Actors Guild (F.A.G.) program he had overseen as Eisenhower's Vice-President. He wasn't going to mention it, but he was sure that now, as President, Kennedy must have been aware of its existence. The room fell silent. Nixon sensed how absolutely alone Kennedy must have felt.

Kennedy tapped his teeth with his finger, as he often did when searching for a solution to a problem, and looked at Nixon and asked, "What would you do?"

Nixon answered without hesitation, "I would find a proper legal cover and I would go back in. Whenever I wanted. To see whatever film I damn well cared to. There are several justifications that could be used. Free Speech, for example. First Amendment Rights. It's a constitutional argument, really. As you know, I think it's important to keep communism out of films, but you should be free to go see whatever damn movie you want. Especially as President. After all, when the President does it, it's not illegal."

Kennedy questioned Nixon's latter statement, but agreed with his constitutional argument at its core. Kennedy shook his head, saying, "Intelligence reports this morning say that Khrushchev is in a very cocky mood at this time. This means that there is a good chance that, if I ever go see *Spartacus* again, or any other film that they consider 'questionable,' that Khrushchev will see me as weak, and I don't think we can take that risk."

"What about a war picture?" Nixon suggested. "Show them how tough you are."

"I don't think I should get involved in that," Kennedy said, "Especially where we might find ourselves someday soon fighting millions of troops in the jungles."

Nixon wanted to press the matter, but didn't. He saw that Kennedy was vulnerable and wanted and needed his support, not an adversary.

Nixon said, "I will publicly support you to a hilt if you ever make such a decision in regard to going to see a war picture, and I will urge other Republicans to do likewise. I realize that some political observers say you might risk political defeat in 1964 if you take a hard line pro-military stance. But I want you to know that I am one who will never make that a political issue if such action becomes necessary."

For a brief minute, Kennedy seemed lost in thought, weighing Nixon's promise. *Christ, I wish I had that on tape*, Kennedy thought, making a mental note to make it a priority to get a tape recording machine installed. Then he shrugged his shoulders and said, "The way things are going, if I can't even go to the fucking movies, I don't know whethuh I am going to even want to be here four years from now."

Kennedy sadly looked out through the door of the Oval Office at the rose garden and said, "Who gives a shit about foreign affairs or the fucking minimum wage in comparison to something like this?"

The meeting had lasted about an hour, and Nixon felt that he had at least lightened his old colleague's burden by assuring him that he would not make Kennedy's taste in movies a political issue. They stood and walked out to the porch that ran alongside the Oval Office. A white House car was waiting for Nixon in the driveway. He looked at it longingly. As they walked, Kennedy told Nixon that he had seen some polls that showed Nixon as a favorite if he decided to get involved in the California Governor's race. Nixon was flattered and surprised that Kennedy was interested.

They shook hands, and Nixon suggested that Kennedy go upstairs and have a drink with his wife, and not to go out to the movies until things clear up a bit. He told him to make use of his private White House movie theater. Kennedy said "OK, Dick. Thanks," and turned and slowly walked back to the burdens and responsibilities of the Oval Office, his hands thrust into his jacket pockets, his head down.

At that moment, Nixon pitied the man who now had to accept a criticism that was not entirely his fault but was nevertheless his unavoidable responsibility. He had never seen a man so crushed as the

Jack Kennedy he saw that day.

The man wants out, Nixon decided, plotting. *Jack just hasn't the stomach for it.*

The Colonel had booked Elvis to fly to Pearl Harbor, Hawaii to perform at a benefit for the Memorial Fund of the U.S.S. Arizona as a favor for some of his friends at the Pentagon, and as a favor to his pal Lyndon Johnson, the former Senator from Texas, now Kennedy's Vice-President. The Colonel's sole condition, without exception, was that all ticket proceeds must go directly to the memorial fund. Every single penny.

Shrewdly, The Colonel also planned for Elvis' services for the benefit to coincide with Elvis' scheduled movie location work there for *Blue Hawaii*.

The Pan American Airlines flight from Los Angeles to Honolulu was scheduled to leave at nine o'clock. Elvis had never been to Hawaii, and even though he was fighting a severe head cold, he was excited about the trip. His troop filled up the entire first class of the plane. The Colonel was with him, along with his band and backup singers, along with the press and the ever-growing entourage of people who traveled with Elvis.

The plane was ready to go, engines revving, and yet nothing happened. Elvis saw two empty seats up front. Nobody came. They waited and waited and waited … and finally, to everyone's surprise, actor James Stewart and his wife got on the plane and took their seats. And the plane took off.

Elvis was well aware that James Stewart, star of *It's A Wonderful Life, Harvey, The Philadelphia Story*, and *Mr. Smith Goes To Washington*, as well as Alfred Hitchcock's *Rope, Vertigo, Rear Window*, and *The Man Who Knew Too Much* (the last three of which were filmed at Paramount), and many others, also had a noted military career. He was a highly decorated World War II veteran who put his Hollywood career on hold for the sake of his country.

Airborne about an hour, Elvis tucked his *Life* magazine

between the seats, and quietly walked up the aisle. He gently touched the stewardess on the back of her shoulder and said, "Excuse me. Miss, do you think it would be out of order if I go up and speak to General Stewart? I've always been such a fan of his."

Brigadier General James 'Jimmy' Stewart

Jimmy Stewart was the first major American movie star to wear a military uniform in WWII. In 1943 he was assigned to fly a bomber to England and immediately began combat operations. While flying missions over Germany, Stewart was promoted to Major. To inspire his troops, Stewart flew as command pilot in the lead B-24 on numerous missions deep into Nazi-occupied Europe. These missions went uncounted at Stewart's orders. His "official" total is listed as 20 and is limited to those with the 445th. In 1944, he twice received the Distinguished Flying Cross for actions in combat and was awarded the Croix de Guerre. He also received the Air Medal with three oak leaf clusters. After flying 20 combat missions, Stewart was promoted to Colonel. He continued to play an active role in the Air Force Reserve after the war, achieving the rank of Brigadier General in 1959. He later lost a son in the Vietnam War.

"Well," she said, "I think he would love it." It was typical Elvis. He was hesitant to bother anybody, even though he was such a big star. Of course Jimmy Stewart was a star too, and had been for decades.

Elvis knelt down on one knee in the aisle beside the Stewarts and they enjoyed a brief conversation. They talked about the new Pearl Harbor Memorial, movies, and music. Stewart jokingly bragged to Elvis that he "played a pretty mean accordion." Then Elvis said "Thank you for your time, Sir. I hope to see you again someday." Stewart, impressed by the polite young man, replied, "V-V-Very well, son. Y-You, too. Thank you for saying 'hello.' N-N-Now, good luck to you, my boy. See you in the movies!"

Elvis returned to his seat, and to his *Life* magazine, where he noticed a small story about newly elected President Kennedy's top ten favorite books. None of which Elvis had ever read or even heard of, for that matter.

When the flight landed at Honolulu's International Airport, more than 3,000 fans were on hand to greet Elvis. There was a thirty-minute wait on the tarmac while one of Elvis' boys hunted the stowaways for the suitcase containing Elvis' gold lame jacket. When Elvis finally stepped onto the short steel staircase he was soon covered with flower leis, tossed by his fans lasso style in the Hawaiian custom. In all the airport bedlam, movie star and General James Stewart was virtually, and gratefully, ignored.

Later, introducing Elvis at the show, a Rear Admiral took the stage and read a telegram from the Secretary of the Navy, thanking Elvis for "his outstanding performance ... as a soldier in the United States Army ..." When Elvis took the stage, wearing his Gold Lame jacket (for the last time) with dark blue slacks, a white shirt, and a blue string tie, the teenagers screamed for almost a minute and a half straight. Elvis, in imitation and fun, screamed back. The sellout concert was one of the longest sets Elvis had played in a long time, forty-five minutes, performing 15 songs, opening with 'Heartbreak Hotel' and closing with 'Hound Dog.'

The Hawaii concert raised over $62,000 to build a memorial to the lives lost aboard the U.S.S. Arizona during the Japanese attack on Pearl Harbor on December 7, 1941, and ended with an announcer proclaiming for the first time, "Elvis has left the building." It would be Elvis' last public appearance until December of 1968, after Nixon was finally elected President.

Filming on *Blue Hawaii* began the next day. Then it was back to the Paramount set in Hollywood to film the interior shots.

There was no rest for the weary.

The Hawaiian Connection

John Wayne was on Kauai in 1962 to film *Donovan's Reef*. In the movie, John Wayne plays 'Guns' Donovan, a former United States Marine who opens a tropical bar in the South Pacific. On April 12, 1961, **Elvis Presley** began filming *Blue Hawaii*, his first movie on Kauai and also his most commercially successful movie. In the film, Elvis plays Chad Gates, who avoids working in his family's pineapple business by working for a travel agency. Elvis returned to Kauai in 1964 to film *Paradise Hawaiian Style*, playing ex-airline pilot Rick Richards who runs a helicopter sightseeing business and finds romance at different Island locations. **Frank Sinatra** first came to Kauai in the early 1950s when he performed at the Kauai County Fair. In April of 1964, Sinatra returned to Kauai, directing and starring in *None But the Brave*, the story of a group of United States Marines who crash land on a Pacific island controlled by the Japanese during World War II.

Despite the Inaugural nightmare, when Sinatra got back to L.A. he still acted like he was 'in' with the new administration, insisting that friends listen over and over again – ad nauseum - to a recording of JFK's tribute to him at the gala. He loved to hear Hollywood big shots ask him, "Frank, what do you hear from The White House," to which he would feign nonchalance and boast that the President always sought his advice.

JFK remained somewhat loyal, too. Eight months after the inauguration, that August, Kennedy flew Sinatra to Hyannisport aboard his Convair campaign plane, the *Caroline*, with Peter Lawford and other members of the Kennedy family and their guests.

Over Bloody Mary's (Sinatra wanted Stoli but the Kennedy's only had the cheap stuff), and sitting in full view of the Atlantic ocean, Sinatra told the President about his interest in making *The Manchurian Candidate*, a psychological thriller based on a novel by Richard Condon about two American soldiers who are captured and brainwashed by the communists during the Korean War.

Art Imitates Life Imitates Art Imitates ...
It is a most ironic fact that the director of 1962's *The Manchurian Candidate*, John Frankenheimer, personally drove Senator Robert F. Kennedy to The Ambassador Hotel in Los Angeles on the night he was assassinated six years later on June 4 1968.

"You see, Jack, one of the soldiers, a Medal of Honor hero, to be played by Larry (Lawrence) Harvey, he was in *The Alamo* with Duke Wayne. Well, anyway, this cat, he's programmed by the communists to assassinate a presidential candidate to ensure that the communist-backed candidate becomes President." Kennedy listened attentively, as he always did.

"And the other soldier," Sinatra continued, "to be played by yours truly here, is reprogrammed by a psychiatrist, and then goes to work with the Feds to stop the plan before it's too late." Kennedy, an avid reader, was well familiar with the bestselling book, but patiently allowed Sinatra to finish before he responded, as he did with everyone.

Then Kennedy spoke.

"Frank," Kennedy told Sinatra in Hyannis that day, "I read the book right after the election. That Condon's a cynical bahstahd in my judgment, but what a story! I absolutely loved it!" He added, "You know, I uh, I really think it'd make a helluva movie …" Kennedy gazed at the ocean and said it again ….

"… a helluva movie …"

He turned back to Sinatra, "Political assassination. What a story, my God …"

Then a thought suddenly occurred to the President, lighting up his face. "Who's going to play the mother?"

"Lucy. Lucille Ball. The Actor's Guild and the studio want me to test some other actresses, but I just love Lucy for this part. I think she'd be just marvelous." Sinatra loved the word 'marvelous.'

[The role of Raymond Shaw's monstrous and overbearing mother in *The Manchurian Candidate* eventually went to Angela Lansbury, who had played Elvis Presley's overbearing mother in 1961's *Blue Hawaii*].

Kennedy considered Sinatra's casting and then turned his attention back to the ocean, and beyond.

Sinatra followed Kennedy's eyes to the water. *What does he see out there? What is he looking for?*

Kennedy was thinking about a woman he once knew in Paris. A woman he still secretly wrote to, and secretly thought about. A woman he hoped to see again someday. *We'll always have Paris.* He smiled faintly until he looked across the lawn at his Secret Service detail. *Christ, security, most of these guys would do anything for me,*

114

but this job is like a goddamn noose around my neck.

He turned back to the ocean, and he recalled verbatim the final verses from his favorite poem-song, 'Greensleeves,' supposedly written by King Henry VIII for his forbidden lover ...

> *For I am still thy lover true -*
> *Come once again and love me ...*

Interrupting Kennedy's apparent daydreaming, Sinatra got back on topic. "I'm thinking about Janet Leigh for the girlfriend, she really digs it too," said Sinatra.

Kennedy paused for another second or so and then turned to Sinatra and asked thoughtfully, "Frank, now, is Janet a blond or a brunette. I can't figure it out. She's blond sometimes when I see her, but then I hear she's a brunette other times, as far as I can tell I just can't ..." [32]

Does the carpet match the drapes? Kennedy had asked him the exact same question about Shirley MacLaine the year before. Sinatra wanted to give him an educated answer but he really didn't know either. "You know what they say, Jack, only her gynecologist knows for sure ..." Kennedy laughed and considered the specialty. *A gynecologist? Now where's the sport in that? It must be like being a commercial fisherman. Doing it for a living takes all the fun away.*

Sinatra's buzzy mind grew a little paranoid with the vodka. He momentarily wondered what Kennedy, with his war record and Purple Heart and all, privately thought about his own draft deferment back in the forties. They'd never talked about it, but Sinatra always wondered what Jack *really* thought. Whether Kennedy held it against him. Suddenly, Frank felt a vodka headache coming on. Drinking in the afternoon sun always did this to him. And then that shitty monotonous and up-tempo Presley 'G.I. Blues' song popped into his head again ...

---

[32] Janet Leigh was a blond in *The Manchurian Candidate* and *Psycho*, and later a brunette in *Bye, Bye Birdie*, a film based upon Presley's early career and Army induction (the film's opening montage includes JFK and Sinatra).

Sinatra shut his eyes and pressed his temples. *Marches. Arches. Purple Hearts. Christ I can't stand this goddamn tune! It's like Chinese water torture!*

"What is it, Frank?" asked Kennedy, concerned, but still lightly pondering a woman's burdensome chore of dying one's hair a different color every so often. *I wonder if some of them dye their private hair too, just to be consistent. What a pain in the ass that must be.* Kennedy quickly glanced at Sinatra's toupee. It was the good one.

"Headaches," said Sinatra. "I haven't been sleeping right. Not for a while. Up all night. Nightmares. The works." He pressed his temples again and gulped his vodka soda with a lime. "No shut-eye at all. Morning either." Sinatra fought it and opened his eyes. He didn't want to waste his time with the President of the United States and Leader of the Free World on dream analysis.

"I'm sorry Jack, you were saying. About Janet … what was it …"

Kennedy looked curious. "Well, have you, uh, heard anything? Are Janet and Tony getting a divorce?" inquired Kennedy. "I saw a, uh, item in *Variety* recently that said, or rather it hinted, that they were breaking up, now Frank in your, uh, judgment what …"

Sinatra heard a wave crash and turned to see it.

"Oh, Janet and Tony," said Sinatra, recovering. "They're splitsville, baby," he said, still watching the surf. Man, this sure beats the desert, he thought.

"Really?" asked Kennedy, leaning forward on the porch in his wicker rocker (pronounced 'wicka rockah'). "Are they separated?" Sinatra indicated that they weren't. Not yet.

"Well, now, what about you and Juliet?" Kennedy was eager to know. "Is it still on?"

Frank turned to face his friend again.

116

"Splitsville, baby." Sinatra exhaled and looked back at the ocean.

Then, Sinatra added, "Endsville," in exactly the same key.

Endsville. The President momentarily turned away, his thoughts elsewhere. Kennedy usually kept these private moments to himself, moments when his own possible assassination or death entered his mind. Though he was still a young man, he had always known sickness and injury, and had already received the last rights of the Roman Catholic Church three times. In a way, sickness and death had become his friend. He had always known them, and thought of them both frequently. Though he never complained. *You never know,* thought Kennedy. I just hope it's quick. *A gunshot would be the perfect way. Endsville.*

"Frank," Kennedy offered. "What do you think of the rule that, uh, for the last hundred years every President of the United States elected in a, uh, year divisible by twenty has, uh, died in office."

"Of that rule Jack I was not aware," said Sinatra.

Kennedy quickly rattled off the President's names and the years they were elected, "William Henry Harrison 1840, Lincoln 1860, Garfield 1880, McKinley 1900, Harding 1920, and Roosevelt 1940."

"Coincidence," Sinatra said. "Dumb luck."

Kennedy dropped the subject and for a few moments just stared off to the ocean and then into space, like he was a million miles away.

My God the sky looks just like the ocean.

He reached for his favorite wayfarer-style, tortoise-shell sunglasses. *Sixty-five, seventy degrees with a nice, light breeze. This is fucking perfect.*

Sinatra was more concerned with his 'reel-life' problem, which was that the President of United Artists, who was also coincidentally national finance chairman of the Democratic Party, had refused to

117

distribute *The Manchurian Candidate* for fear that it was too politically explosive. He explained it all to Kennedy, as Kennedy tapped his teeth.

Sinatra picked up a handful of sand and let it fall through his fingers, saying, "You see, Jack, I bought the film rights. I own it. We just gotta get it made, jack." Then, he added, "Jack."

"But this guy, and I know you know who I mean, he won't ..."

"Let me take care of this right now," Kennedy said. "He owes me one." *Businessmen. Goddamn Businessmen. They're all the same, whether it's U.S. Steel, Texas oilmen or Hollywood executives.* Kennedy chuckled to himself a little. *Thank God I was a political science major. Dad always said businessmen were sons of bitches. But I never knew how bad they were until I won this goddamn job.*

After carefully listening to Sinatra's predicament, The President of the United States then stood up, retrieved the private telephone, and placed a personal call to the President of United Artists, telling him that he was "on vacation in Hyannisport with Frank Sinatra as we speak and that he wanted to see *The Manchurian Candidate* made into a film and distributed nationwide as soon as possible." (The film began production soon thereafter). [33]

Sinatra looked up. "Thanks pal, I owe you one."

"Frank," Kennedy said, gently placing the phone down on the receiver. "How can a friend be in debt? After all, what are, uh, friends for?" Kennedy added, "Frank, let me ask you ... in my job, how often do you think I get to make a decision that comes from me. That isn't one-hundred percent reactive, forced upon me because of unseen, unpredictable events? It's like I'm a goddamn actor, for crissakes!"

Sinatra was intrigued, eternally grateful, but with his headache, all he could do was shrug.

---

[33] When released in 1962, *The Manchurian Candidate* was a box-office flop, failing even to recover its costs. It was pulled from distribution two years later, after JFK's assassination.

"Right. None. So thank you for letting me do something *I* want to do. For a change. I can't remember the lahst time I could do *that*. You don't owe me a goddamn thing. But listen to me, and please do not take this personally. Frank, I can't have you to the White House for a while, or come out to California. The fucking papers are just waiting to pounce all over me. I can't even get properly laid anymore, everything's either in a closet or hit and run. I feel like I'm in the fucking state pen, or the nuthouse. Actually, the goddamn nuthouse might be more fun! As it is, I can't even take a piss without one of these fucking agents practically holding my dick for me. So I pretty much just go where all these guys tell me to go. They have a job to do and I have to go along with them. I have to. Besides, believe it or not, and I know that you, uh, believe it, I have too many enemies now to do uthuhwise. Bobby has a gigantic hard-on for the boys. And you know the boys I mean. It's all black and white to him. Always has been. And I can't stop him or tell him what to do, despite what everyone assumes. And now, neethuh (neither) can Dad. So If someone wants to take me out, then that's the ballgame. There's some crazy bahstahds out there, and you know who I mean, and they play for fucking keeps."

When Kennedy's run-on ended he attempted a weak grin and raised his eyebrows. He thought about saying, 'So, here's looking at you, Frank.' But thankfully, he didn't.

"Okay, my friend?" Kennedy signed. "It's a tough, uh, gig, but we'll get they-uh someday ..."

Sinatra shook Kennedy's hand and held it. Then he smacked him upside the shoulder. He understood. *Cops*. Sinatra hated cops.

"No problem, buddy, boy. Forget about it. A friend is never an imposition." *Man, this guy sure ain't his father's son, that's for sure. This guy 'got a little class. He ain't like his father OR his brother.*

Sinatra was thrilled. He was back, jack. Why, if he wasn't drinking he would have called for a banana split he was so happy. But he still couldn't for the life of him get the words from Presley's shitty 'G.I. Blues' song out of his head ... he rubbed his temples again ... *I tell ya, if I hear this goddamn mutha song one more time I'm gonna*

119

blow my own fuckin' fuse

Inside the Oval Office, after first making sure the switch for his newly installed tape machine was in the 'OFF' position, JFK pressed a button on the Bell Telephone console on his desk, and called for his Special Assistant for Latin American Affairs. Within seconds the eager young aide arrived at the Oval Office, out of breath, his shirt-tail loose. Kennedy hovered over his wood desk, handsomely carved from the timbers of nineteenth century British ship, *Resolute*, bracing down on it with one hand, impatiently and methodically tapping it with his gold-plated presidential lighter in the other. Like a metronome.

JFK stood erect, and began to tap his teeth with a pencil. *What would our old boy Commander James Bond do if faced with a situation like this ....*

Kennedy looked scared. His complexion was sallow, eyes bulging. The demands of the office had already aged him. His face had never looked more grave.

The President wanted miniature Cuban cigars, 1,000 to be exact. "Mister, you have 24 hours to round them up ... and get me an extra 200 just to be safe. Twelve hundred."

Kennedy glanced at his 8-carat gold Lord Elgin wristwatch, pulling gently on its thin and narrow alligator strap momentarily to let his forearm breathe. He always wore his watch further up his forearm, off his wrist-bone. Kennedy never wore jewelry, but the watch was a necessity, and it was less irritating to him that way. He thought again about the cigars. "No, make that *less* than 24 hours, to round them up. Go."

Kennedy was desperate. If his aide failed he would have to settle for domestic cigars, which were inferior in both taste and quality. He cherished his miniature Cubans, smoking four or five per day. But he remained positive that the mission would be carried out successfully. Through it all remained firm, confident and optimistic.

Kennedy addressed the aide formally, "And let no one doubt that you have the moral fortitude and strength and viguh that is so necessary and even imperative to accomplish this most daunting and noble task that has been, uh, set forth ..." The young aide stood dumbfounded, thinking he was being pranked as usual.

It was short notice for such a big request, but then again JFK had a pressing reason for procuring the stash of tobacco in such a timely fashion. He was about to sign an embargo prohibiting any Cuban products from entering the country, including his beloved miniature cigars.

The embargo was born of a nasty spat that the United States was having with Cuba and its fears that Fidel Castro represented a growing threat to America's security. But before Kennedy could act, he needed his aide to complete his assignment. Hopeful that his aide wouldn't let him down, Kennedy retired for the evening alone in his private quarters (his wife, Jackie, was away with the children), where he ordered up a sliced turkey sandwich and a cup of fish chowder for supper, and relaxed as he listened to some Rosemary Clooney and Judy Garland records. Mostly standards and show tunes, which he loved, and Irish songs ...

It's a long way to Tipperary,
It's a long way to go -
It's a long way to Tipperary
To the sweetest girl I know!

The next morning, the young aide, one of Kennedy's best and brightest, didn't let him down, as he had managed to scrounge up and deliver to the Oval Office 1,200 cigars by 9 AM.

Cigars in hand, Kennedy then signed the embargo, making Cuban tobacco off-limits to all Americans.

All except one.

And his gainfully employed aide.

The Cuban Missile Crisis

In October of 1962 an American U2 spy plane secretly photographed nuclear missile sites being built by the Soviet Union on the island of Cuba. Because he did not want Cuba and the Soviet Union to know that he had discovered the missiles, Kennedy met in secret with his advisors for several days to discuss the crisis. After many long and difficult meetings, at the urging of his brother Bobby (the Attorney General), Kennedy decided to place a naval blockade, or a ring of ships, around Cuba to prevent the Soviets from bringing in more military supplies, and demanded the removal of the missiles already there and the destruction of the sites. After the crisis was revealed to the public by JFK's televised address on October 22 and for a week afterwards, the world waited, hoping for a peaceful resolution. Finally, recognizing the devastating possibility of a nuclear war, Khrushchev turned his ships back. The Soviets agreed to dismantle the weapon sites and, in exchange, the United States agreed not to invade Cuba. In a separate, secret negotiation, the U.S. also agreed to remove its nuclear missiles from Turkey.

Kennedy opened his first box of his new Cubans and thought about how he'd spend his evening alone.

Maybe I'll take a hot bath and then have a cigah up on the balcony ... or maybe I'll hit some golf balls out on the south lawn and take a dip in the pool ...

[In 1961, Joe Kennedy had commissioned a 97-foot mural of the French Riviera on three of the four walls surrounding JFK's private, indoor White House pool. The fourth wall featured a large mirror].

JFK loved the nice, smooth, almost mealy taste of the cigars. They even seemed to settle his irritable stomach. He loved the aroma, the smoke, the romance of it all. For some men, it was the glass in the hand. For him, it was the cigar. He reached into the box and grabbed a handful of his miniature Cubans and one of the extra lighters from his desk, checking it for fuel first.

He then crossed the room of the Oval Office, closing the door behind him. *Maybe I'll just go up to the quarters and watch a movie. Put on a record. Make a sandwich. I thought I'd have a copy of Mutiny On The Bounty by now ... but, goddamn actors ... they haven't finished filming the goddamn thing yet.*

An aide excused himself for the evening, saying, "Good night, Mr. President." A Secret Service man nodded and said, "Good evening, Mr. President." As Kennedy walked toward the elevator he noticed a *Life* magazine in the waiting area. Liz Taylor was on the cover, again.

She left Eddie Fisher for Richard Burton? Can you imagine having your affairs splashed all over the tabloids like that, I mean Jesus Christ, my God, I am so fortunate that I am not a goddamn actor or a movie star ...

And as JFK began to hum to himself the opening lyrics to *I Love Paris*, he wondered if Sinatra had ever dated Liz Taylor. He had always meant to ask Frank about that.

Then he thanked his lucky stars that he was just a politician, and decided to send a car to go collect his Washington mistress.

Sinatra's telephone rang. It was Peter Lawford, and he was pissed, as they say.

"Christ, Peter, it's not even noon yet!" yawned Sinatra. "Jeekers creekers, let me wake up first!"

Lawford was busting at the seams. He excitedly told Frank that the President wished to stay at his Palm Springs home during an upcoming trip scheduled for March.

Ecstatic, Sinatra immediately began a massive construction project for the President's stay, envisioning his home as the western White House. He built separate cottages for the Secret Service men, installed a communications bank with twenty-five extra telephone lines, poured a huge concrete helicopter pad, put up a flag pole, and even had a solid gold plaque inscribed 'John F. Kennedy Slept Here.'

Then, just weeks before the trip, the White House had a change of plans, saying that the Secret Service preferred that the President stay at the home of Bing Crosby. It was safer, they insisted. Sinatra was furious. He pleaded with fellow Rat Packer and Kennedy brother-in-Lawford to intervene on his behalf.

"Now Peter! Call Jack now!!" Sinatra ordered him.

The President's secretary took the call and told JFK, "Peter Lawford is hysterical."

"He's funny, but he's not *that* funny," quipped Kennedy, as he pressed one of the dozen or so plastic push buttons on his elaborate Bell Telephone, 'Call Director,' rotary phone.

"Jack, it's me, Peter. Jack, Frank is very upset. Very upset. This bit about Bing Crosby. Jack, now, you realize Bing Crosby is a Republican, I mean ..?"

"Peter, I don't care if Bing's a Red-Chinaman, the Secret Service likes his place better than Sinatra's place and that's that."

Kennedy was unconcerned. He had bigger fish to fry. The CIA. Hoover. Castro. The Russians. The Mafia. The threat of global nuclear war. Trying to find a way to get Marilyn Monroe properly into the sack, just once.

Christ, this office is like a goddamn prison. Goddamn Secret Service crawling up my ass every step I take ...

Maybe I can get Marilyn over to Crosby's house? Christ, this is like trying to get a fucking audience with the Pope!"

"Peter, we'll go where the Secret Service wants us to go," he suddenly said, fingering the tightly wound telephone cord and pulling at it's extra slack. "In my judgment, it's fair to say that it's their problem, not ours."

"Plus, Bobby doesn't really like Frank. And frankly (The President smiled at his pun), I don't feel like listening to him." JFK had wanted to say 'call Dad,' but he knew that wasn't an option anymore. They couldn't go to dad anymore for help.

Thank God for Bobby. Blood is the best security in this business.

"Talk to you later, Peter. Bye," JFK abruptly concluded as he cradled the phone on the receiver. Then, as an afterthought, the President called out to his secretary, "Does, uh, does Crosby have a pool? Check and make sure that he ..."

"Yes, he has a heated pool Mr. President," she immediately replied. "I already checked. And Mr. Crosby will be away that weekend. You will have the house to yourself." *Jesus, I wish all government employees were this efficient. I can't get half these people*

127

to get a goddamn thing done on time and here she is getting me answers before I even ask the goddamn question. After the President considered how invaluable his personal secretary was, he thought about Marilyn, picturing her ass in his mind, and he grinned.

So Lawford went back to Sinatra empty-handed.

Then Frank called the White House himself.

"The President is very busy, Mr. Sinatra. I will be sure to tell him that you called," he was told.

Then Sinatra went back to Hollywood empty-handed, embarrassed, and feeling completely and utterly disrespected.

"Secret Service fucked it all up," he told everyone, trying to save face. "The White House cops said Palm Springs is vicious. They were afraid of dessert snipers," he said, trying to laugh it off. Although few others were surprised, inside, Sinatra himself was blindsided. He felt as though his heart had lost its mind.

It was over. Sinatra thought JFK would be faithful to him, and JFK had dumped him, like he was a dame. Sinatra was livid.

So that's how it is. Quid pro quo. Jack got the gig, and now I'm out.

He knew the game. It was strictly business, Sinatra tried to reason. He understood it, gradually, in time. But he was still insulted. Blindsided. He remembered how Dean Martin had warned him early on, "Frank, these guys (the Kennedy's) are gonna fuck you."

And they didn't even kiss him first.

"No goddamn loyalty these shanty, lace-curtain Irish bastards. No goddamn loyalty."

In a fit of passion, Sinatra grabbed one of the worker's sledgehammers and strutted over to the helicopter pad, talking to himself with steam coming out of his ears. "Crosby! Crosby!! That has-been isn't even a Democrat he's a mutha Republican. One song! *White Christmas*!! Big fuckin' deal!!"[34]

"So Jack's going to Crosby's in March?! It must be an Irish thing, Sinatra thought. It's because I'm Italian. I knew it. The Old Man's such a goddamn bigot!! Why that Irish mutha!! Well Happy Saint Patrick's Day you son of a .....!!!!

Sinatra took the sledgehammer off his bony shoulder and struck the concrete with a thud, thinking he sprained or maybe even broke his hand and wrist in the process. But he hit it again, and again and again. Never making a dent or even a crack. But he felt better doing it. Although he was almost out of breath, he started to sing as he swung the heavy hammer ...

Oh Dan-ny Boy (SLAM)

The pipes (WHACK) the pipes (CRASH) are call-all-innn' (BANG-BANG)

From glen to glen   (WHAM)   and down   (THUD)

The mountainside ...

(Sinatra wrenched something in the center of his chest, near his sternum, and stopped for a second and sat down on the edge of the helicopter pad, for a second he thought he was having a heart attack).

K-E double N-E-D   FUCK!!!!!

You no good lying SON OF A BITCH

Oh why can't somebody   WHACK   JACK

Hit 'em right in the BACK (And that was it, at that very moment, right in the middle of a fairly decent James Cagney

---

[34] Sinatra had idolized Crosby from the beginning of his career, and the two eventually became good friends, co-starring in 1955's *High Society* with Grace Kelly, and again in 1964's *Robin and the Seven Hoods*.

impersonation, that Sinatra decided to be a Republican, right then and there …)

"… You mutha*$&$#@ damn*&@#$# mick f#*$ aaarrrrrrrgggggghhhhhhh!!!!!"

The only person who maybe could have intervened, the only person who understood Hollywood and Sinatra, who understood 'business,' who would maybe hear him out and listen to him, maybe make another deal, prevent the inevitable, was former Hollywood producer-bootlegger-Ambassador Old Man Joe Kennedy. For it was the Old Man who had originally made the deal with Sinatra's in the first place.

Unfortunately, Old Man Kennedy had been struck speechless and paralyzed on his right side by a stroke on December 19, 1961, just a few months before.

Sinatra was on his own.

But Sinatra was NOT on his own.

For Kennedy's list of enemies was very, very long indeed.

The Paramount Lot

The Paramount lot in 1962 sat on the exact same spot where a young Joe Kennedy oversaw 'quickie' film productions back in the late 1920's and '30's, as President of the original RKO Pictures. RKO (Radio-Keith-Orpheum) Pictures was one of the biggest studios of the Hollywood 'Golden Age,' It was formed after the Keith-Albee-Orpheum (KAO) theater chain and Joseph Kennedy's Film Booking Offices of America (FBO) studio were combined under the control of the Radio Corporation of America (RCA) in 1928, in order to create a market for the company's new sound technology for 'talkies.' In 1948, RKO was taken over by Howard Hughes, who then sold the company in 1955 to the General Tire and Rubber Company, who then sold the studio lot in 1957 to Desi Arnaz and Lucille Ball's Desilu Productions. The sale symbolized the cultural change in Hollywood from film to the new age of television.

One day, while filming *Girls! Girls! Girls!* on the Paramount set, Elvis and the boys saw fast approaching none other than John Wayne himself, dressed in his usual costume cowboy regalia and white ten-gallon hat, walking towards them from behind the shoeshine stand. He was working on an adjacent set shooting *The Man Who Shot Liberty Valance* with Jimmy Stewart and Lee Marvin (The central plot of *The Man Who Shot Liberty Valance* is of a man (Wayne) who resorts to violence and gunplay to resolve problems, albeit for good and noble causes).

"Look!" punched one of the boys, "Over by the Irish kid!! Behind the shoeshine boy!! It's John Wayne!!!"

Elvis and the boys took a step back in awe, like they were star-struck, which they really were. 'The man himself,' Elvis whispered.

Wayne turned in mid-stride, stopped, smiled and said, "Excuse me, you're Elvis Presley, aren't you?" He had heard Elvis was on the Paramount lot.

Elvis said, "Well uh yessir, sir … and uh I-I-I know who you are, Mr. Wayne."

Wayne held up his hand and said, "Gimme a minute, son. I'll be back in a second. I gotta hit the head." [35]

"Yeah?!" said Elvis. "Me too!" Even though he didn't really have to. He just wanted to talk to the legend.

Standing side by side at the men's white, make that yellowed white, porcelain watering trough, focusing on his business at-hand, Wayne studied the old wood wall right in front of him, going over the

---

[35] 'Head' is a slang Navy term for bathroom.

carved-in names of the stars of yesteryear … 'Rudolph Valentino.' *Pretty nice handwritin' for a man who couldn't talk.* 'Gary Cooper.' *Ol' Coop.* 'Mae West.' *In the men's room!? Well, I'm not surprised.* 'Ward Bond …'

Wayne got awful quiet when he saw that.

Life goes too damn fast, too damn quick to lose good, young men like ol' Ward.

Wayne turned his back to Presley and wiped an eye and gave his nose a sniff and finished up his business and stepped back to fasten his britches and said, "If you wanna stick around in this here town, let me give you a friendly bit of advice, son." Elvis held onto himself, nervous, afraid that Wayne would notice he was without stream. "Talk low, talk slow, and don't say too much," drawled Wayne, before giving himself a gentle shake before carefully zipping up.

"You'll last a lot longer in the business that way."

Elvis pretended to give little Elvis a final shake and said, "Thank You, Mr. Wayne, thankyouverymuch," as he turned to face Wayne to shake his hand.

Wayne backed away quickly and turned on his heels, instinctively giving his hands a quick rinse under the bathroom's old spigot sink. He glanced down at his wet boots.

"And," Wayne added, "Never wear suede boots."

"Suede … what … why's that Mr. Wayne?" asked Elvis, confused.

"Because one day, son," said Wayne. "You'll be taking a piss, and the guy next to you will recognize you, and he'll turn toward you and say, 'Mr. Wayne!!!' and piss all over your brand new special-order suede boots."

Wayne kicked his boots through the sawdust and dirt on the bathroom floor.

Then Wayne turned and grinned at Elvis, "And who knows, kid? We may get another chance to work again someday. You know, life is long. Might be another *Rio Bravo* somewhere down the line. Just tell that manager of yours, don't be so greedy next time …"

And John Wayne went on his way, one leg in front of the other, with the physical grace of an oversized dancer, through the open rest room door and out into the California sunlight.

'Rio Bravo'!? thought Elvis.

Oh no, oh my God, no. Colonel. Damn Colonel. Damn thievin' lyin' Colonel …

Elvis fastened his button-downs.

The entire cast and crew and other assorted onlookers stood silent, some almost embarrassed for John Wayne, the world's Number One movie star, as the tyrannical director John Ford mercilessly derided him in front of both peers and public.

"Duke, look at you - you big monkey!! Do it again!! Alright! Cameras!! TAKE Nine-Hundred and Seventy-Two!!" barked Duke's mentor and director of three decades, John Ford, sitting comfortably in his canvas director's chair, one leg crossed over the other, like he was ready to take his afternoon tea.

"I take you out of eight-day westerns and silent pictures and make you what you are today -- a legend in your own mind!! And this is all you give us!! Now speak up goddammit you big baboon!!"

Director 'Pappy' John Ford

Renowned for his intense personality and eccentricities, director John Ford, in a career that spanned more than 50 years, made over 140 films. He was the pioneer of 'location shooting' and the 'long shot,' which frames characters against a vast, harsh and rugged natural terrain. Also, during World War II, Commander John Ford, USNR, served in the United States Navy and made 'propaganda' documentaries for the Navy Department. Ford eventually rose to become a top adviser in the Office of Strategic Services (OSS), a WWII wartime intelligence agency and the precursor to the CIA. After the war, Ford became a Rear Admiral in the U.S. Naval Reserve.

As a director, Ford was merciless in his use of callous motivational tactics on his actors, especially his star protégé, as he mocked and ridiculed Duke mercilessly for failing to serve in WWII, while co-stars Jimmy Stewart and Lee Marvin had been honorably discharged (Marvin had been awarded the Purple Heart) and publicly regarded as a highly decorated war heroes.

Ford flipped up the black eye-patch he wore over his left eye,

134

"Duke, tell us, just how rich did you get back in the forties while Jimmy and Lee here were risking their lives overseas for their country?" The brutal little dictator Ford taunted him, waving about his white linen handkerchief at Wayne in mock surrender.

Blindly loyal and ever deferential to Ford, Wayne turned the other cheek and instead took out his frustrations verbally on Woody Strode, the journeyman black actor who played Wayne's sidekick, Pompey, in *Liberty Valance*. Strode, as it turned out, like Stewart and Marvin, was also a proud, decorated World War II veteran.

Moments later, boiling inside, Wayne unleashed on Strode during a key action scene. In the brief confrontation Wayne almost lost control of their team of horses and knocked Strode away when he tried to help. When the horses finally did halt, Wayne fell out of the wagon, and then almost started a fight with Strode, who still had the body of his UCLA playing days and was much stronger and physically much tougher than the fifty-five year-old Wayne.

After a tense standoff, Wayne got a hold of himself, and told the actor, "Forgive the hot head Woody, old Pappy sure knows how to push my buttons. Now let's get back to work, pilgrim, before he gets under my hide again." Wayne coughed and cleared his throat and thought for a second if he'd ever direct again. If he'd ever again be the man in charge.

"C'mon, pilgrim. Let's get back to work. We gotta act professional-like," Wayne was overheard saying.

Kennedy's 45th Birthday Party was televised before a crowd of thousands at Madison Square Garden, where Marilyn Monroe sang her indelible, breathless and sultry rendition of "Happy Birthday, Mister President." (Ever the good sport, the troubled, soon-to-be-jilted Monroe even paid for her own thousand-dollar ticket.)

During the program, which also included Jimmy Durante, Peggy Lee, and Bobby Darin, JFK coolly admired Marilyn's ample ass behind his tortoise-shell shades, but privately, he was embarrassed at the display. *Christ, of all the birthday parties and all the sports arenas in the all the cities in all the world, she walks into mine.*

For the cameras, though, he quipped, "I can now retire from politics, after having had 'Happy Birthday' sung to me in such a sweet, wholesome manner."

Afterwards, Marilyn called the White House incessantly. Every day. So Kennedy did what most men who wanted out of a relationship would do, and what his wife told him to do. He stopped taking her calls and he never saw her again. Besides, he had other things on his mind. The new James Bond novel, *The Spy Who Loved Me* (in which Ian Fleming mentioned 'Jack Kennedy' by name) was out, and he was eagerly awaiting the release of the first James Bond film, *Dr. No*, made at his own request, which was to star a British newcomer named Sean Connery.

Also, *The Manchurian Candidate* was due to be released, and his brother-in-law Peter Law ford had a role in the new all-star cast epic film about the Normandy D-Day invasion, *The Longest Day*, which also featured Connery, and a cameo appearance by Wayne, was going to be available to him within the next few months. [36]

---

[36] JFK privately viewed *The Manchurian Candidate* at the White House on the evening of August 29, 1962, the exact same day that a U-2 spy plane over Cuba reported eight near-operational missile installations.

Before JFK knew it, the summer of 1962 was almost over, and on August 5th, the gifted method actress was sadly gone.

Robert Kennedy, Marilyn Monroe & JFK the night she sang 'Happy Birthday' to the President at Madison Square Garden, May, 1962.

Hollywood producer-bootlegger-diplomat-businessman, father of JFK, and the consummate master of the perpendicular hat-hold, Joe Kennedy.

Colonel Tom Parker, Elvis' manager.

John Wayne. The Duke. 1960.

Frank Sinatra, March 1960

One of the three televised JFK-Nixon debates of 1960. Kennedy's obvious charm and good looks made him an easy guest in American living rooms.

Method Actor Marlon Brando on the Washington Mall during a Civil Rights rally in August of 1963.

President Richard Nixon and John Wayne in 1973.

Brigadier General and actor James 'Jimmy' Stewart.

Russian theatre director Konstantin Stanislavsky (1863-1938), founder of 'The Method' acting technique, shown here sitting very convincingly.

Nixon confidante Bebe Rebozo confers with the President circa 1973.

Elvis Presley in 1957's 'Jailhouse Rock.'

An absolutely ecstatic TV variety show emcee
and gossip columnist Ed Sullivan.

The 'WANTED FOR TREASON' handbill circulated in Dallas on November 21, 1963, the day before the assassination.

November 22, 1963

144

ACT II

THE SCRIPT

'THE CONSPIRACY'

JANUARY 9, 1963[37]

John Wayne and many other show business people received engraved invitations to join Mrs. Richard Milhous Nixon in celebrating her husband's fiftieth birthday on the ninth of January in the year of our Lord nineteen hundred and sixty-three.

The reception was held at Nixon's estate in Beverly Hills, California, and the festivities would go on all day and long into the night. Along with his heightened sense of mortality at reaching the half-century milestone, Nixon was still a bit depressed after losing a bitterly waged California gubernatorial contest against Edmond 'Pat' Brown just two months before. A celebration was just what he needed to lift his dampened spirits.

And so on that day the friends and business associates of Richard M. Nixon came to honor him. They all brought with them envelopes of all sizes filled with cash, no checks. Inside each envelope was a small card or note that gave the identity of guest.

Richard Nixon was a man to whom everybody in California came for help, and he never let them down. As Vice-President, he had never made an empty promise nor offered the excuse that his hands were tied by more powerful forces in the country than he himself. He

---

[37] Elvis Presley's birthday is January 8th.

only asked one thing in return: Cash. Because only with cash could he regain his power: The power that had been stolen from him by John Kennedy.

Even though he was once JFK's House and Senate colleague, Richard Nixon found himself publicly humiliated by Kennedy after the unfortunate outcome of the 1960 election, just like he'd been humiliated by good looking rich kids his entire life; from his youth in Yorba Linda, California to Whittier College all the way to the race for the Presidency. But after the fraudulent 1960 election, and especially after taking another beating in the governor's race, and at Kennedy's suggestion, no less, Nixon vowed to the public that he wasn't going to let himself get kicked around anymore.

On this festive day in 1963, Richard Nixon stood in the doorway of his Beverly Hills home to greet his guests, all of them known to him. Many of who felt it appropriate to call him "Dick" to his face. Even the caterers were known to himself and Mrs. Nixon. The bartender was a lobbyist for the liquor industry whom Nixon had known from his days in Congress. The waiters were all out of work actors and dues-paying Film Actors Guild (F.A.G.) members. Except one, a young, Irish lad hired as a personal favor to John Wayne, who had first met the kid on the set of *The Quiet Man* back in 1952. The grounds of the property had been decorated by the Nixon's two daughters, and their friends.

They were all welcome on that day. No one was refused entry. And the guests so remarked at how relaxed and fit Nixon looked that one might have thought his suit was custom made.

As Nixon stood greeting his guests, a green and white trolley bus came to an abrupt stop at the edge of the driveway. It was a sightseeing bus filled with curious tourists and photographers. One guest, Frank Sinatra, turned to Nixon and said, "Goddamn paparazzi don't respect nuthin'!"

Nixon shrugged and said, "My property line runs along the stone wall. I don't own the whole street. I wish I did though … (inaudible) keep those nosy commie bastards away."

Although Nixon didn't disapprove of Sinatra's behavior, he was well aware that the rules of society are not fair, and he drew much comfort from knowing that there comes a time when even the most homely and awkward of men can again seize power. This thought was very much on Richard Nixon's mind on his fiftieth birthday. After all the guests had arrived, and the one-man band began to play, Nixon turned towards the patio to walk among his people.

A hired waiter, the Irish lad who knew Wayne, walked in behind Nixon, attempting to gain his attention. 'They're out of Jack Daniels,' he said, at the suggestion of Sinatra. Nixon, clearly displeased at the boy's proximity, told him, "Son, why don't you go around and make sure everybody has a drink, like a good boy, or else I'll call the union." With that, he patted the young man's shoulder, and the waiter named 'Fitzy' then disappeared into the crowd.

Some of the guests urged Nixon to play a tune on the piano. It was a request he would have been happy to oblige, but the day's entertainment was to be faithfully provided by the accordion-laden chest of Nixon's friend and longtime supporter Jimmy Stewart, and his solitary one-man band.[38]

As Stewart walked and slowly pumped the music box, he nonchalantly hummed and softly whistled the lyrics whenever possible. One song, in particular, he sang …

> *Buffalo gals won't you come out tonight …*
> *Come out tonight …*
> *Come out tonight …*

Stewart moved among the people casually, ever the keen observer, as he watched the afternoon's proceedings …

From behind the drapes of Richard Nixon's study on the far side of the house, Bebe Rebozo watched the revelers with a cautious eye. The walls behind him were stacked with history books, joke

---

[38] Stewart played the accordion on film in 1957's *Night Passage*, co-starring fellow WWII veteran Audie Murphy. He also played jazz piano alongside Duke Ellington in Otto Preminger's classic film noir, *Anatomy Of A Murder*.

books, photo albums, boxed and banded decks of cards, tape recorders, and most sparingly, law books. Rebozo was Nixon's friend and acted as the go-between, or 'buffer,' between Nixon and those who sought to gain his favor. He and Nixon had taken many bribes and payoffs in this room, and so when he saw Nixon return under the patio canopy he knew the Vice-President would be coming to see him. This was to be a "working" party. Rebozo went over to Nixon's desk and picked up a yellowed piece of White House stationery containing a list of people who had asked to meet with Nixon privately. When Nixon entered the room, Rebozo gave him the list. Nixon read it and said, "This is fine…Leave Sinatra til the end."

Rebozo left the study and went outside to where the major donors were waiting   He pointed his stubby finger at Colonel Tom Parker, the renowned manager of Elvis Presley.

During the mid to late 1950's, when Colonel Parker was making money hand over fist with Presley, he was at the mercy of Vice-President Nixon, the man who could have him deported with the blink of an eye. Not being a United States citizen, Parker had never paid a dime in taxes: A fact that wasn't missed by the Internal Revenue Service. As a result, Parker ended up paying more than a fair dollar or two to the cunning politicians and government officials who promised to keep his little secret, for a price. And as Parker well knew, everyone has their price. Nobody but nobody knew that better than the Colonel. Deported, Parker would have nothing. And he would do anything to prevent that from happening. And that meant that Elvis, his 'boy,' would be willing to do anything too, including enlisting in the United States Army.

Nixon greeted Parker politely. The Colonel had long been a Nixon supporter and the now ex-Vice-President was thankful for the large cash amounts Parker had given him over the years.

Rebozo handed Parker a glass of whiskey and a hand-rolled cigar, illegally imported from Havana. Parker nodded his appreciation and began to tell Nixon his story. Parker expressed his concern about the Kennedys. He was worried that a Kennedy second term would be his ruin. Parker was concerned that his illegal alien status would soon be discovered by the overly zealous Administration, and that all he had

148

worked so hard to gain in America, Parker's land of opportunity, would be lost. He feared bankruptcy and deportation. Nixon paced the paneled study while Parker spoke, at one time picking up a deck of cards and cutting it once. His mouth tightened with insincere empathy to keep the portly promoter talking.

When Parker was done, Nixon smiled and said, "You know, Colonel, I can call you Colonel, right?

Nixon knew that Colonel Tom Parker was born in Holland (his name at birth was Andreas van Kuijk), and was without U.S. citizenship. He also knew that 'The Colonel' was only a nickname, not an official rank. He was just a 'Kentucky Colonel.' The United States armed services, or any country's armed services for that matter, were presently total strangers to The Colonel.

Nixon continued, "Well, now there is a way you can put an end to your worries. As you know, I still have many (unintelligible) friends in government, but they don't work cheap. We'd have to agree on a price, a trade off, if you will, and your worries will then be put to rest. You've worked hard in this country ... you deserve to stay here and enjoy it a little, isn't that right, Bebe?"

Rebozo smiled broadly. It was just like Nixon to give him credit when he could. Without really saying it, Nixon had just congratulated Rebozo for his hard work too, and the loyal Cuban immigrant appreciated it. Rebozo thought to himself, why do I love this man so? My guy has no charisma, can't hold his drink, doesn't smoke, doesn't chase women, doesn't know how to play golf, doesn't know how to play tennis. He can't even fish. But Nixon did readily admit to one vice, one hobby, as it were. Poker.

Oh, how I adore this man. How I do so love him.

Nixon viewed poker as a metaphor, learning life lessons wherever he could. He found it instructive as well as entertaining and profitable, and learned that the people who have the cards are usually the ones who talk the least and softest. And that those who are bluffing tend to talk loudly and give themselves away.

149

Bebe worshipped Nixon, and hated Nixon's enemies.

Nixon reached across the desk to shake Parker's liver-spotted hand, saying, "I'll try to take care of this mess for you, but I may need your help on something soon … I hope I can count on your support?"

"Yes, Sir," said The Colonel, grinning like a child as he bowed his head with reverence.

"Thank you, Mr. Vice-President."

Rebozo laughed and walking him to the door, said, "That's a good deal Colonel, you are a very smart man." Then Parker shook Rebozo's hand too and marched off to the champagne fountain.

Rebozo asked Nixon, "Who might I give this job to?"

Nixon replied, reaching for a dried fig from a government-issued 'snack' bowl on his desk. "Immigration. But wait until Spring, maybe later. We'll have to make sure he holds up his share of the bargain."

In the meantime, Stewart continued easing his way through the partygoers, squeezing Nixon's favorite selections in-and-out, 'Victory At Sea,' 'The Battle Hymn Of The Republic,' some classical Beethoven and Tchaikovsky selections, and 'Happy Days Are Here Again,' which he knew was Nixon's favorite all-time 'popular' song.

Next on Rebozo's list was a case of vast importance. Pat Nixon had wanted a new overcoat for what seemed like ages. She was requesting $100 from her husband so that she may purchase a new one. She came in, looking alert and perky despite the long hours she had spent preparing this 'surprise' party on her husband's behalf. As far as Nixon was concerned she looked perfectly fine in her old Republican cloth coat, but being his birthday, and as he was surrounded by all of his colleagues and major contributors, he acquiesced.

I would do anything, Anything, for this woman.

Nixon reached into his pant's pocket and pulled out a roll of bills. He only had ninety. Wearing a conceived look of disdain, Nixon asked Rebozo for a ten-dollar loan. Bebe then put a ten-dollar bill to Mrs. Nixon.

Again, Rebozo quietly admired his boss and friend. After all, how many men would go to the trouble of asking a friend for ten dollars so their wife could buy a new coat. Richard Nixon was a very big-hearted man to do such a thing.

Nixon asked who was next. Rebozo said, "He isn't on the list, but John Wayne wants to see you. He knows you're busy, but he wants to say hello to you in private."

For the first time that day Nixon looked panicked, "Bebe … is this (inaudible) absolutely necessary?" Rebozo had no answer. He tossed his shoulders and cast a frightened eye, saying, "I'm not gonna tell him to leave." Nixon hung his head over the desk and motioned for him to bring Wayne in.

Outside on the patio, everyone stole glances at the deeply lined, carved granite face of Hollywood's most enduring legend. Nixon's daughters stood star-struck and said each other, "Wow, a movie star!" They both gazed up at Wayne, equally silent, wonder how such a nice old man could kill so many men every Saturday afternoon.

"He's friends with Daddy?!" chirped the younger of the two.

"Yup," answered the other with the proud air of a oldest child, "I heard Daddy says it's a good thing John Wayne isn't a politician or we'd all be out of business."

In 1963, John Wayne had just come off his biggest decade in movies since he started in the business back in the thirties (By 1939, Wayne had appeared in no less than sixty films). He'd met success through hard work. Simple as that.

And Nixon knew that The Duke had certainly paid his dues.

With almost three decades of films under his belt, in 1960, Wayne was poorer than he had been when he first started making pictures back in the 1930's.

By 1963, largely due to mismanagement of funds, overly generous charitable donations, and a couple of ex-wives who took him to the cleaners, Wayne was about as broke as a wood wagon. He needed some dough and he needed it fast. To prove and recover his worth, Wayne still had an obsessive hankering to direct again. All he needed was a break.[39]

Rebozo led Wayne inside, walking just behind him and to the right, afraid of treading into the hurried steps of the immense actor's purposeful, yet graceful, gait. Wayne strode into the room and with his eyes never leaving Nixon's, he handed over a heavy leather satchel and an envelope ripe with cash, and a satchel. Nixon greeted Wayne the way he had greeted heads of state while Vice President, with a combined gesture of awe, adulation, and respect. And with every unspoken word and steady gesture, the tough, prideful and noble Wayne communicated to Nixon one thing and one thing only. He was available should Nixon need him. He was with him. One hundred percent. The cash and the gold bars and silver coins and medallions in the satchel were almost insignificant. As Nixon received the gift, Wayne's rugged visage melted into a friendly, almost bashful smile.

When Wayne backed towards and through the doorway Nixon fell into his seat. The meeting with Wayne had taken all the wind out of him. In all his years of politics, he had never met anyone who filled up a room simply by entering it more than John Wayne.

"Is Sinatra the only one left?" Nixon asked Bebe.

Nixon and Rebozo of course knew that Frank Sinatra, the temperamental Italian-American crooner-actor and more recently the star of the critically acclaimed 1962 film *The Manchurian Candidate*, had helped to raise untold sums of money for JFK on the campaign

---

[39] Also, rumors persisted claiming that his mentor, John Ford, the legendary director with whom Wayne made many films, primarily westerns, had assisted him in crafting *The Alamo* epic.

trail. They were also well aware that, after being inexplicably shut out of JFK's inner circle, Francis Albert Sinatra, sought revenge.

Sinatra followed Rebozo to the study and found Nixon seated behind his desk. Nixon acted quietly hostile to Sinatra, not bothering to offer him even a handshake. Sinatra looked at Nixon and implied that he didn't want to speak with Rebozo in the room.

"We all know of your misfortune," Nixon said.

Sinatra was serious. He spoke without flinching, "Can I talk to you alone-like?"

"Why, Bebe's my friend, you know that, Frank," said Nixon calmly.

Sinatra lowered his head and shook it gently, wishing he could have Nixon's ear in private, but such was not the case. Then he began to speak in a low, soft voice. The voice he used when he sang songs like *The Last Dance* or *All the Way*. The voice he used to make people feel in love.

Sinatra began, "I believe in this goddamn country. I've made a lot of dough here. Money my parents never could've dreamed of. I met a politician, not an Italian. I hung out with him. I drank and picked up broads with him. I raised a few million for him. He did not properly thank me. I accepted this without protest. The fault is mine. A few months ago his little brother, or his old man, somebody, tells me to take a hike. They took advantage of me. They hurt my pride. I was shattered. Over and over again I asked myself, 'Why? How could Jack do such a thing? And I cried."

Sinatra could not speak any further. Tears filled his eyes as his talking voice weakened.

Nixon, appearing all but fed up at Sinatra's emotional display, looked at his Timex watch as Sinatra continued.

"Why did I cry? I am an only child, and he was like a brother to me. He had charisma. I trusted him, and now I will never trust him again." The color had left Sinatra's face. He had suffered from insomnia due to the vivid nightmares he had been suffering ever since airing his 'Welcome Home Elvis' TV special and throughout the filming of *The Manchurian Candidate*. He was visibly fatigued.

Nixon's eyebrows collided, "Geez, you sound like a fag for crissakes, you're not one of these queers, are you Frank? ... you're acting very emotional, very ... feminine. Tell me, has your mind failed, what with all that gallivanting around with those ... showgirls?"

Sinatra was so agitated he barely heard him. Nixon was taunting him now, so much so that Rebozo almost laughed out loud.

Sinatra felt numb. "I went to the Mafia like a good Italian," he weakly responded, "They told me it was my problem, that I had to fix it. I left him messages. Jack was warned. But he never said he was sorry. That he'd make it up to me. I never heard from him again. I felt like a fool. And then I said to myself. 'I will go to Vice-President Nixon for justice.'"

Nixon held himself up straight and looked Sinatra right in the eye, "Why, uh, why did you go to a gang for help? Why didn't you come see me first?"

Sinatra babbled almost incoherently, "What do you want? Just say the word. Pick a number. I just want this mick bastard taken care of!"

Nixon's voice hushed, "What do you mean, taken care of?"

Sinatra glanced over at Rebozo before stooping forward to whisper into Nixon's ear. Nixon cradled his chin in his thumb and forefinger. When Sinatra was finished Nixon wrapped his arms around his own hollow chest and stared into Sinatra's wet, blue eyes and muttered, "The Big Casino in the sky?! Frank, that's implausible. Out of the question. I'm not a crook, I'm an attorney."

Sinatra held his ground, "I am talking green Vegas money here, Mr. Vice-President. Whatever you need. Name it, it's yours."

Rebozo coughed to hide his guffaw. Sinatra had taken liberties no one had dared to take before. Nixon pushed himself slowly from his chair. His eyes looked cold, lifeless, as he said to the crooner, "You didn't back me in '60. You never sang on my behalf ... there was no 'Dick's got hiiiiigh hopes' ... speaking frankly, er, Frank, I wonder if you're even registered."

Nixon began to try to croon Kennedy's campaign lyrics, vocally mocking Sinatra,

> *You sang for pretty boy Kennedy, why?*
> *It seems he was Sin-a-tra's fa-vor-ite guy*
> *Now you say you want to whack - Jack*
> *Frank, you got way, way off, track ...*

Sinatra tried to interrupt, "Registered? I voted plenty of times, c'mon, what the ...?" But Nixon waved him off and continued his terrible, terrible singing ...

> *Frank, what happened to those Hiiigh Hopes?*
> *Those pecan and apple and lemon mereigne pie*
> *In the blueberry skyyy kind of hopes ....?*

Nixon drew a breath and jabbed a crooked finger at Sinatra, "NO, no, I understand completely. You wanted to sing, so you sang. You didn't care who you sang for, or what the consequences would be ... tell me if I'm wrong now Frank, I mean, you knew who you were singing for, am I right? Uh, I'm not being to pushy now, am I Frank? Hmmmm. Welll?"

Sinatra was clearly humbled. Nixon went on, "And now it seems, I'm your guy! I'm the candidate all of a sudden! Is that it?! Well let me tell you, Dick Nixon isn't running for anything today. I've said it before and I'll say it again, nobody's gonna be kicking this fella around anymore! Nobody! Dick Nixon is fifty years old today and he's out of office ... driven out by that ... that ... errr ... Kennedy." Nixon wagged his jowls and continued speaking in the third person, "Christ" he swore, "What in hell did Dick Nixon ever do to you, to drive you so far to the left?"

155

Sinatra's face filled with rage, rage he had held inside him ever since being ousted from the Kennedy camp, "I just want what's best for this country. I can't stand to see that crumbum's face on TV no more."

"Then tell your old friend to straighten it out," said Nixon, tapping his desk methodically with a gold envelope opener given to him by the Mail Handlers Union, "But no, Frank, you want more than that. And that's not right, what you're asking. I know how you feel Frank, believe me, Nixon knows better than anyone how you feel, yes, but uh, that is not the heart of the matter. Life isn't easy. I learned that a long time ago. You've got to move on. Onward and upward. As T.R. (Teddy Roosevelt) always said, 'A man is not finished when he is defeated. He is finished when he quits.'"

"But it ain't right, what he done."

"Right?!" replied Nixon with arched brows, "Right? You got what you wanted. He won the general election. He never told you you'd be on for the full term, did he?" Nixon smiled faintly, "No, I didn't think he would have."

"He whacked me, I'm gonna whack him back," said Sinatra, clipping one open hand with the other.,

"Whack?" Nixon shuddered, "Frank, you're very excited right now." Nixon gestured towards the lawn, "Go out there, maybe, have a drink. I don't have any Jack Daniels, but try the house bourbon ... say hello to a girl ... it's out of our hands. He's in, we're not." Nixon's injection of the plural 'we' was not lost on Rebozo, or Sinatra.

"Pick a number ... any number," said Sinatra.

Nixon took two steps over to the curtains and gently tugged at their length as he exhaled a long stream of air from his lungs, "Frank, if you had backed us in '60 it may have been different, then we'd both be back in Washington, right now, as we speak, but I ... uh, I have nothing more to say."

Sinatra approached Nixon, saying humbly, "I'm with you now babe, ain't I?"

"Well done," said Nixon, motioning Bebe to show him to the door. "That'll be fine, now, uh, I'll, I mean, Bebe will be getting in touch with you soon to discuss that figure you spoke of, Bebe will arrange everything."

Rebozo closed the door behind Sinatra and turned to face his friend, "What will I be calling him about?"

Nixon jutted out his jaw and said, "The time has come for a payback. I want you to fly out to Vegas next week and see this Parker fellow, tell him it's time for us to use that Presley boy."

"What about the publicity," moaned Bebe, "the kid's famous, the papers will be all over it!"

Nixon drew his index finger along his right temple, "Too famous. He's too obvious a choice, it'll never be questioned."

"Parker will never agree to it, no way!" chimed in Bebe.

Nixon got comfortable in his chair and smiled like the cat that ate the proverbial canary and said. "He has to. Besides, we have a fine newspaperman on the payroll. All I have to do is give Sullivan the go-ahead and he'll be all done anyway. We have information, right now, that Presley takes sleeping pills, prescribed of course, and I know for a fact he's harboring an underage girl. Daughter of an officer in the military, no less. And there's stories, listen to this one, that he's been seen around town driving a commie-pink Cadillac to boot!"

"But he's a veteran?" asked Rebozo. "Kid's like a war hero."

"True Bebe. He is a veteran. But he's no hero." Nixon thought for a moment about Presley's anti-establishment antics and the despicable sex acts he was rumored to perform on stage.

"Newspapers might like a story like that," said Rebozo licking his lips. "You think the kid's reliable?"

"Yes, I'd say so," said Nixon confidently. "But we're not relying on him … we're using him." After a moment he asked Bebe if there was anything else they had to discuss.

"Oh yes, Howard Hughes called, said he was sorry he couldn't make it but every time he left the apartment he had to go back to make sure it was locked. Checked the lock about three hundred times. Said you'd understand."

Nixon shook his head with a curious fury, "He what?!" He knew Hughes was a lunatic but he'd never heard this one before.

"He sent a card though," said Bebe, "You know … if we're going to go ahead with this thing, we should talk to him soon. This month, I'd say."

"Next month," answered Nixon, stretching his legs and checking his Timex again as he lifted and casually placed his scuffed and worn black wing tips up on his desk, "All in due time. But first thing next week I want you to go and tell that buffoon Parker that it's time to enlist, err make that re-enlist, the boy. Now go on out there and enjoy yourself, okay Bebe."

Outside, Jimmy Stewart continued to move unobtrusively among Nixon's pleased, optimistic crowd …

… come out tonight… oh, won't you come out tonight …
… Buffalo gals won't you come out tonight …
And dance by the light of the moon …

And then Stewart's squeezebox finally fell silent.

Happy days were here again.

When the Film Actors Guild (F.A.G.) was founded in 1933, its purpose and goal was to eliminate the exploitation of Hollywood actors who were being forced into oppressive multi-year contracts with the major movie studios that did not include restrictions on work hours or minimum rest periods, and often had clauses that automatically renewed at the studios' discretion. These contracts were notorious for letting the studios dictate the public and private lives of the performers, and most of the contracts did not have any provisions that allowed the performer to end the agreement.

Through the years, as the Cold War intensified, and as the Guild's political power and influence expanded, it was expected by the U.S. government to assist in purging the motion-picture industry of Communist party members.

In 1947, after suspected communists working in the Hollywood film industry were summoned to appear before the House Committee On Un-American Activities (HUAC), which was investigating Communist influence in the Hollywood labor union (i.e.: The Hollywood Ten), the politically divided Guild voted to force its officers to take a non-communist pledge, saying publicly, "We will not knowingly employ a Communist or a member of any party or group which advocates the overthrow of the government of the United States by force or by any illegal or unconstitutional methods."

However, by 1952, after elected union officials had failed to 'clean their own house,' certain frustrated, rogue elements of the Guild, working on their own behalf and without union sanction or approval, took it upon themselves to root out suspected communist infiltrators within the organization, especially any actor rumored to be studying 'The Method.'

These same clandestine agents, working unchecked without audit or oversight, then sought to broaden their powers, and they began to search out and employ union 'double agents.' Ultimately, with

159

invisible power at their disposal, and to further their zealous cause, they then began to seek out robot actors in earnest. Their misguided hypothesis being that a properly trained, susceptible, hypno-programmed subject, under the supervision, suggestion, and manipulation of a professional hypnotherapist (or high school acting coach or the equivalent), could involuntarily perform against their will, no matter how horrible the script or it's accompanying score. These rogue F.A.G. agents privately funded and administered the covert program under the vague and unrestrictive governance, "To Protect and to Act," and any suspicious or non-dues-paying actor or other industry worker was considered their enemy.

Mainstream Hollywood hadn't become aware of the mind-control scenario until late 1960, when Richard Condon's best-selling book *The Manchurian Candidate*, was being discussed as a potential film.

Unbeknownst to the young Elvis Presley, on October1, 1958, he had already been enrolled to take part in the secret, highly classified, mind-control program in Germany. He had been recruited by F.A.G. at the request of The Colonel, who, acting as Elvis' primary handler, used the opportunity to keep his most vital and lucrative interest, under his arm. The arrangement was developed and managed independently by the Film Actors Guild, and fully sanctioned by the Motion Picture Art and Science Commission, and Vice-President Nixon.

Elvis was the perfect mind-control subject, and his passive personality worked like clay in The Colonels hands. Always open to suggestion and searching for answers, Elvis could be hypnotized by the swami Colonel within minutes. Most Presley insiders dismissed the act as just anther one of The Colonel's old carny tricks, which oftentimes had members of Elvis' entourage barking like dogs or scratching like monkeys under even the most mild, hypnotic suggestion.

But the fact is, it worked, and The Colonel actually held power over people and got them to do things they wouldn't necessarily do otherwise. Elvis' 1956 episode of him singing to a basset hound on *The Steve Allen Show* was such an example. The Colonel, at Steve

Allen's misguided request, had hypnotized Elvis into donning a tuxedo in order to sing 'Hound Dog' to a basset hound. Hence the top hat and tails, and the embarrassment.

When one studies Presley after his two-year Army stint, the change from his once raucous musical style is obvious. Honorably discharged, he refrained from recording typically aggressive, pseudo-macho type songs like 'Heartbreak Hotel,' and 'Hound Dog,' 'King Creole,' and 'Trouble,' in favor of Latin-inspired ballads and mindlessly hypnotic sing-a-longs such as 1960's 'G.I. Blues.'

The huckster Colonel employed his most dangerous game throughout Hollywood, and although Nixon wasn't a member of The Snowmen's League, for he knew better, as Vice-President under Eisenhower, it was Richard Nixon who acted as the White House conduit to the Film Actors Guild. It was Richard Nixon who had firsthand knowledge of the communist brainwashing program, and of Elvis Presley's unknowing participation in it. Nixon had control over the program, without being controlled by The Colonel.

After enjoying three years of civilian life, there he was, the perfect subject, at the complete mercy of The Colonel, ready to take orders, and ripe for the picking. In 1963, Richard Nixon and the rogue planners could not have found a more suitable and compliant subject.

As a dues paying member of F.A.G., Elvis was now in the most dangerous of worlds. He was acting out The Method's pro-Communist pantomimes under the soon-to-be assigned command of a violently anti-Method Acting cabal and dominated by mind-controlling manager-promoter blackmailed by a plotting, exiled head of state.

Elvis Presley.

The Memphisian Candidate.

All he needed was the right script.

Upon greeting Sinatra with his customary weak handshake, and without a smile or saying a word, Nixon watched as Sinatra opened his alligator attaché case and removed an oversized, yellow manila folder, which he had placed on Nixon's desk.

Nixon turned the folder over three times, examining it closely. Comfortable that there was no indication of any bugs or electronics, he opened it and removed its contents, all checks, all made out to 'The Committee to Elect Richard Nixon.'

"Just sprinklin' the goodies," said Sinatra, absolutely beaming with pride.

Nixon looked at the first donation. Helen Hayes $500. Nixon smiled. Helen had worked very hard for him in 1960.

Next, Mervyn LeRoy $500. LeRoy was yet another Hollywood supporter who had helped Nixon in 1960. He was a director and producer. Back in the 1930s, Nixon knew, LeRoy had directed Edward G. Robinson in *Little Caesar* and had even produced *The Wizard of Oz*. He also produced *The FBI Story*, starring Jimmy Stewart, which was one of Nixon's favorite movies, and *Gypsy*, which wasn't.

Gary Cooper $500. "Gary Cooper!!" Nixon yelled. "I thought that son of a bitch was a communist! And dead to boot! *Well, if dead men can vote for Kennedy they may as well be able to make campaign contributions to me.*

"Frank, you've really outdone yourself here!"

There were more campaign donations. Rosalind Russell, Robert Montgomery, Robert Cummings, Robert Taylor, Irene Dunn, Cesar Romero and even former silent screen star Mary Pickford. Not exactly the 'cool' Hollywood set, but contributors nevertheless.

"Keep going, baby," motioned Sinatra. "There's more bangles and baubles where that came from."

And the checks kept right on coming. Red Skelton, Dick Powell, June Allyson, Robert Young, Cyd Charisse, Johnny Mathis, and even Efrem Zimbalist, Jr.

"Wowie, Frank! This is real campaigning! You may have a second career here!"

Sinatra had wanted to approach Dean and Sammy, but then decided that he didn't want to get the boys to get too mixed up in all this just yet, or ever.

Then the biggie. Sinatra had tucked this last check way down deep in the bottom in his jacket pocket. With a big smile, he handed it to Nixon.

The last check, for $25, was signed, 'Bob Hope.'

"$25!!!" Nixon looked like he was going to cry.

Nixon had first met entertainer Bob Hope in the 1950s when Nixon was Vice President. Hope had been a friend and supporter ever since. But even the excessively frugal Nixon knew what a legendary world-class cheapskate Hope was.

"How in blazes did you get Bob Hope to write a check for $25?" asked an incredulous Nixon.

Sinatra just shrugged as if to say 'nuthin' to it,' but added that he practically had to sign it for him.

Nixon sat back and took full measure of the new man who stood before him. Frank Sinatra, Republican. And Nixon knew that Sinatra was even more than eager for revenge now, having just been further victimized by the ruthless Attorney General Bobby Kennedy, who had recently initiated a full investigation of Sinatra's business relationships and financial holdings, causing him to lose his nine-percent interest in The Sands hotel and casino in Vegas, his home away from home and one of the strips biggest moneymakers.[40]

"Now … are you ready to go for the big enchilada?" asked Nixon. "The donation that could singlehandedly elect us … and then re-elect us again? … The fundraiser to end all fundraisers …?"

Sinatra's eyes lit up. "You just told me who we're gonna hit?" he said.

"Hughes …"

Nixon nodded to Sinatra, "We could get it in cash. I know where it could be gotten. And I know that you know where it could be gotten. The question is who the hell would handle it."

Sinatra was practically falling out of his wingtips to get Nixon's attention, to the point where he literally started to raise his hand and wave. Nixon noticed the excitable song stylist raising his hand. He played to Sinatra's infatuated ego, "Of course, we'd need to hire a professional for that kind of job, maybe even a burglar … to get that kind of money … isn't that right Frank?... Frank?"

"Yes, sir," answered Sinatra, complimented by the attention Nixon was granting him, he'd always imagined himself as a tough guy. Albeit one with bodyguards.

"Would you be able to take care of this," Nixon asked, "He's so isolated. You're one of the few people he communicates with. Could you maybe, talk, to (inaudible) Hughes?"

"No problem, buddy," said Sinatra, "It's one phone call. I'll take care of it."

---

[40] Later, in 1967, Howard Hughes purchased 'The Sands,' forcing Sinatra to take his show elsewhere. It had been a long time coming, since the two had privately feuded ever since Sinatra had found out Hughes had dated Ava Gardner.

Both men knew that by 1963 Howard Hughes had earned himself a reputation as an innovator, inventor, businessman, playboy and kingmaker. Born in Houston, Texas and orphaned at age eighteen, he readily promoted himself as the ultimate entrepreneur, seeking to obtain every worthwhile thing that came within his eager grasp. First Hughes Tool Company. Then Hughes Aircraft Company. Then show business with R.K.O. Pictures. He'd done it all.

Cross My Heart

In producing the film, *The Outlaw*, Howard Hughes also became single handedly responsible for elevating (in addition to lifting and separating) the female breast to the revered position in American society that it holds to this very day. Hughes designed a steel underwire push-up bra for sweater girl Jane Russell to wear in the film. Hughes, an airplane designer, adopted modern technologies to up-lift the contour of the bosom. The film's release is delayed for three years because of Russell's sensuous portrayal, and Hughes finally decides to release *The Outlaw* without a Motion Picture Code seal. It marked the beginning of the end of film censorship.

Then Hughes bought up virtually all of Las Vegas and it's surrounding real estate. He also held a controlling share in Trans World Airlines (TWA). With Hughes around, nothing worth anything was safe from his grasp. Howard Hughes had also learned very early in his career, that political leanings had little if anything to do with striking deals with Washington bureaucrats. But from 1950 onward, Hughes had lived the life of a recluse, and his business relationships had oftentimes suffered as a consequence. The tormented American industrialist-aviator, having seemingly conquered it all, had become fearful that his empirical fortune was growing out of control. Hughes had become paranoid, living like a hermit in a Las Vegas hotel room.

Sinatra had recently lost his interest in The Sands hotel, so he had turned to Howard Hughes for help. Hughes had been buying up most of the Vegas strip, and Sinatra felt such an alliance would prove beneficial down the road. Hughes, too, saw Sinatra as a bonus feature attraction that would fill seats in his newly acquired casinos. Despite their personal grudges, their relationship was at present a mutually beneficial win-win situation.

Nixon turned on his heels and walked over towards the window, "Would we, uh, need to *meet* with Howard on this," stammered Nixon, poking his index finger through the curtains and peeking out onto the traffic, "You know, just to go over this thing, details and what have you?"

"No," said Sinatra, "As far as Mr. Hughes is concerned, this here's dirty money and he doesn't want any part of it."

After a moment of silence, Nixon turned away from the window and began to point his finger at Sinatra, "Now Frank," he said, "There's no need to disparage what we're trying to accomplish here with remarks like that, with ... [inaudible] aspersions, if you will." Nixon very well knew that Hughes was known to offer massive cash payoffs to influential state officials in return of IRS leniency and government defense and aerospace contracts.

"Hey, Clyde ..." the cocky Sinatra was clearly taking liberties with the former Vice President, "Don't worry, it's no problem. I'll get it out of the safe, the one where he keeps all the dirty money."

Ignoring the 'Clyde' comment, Nixon spoke quickly, spraying a bit of spittle as he began, "Now Frank, I thought we agreed not to speak in such a manner. We're all here for the same [expletive deleted] reasons."

Then Nixon stopped. His eyes widened. "The safe. You've seen it? Does Howard tell you what the ... what the, the dirty money's being used for?" Nixon continued, looking genuinely concerned.

"Does he tell me!?" laughed Sinatra, "He calls me like two or three times a week."

"Calls you? What do you mean *calls*?" asked Nixon.

"We talk on the phone. I haven't seen him in years though. At least since '59."

Nixon was really concerned now, "Frank. Is everything … okay? I mean … I've heard stories…"

"No, Dick. Relax. Everything's fine. It's just that he can't leave the room," said Sinatra to Nixon's amazement, "It's the doorknob, see. He says the doorknob's got germs on it, same as the money."

"Germs!" said Nixon, crinkling his rubber lips with disgust "Jaysis! Doesn't he have any help come in and … tidy things up. I know Pat has a woman come in on Thursdays … a Latin American woman … she's very reasonable … I could get you references?"

"No, sir, nothing like that" said Sinatra, picking up the empty manila envelope. "The germs are in his imagination. It's all in his head."

Nixon smiled after hearing that and looked at Sinatra and said, "Well … we'll just have to tell Howard we're *laundering* it for him." Nixon laughed nervously and threw his arms up in the air and then slammed them down against his sides.

That night, back at his desert home in Palm Springs, Frank Sinatra tossed and turned violently in his sleep, night sweats spitting off his face, gasping and sighing, as if he were having a fit.

In the dream he was in the Army with Elvis. The other soldiers were giving Elvis 'The Treatment' because he wouldn't sing.

"I can soldier with any man," Elvis retorted to his superiors, again and again.

Elvis frowned slightly. He hopped once, changing stride, only then realizing he was out of step.

"Presley! This is a drill, not a southern picnic! Get in step!"

Presley awkwardly hopped again, changing step. Then he marched along, singing 'Witchcraft' as he snapped his fingers out of beat.

"Platoon -- Halt!" Elvis and the men around him came to halt.

"Presley! Step out!"

Elvis stepped to the front.

"Maybe all that shaking's made you crazy! You march like a drunken loony bird! Private! Take this man to the track. Send him 'round seven laps double-time, rifle at high port!"

Elvis ran around the track, his rifle at high port, wearing a slightly contemptuous smile.

Sinatra awoke, startled and frightened, as if he were in a trance. His head jerked.

"The kid's been away for two years," spoke Sinatra aloud to himself, "And I get the feeling he really believes what he's doing."

He shook his head violently, trying to get back to reality. The dream was too real. He had been there. He knew the place. He felt it in his gut. But where was it? When?

Drenched in sweat, Frank Sinatra fell fast back to sleep.

Elvis had just stepped out of the bathroom.

"Good morning, sunshine!" Sinatra shifted his jaw and smirked and gave his cigarette a tug. It was three in the afternoon.

Elvis' mouth fell open. *How the heck did Mr. Sinatra get into my house?*

Elvis put down his boxing gloves and bathing suit and pushed his greasy mess of disheveled hair back in place the best he could. He looked down at his crazy mismatched wardrobe. Half dressed in a matador outfit consisting of a crisp collared white shirt, with a black string tie, and a hip-hugging red matador jacket with a red cumber bund. And boxer shorts. And he was wearing a cape, unsure if he was preparing for his role in *Fun In Acapulco* or *Kid Gallahad*.

"Man ... dig the ensemble!" said Sinatra, before adding, "Hey kid. How's your Bell and Howell?" [41]

Elvis stood speechless.

"So tell me," mimed Sinatra, doing his 'Amos and Andy-Steppin Fetchit' bit. "Who *does* wear the pants in this family anyway? Cuz whoever done wears 'em has up and lef' town!"

Here we go again ... thought Elvis. Fearing another John Wayne episode, Elvis gave his boxers a quick peek just to make sure that his front man was tucked away safe behind the curtains.

"You know, boxers oughtta be sewed shut," Sinatra mused. "You only pull 'em down when you gotta go, anyway. Right? So why with all the aggravation?"

---

[41] Sinatra-ese for "How's it hangin'?"

It occurred to Elvis that maybe Sinatra was looking for a check for a politician or something. Maybe President Kennedy or Saint Jude's Hospital or something like that. Elvis thought he had heard from someone a while back that Sinatra was a big political guy around town, having fundraisers and golf tournaments and that sort of thing. Elvis would just as soon keep his political ideas to himself, not that he had any. He'd ask The Colonel for some money for Kennedy, since he knew he was already freinds with Kennedy's Vice-President, anyway. And he'd be happy to call his daddy for a charity check, if that was what Mr. Sinatra wanted.

"You gotta get some new help kid," said Frank. "That bellboy of yours gave you up for a five. For a ten-spot he wouldda sang chorus."

Elvis was embarrassed. And he *hated* being embarrassed. He grabbed a comb and started slicking back his damp hair while he grabbed a stray pair of pants.

Sinatra seemed to be in an extra ball-breaking mood, and it showed in the cock in his walk as he strolled around the foyer as Elvis fished for his pant leg.

"What gives with the duds? You look like Batman on a bender. What are ya, waitin' tables today at the beach or something?"

Elvis wasn't just embarrassed, he was nervous too. *Fun in Acapulco* called for some stunts, and he wanted to do it himself. Like a trapeze drop from twenty feet. And he insisted, over everyone else's dead body, that there wasn't going to be a stuntman, either. Elvis wished himself to laugh at his mismatched costume but he couldn't. So he just gave Sinatra a blank expression until he had something to say.

"You alright kid. You got a bird tucked away here or something? I walk in on you?" For the first time since arriving Sinatra actually appeared apologetic.

"N-n-n-n no, Sir. I just got a lot goin' on right now. We just started shootin' this movie, a-a-and I play a singin' fisherman , no a singin' boxer, uh, singin' tour guide. I-I-I'm playin' a singin' cliff diver, no, I mean a singin' trapeze artist, aww shoot … I mean …"

Sinatra approached Elvis quickly and held his arm firmly. "Listen kid, relax, relax. I know you're workin' hard. I just came over to say hello. I wanna talk to you. I got something on my mind. And it's been bothering me. Big time."

Sinatra sat him down on the couch and he pulled the ottoman up so he could talk to Elvis up close. The short show was over. Sinatra was out of gas with barely any sleep, no naps, and nothing else but work, Jack Daniels, and cigarettes.

"Listen. I've been having this dream, see. A nightmare. It's a real swinger of a nightmare too. And it's getting' worse. And I was just wondering if you … well …"

Sinatra didn't know how to tell him. Now *he* was embarrassed. *What the hell am I doing here. I must be out of my mind. Tellin' the kid I'm having dreams about him, like I'm half a fag or something ...*

Sinatra ran his fingers through the real hair on both sides of his head and put his elbows on his knees and his face in his hands.

Elvis looked down at him and said, "Don't be embarrassed Mr. Sinatra. It's okay." Although he was more of a daydreamer, Elvis had had nightmares, too. Real scary, end-of-the-world type nightmares. Trees falling down. Roller coasters flying off their tracks. People screaming, needing to be saved. Like it was World War Three or something. But he figured they were from his medicine. He didn't give it much thought. He'd just cut down a bit on the medication the next time. Plus, it was personal. He'd just as well keep it to himself.

Elvis gave Sinatra's shoulder a pat and a squeeze. "What happened, Mr. Sinatra? You're workin' too much, I bet. Man, you never stop, do you?"

Elvis was right. Frank's schedule never gave up. Sinatra always seemed like he had just got back from somewhere and was on his way to someplace else, everyone said it. Always in between gigs, dates, meetings and meals. Always go go go. He had three movies set for release this year alone and maybe half a dozen albums. In fact, the one he did with Count Basie had just come out a week or two ago, and it was doing gangbusters. 'The Sands' every night with Sammy and Dean. The charity shows for the boys in Chicago that never seemed to end. True, he was beat. Hadn't even seen the kids since Christmas. But there was more to it than that.

Frank lifted his head. "You remember when I had you on my show, when you got back from the Army?"

"Yeah, sure I do," said Elvis. "First time I met you. I was so nervous I thought I was gonna flop and die right there on stage."

Sinatra closed his eyes and nodded up and down. "Yeah right right … and then me and the boys and you did a few numbers and then we all went home, right?"

"Yeah. I went back to Memphis." Elvis' face got all screwed up. "Mr. Sinatra, what are you talkin' about? Why'd you get all dressed up in that suit and felt like you had to come see me and tell me that today? Is everything okay?"

Sinatra looked down at his sleeve and slacks, "Naw, this here's my everyday rags. I had a business meeting down Warner Brothers earlier. I just, see … it's like this, kid … I haven't been sleepin' right. Not for a while now. And it ain't just show biz neither, bud. Something's up. Up *here*." Sinatra tapped the side of his head with his index finger.

"And I think that that Captain Blubber boss of yours did it. I think the bum slipped me a mickey."

Elvis tried to make sense of Sinatra's words. *Captain, Captain … Colonel? …*

He didn't know what to say. His whole face was a question. He forced some words. "What's this got to do with …"

173

"I'll get into that in a minute. But kid, listen. You gotta promise me something. You gotta drop that bum. He's no good. I know." Sinatra tapped his head again. "I hear things."

Elvis tried to stand up but Frank reached for Elvis' waist, and Elvis sat back down.

"Look. I dunno what kinda mindgame this cat plays. Whether it's abracadabra circus stuff or the real McCoy, like in Korea. Remember, I was in the movie, Charlie."

Sinatra's mind privately rattled off some words that had been stuck there for some time … *no hypnotized subject may be programmed to perform an act that is abhorrent to their own moral duty …*

"And that fat pimp manager of yours, he's like a mind-reader, I've seen it. I studied it last year and I know. And I'm telling ya that something in Denmark has gone berserk, baby. And I'm not sure yet about the whole thing. But I think you … we … might be in some trouble here, cowboy."

Elvis stood up fast. He needed some breathing room to think. He wanted some space for a second. "You want somethin' to drink. A Pepsi or anything? A milkshake?"

Sinatra rubbed his tired face and reached inside for a smoke. "Yeah, yeah, kid. A Pepsi. That'd be swell." Sinatra pulled straight his orange striped tie and sighed heavy. "Milk is bad for you. Just ask Pat Boone …"

Elvis went into the kitchen and leaned against the refrigerator. The Colonel. *What's that greedy double-timin' bastard done now?!* He went into the bathroom and quickly zipped open his leather satchel and then hurried back to the kitchen. He opened the fridge and grabbed two bottles of Pepsi, which he popped open before returning to the den.

Sinatra went over to the bookcase. "Kid, what's with all the books?" he asked. "You're all over the map here. Karate books. *The*

Bible. Prophecies … Spanish for Beginners … The Book of Numbers … What the hell is this stuff? You got some kinda interests kid."

Elvis took the *Book of Numbers* from Sinatra's hand, gently, replacing it with a Pepsi, and brought it back to the bookcase. He was trying to learn some Spanish for the movie, but he didn't feel like telling that to Sinatra.

"Oh, I don't know. I guess I just kind of like all that stuff. Karate especially. I found out about it over in Germany. I found out about *a lot* over in Germany." He laughed quietly to himself and then stopped. "There's a birthday card around here somewhere. They called me 'King Karate' on it." He chuckled nervously and looked around the room once and then again, remembering he had promised to give the Irish kid down at the lot a few lessons.

Sinatra rubbed his hand. The one he broke in the karate scene in *The Manchurian Candidate*. Someone forgot to tell the prop man to go get a breakaway table. *Dummies.*[42]

Sinatra felt nauseous, bloated. He took a swig of the bubbled soft drink and swallowed hard. He usually wasn't one for carbonated beverages, but he thought it might get a burp up, give him some relief. *Tired. Sick and tired.* He made a mental note to grab a steam later on, or maybe get his wingtips shined.

"Listen kid." Sinatra held the bottle with both hands between his legs. "What I see going on here. What my gut tells me about this guy. This riverboat gambler of a manager of yours, or whatever you wanna call him, is not good. And I dunno about you but I always trust my gut. Not much else, but that I do."

Trust your gut. Elvis thought about his mother. *Always trust your gut. It knows things*, she always said.

---

[42] *The Manchurian Candidate* was the second American motion picture to feature the sport of karate. The first was 1955's *Bad Day At Black Rock*, starring Spencer Tracy (another one of JFK's favorite films).

"What I'm sayin' kid, is you gotta make a decision. You gotta start usin' some of your star power and start callin' some shots for yourself, before it's too late." Sinatra knew this much was true. He'd lived it.

Elvis had nothing to say. If it were anyone else he would have said 'I'm just a country boy with a six-string singin' a song.' But he wasn't talking to anyone else. He was talking to Frank Sinatra. And Mr. Sinatra had a bullshit detector like a Russian satellite.

"Decisions. Let me tell you. You're better off alone. Make your own deals. Pick your own movies. You gotta bag this hot air balloon blimp. This pimp. I had to do the same thing myself back in the day. What's this bastard take? A third? A half? Plus percentages?! No way, baby! Same as Dorsey." Sinatra looked around, paranoid. "And look where he is now … Kaput. Big casino upstairs, the poor bastard. I just see it comin' kid. Same thing. And I don't wanna see you make any mistakes. We're all in this show together, right."

Elvis wasn't paranoid, but he was close. He trusted Mr. Sinatra but he didn't trust him.

What does he care. He must want something from me. Girls? Can't be girls. He's loaded with them. What is it?

He remembered what Sinatra had said about him back in '57.

And I never gave it back to him. I always treated him as an elder, with respect. I said, "I admire the man. He has a right to say what he wants to say. He is a great success and a fine actor, but I think he shouldn't have said it. He's mistaken about this. This is a trend, just the same as he faced when he started years ago."

Sinatra saw Elvis' wheels turning. "What's he got on you?" Sinatra questioned. "You knock somebody up?" Sinatra's eyebrows shot up fast. "You knock somebody *off?*"

"Nope," Elvis said, a little too quickly. "Nuthin' like that. It's just the way it is. Deal's a deal. Just like it says. Right there in black and white. It's a joint venture." It seemed like the right thing to say,

176

even though Elvis had never actually seen the contract. Never read it all the way through, that is.

"Joint venture, my ass. Yeah. HIS joint!" Sinatra hated phony lying bastards like Captain Blubber.

Elvis didn't want to admit it, but in the bathroom he had taken another tranquilizer. Deep inside he knew the pills were starting to go a bit over the top. But it wasn't like he really needed the pills. *It's not like I'm sniffing cocaine or smoking marijuana or anything. It's all prescribed medicine. I can take it or leave it if I want to.* It was just that he took them sometimes if he needed to get some sleep, and then if he really needed to stay awake he took some of the little white ones. But he would never have said anything to Sinatra. It wasn't a big deal or anything.

Ordinarily, Sinatra might have noticed it. He was nothing if not aware. But he was too overcome with severe fatigue. He saw the puffy face when he walked in but just figured the kid had put on some weight or had just woken up. Sinatra wished he himself had just woken up. Man was he tired.

Sinatra stood up to excuse himself, taking Elvis' hand into his own.

"Listen, kid. I want you to call me. Anytime. You need help. You need something taken care of. Some*body* taken care of. You want some advice. You just buzz me, okay pal. Ring-a-ding-ding, and I'll come runnin.' Sometimes this town can be a little hollow, like 'Alonetown.' You know what I mean? And you might need someone in the foxhole with you, just like in the Army, okay kid?"

Army. Just the word triggered a lifetime of horror to Elvis. *Where I wasted two years of my life. The same people who almost wouldn't let me go to my own mother's funeral. The Army.* He wondered if Sinatra had ever served. He didn't think so.[43]

---

[43] Sinatra was declared 4F (not qualified for service) and did not serve during WWII, the reason listed was 'punctured eardrum.'

He wanted to tell Sinatra, someone, anyone, how lonely he got. How empty he felt out here in Hollywood. How even with his friends around him and all the girls and all, how he felt like his life would never feel the same again. But he figured Sinatra would never understand. Guys like him never got lonely.

Just like in the Army. Elvis sighed.

"Lord Almighty, Mr. Sinatra," said Elvis out loud. "I sure hope not."

*O*ne afternoon the following week, Richard Nixon, Bebe Rebozo and Frank Sinatra boarded Sinatra's private plane, the 'El Dago,' in Beverly Hills for a short, little fundraising junket to Las Vegas.

Inside, the El Dago was like a flying hotel room. Miniature Stoli bottles and Jack Daniel's nips all lined up and ready to pour. And plenty of ice. Not crushed, not cubes, a nice in-between.

When Nixon and Rebozo arrived a few minutes late, Sinatra's private pilot whispered "Frank, what gives with this guy? You don't wait for nobody."

"This man is gonna be our leader someday," Sinatra said confidently. "You watch and see."

Rebozo and Nixon had brought their own Pepsi-Colas and were enjoying them on the couch. Sinatra poured his customary Jack Daniels, letting the ice sit and swish around his glass for a few minutes, so the flavors would blend.

Then surprisingly, at Nixon's urging, Sinatra broke into song. Even though it was mid-afternoon, to Sinatra, it was the dawn of new day.

"Okay baby, Post-time! Let's start the action!"

Sinatra sang lead with Nixon, Rebozo and Frank's pilot on chorus.

(Sinatra, using his singing voice, as he ad-libbed another classic ...)

Everyone is waiting for Dick
Cause he knows what makes the USA tick
Everyone wants to back - Dick

179

Up his sleeve's a nifty new trick!

'Cause he's got high hopes
And he's – no dope ....
Nineteen Sixty ...

(Sinatra looked at Richard M. Nixon and shrugged ...)

... Sixty-Something's the year for his high hopes.

(Sinatra then turned admiringly to Nixon ...)

Richard Nixon - You just can't kick him around!!!

(Then Sinatra secretly drew a lungful of air in through a small corner of his mouth, a little breath control trick he learned from his days with Dorsey ...)

Richard Nix -   he just keeps rollin' - a

They'll all buy tix -   he just keeps rollin' - a

My man Dick Nix -   he keeps on rollin' along ...

When the DC-6 landed and came to a halt, the three men tightened the knots of their ties (Sinatra then realized he had forgotten to wear a necktie), disembarked the plane, and hailed a cab for The Desert Inn, secret home of Howard Robard Hughes, gazillionaire.

Ring-a-ding-ding!

In a rare instance of dress code neglect, Frank Sinatra had forgotten to wear a tie.

Initially denied entrance into the VIP room by Hughes' surrogates because of his neglect to wear a proper neckpiece, Frank Sinatra and his friends were temporarily relegated to second-class status and force to enjoy the hotel lounge and piano bar with the small-time players and tourists.

After a few extra bourbon shooters, Sinatra, fuming, excused himself, and decided it was time to go upstairs and get the one million from Hughes in cash.

Enough of the bullshit.

Telling Nixon and Rebozo it might be better if they waited in the lounge, he took the elevator to the Hughes' ninth floor private residence, showed his meager credentials to security, and knocked on the door of Hughes 13th floor room.[44]

Sinatra chirped up. "Howard, you in there? It's me, Frank. How's your bird?"

There was no answer. Then Sinatra remembered about the doorknob. So he returned to the lounge and scrawled a message on a Rebozo's bar napkin, and after making small talk with a few dames,

---

[44] John Wayne had called Hughes an "asshole" in public at The Desert Inn one night in the early 1950's, and Hughes had never gotten over it. Hughes had also dated one of Wayne's great loves, the enigmatic actress-singer Marlene Dietrich, who had also been linked to Sinatra, JFK, and JFK's father, Joe Kennedy.

Sinatra returned to Hughes' bolted door, this time accompanied by Nixon and Rebozo.

The napkin read: *RN4PREZ - 1 million clams*
                                 Whaddaya say? - FAS

Sinatra looked at the note with pride and for no apparent reason began speaking into the door knob, "Howard, I know about the germs and that kinda stuff, so I'm gonna put a note under the door, okay pal? Here goes…"

Frank slid the folded napkin under the door, catching his gold signet pinky ring on a piece of carpet fiber in the meantime, "Sonofabitch!!" screamed Sinatra, trying to free his hand from the rug.

With that, the napkin promptly returned, appearing under the door wrapped in a plastic sandwich bag, empty. "There will be no foul and odorous language in my company," came the echoed voice behind the door. The voice of Hughes himself.

Sinatra looked at the others and said, "What gives with this joker?" Nixon shushed him to mind his mouth and tapped on the door gently.

The voice returned, "What is it that brings men of such prominent public stature to my primary residence?!"

Sinatra opened his mouth to talk, but Nixon drew his hand to his chapped lips in an attempt to silence the hot-tempered singer-actor.

Then Rebozo quietly intervened, "Sir, we came here from Beverly Hills, and we'd just like to talk to you about getting my friend back home again."

Silence.

"He's lost is he?" said the man behind the door, "If he is lost, why then travel thirteen stories to see me, why not just ask the woman at the information desk in the lobby. Did you not see her?" The men all looked at each other and shrugged.

The humble Rebozo again spoke up, "A mere hourly worker cannot help us Sir. We will only be able to help our friend with the generous assistance of a rich and powerful man like yourself." Nixon winked at Bebe. The little Cuban was a goldmine to him.

"Please sir," Bebe continued, "We only wish to help our friend here. This is all." Sinatra snarled at Rebozo, thinking he was getting shortchanged.

Hughes' voice was louder, "I have neither the time nor the energy to entertain men with mortal wants and desires, I have a business to run, a corporation, a conglomerate, an Empire!! Sinatra, Nixon and Rebozo jumped back against the opposing wall, frightened at Hughes' heightened vocal inflection.

"Hey," whispered Sinatra, "It's worse than I thought ... this cat's flipped."

Nixon prodded Bebe to take the floor again and gently pushed his friend towards the door. Bebe pressed his ear against the shut barrier and wrinkled his nose, "Hey, Boss," he said to Nixon, "I smells something funny in there." He sniffed again.

"Smells like low tide in Miami." Nixon and Sinatra rushed to join him, and all three men sniffed the door's entire casement. Sinatra smelled something else. He thought he smelled chocolate.

"What are you doing there?!" intoned Hughes as he peered through the eye hole, "Get away....away with you all...back, step back from my suite this very instant!!"

Sinatra clenched his ring-ridden fist and calmly challenged the inanimate and defenseless door. Hughes childishly chanted, "I would if I could but I can't so I won't." Again, the men exchanged glances and shook their heads in disbelief.

"You can't open the goddamn door?!" chanted Sinatra, feeling a need to show off in front of Nixon. "Hey, Howard, c'mon, step out here and say hello to the boys." After waiting a few seconds or so,

Sinatra grew impatient. "Here, I'll open the damn door for ya!" Sinatra braced himself for what could very possibly be a very ugly replay of his wrenched sternum, cement versus sledgehammer incident.

"No, get away....they'll get you if you touch them!" cried the ever eccentric Hughes.

"What?" said Nixon and Rebozo at the same time.

"The germs!" replied Hughes, "They're all over the doorknob. They're everywhere. I can never be rid of them." Hughes had become so paranoid that even Nixon and Sinatra took notice.

Then, Sinatra, confident that the hotel's walls and doors were poorly constructed and paper thin, took two short steps back and planted his foot before jumping against the door, cracking it open instantly despite the apparently frail condition of his slight physique.

Nixon screamed, "A Break-In! No!"

As the door swung open and the three men turned, their faces became taut with fear. They'd now succeeded in pissing off the richest man in the world, and they were about to catch his fiery wrath. Upon seeing him, they stopped in their tracks, and their collective jaws dropped as they stared in full and utter disbelief at the long, skeletal figure that appeared before them.

"Howard?" sighed Nixon, "is that you?" Rebozo and Sinatra felt as though their hearts had stopped.

There stood billionaire recluse Howard Hughes, scantily clad in a blue hospital gown with matching paper slippers. His gray-white hair was unruly as all hell and his overall person most generally unkempt. Behind him the hotel windows were cloaked in tin foil, and the entire room was completely devoid of light, man-made or natural. Everything inside the room was shrouded in cellophane … lamps, tables, chairs, even the floor beneath his sanitary feet. And against the far wall lay his king-sized bed, encased within a dome of opaque plastic.

Hughes was no mere 'clean-freak.' He clearly had a serious issue with personal hygiene.

Nixon paid particularly close attention to the lamps and their wires and cords.

Just below the closest windowsill sat a gold-rimmed, marble-bodied dry Jacuzzi. In it swam cash. Cold, hard cash, and lots of it. And all of it veritable, serial marked American currency. Crisp, brand new bills, hot off the Treasury presses. Beside it, against a commercial-sized air conditioner unit, stood stacks and stacks of chocolate bars, all unwrapped, like dipped gold bars. Thousands of them, in human sized-towers, row after row after row.

"Whoa ... that's a lot of jingle, baby," said Sinatra before venturing, "Howard? Man, what's happened to you kid, you eatin' alright?"

Hughes looked down at the ink-stained bar napkin with distain, and hung his shaggy head as he nodded to the left and right, "I am a sick man...very sick...sicker than you know." He was holding a specimen cup half-filled with milk, with a thick wad of Kleenex tissues between the cup and his palm.

The three men shrugged as if to say, 'No, we got a pretty good idea.'

Hughes continued with a voice full of sorrow, "True. I am a rich man, yes, but I am an empty man. I only have what you see before you. My money is in places I will never know. Overseas ventures. European banks. Real-estate worldwide. All I really have to my name is this room and the tub of money there which is too contaminated for me to even touch."

"Jesus Christ!" said Nixon, turning to Sinatra, horrified, "Frank...I never knew?"

Sinatra raised his shoulders and turned up his palms, "Like I had an idea?"

"Howard," Sinatra continued, "You gotta get a hold of yourself kid, get some air, run around a little. Go to the track …"

Hughes managed a weak smile and nodded no, "It's too late for me," he said, "my time has come and gone. There are many things I have done in life and so few I wish to attempt. I have become a prisoner of myself…of my own…demons."

Before Hughes lifted his head Nixon motioned Sinatra to start talking money, before it was too late. Sinatra asked, "Howard, I'm real sorry about that and everything, but can ya help us out, we needs some dough in a bad way…"

Hughes face lit up a bit, he seemed happy to have the chance to help out his fellow man, "What can I do for you? Tell me, why do you three men need a million dollars?"

After a thoughtful pause, Sinatra spoke first, ignoring the plight of his colleagues, "I wanna get my respect back!" he said.

Hughes replied in measure, paternal tone, "Francis, in order for a man to regain respect, he must possess it to begin with. No. I cannot grant you respect. To gain the respect of other men takes much time and conscious effort, and is something that is difficult for the arrogant and ill-tempered to achieve, but there is one thing I can give you…class, something that can be worn like a simple garment and discarded at will."

Then Hughes reached behind him and pulled a very old and very wide paisley necktie from under a strip of cellophane, "Here Francis, this is something ordinary working men take great pride in wearing, it will give you an air of noblesse oblige that may be fleeting, but that is impossible to assume without it. It will also get you into some of the best joints in town …what were you thinking when you left the house?"

Hughes shook his head and turned to Nixon, "Dick, my old benefactor, to whom I owe many a government contract and occasional pardon, what brings you to my room this evening?"

Nixon filled his chest up big and drew a long sigh, "I wish to regain my power base and win back the Presidency that was stolen from me by that baby-faced pretty boy ... that ...that...er ...Kennedy!!" Nixon was livid, consumed with jealousy and hatred, two traits that don't come across all that well on TV.

Hughes took a tenuous hold of Nixon's forearm, "What you want is not the Presidency, per se, what you wish for is something common in the intentions of the morally weak and incurably insecure. What you want is power, something even I cannot grant to any man. However, I can give you something which will give you a temporary sense of power, so that you may discover that it is indeed an illusion."

Hughes again reached behind him under the cellophane and, bringing his hand forth, casually dropped a stream of poker chips into Nixon's outstretched hand, "Take these," Hughes said, "Compliments of the house. And while you're enjoying them, stand back a moment, and reflect. You will soon learn, after experiencing that brief and intoxicating rush of power, just how fleeting it really is."

Nixon scrunched up his face and said quickly, "I already know how [expletive deleted] fleeting it is, believe me, Nixon knows!!" He stuffed the chips in his jacket pocket and turned away, disgusted.

Then Hughes approached Bebe Rebozo, Nixon's obedient and loyal little concierge who until now had stood quiet in the hall, without even uttering a sound. Hughes took hold of the man's stubby fingers and said, "And you, you who have remained silent until now, but surely there is something that you wish for, something for yourself? Is there not?" Hughes was impressed by Bebe's quiet manner. He wasn't a bit as self-impressed as the other two.

Bebe spoke, "I only want for my friend to get back to Washington again. To his white house. Where he belongs."

Hughes slowly walked back towards the dry Jacuzzi, his bony rear end in full public view. Stopping to steady himself on a table at the room's halfway point, he completed his journey. With trained, sterile hands, he opened the sliding door of his custom-made stainless-steel autoclave, and from which, and using only his elbows, Hughes removed a surgeon's tray holding no less than ten shrink-wrapped plastic packets of $100,000 each. Exactly one million dollars in cash.

Despite his frail mental condition, Hughes had a memory like a Republican elephant. For he too had a deep seeded dislike for the Kennedy's dating back to the their Hollywood days. And the overly sensitive, romantic Hughes' fury only grew over the years.[45]

With his tender arms chafed raw and his two pale and wiry hands still held high in the air, Hughes returned to Rebozo and patiently waited while Nixon's appreciative aide filled all his available pockets with the tray's contents.

When Rebozo was finished, Hughes draped his long arms over the immigrant's shoulders, facing him. "Because you selflessly ask nothing for yourself, and your only wish is for your friend's safe return home, I have given you the greatest gift of all. Use it wisely, for good and not evil, and you shall prosper accordingly. I sincerely hope you are able to get your friend home again."

With that, Sinatra reached down and grabbed the bar napkin, tucked it into the instep of his black loafer, and said to the others, "Let's split!" Sinatra had no problem ripping off Hughes, who he knew had once been engaged to his notorious flame and femme fatale Ava Gardner.

"Yeah, thanks Mr. Hughes!" yelled Rebozo, as the three men bolted three-wide down the hotel hallway and ran for the elevator, wondering how the hell a complete nut job like Hughes ever made a dime. Upon reaching the lobby, Sinatra palmed the bellboy on the hush-hush, with a twenty-dollar bill that he had pre-folded three times into small squares and passed off in a subtle handshake, as was his custom.

Nixon waited with arms crossed as he cashed out his chips at the cashier's window while Bebe looked on, amused.

---

[45] Joe Kennedy had romanced actress Billie Dove. She was living with Hughes at that time.

"Let's get going fellas," Frank said, looking at his watch "I gotta get into my duds for the dinner show over at The Sands."

The next morning, after having a long, private conversation with Nixon about Kennedy, Sinatra and Nixon shook and agreed to have Sinatra's private pilot fly the 'El Dago' to Mexico, to deposit one million dollars in cash into a safe deposit box under an assumed name. And to protect and insulate himself, without mentioning Wayne, Nixon gave Sinatra full creative control to work on Nixon's comeback project.

A new, revised script was about to be written under the sole supervision of Mr. Francis Albert Sinatra.

The Chairman of the Board.

Richard Nixon and his beloved cocker spaniel, Checkers, were in New York. After placing a call to Ed Sullivan, the two planned to secretly meet at the Theatre. Per Sullivan's request, Nixon had driven himself, and both knew instinctively, of course, not to say a word to anyone about the secret meeting.

Although he was planning on moving from California to New York City soon, to ostensibly open his law practice and re-start his legal career, Nixon was still very much unfamiliar with the bustle of the city, and he began asking pedestrians for directions, and without much success at that, for unbeknownst to Nixon, he was asking directions to the Ed Sullivan Theatre while standing directly beneath the huge marquee reading 'The Ed Sullivan Theatre.'

He approached an old janitor who was sweeping just outside the Theatre's entrance.

"Excuse me" Nixon asked the custodian, "How do I get to the Ed Sullivan Theatre?"

After glancing up at the huge marquee and giving Nixon a once-over, the custodian answered very predictably, "Practice!" to which a furious Nixon muttered "Commie social-planning liberal do-gooder immigrant bastard," before he and Checkers, who was really starting to show his age and had just thrown up a little bit on the sidewalk, stepped hastily inside the Theatre.

"Practice … I *love* that line …" the old janitor laughed to himself as he swept Checkers tiny chunk of doggie vomit into his trusty dustpan. "Practice! ... it never gets old." The janitor giggled and hugged his sides.

Nixon knew that unlike himself, Gossip Columnist-Variety Show Host Ed Sullivan had spent most of his life in New York City. And Nixon surmised that, perhaps during Sullivan's early childhood, he had discovered two things about himself ... that he liked show business and that he liked money, two things which Sullivan, nor Nixon himself, never had much of as a boy. Entering the building, Nixon tried to imagine himself as one of the common folk. As a public person he could no longer do and enjoy the things that everyday people enjoyed. So he imagined himself taking the official Ed Sullivan Theatre tour with Checkers, as he fished his pockets for a nickel, which he was sure was the going rate.

Then he passed the ticket window and saw the price of the tour.

"Twenty-five cents!" he exclaimed, dropping his nickel. "Why that's highway robbery! There should be an investigation! A commission!" He reached down for his coin. "New York, New York," he pitied, "You drop a nickel and it costs you a quarter to pick it up."

"Screw it!" Nixon sneered. "I'll take the goddamned tour myself!"

He combined his gathered knowledge of both Presley and Sullivan as he began guiding his own his extemporaneous tour ... "Ed Sullivan parlayed his incurable ambition into bread and butter quickly," Nixon began. "And by 1933, Sullivan had fast emerged as a noted gossip columnist, writing for *The New York Daily News*. In that role, Sullivan became privy to the dirty, [inaudible] celebrity secrets that allowed him to compromise them and hold Hollywood hostage at the drop of a felt tip pen or the keystroke of an IBM Selectric.

"Yes! To Sullivan, journalistic blackmail was a really big shew." Nixon was particularly proud of that line. And without a speechwriter, too, he thought, oh this is fun. He continued his imaginary tour with the slow moving and gratefully deaf Checkers ...

"In 1948, Sullivan felt it was high time to take full advantage of the power he held over the entertainment industry, and in that same year he aired a variety show that would become known as *The Ed Sullivan Show*. To refuse appearing on the program was to risk show business suicide. One of the biggest [unintelligible] ever to perform on Sullivan's show was Elvis Presley.

"In 1956, Colonel Tom Parker had managed to book Presley for three appearances at an unprecedented fee of $50,000. And on [inaudible], 1956, Sunday night at 8:00 PM, Elvis Presley was brought onto the stage of The Ed Sullivan Theatre, after he was mistakenly introduced to America as 'Elvin' by actor British [expletive deleted] Charles Laughton, a last minute fill-in for the [inaudible] morose emcee, who was home recovering from a serious car accident.

"The high-priced deal was a brave and [expletive deleted] move on the part of the Colonel, and Sullivan insiders suggested Parker and Presley say good-bye to their once and future careers for the high-priced insult.

"But it worked, [unintelligible]. Sullivan was above all a businessman, and although he was furious after being stuck up by The Colonel, after he saw his ratings virtually shoot through the roof of [unintelligible], as far as he was concerned, Elvis was gold.

"But in the era of Eisenhower," Nixon shuddered, "Conservative armchair America still remained in doubt."

Nixon saw a door to the main theatre entrance. *Ah, here we are ... just in time.*

Upon entering the studio itself, Nixon saw Sullivan down on the stage, and proceeded down the aisle, trying to hastily finish the imaginary tour in his mind,

"… And all that changed four months later, when the nation witnessed Elvis' third and final appearance on Sullivan's variety show. This time, Sullivan took time to tell a still skeptical nationwide TV audience of concerned American parents that Elvis was 'a fine young boy' and that he was 'thoroughly all right.' With Sullivan's approval, Presley's career became legitimate, and his status grew to mythic proportions almost overnight. In return for Sullivan's prime-time endorsement, Colonel Tom Parker would be forever in Sullivan's debt."

"Hello, Ed," Nixon hushed, raising both arms high in victory and almost choking Checkers to death with his own leash in the process.

"Dick, how about a little makeup? Don't be shy … perhaps, just a dab?"

Nixon rolled his eyes. *Makeup jokes. Here we go again …*

"You know, Dick, if you'd let them make you up the night of that first debate, *you* might be president now." Nixon thought again about buying a vacation home or two, maybe in San Clemente, or Key Biscayne. If I only had a tan the way Kennedy did, then I wouldn't even need makeup, he thought.

"Ho ho, ha ha, oh, that is a good one, Ed … now … ahem, let me inquire, is your undertaker presently taking on new clients?"

It was their regular routine, The Ed and Dick Show.

Waving his guest onto the presently empty 1200-seat theatre's bare stage, Sullivan began his own introduction of sorts, "And now, ladies and gentlemen, right here on our stage, former Vice-President of the United States of America and communist witch-hunter, Richard Milhous Nixon and his geriatric cocker spaniel, Checkers!"

Nixon's eyes darted all over the stage, bandstand, across the catwalk high above. *Where are the bugs? They have to be somewhere!*

"How about giving them a big welcoming hand folks, he's been through a lot this year, especially after Pat Brown kicked his ass in the California gubernatorial race. And we hear you hit the Big 5-0 … Wow … that must have been a tough one for you, honestly, you don't look a day over forty-nine and a half … So, Dick, why don't you and Checkers come on out and say hello to the folks…"

Nixon awkwardly cleared his throat, pulling the heavy stage drapes shut as he looked about the huge amphitheater, which he was confident had been bugged, as he continued talking, choosing his words carefully, after clearing his throat.

193

"Ah, hmmm, Ed, I would like to discuss something very serious with you. Something that affects each and every one of us in this room."

"There's no need to be nervous. It's just me and you Dick. And don't worry, we're taping tonight's show."

Nixon shivered, "Jaysis!" He cleared his throat a second time, for his phlegm was deep, and continued, "Yes, the two of us, Ed, you and I, that's right…uh, today we are faced with a problem of such magnitude that I'm afraid if it isn't stopped now, it could tear apart the entire country as we know it."

Sullivan, although listening attentively, motioned Nixon that it was time to start performing his trained dog act. "So, what is it that you two have worked up for us tonight?"

Nixon tugged on the leash of the motionless dog.

Checkers was black and white, spotted and as Sullivan surmised, since he was almost eleven in dog years (mid 70's in human years), the elderly animal was incapable of performing any tricks. But Nixon's mind was elsewhere.

"I'm afraid we have a Communist in the White House," replied Nixon with a stiff upper lip, one that was not at all sweaty.

Sullivan erupted with a unanimous roar of agreement, trying to bait Nixon, "Tell me about it, he's as red as they come. This is all off the record, of course."

"Of course, Ed! Of course!" said Nixon. *Are you kidding, Ed, my whole life is off the record!*

At Sullivan's urging, Nixon began dragging Checkers around the stage, like a senile Westminster show dog, as he spoke to Sullivan. "But the public seems to be responding to him, and the polls don't really reflect that…not that I pay much attention to polls. Never did, really…"

Sullivan stood with his arms stiffly at his sides, watching the dog with a critical eye. "He does handle himself very well with the press. Comes across very polished, I think."

Nixon looked askance, becoming suddenly suspicious of the famed emcee. He replied in a hushed tone, "Yes...well, anyway ... it's not only that, I mean (inaudible) I wish that was it, but there's more. I heard he was taking acting lessons for his speeches, you know, that 'Lee Strasberg' Jew commie type stuff, trying to make himself more believable for the press conferences, that sort of thing."

"You mean Method? Jesus Christ, a Russian Jew ... it's worse than I thought. Christ, he must be a commie." Sullivan stuck his finger in his ear and pulled something out and looked at it. "Well, he really has a presence to him. He must've studied somewhere, right? I have some contacts down at Strasberg's outfit, that Studio of his, there may be records of him. Of course, records can be destroyed."

Nixon looked like he saw a ghost, pretending like he was in shock at the possibility of such a thing.

"You know," Sullivan continued, thinking, "He does that thing with his jacket button. You know, like he twists it. And that hand in the jacket pocket thing. Reminds me of Cary Grant. Very quick on his feet, too. Reminds too me at times of a young Cagney, very fast on his feet, and great comedic timing ..."

Nixon grew frustrated. "The issue is ... he's a pinko all right, right down to his boxer shorts," confirmed Nixon.

Sullivan had been considering boxers as of late, and thought for a moment about how his cotton briefs sometimes rode up on him. And how frequently, under the hot studio klieg lights, when his crotch got a little sweaty ...

Sullivan looked at Nixon's face. "He wears boxers? Really? Not briefs? Why I heard from ..."

"The Method!" said Nixon, forcing the word. He shook his head in disgust. "Duke Wayne told me all about it. It's ruining the acting profession."

"So the rumors are true," Sullivan said. *Kennedy was conferring with Brando.* A known, perhaps the best-known, living method actor in post-World War II America. *My God! The Leader of the Free World is taking his marching orders directly from the Communists!*

Sullivan and Nixon faced each other and wrapped their arms across each of their respective chests, cradling their chins in their hands. Two cool dudes. It was a rare 'Kodak' moment.

"Things have to change," began Nixon. "And they have to change quickly. If we wait too long we'll be into the next election. And we just can't afford to re-elect him. Think about what he's likely to do in his second term as a lame duck. He's liable to make Brando Secretary of Speech and Elocution, for Christ sakes! Then Bobby for eight years. Then Teddy for another eight. That's their plan, you know. President Kennedy's until 1984. It'd be the ruin of the country. The end of the republic! And they've got about eight-thousand kids. Christ, they're like rabbits! They could colonize Mars and take over the galaxy!"

"If he gets re-elected he'll sell Uncle Sam right up the river," said Sullivan, motioning toward the general direction of the Hudson.

"He's doing it already." Sullivan knew Nixon was up to something and he liked it already.

"When?" Sullivan ventured.

"Soon" said Nixon, "It's got to be soon."

They both laughed nervously and then stopped

Nixon looked a bit worried, "Any … ideas?" he asked.

"What's on your mind?" asked Sullivan, his eagerness raising Nixon's eyebrows, despite his actually not having said anything.

Nixon's face lit up the best it could. He reached down to pat the dog. Sullivan was waiting for more. But Nixon said nothing.

Sullivan's forehead wrinkled, "What about Sinatra? Is he exposed on this thing?"

"Without question. Like a naked jaybird," said Nixon.

"What exactly *is* a jaybird?" asked Sullivan unassumingly.

"I don't know," Nixon whispered, his eyes leering about. "I just don't know."

"Well. Good." *So if the project fails Sinatra gets it. Well that's just dandy.* Sullivan was still ticked at being beat out by Sinatra for Elvis' 'Welcome Home' debut.

Sullivan furrowed his brow. Nixon knew what he was thinking. Nixon shrugged his shoulders and looked around the theatre in a paranoid manner, "Ed, I uh, I have something [unintelligible] in mind, something I don't want you to act on, not yet. Colonel Parker has agreed to help us out."

Sullivan's head nodded repeatedly in firm acknowledgement as Nixon told him the outline and proposed treatment for the script. "That part's all set you know, but, uh, we're going to need some assistance on the back end, so, if you could, try to do whatever is in your power to take the spotlight off Presley, you know, keep things quiet for him for a while, at least until this thing blows over … for the good of the country, national security and so forth…"

"But don't concern yourself with Sinatra. He is a valuable asset to us. I'd rather have him in our camp than out. If he gets blamed it will be perfect. But Ed, keep your eyes on the big prize. We play our cards right," said Nixon. "There's a big pot for everyone, yourself included, after the hand's played."

Sullivan took both of Richard Nixon's sweaty hands firmly into his own. "Done," he answered.

After a brief pause, Sullivan asked, "Does the dog do *any* tricks?"

Nixon looked at the old dog fondly and scratched its head and said, "Believe you me, there was a time when that dog performed miracles." Then he added, "You know, the girls just love him … he's one gift we're going to keep."

Nixon scratched under the dog's chin "Isn't that right, Checkers?"

He reached for his hanky. There was still a little throw up left.

Nixon's 'Checkers' speech was an address made by then Senator Nixon on television and radio on September 23, 1952. Nixon had been accused of improprieties relating to a fund established by his backers to reimburse him for his political expenses. With his place on the Eisenhower's presidential ticket in doubt, he delivered a half-hour television address in which he defended himself, attacked his opponents, and urged the audience to decide whether he should remain on the ticket. During the speech, he stated that regardless of what anyone said, he intended to keep one gift: a black-and-white cocker spaniel that his daughters had named 'Checkers.'

Ann-Margret, Hollywood's newest and sexiest performer, was going to sing for the President on his 46th birthday. Kennedy, always on top of the latest gossip, already knew all about her. Though he preferred blondes and brunettes, he had always found redheads to be especially elusive and unpredictable, and it was a quality that had throughout his years intrigued him.[46]

Discovered by the legendary comedian George 'Say Goodnight Gracie' Burns in Las Vegas in 1960, the twenty-two year-old Swedish born actress-singer-dancer had already made three films, *State Fair, Pocketful of Miracles*, and *Bye, Bye, Birdie*, a musical-comedy based on Elvis' own early career and Army induction (co-starring Janet Leigh, Ed Sullivan (as himself) and featuring an introductory, photographic montage that included both JFK and Frank Sinatra).

In only three short years she had fast become the new talk of Hollywood, so much so that she had been asked to perform for the Commander-In-Chief, through an aide and at his request, before a very private, exclusive audience at Washington's luxurious Waldorf-Astoria hotel. The red-haired actress-singer-dancer agreed, of course, and with a sexy, sultry, pouty innocence sang *Baby, Won't You Please Come Home*, to the grinning President as he sipped a cold glass of Heineken beer and enjoyed a long cigar at the head table …

I've got the blues
I feel so lonely
I'd give the world
If I could only
Make you understand …

---

[46] Marilyn Monroe had infamously sang at JFK's forty-fifth birthday party at Madison Square Garden the year before, just three months prior to her mysterious, untimely death.

This time, JFK had ordered his aides in advance, his birthday party would be a small, private affair, and it was not to be filmed or televised. Now in the third year of his Presidency, Kennedy purposely limited his appearances with movie stars, as he had suggested to Sinatra that day in Hyannisport, fearing that too much celebrity chumminess might be unseemly to registered voters and the press.

The captivatingly beautiful Ann-Margret stared seductively at not only the President, but everyone present, male and female alike, and continued to coo and croon the blues ..

> *When you left you broke my heart -*
> *That will never make us part.*
> *Every hour in the day you will hear me say -*
> *Baby, won't you please come home?*
> *I mean, baby, won't you please come home?*

The President glanced over the heads of the small gathered crowd and saw Brando in attendance, way in the back. Brando waved and smiled, laughing hysterically. Kennedy did a quick underhanded wave and winked back, and then focused on relighting his cigar.

Brando. Well, what do you know? Kennedy laughed to himself.

Marlon Brando, why you little hot shit ball-breaking sonofabitch. Mother of God, that crazy little bastard shows up everywhere, like a bad penny.

The President then re-focused his attention back to Ann-Margret …

> *Baby, won't you please come home?*
> *'Cause your mama's all alone -*
> *Baby, won't you please come home?*
> *I need money -*
> *Baby, won't you please come home?*

After the show, one of Kennedy's aides approached the President accompanied by the gorgeous redhead. Wanting to flirt with the singer about the 'I need money' line, Kennedy fished his trousers for his billfold, but as usual, the trust-fund millionaire President had no money on him.

"Mr. President, this is Miss Ann-Margret."

Kennedy gave the young lady a polite once-over, rethinking his strategy.

Well, what do we have here? ... a cute little red-headed cross between Grace Kelly and Jayne Mansfield, with a little attitude thrown in ...

"Oh, I've met Ann before," he said. And she courteously replied, "No, you haven't."

And Kennedy casually said, "Of course we've met before."

And Ann said firmly, "No, sir, we haven't."

And Kennedy said, "Well, uh, in my judgment, it is my firm, uh, belief that of course we have, uh, met."

And then Ann looked straight at him, smiling, and said, "You meet a lot of little girls, Sir. I only meet one president. I would remember."

With that, she bounced away. Kennedy leaned back and studied her backside.

Ah, the old game. Give a wolf a taste and then leave him hungry. Jack boy, my friend, she's got you dangling.

He felt a slight stiffness coming on. Unfortunately it was in his back.

Sir. God I hate it when they say that word.

Ann-Margret knew he was watching her walk away without even looking.

Then Kennedy tilted his face to the side, squinting.

I wonder if she's a real redhead.

Finally, he conceded that, yes, of course she was a true redhead.

She's, sexy, tough, and elusive. She must be.

Here's looking at your ass, kid.

The President released a cloudburst of smoke.

Elvis and Ann-Margret began filming MGM's *Viva Las Vegas* in Hollywood. Even before filming began, the press had already dubbed her the 'female Elvis,' and by all indications she was all of that - and more. She was strong, confident, hot as a pistol and full of dynamite. Men would have died for her.

The night before the first day of filming, Elvis had invited his randy, redheaded co-star to his rented Bel Air home in order to get acquainted.

Elvis' friends couldn't wait to feast their eyes upon her in person. "Man, she's fine, I'd give a week's pay just to …" said one of the boys. "Dig those legs," said another. And a unanimous "I can't wait to get a look at her up close."

"You ain't getting' a look at nuthin'," said Elvis, laying down the law. "I want you guys out of here, and I mean *all* night. And that's an order."

"Get lost? Us?" the boys collectively asked. "Well," they agreed. "There's a first time for everything."

They all knew right then that this one was different. "Okay, okay. We'll get lost," they winked at each other. But boys will be boys.

Even after just one brief meeting in person, back on the set, Elvis already sensed that this one was special. Little did he know he was about to meet his match.

When she rang his bell that night, they had each other at 'Hello.' It was the kind of immediate, all-over-each-other, passionate chemistry that comes but once, or maybe twice, in a lifetime.

Ostensibly, the date was intended to get to know each other a little and to go over the script, which Elvis already knew by heart. But all bullshit aside, upon greeting each other, and embracing each other, and maybe a minute of chitchat, the going over the script part was, well, taken out of the script.

"You smell like baby powder," Ann said to Elvis.

"So do you," Elvis said to Ann.

Ann grinned a real sexy grin and gave him a sly, come hither stare. Elvis smiled suggestively.

Elvis heard something outside, and he quietly excused himself to Ann, and went into his bedroom. The boys were outside, peeking through the dark window trying to sneak more than a glance at their boss and Ann. "Where'd Elvis go?" They asked each other.

The four boys stood and wondered.

Suddenly. Elvis was standing behind them. One of the boys had managed to quickly scatter, but before the other three could react Elvis had effectively and efficiently karate chopped and kicked them to the ground. They weren't hurt, but they were disabled. Elvis wasn't mad, but he wasn't pleased either. After all, orders were orders.

He went back inside to Ann, while the boys recovered and made alternate plans for their evening.

"What happened, baby? Where were you?" asked Ann.

Elvis slid back to where they had left off and said, "Damn raccoons."

After sharing a few hours of sis-boom-bah-zowie aye-aye-aye, and tender intimacy, Elvis found himself lovingly vulnerable, fully trusting her, and feeling as though he could confide in her like no one since his mama.

He knew this was no usual tryst. Juliet Prowse this was not. He knew Ann was different, that she was 'the real deal.'

Deep into the evening-morning, laid out on a couch with cushions tossed about the room, the two of them, all tangled up together, dozed for a bit.

When Elvis opened his eyes, he smiled and kissed her forehead, quietly waking her.

"Why did you do that?" she asked.

" 'Cause I felt like it," he answered.

"Your lips are soft when you kiss."

Ann looked around the room. "What do you pay for this place? Must cost you a fortune."

"Ah, ah, ah … I'm not sure. One thousand … I mean, fourteen hundred a month, I think," said Elvis. The Colonel and his daddy took care of the bills and money stuff, but he had seen them. Most of them anyway.

Then he said it.

"You ever think about gettin' married?" *Shoot, I said it.*

Too late. It was already out there. The words had crossed his lips.

Ann was shocked but remained poker-faced and unfazed. No flies on Ann.

"No. I need to think about my career. I came here to be a star, not a housewife." *Oh my God, no, she thought. Marriage means kids and diapers and, why I don't even know who I am yet. I want to be somebody first.*

Then she raised her coiffed, penciled brow and asked, cockily, "You?"

"No, me neither," answered Elvis, embarrassed at having asked and unable to meet her eyes.

He remembered how his mama told him never to marry a girl in show business. She told him their careers would clash. That it wouldn't work. For once, he thought, he hoped, that mama was wrong.

Between a rock and a hard place. Story of my life. Here I am with a woman I can finally love, see myself with forever, and back home in Memphis, the rest of my life is already planned with that little jailbait brat. He silently cursed The Colonel yet again.

"Kiss me," Ann said, distracting him.

He kissed her. And then again.

She ran her fingers though Elvis' hair, and then pulled back, giving him a 'come hither' stare. He stared into her eyes and wished he could stay in L.A. and be with Ann forever. He stared at her hard now, right into her eyes. He felt like asking her to marry him right there. But he knew he couldn't.

Elvis held Ann's hand and kissed her palm, looking at it.

"You know honey, you have a long lifeline," he whispered. He had recently read a few books on astrology and the like, and had developed a bit of an interest that kind of stuff.

Ann took Elvis' hand examined it in return.

"So have you." She hoped it was true, and kissed his hand and held it against her flushed cheek. She wasn't about to get married anytime soon. But when she did, it was going to be to one man and one man forever. That she knew.

The lamp dim, the TV off, they cuddled on what remained of the couch and talked about 'the business' until after midnight. Their hopes. Their dreams. Elvis, knowing she was smart as a fox but still somewhat new to the industry, talked about the importance of having a manager.

"I hate the thievin' bastard ... but without the Colonel I'd still be drivin' that truck or pickin' up popcorn at the Loews movie theatre back home. It was only fourteen bucks a week ... but man, I had all the popcorn I could eat!"

Ann chuckled.

But it had been more than that, Elvis knew, it was mostly luck.

There's a hundred guys with more talent than me. Thousands. This whole thing could end today and I could go back to drivin' a truck tomorrow.

He could hear The Colonel in his head.

Stick to the plan, son. Just stick to the plan. Business is business and time is money, son. Time is money. Everything will go just as I said it would all along just Stick With Me and Pay-Your-Taxes, son. Pay-Your-Taxes. Don't Forget to Pay-Your-Taxes.

Then, before he could catch himself, Elvis blurted out that maybe she should sign on with The Colonel. But just as fast as he said it, he stopped himself.

What am I, crazy?

He told her how The Colonel takes fifty percent, probably more, of every dollar he makes. Ann gasped and held her hand to her mouth. "That's horrible. Why, that's *criminal*. Elvis, I'm so sorry ..."

"It's okay. It's only money, honey," he said, meaning it. Ann jabbed his shoulder bone with her palm, "Only money! Elvis, do you know how hard it is to *make* money?"

"I didn't make it. It's show business money, honey. It's like I won it."

"Well, when you to earn your money, it's hard work. Believe me."

She added, "You want to go earn it!! You should try dancing some yourself!! It's like you don't even have to try!!" She tried to sit upright but lost her balance in their cushion-less cocoon.

"Yeah, well you should try some 'gettin' up off the couch' yourself!"

His embrace held her tight. She rested her hand on his arm and closed her eyes against his chest, smiling.

"Will you be my girl?" said Elvis in absolute earnest, like he was thirteen.

Ann smiled and never blinked. She was wary of being owned but knew he didn't mean it that way. "I have dancing scenes tomorrow. Rehearsal."

He tapped her rear. "Let's go for a drive after …or something … let's get the Harley's!"

"Or something …??!" She looked at him knowingly. "Elvis, it's after midnight?" She stopped, surprised. "Wait. Harley's. You have a Harley? I love Harleys!"

"Five of 'em. And so what if it's midnight?!" He chuckled. "Midnight's early, baby. Come on. I know a place …"

"Maybe next time, keep the bike warm for me," said Ann, strong but coy, mischievous. She punched him in the chest. "And you, stop calling me baby!"

"Oh … okay … Rusty …"

And for what seemed the first time in a long time he smiled bigger than ever and grinned that big, cheeky, boyish, lopsided grin of his.

Heading home to the safe confines of the White House with Jackie one Saturday afternoon, President Kennedy was sitting comfortably in the back of his long, black Presidential limousine, the new, custom-built SS-100-X, plush, suicide-door, Lincoln convertible (in fact, as a youth, JFK's very first car had been a Lincoln), when he glanced out the window and saw a boy in the backseat of a nearby car holding a large motion picture camera against the back window, its lens pointed at the President.

JFK's muscles tensed. He pressed a secret button to make sure the seat was a low as possible (it had been designed to rise 13" high so Kennedy could be elevated during parades, without having to stand up). *Bond gets really cool, custom-made gadgets. And The President of the fucking Free World gets a seat that goes up and down. Like I'm at fucking Paragon Pahk* (Park). *Wow, what a goddamn thrill.*[47]

Kennedy looked at the boy and smiled politely through the glass window. *Hello you little bahstahd* (bastard).

Jackie sensed his annoyance, "Jack, it's only a child with a movie camera," she assured him.

The President took a deep breath and reassured himself, as he always did in these circumstances. *I will not live in fee-yah (fear). Whatevuh shall be, shall be. Que Sera Sera.*

He started to hum the song quietly to himself. He thought about Doris Day. Then Rock Hudson. Then he stopped humming ...

And then his restless mind moved on.

---

[47] Paragon Park, an amusement park located at Nantasket Beach in Hull, Massachusetts, where the Kennedy's had summered prior to Hyannisport, was home to one of the oldest, wooden roller coasters in the United States.

By mid-filming The Colonel was furious. *Viva Las Vegas* was taking forever to finish. They were over schedule and over budget. Elvis wasn't taking his calls, out every night carousing with Ann and the boys. The Colonel was starting to feel his reign loosen. And he needed to tighten it.

"*Your* business is *my* business and business is business. And this here is business!!"

As The Colonel went over the dailies one night (as his bullshit, paid, 'Technical Advisor' contract allowed) before he hit the casino, he noticed that Ann-Margret was getting the same, or more, exposure as Elvis. More close-ups, more songs, more dance numbers, more dialogue, and more laughs. The works.

"Who does this little woman think she is! This here's an Elvis pitcha!!" The Colonel was mad as hell. He didn't feel threatened by Ann, just very annoyed. She was, in his mind, just a woman, so he ignored her like all the rest. He instead directed his blame on the director. After all, it was the same guy who directed her in *Bye Bye Birdie*. The Colonel figured it was one of those asinine 'matters of the heart' that those emotional types tend to fall into.

Must be in love with her, the dumb jackass. No wonder the ninny made such a fuss over her.

The Colonel made a mental note not to make the same mistake twice and sent the thought into one of the drawers in the cabinet of his mind. He then paced the set quietly, staying a way's away, out of everyone's sight but keeping everyone well within his.

The day's shoot was dragging. Lots of close-ups. Take after take after take. Plane engines overhead. The practically antique MGM set from the 1930's falling apart at the seams. Rookie per diem dancers out of sequence. And Elvis. Spitting out his dialogue like he was on fast forward. Drumming his fingers against his thighs. Nervous. Racing. Like he had to be somewhere else. And completely one-dimensional. Without cadence or intonation. And Elvis knew it too.

Elvis knew he could do better but he was too jacked up and too mad at the script's predictable dialogue and too goddamn distracted to do anything about it. Although he had a photographic memory for scripts, Elvis had the attention span of a moth, everyone knew that. And without Ann opposite him in a scene, or anywhere, he was lonely and completely bored. That, and the fact that he had heard a rumor earlier in the day. A rumor that was grating on him, hard.

The story was this … the Paramount shoeshine boy, in a rare, but entirely well-intentioned departure from his normal code of secrecy, had mentioned to one of the boys that the famous Director Elia Kazan had casually told him that he thought Elvis could be a serious actor given the right screenplay and a good director. This was THE Elia Kazan, director of *On the Waterfront, A Streetcar Named Desire, East of Eden.* He had directed Brando, Dean, and even Montgomery Clift (in *Wild River*), the top three method acting legends.

Unfortunately, as the story went, when word got back to The Colonel about this, The Colonel told the shoeshine boy that if he ever let Elvis know about this he'd see that he never worked in Hollywood again. Period. Word had gotten back to Elvis that morning.

Elvis exploded on the set. When the director called for an umpteenth take on a casino scene that should've already been in the can, Elvis lost it, tipping over one of the scene's crap tables and flinging a pot full of casino tokens across the set, pelting the cast and crew.

"Screw this shit!" He said, karate-chopping a roulette wheel. "Screw it all!"

Elvis stormed off the set, grabbing Ann by the arm as he left. Within seconds they were giggling. There were only a few days left of shooting, Elvis justified.

They'll get over it.

He gave it one last thought, then bolted over the set's thresh-hold, "Aww, who the hell cares!"

"Come on Thumper … let's split …"

Elvis hopped on his motorcycle and Ann straddled in tight behind him and they raced off as one, away from the old Paramount lot and out of town, speeding dangerously, thrillingly, high into the Hollywood Hills.

He knew a place.

Elvis' destination, though Ann didn't yet know it, was The Griffith Observatory and planetarium, just beyond Griffith Park, beyond the legendary white 'Hollywood' sign that stood against the hills. The site that had been made cinematically famous in the 1955 teen film classic *Rebel Without A Cause.*

[The undeveloped land adjacent to the famous Hollywood sign, with its stunning 360-degree view of the Los Angeles Basin and the San Fernando Valley, was owned by Howard Hughes, who purchased it in 1940 to build a love nest for then-girlfriend Ginger Rogers].

As Elvis and Ann wound through the Hollywood hills Elvis was reminded of the late James Dean, just as he had been all during the *Viva Las Vegas* race car sequences they had shot just two weeks earlier.

Dusk had approached when they pulled into the Observatory's south lot off Canyon Road and dismounted the bike. The grounds of the Observatory included a magnificent Greek amphitheatre. It was striking. Breathtaking. He hadn't told Ann that this site was like a shrine to him. An acting shrine. *His* acting shrine. At least it used to be, anyway.

They walked slowly, almost shuffling hand-in-hand over towards the Observatory's southern slope that overlooked the twilight skyline of downtown Los Angeles.

Ann glanced up at him briefly, but continued walking.

Elvis felt her gaze. "Hey, didn't I see you before someplace?" Asked Elvis, kiddingly.

Ann smiled but deliberately ignored him. She'd heard this story before.

"Hi," Elvis said, straight-faced.

"I saw you before. Where was it?" He scratched his chin.

She smiled and kicked him in the butt with her other heel as they walked.

"Hey, I know where it was ..."

"Where WHAT was," said Ann, playing along.

"Where I saw you. I think it was in a movie?" Elvis pretended.

Ann gazed up at him. *God, I love him so much, she thought. Why can't he ever believe it when I say that?*

"It was that movie with that real good lookin' actor. You know, the tall dark and handsome one ..." said Elvis, deadpan.

"Ohhh ... you mean *Viva Las Vegas*. Hmmm. What *was* his name ..?"

They kissed.

Elvis took off his costume jacket and smoothed it out on the grass. Then they lay down together on the grassy slope, and kissed some more.

Catching his breath after a particularly long make-out session, Elvis exhaled and pretended to yell, "Stella-a-a!"

Ann nudged him, laughing as she always did. "Steady Marlon!"

Elvis was over the moon.

She's fun. She's hot. She doesn't try to change me, tell me what to do. Doesn't break my balls. Doesn't smoke, doesn't drink. She says she doesn't like it when I call her 'baby' but I know that she really doesn't mind. She likes it when I calls her 'baby' or 'bunny' or 'rusty' or 'thumper.'

He could tell. After all, he reasons, she calls me 'baby' … Elvis' mind was racing. He wanted a new life. One without the Colonel. Without that other little girl breaking his balls.[48]

Elvis imagined a happy life with a woman he really loved and who loved him back, a life with good movies and good scripts. Outdoor *and* indoor concerts. Not just state fairs. Football stadiums. World tours. Oscars. Grammys. Respect. Record ownership, like Sinatra. Like Ray Charles.

Even though he knew their careers would clash. Just like mama said. He knew it was true, but his gut told him otherwise. He wanted normalcy. Structure. Security. Four walls around him. Someone to lean on. And he wanted that someone to be Ann. Elvis hadn't known normalcy since the first Sullivan show. Back in 1956. He remembered how the next day he was mobbed in New York City. Normal was over the day after that show. Gone.

He looked down at the lights of the city and felt like he was in heaven. This is it, he thought. This is what it must be like. Mama must be in a place like this.

---

[48] When Elvis did eventually get married in 1967, Frank Sinatra loaned him his private plane so he could fly from Beverly Hills to the wedding in Las Vegas without publicity.

His unquiet mind raced. He worried that someday Ann would be gone from his life too. He pictured it. Pictured her kissing some other guy on a set, in a movie.

He felt sick.

He snapped back to reality and looked at Ann. He pictured his mama at their wedding, with him singing *I'm Walking Behind You On Your Wedding Day* to them. He knew it would never happen, but he could dream. So dream he did. Right there high up in the Hollywood hills, right where James Dean once stood, he dreamed.

Ann was thinking too. She thought about how she wanted a simple private life. Quiet. And she knew Elvis' world would never be simple. Or private. Or quiet. He was too big a star. And she saw the pills. She sensed something wrong sometimes. His temper on the set. Throwing things, plates, screaming. His insomnia. His energy. She knew it wasn't all real. Sometimes it scared her. But she loved him. Loved him like she had never loved a man before, maybe more than she never, ever would either. But she had to be sure.

Elvis got angry. Mad that he was trapped. *If only* ...

A trace of concern crossed Ann's face.

Elvis grabbed a clump of grass and scattered it.

"I swear, sometimes, I dunno, sometimes I just wanna hold you forever! Ann, what am I gonna do?! I'm homesick but I can't go home again, back to Memphis. Not without you. It'll never be the same. Baby, I can't go home ..."

"Neither can I, baby" she answered. "Neither can I ..."

He turned and looked at the Observatory. He pictured James Dean ... right there ... in his red barracuda jacket.

"I'm gonna fire The Colonel tomorrow," he said. "I'm out of gas. I'm done." He was so frustrated and felt so helpless and imprisoned he felt like crying.

Then he sucked in some air and summoned one last bit of fight.

"That's it!" Elvis told himself and Ann. "That two-faced thieving snake-oil salesman is gone tomorrow. You hear me! Just watch …"

She leaned into him and he quieted.

"There's something I should tell you, Ann," he said.

"I know already," she replied. "I know." I love being here with you, she thought.

The moon lit up the planetarium behind them.

He sighed. She had soothed him. Calmed him. Just like mama. How did she do that?

Ann held him tight. "I love you Elvis. I really mean it." She grabbed his shoulders. She wanted to shake it into him.

She kissed his lips gently and looked into his face. He kissed her and held her tighter, closer.

This is it. I'm never going back.

Viva Las Vegas was finally wrapping up. Its final take involved a scene where Elvis has to break up a crowd of drunken, rowdy Texan convention-goers in a small casino on the Vegas strip. In the scene, Elvis sang 'The Yellow Rose of Texas,' after he invokes the names of Texas legends in the process to get the reveler's attention ...

"Sam Houston ..."

"Davy Crockett ..."

"... and ... John Wayne ..." [49]

"Hooray!!!" All the rowdy actors yelled on cue.

Then Elvis beckoned to the boisterous crowd of Texans, and sang, 'The Eyes of Texas re Upon You' ...

---

[49] Wayne was actually from Winterset, Iowa. His father was a pharmacist.

When the movie was eventually wrapped and 'in the can,' as they say, Elvis and Ann and the boys and their respective dates all met up at Elvis' hotel suite, before heading out to catch Sammy Davis Jr's midnight show over at The Sands.

Towards the end of Sammy's show, champagne arrived at Elvis' table. "Compliments of the two gentlemen over there ..."

The maitre de motioned over to Mr. Frank Sinatra and Mr. Dean Martin, who were knee-deep in bourbon and scotch, front and center, just a few tables away.

The maitre de added, "The two gentlemen kindly ask that you and your party please join them."

Elvis looked over at them and then back at the maitre de quickly.

No Juliet. No Mrs. Martin. Just the two of them. Stone drunk.

"Tell them I said thank you, thankyouverymuch. But that we were just leaving." Elvis braced his palms against the table to stand. His entourage stood with him.

Just like I thought. They just want our women. What do they think I'm stupid? I got eyes in my head.

He pushed his chair in and led his group to the door.

As Dean chatted up a cocktail waitress other than his own, Sinatra smiled pleasantly at Elvis' back and then glared.

First Juliet. Then he tries to top 'Ocean's Eleven' with this French Vegas movie he's making. I try to help the kid and now I get disrespected at The Sands? On my home turf! Phew! This kid's really getting under my skin here a little bit.

Sinatra looked up at the young waiter and then at his plate, jerking his thumb into his stomach. "Easy on the garlic, buddy boy. Easy on the garlic. Atta boy. Nice and easy."

Sammy was finishing the celebrity impersonations part of his act, and was now doing a better-than-passable Sinatra. He started to sing 'Witchcraft' …

Sinatra rapped Dino's shoulder as he watched Elvis and his party leave, "I believe that this Presley kid here is starting to a little bit irritate me." Dino in turn tried to redirect Frank's attention and motioned to their virtuoso friend Sammy, still singing his jazzy high-hat version of Sinatra's hypnotic song on stage.

Then Sinatra stopped cold, as if in a trance. He seemed in a daze, hearing no words or lyrics, just lost, as Sammy snapped his fingers slowly to the drummer's beat.

"The kid's been away for two years," Sinatra said robotically right there at The Sands and to no one in particular, "and I get the feeling he really believes what he's doing."

Then, shaking his head violently, Sinatra snapped out of it, eyeing his dinner plate.

"Frank baby," slurred Dean when he saw Frank attack the plate. "But I thought you got too hungry for dinner at midnight!"

Sinatra cracked up, fired a spoon-flung missile of sautéed shrimp at Dino, and then proceeded to fork his scampi.

The Rat Pack

In their early '60's heyday, Sinatra and Dean Martin and Co. kept a ridiculously hectic schedule. They started filming their various movies at 8 am, which continued until 5 pm. They then flew to Las Vegas via helicopter (they shot their movies in Las Vegas or in neighboring California), where they did their nightclub act that lasted until two in the morning. They'd carouse in between. Then, the following day, they'd do it all over again.

*O*ne night, after awaking at the crack of dusk, as he soaked his aching feet in a pot of Jack Daniels for medicinal purposes, a lonely and guilt-ridden Frank Sinatra placed a telephone call to a highly intoxicated Peter Lawford. Some nights he was afraid he'd cut so many people out that there'd be nobody left someday. It was on these nights that he would often drink and dial.

Lawford had been entertaining a few friends at the house that night, and in an effort to patch up old wounds, he invited Sinatra to stop by. The two hadn't spoken since the Crosby incident.

"Yeah, Dean and Sammy there?" asked Sinatra, trying to get himself genuinely interested.

"Dean's here, Sammy couldn't make it," replied Lawford, "He's home learning how to spin dreidles. Why don't you come on over? The Irish lad has your bourbon already poured."[50]

"Sure, Peter," said Sinatra, "You want I should bring a date?"

"No," said Lawford, "Plenty of broads here. You'll have your pick of the litter."

"Okay pal," said Frank, "See ya then."

"Grand."

"The President there?" Sinatra asked, a trace of hope in his speaking voice.

---

[50] A dreidle is a Jewish toy resembling a spinning top. Sammy Davis had converted to Judaism.

221

"No," said Lawford, already somewhat lubricated, "Not yet anyway. So there's still plenty of chics available, old chap. You may have your pick of the lot."

"Yeah. Right, old chap. I heard you the first time, Peter," said Sinatra, losing interest. "Maybe some other time."

"Okay, mate," said Lawford.

"And Peter …" added Sinatra, his voice trailing off … "Say goodbye to the President for me … and say goodbye to yourself to … I'm gonna go dark for a little while … you know what I mean …"

"Yes, sure Frank. Bye now." Lawford looked at the phone for a second but didn't think too much of it. He knew Sinatra was one complicated cat. Plus, he really had to take a piss. Lawford hung up the phone on his end.

Frank Sinatra hung up his phone, having decided to stay in. He was lonely, but he was getting used to it. He had stopped fighting it years ago.

Besides, he had just received some frozen, mail order tomato sauce from his favorite restaurant, Patsy's, in New York City. There was some leftover pasta in the fridge, or maybe a little leftover Fettuccine Alfredo would hit the spot? It was always better the next day, anyway.

Sinatra called his kids, put a Billy Holiday record on the turntable, and then looked around for some Chianti.

The President was on the phone in his private residence on the second floor of The White House. Mrs. Kennedy was in Hyannisport with the children. JFK said to his steady mistress, "A car will come to collect you at midnight, and (he kidded) please look innocent and virginal, remember, you'll be in the hands of the Secret Service." He said 'bye' quickly, as he usually did, as he hung up the phone.

As usual, Kennedy loved the independence, but hated being alone in the White House at night, or anytime, for that matter.

He quickly remembered what his brother Bobby had told him. *Jack, you've got to be careful. One of these girls could be a Russian spy.* But Bobby didn't understand, that was what he loved about it. The intrigue. That's what made it so much fun.

The President's longtime, loyal aide stood nearby, next to the large wood-consoled RCA television set. The screen flickered and then came to, and Kennedy saw the black and white image of a cowboy.

"No, no more Westerns, not tonight, my God that isn't that *Bonanza* is it? I don't know how they ever get laid on that show, Christ, I haven't seen a woman on it yet!" As it turned out, it wasn't *Bonanza*, but his aide turned the knob counterclockwise nevertheless.

The Beverly Hillbillies … "Oh my God, not those silly bastards, give me a break, my God, Christ, shut it off!"

Kennedy turned his head about the room to and fro, looking for something to catch his interest.

There were no major sports events that evening so the aide searched for some local news. A commercial for Pepsi-Cola and a plug for *The Dick Van Dyke Show* flashed momentarily but Kennedy, exasperated, and only after quickly studying how sexy Mary Tyler-Moore was in those hot little Capri pants of hers, strained to get up out of his chair and waved aside his aide, walking the seven or eight feet across the room to turn off the television set himself.

"Dammit I missed Cronkite again!"

It was Wednesday night and even though there were three major network channels to choose from there was absolutely nothing on TV. The day had been long and the President needed to somehow unwind. He had been in meetings regarding the situation in Vietnam most of the day. He was beat.[51]

Earlier, Kennedy had briefly chatted with Marlon Brando and with other celebrities, Paul Newman, Charlton Heston, and other activists who had promised to support his long-awaited civil rights program. After the dinner a secret service agent told Brando that the President wanted to meet with him upstairs after the reception.

The President began to read his advance, autographed, copy of Ian Fleming's latest Bond offering, *On Her Majesty's Secret Service*, had just arrived from Istanbul, Turkey, where Fleming had written that he was presently visiting the set of *From Russia With Love*, the second Bond film starring Sean Connery. Kennedy creased over a tiny corner of the page he had just finished, a few paragraphs about some Irish girls and their susceptibility to food allergies, which in turn caused him to again ponder the source of his own digestive ailments.

Maybe we should plan a little Middle East trip one of these days.

He thought about the secret missile agreement. *Christ, Turkey sure did save my ass with those missiles last October.*

A Secret Service agent led Brando up to Kennedy's second floor private residence.

---

[51] On October 11, 1963, Kennedy signed NSAM 263, initiating his withdrawal of 1,000 troops out of roughly 16,000 Americans stationed in Vietnam. Other documents, including planning documents from the spring of 1963, suggest that this was his first step in a planned, complete withdrawal.

The agent escorted Brando in and Kennedy at once looked up and closed the hardbound book, standing awkwardly as he did to greet his guest.

This should be interesting, though the President. Let's see if I can get a reaction out of him this time.

Kennedy gave Brando's hand a firm and perfunctory shake with the James Bond novel still on his mind, sardonically quoted verbatim, "And I've never been to Istanbul ..."

Brando stood confused, but went along, smiling wildly, mumbling, "You've never been to Istanbul?"

Kennedy kept a straight face. "Where the moonlight on the Bosphorus is irresistible ..." [52]

Kennedy tucked his chin into his neck and laughed but decided to keep his private joke to himself.

Brando could never play Bond. Too much of an actor's actor. Rex Harrison was too old, he had agreed, so was Cary Grant, as perfect as he would have been otherwise. Richard Burton didn't look the part, and like Brando, he was too much of an actor's actor. David Niven could have pulled it off. But Connery should always play Bond, he thought. Every time. And he was very good in that little role in 'The Longest Day' too. I almost forgot about that ...

Kennedy never ate at the formal dinners because he was too busy shaking hands or speaking, and he preferred eating later while relaxing with an aide or close friend. His aide brought him his grilled cheese sandwich from the hotplate, a holdover from Kennedy's bachelor days, and then returned to the kitchenette's narrow counter to add some milk to Kennedy's steaming bowl of Campbell's tomato soup.

---

[52] The Bosphorus, also known as the Istanbul Strait, is a narrow river that forms part of the boundary between Europe and Asia.

When the aide placed the soup bowl and saucer before the President, Kennedy reached for an open bag of saltines on a nearby chair and put a handful of them on the saucer, against the bowl.

He smiled at Brando sheepishly as if to say, *Yes, the wife is out of town. Isn't it obvious?*

Brando considered the situation for a moment, thinking to himself that Mrs. Kennedy was quite a striking woman.

"What would you like Marlon? We'll fix you up whatevuh you like. The White House kitchen is available and, uh, willing, and at your full disposal tonight. Now don't you go and tell me you've already eaten because I know that there is, uh, no way that you did nothing but pick on a few little appahtizahs and maybe have a few cold drinks downstairs …now … what shall it, uh, be? How about some chowdah? Perhaps a little chowdah to start with and then maybe a lobstah sandwich with some, uh, potato chips? Or would you rathuh steak? A filet with a baked potato or perhaps the, uh, Boston favorite with some baked beans …"

Kennedy was restless. *Where's the music.* He asked his aide to put on some records.

"Anything but that fucking *Camelot* album! My God, I can't stand that fucking song! It's all Jackie fucking listens too!"

Kennedy's eyes lit up. "Where's that new Sinatra record, the one with Count Basie?" His aide began searching.

Brando was a little rattled by all the attention, but hungry nevertheless, "The chowder sounds exquisite." Kennedy chuckled at the word. His aide was opening drawers, still looking for the album. "There's a picture of them on the cover, Sinatra has that hat on …"

The President licked his lips "And a cold bee-yah …" said Kennedy to his aide. "A Heineken! And, uh, a little ice, too." *Damn things never get cold enough.*

Brando had balls. He flagged down the aide and said, "And a red wine ..."

"Yes, and a, uh yes, a red wine for Mr. Brando," repeated Kennedy honestly, offhandedly. "Yes."

Kennedy wanted to suggest white wine, but didn't. *Red wine with fish? Well, that should have told me something* ... Kennedy imagined his wife grimacing and shaking her head in disgust. The aide found the album and carefully placed in on the hi-fi's turntable. After a few seconds, Sinatra was singing 'Pennies From Heaven' perfectly. Flawlessly.

The chowder arrived from the downstairs kitchen within minutes, and like the soup it was piping hot. Oyster crackers on the saucer. A carafe of burgundy was placed before Brando, a crystal glass beside it. *Mrs. Kennedy would have insisted.*

As they ate together and shared a few drinks, Kennedy asked Brando about movies. *Mutiny On the Bounty,* "Tell me, why in the hell did it take so goddamn long to make? Did the studio hold it up?" They talked about *The Ugly American,* "Our diplomats, especially in southeast Asia, need to be educated before they go into that, uh, kind of work." Kennedy added, "Do you know, I sent a copy of the book to every single United States Senator during the campaign." He added, "The thing is, I should have only sent it to the, uh, ones who can, uh, read ..."

Sinatra was singing away. *My God this is a good record!* JFK was getting into great spirits, unwinding, enjoying his soup and his beer with Brando, whom he considered, from what he had heard, to be "the greatest womanizer in the history of Hollywood," and who aside from the brief, tense chat in 1960, he had never really met. At five-nine, he was shorter than the six-one Kennedy, but still taller than Sinatra and most of the other Hollywood stars, most of whom were tiny.

Hollywood, the land of the little people.

'I Only Have Eyes For You' kicked in next on the record

player. *My God, this is Frank's best recording yet.* And the President, as usual, was full of curious, gossipy energy, "Marlon, which, uh, actresses do you like the best? Who are the best to work with? Who are the, uh, best in bed? Is it true, the story that you were never actually inside the taxicab there with Rod Steiger when they shot that, uh, scene? Who are you sleeping with? Tell me, Marlon, are you, uh, getting any?" he kidded in all seriousness.

Brando stood up, nervous, mumbling almost incoherently. "I keep thinking Abraham Lincoln's going to jump out at me from behind a curtain somewhere."

"Marlon," Kennedy laughed, "Now will you just, uh, sit down here and finish your suppah?"

Brando frowned and squinted. *Is it the Heinekens or does he talk like this all the time. Mother of God, I can't understand a fucking word he's saying ...*

Kennedy listened to Brando attentively. More attentively than usual because of his mumbling. They talked a bit about civil rights, living in New York versus living in L.A., their shared Irish heritage "on my mother's side," mumbled Marlon, and the plight of the Native American Indian.

"For a subject worked and reworked so often in novels, motion pictures, and television," mused the President, "American Indians remain probably the least understood and most misunderstood Americans of us all."

Brando grinned. He had an ally.

Kennedy started calling Brando "Chief," and Brando called Kennedy "Chief" in return. They were having fun.

Then JFK thought he noticed, if only for a second or so, that Brando was imitating him. Something he did with his hand. Like he was reacting to something Kennedy was saying or doing. He studied Marlon's face for a moment and changed the subject very quickly. "Don't even think about it," he said, smiling, shaking his head.

"You're getting too fat for the part." Sinatra was singing 'My Kind Of Girl,' humming at the bridge of the song.

"What part?" asked Brando, surprised, laughing out loud.

"That's not important. It's the fat that's important," said the President.

"Are you kidding?" asked Brando, trying to get a reaction out of Kennedy. "Have you looked in the mirror lately? Your jowls don't even fit in the frame of my television screen. When they go in for close ups, they lose your face. It looks like a big fat redheaded pillow! It looks like the moon!" Kennedy hated his new jowls but wouldn't trade the medicine that caused it for the world.[53]

When Marlon stooped down and attacked his chowder, Kennedy tilted his chin out, jokingly, and challenged him. He figured it was about time to break Brando's balls and get a nice, little reaction out of him for a change, "Chief, have you gained weight? Looks like you've put on a few." It was high school stuff, but it was all Kennedy had.

Brando, still chewing, beamed with boast as he clenched his silver soup spoon and made a muscle, "Nary an ounce."

Kennedy grinned and cut into his baked potato. "Then I must've got some bad intelligence information," he laughed.

"Why, I bet you weigh more than me!" Brando wagged his finger. "Where's the scale!" Kennedy clapped his hands and stood to summon his aide. Sinatra and Count Basie were going gangbusters on the record player.

When the bathroom scale appeared, Brando stood on it, realizing he was a bit lightheaded, and checked in at one-hundred and eighty-seven pounds pounds.

---

[53] JFK's 'full face' was the result of the 'Prednisone' steroid injections that Kennedy received to combat his periodic flare-ups from Addison's Disease, and to increase his strength and energy.

In his stocking feet, Kennedy weighed in at one seventy-three. Fourteen pounds lighter.

"Let's do another take," Brando said. "I think I can be lighter! C'mon, one more take!" He tapped Kennedy's stomach gently with his knuckles. Kennedy flinched. He didn't like people touching him unexpectedly. "One seventy-three!" Brando ranted. "You can't lead a country at one seventy-three! Hell, in *Desiree* I played Napoleon at about one seventy-eight! And I played Julius Caesar at one-eighty!!"

Kennedy laughed at the scene. He still couldn't believe that Brando hadn't seen him put his toe on the scale.

"Good God," said Brando, kidding the President, forgetting. "You're almost as skinny as Sinatra!"

Kennedy listened to Sinatra on the record player. He weighed his Heineken bottle in his hand, biting his lip as he spoke. "Marlon, let me ask you, how is Frank? Do you see him around town at all?"

"Uh, no, not since we did *Guys and Dolls*. Not directly anyway." Brando laughed, "We go to the same shoeshine boy."

"Fitzgerald? The Irish kid?" asked the President, shifting his weight onto his left foot, silently favoring his aching back a bit, and remembering again to ask someone soon about building him a lift for his left shoe. *Who cares about the fucking gadgets at this point, I'm only forty-six fucking years old, I just want to be free from of the pain.*

"Yeah, that's the one! Fitzy!" exclaimed Brando. "Good kid. Anyways, Frank's still mad, you know how Frank is, you know the story ..." said Brando, palms up. [Sinatra always felt that Brando's Sky Masterson role in 1955's *Guys and Dolls* should have gone instead to *him*, and that *his* Nathan Detroit should have gone to Gene Kelly, his co-star in the 1940's musicals *Anchors Aweigh*, *Take Me Out To The Ballgame* and *On The Town*].

Kennedy listened and nodded as he reached for a cigar and searched again for his ever-disappearing lighter, anticipating Brando's next words as he pictured Gene Kelly as Sky Masterson.

Brando chose his words carefully, squinting, as if he were reading his lines off cue cards on the opposite wall, knowing that the President and Sinatra had a past. "Now, let's see …" Brando slowly placed his hand on the President's shoulder. "See, Frank's the kind of guy," Marlon began, "That when he dies … he's gonna give God a bad time for making him bald."

Kennedy smiled faintly and tossed his head in a knowing way that showed he understood.

Brando jokingly pushed Kennedy aside. "Now lemme do just one more take, I can do lighter, I know I can, c'mon, just one …"

"Chief … I knew it!" exclaimed Kennedy, shaking his head in disbelief. "Oh you sly fox …" He wagged his finger at Brando accusingly, "I knew it, I knew it all along …"

"What …?" Brando's face was guilty, there was no hiding it.

"You're not an actor!" smiled Kennedy, enjoying the one-ups-man-ship. "You're a movie star!"

Brando curtsied and then properly bowed in reverence. "Guilty as charged, Mr. President … you fat sonofabitch!!"

At that, the record ended and after a few seconds went back to the groove of the first track. Kennedy thought about telling Brando that he had his toe on the scale, but then got distracted and remembered that he wanted to ask Marlon his thoughts on the recent Nuclear Test Ban Treaty, and to see if Brando had any experience with Asian women in the Pacific.[54]

But what the President mostly wanted to learn about was 'The Method.'

---

[54] 1963's *PT-109* starred Cliff Robertson. Robertson was personally selected for the role by President Kennedy.

One Degree of James Gregory

Character actor James Gregory co-starred in 'The Manchurian Candidate' with Frank Sinatra (1962), 'PT-109' (1963), 'The Sons of Katie Elder' with John Wayne (1965), and 'Clambake' with Elvis Presley (1968). In second place is Gig Young, who appeared with Wayne in 1948's 'Wake of the Red Witch,' Sinatra in 1954's 'Young At Heart' (with Doris Day), and Presley in 1963's 'Kid Galahad' (Elvis fell madly in love with Gig Young's then wife, Elizabeth Montgomery of TV's 'Bewitched,' during filming).

Having stayed up all night drinking and thinking his way through yet another bourbon-soaked quiet spree and beating the orange desert sunrise into yet another new day, Sinatra tossed and turned atop his bright orange 800-thread hand-made imported cotton Egyptian sheets, drenched in pure Kentucky-distilled sweat.

This time, Elvis was marching with his platoon, wearing only a pink bathing suit and a light smile of pleasure on his face as he moved along. Another soldier, bringing up the rear, was leading the cadence in a wonderful baritone …

> *Hey, Hey, Captain Jack …*
> *Meet me down the railroad track …*
>
> *With that weapon in your hand!*
> *With that weapon in your hand!*
>
> *I'm gonna be your killin' man!!*
>
> *Sound Off !!*   *1 - 2 !!*
>
> *Sound Off !!*   *3 - 4 !!*
>
> *1 - 2 - 3 – 4*   *1 - 2   3 – 4 !!*

The flag bearer, wearing a black bearskin hat and a red, flowered Hawaiian shirt, unfurled the red Russian flag with the yellow hammer and sickle emblem. They were all marching on an open beach. Paper American currency had washed up on the shore as far as the eye could see. They were all snapping their fingers out of beat. And all the men, with the exception of Elvis, were in perfect formation.

The Sergeant yelled, "Presley! Get in step, Presley!"

Then all of a sudden, Elvis, is in his Army dress greens, his

233

chest covered with medals for bravery and pins for marksmanship, and shoulder stripes for rank, bolted out of Jilly's saloon on Manhattan's upper east side and ran like he was on fire clear across Central Park, and then he jumped into a cement pond with a terrific splash.

Sinatra awoke, realizing he was still at home, in California. But when he awoke, it was with a foggy, foreboding sense of déjà-vous, all over again.

He was worried about the script. They were way behind schedule. And he worried about the headstrong Wayne, and how he could approach him.

It was Autumn in New York, and Richard Nixon's Sunday was already planned and scripted. He would be holding court with each of the three, key members of his 'election' team in his newly acquired New York Law office in lower Manhattan, without interruption. As he waited for his first meeting, he sat in a high-back leather chair in his office study, patting his beloved black and white cocker spaniel, the aforementioned and talentless 'Checkers,' and the poor dog wasn't getting any younger, either.

There was a knock on the door.

"Come in Mr. Parker. Come in." called Nixon from his study as he readied himself.

The Colonel was dressed in white, looking more like a renegade ice-cream man than the ruthless negotiator he was.

The Colonel sat himself opposite Nixon. Now they could get down to business.

"Now, Mr. Parker ..." Nixon began ...

"One million dollars!" exclaimed The Colonel in haste, "And I say at least twenty-five percent of that goes to mah boy! That's up front money too!"

Never making direct eye contact with The Colonel, Nixon paused for a moment, gathering his thoughts.

Ignoring Parker, Nixon spoke quickly, spraying a bit of spittle as he began. There was some thick black hair in his ears too, "Mr. Parker ... do not speak ... please refrain from speaking until I am finished. Do you understand?" Nixon looked at Parker and then looked away.

"Good. Now, Mr. Parker. Issue One. If this project, this agreement, is successful, if everything goes one-hundred percent according to plan, you will receive $3 million dollars per year for the next five years. In exchange, you and your client will be obligated to participate in a minimum of three films each year during each of those five years, until 1968. Of course, each film will have a sound recording of songs attached, for our friends at RCA, naturally. No risky 'dramatic' investments either. No more *Wild In The Country* ... no more *Flaming Star*. He had his chance. NO MORE dramatic films. None of that artsy social propaganda intellectual 'message' bullshit either. Strictly family films. Family entertainment. Singing. Dancing. Some light humor, but nothing off-color. No foul language. Nothing Blue! And no political statements!"[55]

Nixon stood up straight. "Issue Two."

"And if, after those five years, and you and your client have held up your share of the bargain. And providing his cover isn't blown. Then your payday will arrive."

"The Colonel is listening," said The Colonel.

"If your cover isn't blown, and everything has gone according to plan, then, Mr. Parker, in 1968, you and your client will be able to come back and go public again, and will be free to perform live again, concerts, perhaps on television, arenas, anywhere, and as often as you wish, providing it is within the confines of continental United States."[56]

The Colonel looked like he had a question, thinking he would ask Nixon for a cash bonus if Elvis was successful in his first take, with only one shot, but then thought better of it.

---

[55] In his Hollywood days, Joe Kennedy had also overseen the creation of RCA Sound and Pictures in 1928, Elvis' future record label.

[56] Five years later, in November of 1968 Richard Nixon was elected President of the United States. The following month, on December 3 1968, Elvis Presley finally made his historic television comeback before a national audience on the *'68 Singer Special* sponsored by Singer Sewing Machines, and televised on NBC.

"And Issue Three. Providing you continue to pay every penny of your fair share of taxes, and then some, and continue our other arrangement ... and then, Mr. Parker, and then you will also be allowed to remain here in our fair land, within the confines of the United States, and enjoy our various freedoms and liberties, without restriction. Providing, that is, that you never waver from this agreement, and you and your client agree to never flee this country. Never. Otherwise, an order for house arrest, which is now pending, mind you, will be issued to both of you, and the IRS will be notified, as well as Immigration."

Nixon pointed to a fountain pen he had laid atop a legal document.

"Do we have an agreement, Mr. Parker?"

Colonel Parker, remaining silent, leaned forward a bit, giving the one-page document a cursory look. Then he picked up the pen, and signed his name, 'Andre Parker.'

"Sign your other name too, Mr. Parker, and then wet your fingertips on the ink pad, and press gently to leave your prints on the bottom of the page."

The Colonel signed 'Colonel Parker' next to 'Andre Parker,' and left a set of prints on the paper beneath his signatures. When he was finished, Nixon handed him a clump of damp paper napkins. The Colonel stood, wiped his fingers and hands the best he could, and asked meekly, "I'll wait to hear from you, Mr. Vice-President?"

"Yes, you will hear from someone very soon. Have your client ready for his assignment."

"Yes, Sir."

In Nixon's law study, John Wayne was sitting before his friend and political alter ego, Richard Nixon, in the same chair Parker had occupied only an hour before.

"Are you staying in town long, Duke? Pat had asked me to make sure to invite you for dinner tonight, that is, if you can make it."

"Well, thanks Mr. Vice-President. I would love to, but I'm just here for the day. After I leave you I have a little dust-up over at a hospital here that I gave a little money to. I called them last night to see if I could stop by and say hello to some of the kids, and they said 'come on over! But then I'm headin' back west. Thanks though, for your hospitality. To your missus too."

This time, Nixon was at ease and relaxed. And as usual, John Wayne was just John Wayne. They've known each other and respected each other for years. Decades. But both men had neither the time nor the inclination for much small talk. It just wasn't their nature. Not now, anyway. Not with serious issues at hand.

"Duke, would that be okay?" shuddered Nixon, "the third week-end in November, the one before Thanksgiving, the twenty-first or twenty-second ... next month ... could that be ... arranged?"

"We could do that" said Wayne, "It'd take some doin' though. Good men don't come cheap…"

"The boy is all taken care of, we finalized that part of it just today," said Nixon.

"The boy," answered Wayne with a grin. Over these past few months he had taken to referring to him as 'Memphis.' He just hoped the kid could shoot. *But I still need one more, maybe two ...*

"One million …? Duke …?" pleaded Nixon. "… Would a million dollars cover your expenses ..?"

Wayne leaned forward and faced the Vice-President directly, "That's a lot of silver, but I reckon that's what we need to get the job done. That is, if we want it done right proper like?"

Nixon thought for a second, and decided he could share his plan for financing the project with Wayne. "We've gone to Hughes for the funding. He has billions, and millions of it in cash, just sitting there in Las Vegas, sitting right there in the middle of his hotel room."

"Jesus Christ!" said Wayne, thinking about all the dough he shelled out to his Mexican ex-wives. "What's he gone loco?" Wayne asked.

Wayne knew Hughes was nuttier than squirrel shit, but he hadn't even thought about Hughes for years. There was certainly no love lost between them. Hughes had always claimed Wayne solely responsible for Hughes' film *Jet Pilot* losing millions in 1957, but Wayne knew he had nothing to do with the box office bomb, it was Hughes obsessive-compulsive disorder (OCD), or as Nixon called it, his 'crackpot make-believe disease,' that caused Hughes to pay so much attention to detail, that millions of dollars were lost in the editing room alone, where the obsessed Hughes toiled for months working to get his beloved aerial fight scenes 'just right.' [57]

"He's very unhinged, unbalanced, shall we say," said Nixon. "But he's always been a supporter of both myself and the party, and we know he's no friend of 'theirs' … so we have reason to believe that he will be 'understanding,' shall we say, of our campaign …"

Wayne, a firm believer of the 'don't write it if you can say it and don't say it if you can nod it' rule, nodded in agreement.

---

[57] Privately, Hughes enjoyed his own RKO production of *The Conqueror,* in which Wayne gave a convincing portrayal of a six-foot four oriental Ghengis Chan.

"That's all good by me," said Wayne. He wasn't in the financial side of the operation, so he rarely gave it a thought. He was more concerned with logistics.

"The boy'll do, but I'll need a team, one shooter alone is a bit of a gamble, and it's one I'd rather not take," said Wayne.

A gamble? Nixon wasn't about to bet his comeback on a gamble. The stakes were too high. He needed a sure thing.

"A team?" Nixon repeated. "How many men do you usually use for this type of work, Duke? I have no experience with this sort of thing, as you know." Although Nixon did look genuinely interested.

Wayne tightened his mouth and thought for a second.

"Ideally, four. Including myself. Four is the perfect scenario. But I've had success with just three. But there's been shoots where I had to do the whole damn thing myself, crackers to coffee, soup to nuts."

Crackers to coffee, soup to nuts, well isn't this just great. Nixon smiled and laughed in appreciation. He was just so happy that John Wayne was in his camp. *My God, what a man!*

Wayne tugged his ear. "But this here's a major production, Sir, the biggest, so if it isn't too much trouble I'd like to ask permission to hire out two, or at least one other man."

"Duke, you are free to make any arrangements that you feel are necessary. That's why I need you, Duke. This is your realm, your area of expertise." Nixon didn't want Wayne to know about Sinatra. Not yet.

Humbled, The Duke said, "Much obliged, Mr. Vice President."

"Now what else do you need, Duke? Whatever you need .."

"Well, we have a time, Sir. But do we have a place yet?" asked Wayne.

Nixon smiled to himself, and then to Wayne. "Yes, Texas. Dallas."

"Is there a pass?" asked Wayne.

"A what?" Nixon replied, confused, thinking Wayne was recalling his college football days at USC. *A forward pass? A lateral pass? The Khyber pass?*[58]

"I'll need a pass, you know, a place to head 'em off at."

"Oh, a pass! That kind of pass. Yes, Duke, sure. Let me check. I thought you meant a pass like a football pass, or a free pass, like a pardon, and I thought to myself, why would Duke need a pardon, why, he's the most patriotic man I know ..."

Wayne smiled and then tried to think, to see if there was anything he was forgetting.

"Now, this here pass ... there needs to be proper cover? I mean, like a boulder or a wall or a picket fence ... these men will be trained, but they'll need cover, they'll need protection." Wayne thought some more. "And a way out, like a back door to get out of there ... if you could check Sir, a railway, a getaway route." Wayne swallowed hard.

"Sir, I can't leave my men, out there in broad daylight, with their rear ends hangin' in the breeze."

Nixon made a mental note to himself, committing nothing to paper. "I'll look into all that for you Duke. Believe you me, you'll have everything you'll need right at your disposal. After all, you're directing this operation."

Directing. Wayne liked the sound of that. Has a nice ring to it, directing does, he thought. He thought about all the movies he had

---

[58] Throughout history, the Khyber Pass has been an important trade route linking central and southeast Asia, and a strategic military location.

made with Ford down in Monument Valley, and a thought came to him, "The coach … will it be an open coach or closed?"

Nixon knew Duke was tired. "Open, Duke. It will be an open car. You can rest assured of it."

"A horseless carriage? Good. It's got to slow down for us, can't have a stampede on our hands."

"Yes, Duke. I mean no … no horses. A car. Probably a state car. A government car. A limousine. It'll be slow, no stampedes …"

Nixon chewed on his knuckles and tried to think. *What else, what are we missing?*

Something suddenly occurred to Nixon. "I think there's a wall there … yes, I believe there is. And I recall that there is a little knoll there too," Nixon said.

"A knoll?" asked Wayne. "That's like a hill, ain't it."

"Yes, a knoll is a small hill," said Nixon. "The 'k' is silent, I believe."

"The 'k'?" asked Wayne. "There's a 'k' in knoll, well I'll be damned. Is it at the beginning or at the end?"

"At the beginning," said Nixon. "K-n-o-l-l. Knoll."

"No Sir, I mean the parade. Is the pass, are the pass and the knoll at the beginning or near the end?"

"Uh, err, towards the end, I believe, would you prefer it at the beginning? I can make arrangements to …" said Nixon.

"No," Wayne held up his hand. "At the end is good. Better, actually," smiled Wayne. "Less people that way. Less witnesses. Less confusion."

"Duke," hushed Nixon. "Trust me. I've never seen a better cover plan in all my life. This will be the greatest hoax ever to be perpetuated."

Wayne caught his breath and stood to shake Nixon's hand. Nixon pushed himself to his feet and met Wayne's grip in midair, from below, giving Wayne the upper hand. No other man had received such an honor from him.

"You're in good hands, Sir." said Wayne to Nixon.

"I know we are, Duke. I always know I can count on you. I will be in touch."

"And Sir, please don't forget to give my best to the Missus."

Wayne smiled and turned to leave. When he shut the law office door, he was surprised to see Frank Sinatra, carrying what looked like a briefcase, walking down the hallway towards him. *What the hell is he doing here?*

"Your head cold?" asked Wayne matter-of-factly as Sinatra neared him.

"No. Why?" answered Sinatra, as he approached Wayne, before glancing upward with an embarrassed look on his face, and he hastily removed the trademark chapeau.

"Sorry, pally," said a temporarily defensive Sinatra, to which Wayne responded firmly, "Never apologize and never explain...it's a sign of weakness."

Wayne cocked his mouth disapprovingly at Sinatra, shook his head twice, and walked deliberately toward the elevator.

With that, Sinatra entered Nixon's law office, hat in hand.

Nixon vaguely and suspiciously asked Sinatra how things were going.

Sinatra cocked his cruel looking mouth and said, "Alright, you want the gig, right? Well, here's the pitch. The job'll get done," Sinatra said, glancing about the room. "But the odds aren't right, yet. We gotta keep doing things my way, see. All or nothing at all. Otherwise, some people might blow the lid on this here magilla, and then this whole koo-koo, cockamamie operation goes kaput. Capiche?"

Nixon listened with flat affect, emotionless, revealing nothing.

"Leave everything to me, like we have been, and it's a lock. A sure thing. Otherwise, it's gonna be Bombsville."

Nixon nodded that he approved, and he did. *Let Sinatra take all the hea*t. *Kennedy's jilted, vengeful friend. The perfect cover* .

"You have my blessing, Frank. You'll need to work with Duke, though." Nixon held up a hand to halt Sinatra's protest. "Now, it's only temporary. Just get him the finished script when it's ready. Then the two of you can proceed on this thing as you see fit. But you get full creative control and final script approval."

A mildly jubilant Frank Sinatra looked down, grinned, squinted, and with his right thumb and index finger removed a stray thread from his hand-woven one hundred percent imported silk shirt. *You gotta love livin' baby, Sinatra said to himself.*

"Yes," answered Nixon. "So, Bebe will be ..."

Sinatra interrupted, "Hey, Dick, whaddaya say we head over to Patsy's for some Clams Posillipo, a little Veal Milanese, maybe a side of manicotti, lay a few bets, say 'hello' to a few dames, and then go uptown to Jilly's for a little hey-hey ..."

"Well, um, Frank, I uh am grateful for your invitation." Nixon threw his hand out from under his cuff and looked at his Timex. "It sounds like an awful lot of fun and all, but I still have work to do and then I have a meeting downtown and then I promised Pat I would ..." Nixon was looking forward to the mouth watering Beef Wellington that would be waiting for him at home, before he settled in for his regular CBS Sunday night lineup of *Lassie, My Favorite Martian* and, of course, *The Ed Sullivan Show*. Then possibly a nice, quiet dry martini or five alone in his dark study listening to some stirring Beethoven or Wagner, while he updated and amended his Enemies List. Just another quiet Sunday.

"No problem pally," said Sinatra as he patted Nixon on the shoulder and said goodbye. *Boy, what a drag. Being a Democrat sure was a lot more fun.*

"See ya Dick, I'll work on Hope. See if we can make it an annual!" Sinatra started to leave but looked as though he had a question.

"Dick, you really gonna run next year, you know, for President, against Kennedy. Or are you gonna wait?"

Nixon kept the straightest of faces, paused a second or so, and said, "Patience. Patience is a virtue, my friend."

"Well, if you do," Sinatra said, "I'd bet the house. He ain't gonna see '64. I'd take the long odds, too. Hundred to one. It's a lock. A sure thing, baby."

Nixon, never revealing his emotion, was both shocked and intrigued by Sinatra's outburst. How much, if anything, did Sinatra know? Did he know about the secret F.A.G. program? But Nixon kept his poker face straight. Then he very carefully smiled a very tight, controlled smile at Sinatra, who then turned to leave.

Nixon gave Frank Sinatra a quick wave goodbye and closed the door behind him, locking it, before breathing a long, deserved sigh of relief.

After the door closed, Nixon laughed at the remark, deciding that Sinatra didn't know about the plan, considering all the checks he had solicited and delivered. *Boy, this Sinatra fellow, he sure has a language all his own! My God, does he give it his all! Tremendous energy. What a valuable asset!* He leaned back in his chair, thinking that Sinatra would be a good man to have in his camp, and then his naturally manipulative instinct took over.

A sure thing. At a hundred to one? Why, that's like pulling a straight flush. With an ace in the hole ...

Nixon checked his Timex. All in all, the three private meetings had taken barely two and a half hours of his non-billable time combined.

Very efficient, Dick. Very efficient.

Nixon smiled and clicked his teeth. He was still, as always, paranoid. But he needed Kennedy out of the picture, and Sinatra and Wayne and Presley were his best hope. *Scatter the blame. The bigger the lie, the easier it will be for them all to believe it.*

Upon leaving Nixon's office building, Sinatra felt vindicated, and confident of his new plan, but as he walked the streets of lower Manhattan, amidst its canyons of steel, he grew nostalgic of the city where he had made his start in.

Passing The Bowery on 'Skid Row,' as the 3rd Avenue El train rattled overhead, Sinatra stepped over a beat up bum on the darkened sidewalk, his face all battered and bruised. Sinatra gently tucked a twenty into the man's ripped lapel pocket, and made his way uptown.

When I first came across that river, this was the greatest city in the whole goddamned world. It was like a big, beautiful lady... but look at her now, she's like a busted-down hooker ...

He thought about Wayne, and how difficult it would be to work with him.

Goddamn egos. Hollywood. Washington. Everyone's such a

goddamned Ego.

Sinatra scuffed the sidewalk with the heel of his shoe, frustrated.

Man, this dyin' thing sure is a pain in the ass.

That night, in his private suite at Manhattan's Waldorf-Astoria, after he called over at Patsy's and asked them to send over some pasta and meatball sandwiches (and milk) over to the homeless guys at Skid Row, and to "put it on my tab," Sinatra called his kids before having three powerful Jack Daniels to try to quiet the nightmares and get some shut-eye.

But even in New York, the Sergeant's nocturnal Treatment of Elvis continued.

"Ladies ... " began the sarcastic Sergeant, "Your rifle's your best friend. Them weapons jam in combat, could mean life or death. You got to know 'em inside out. Now I want you to strip them weapons and put them together again."

The Sergeant held up a government-issued stopwatch, a Timex.

"Go!"

The men start taking their rifles apart as fast as they can. Presley was efficient and brilliantly fast, the others were fumbling and slow. A few men looked over at Presley, admiring his speed.

Presley finished the job and stood at attention, his disbanded rifle on the ground before him.

"Fair enough, Private, now let me see you put it back together."

Elvis' hands quickly started to work over rifle parts, putting them together, as he hummed the lyrics to 'Witchcraft' ... "hmm hmm hair ... hmm mmm mmm mmm-mmm stare ... hmm hmmm mmm-mmm bare ... common sense hmm hmm hmm-mmmm ..."

Reassembled, the rifle is in his hands again. Elvis stood up at attention, holding the weapon at half-port. The rest of the men were still working over their rifles. A few others were staring up at him, as if in awe.

The Sergeant grabbed the rifle from Presley, and turned his back to him, pretending to squint along the barrel. His thumb then adjusted the rear sight to one side. The Sergeant then turned around and threw the rifle at Elvis, who caught it, staggering back.

"Your rear sight's way off! You'd be fifty feet off your target at three hundred yards! That's what comes when a soldier don't know how to assemble a rifle." He leaned into Presley, "You better get down to the track and carry it around a few times. Maybe that'll teach you ..."

Again, Presley, as ordered, ran the track in the hot sun, his rifle held before him, his smile faint but visible. Sinatra, in uniform, sweeping the barracks porch, watched from afar in anger.

Asleep barely an hour, Sinatra then suddenly awoke and bolted upright against his headboard.

"The kid's been away for two years," he said to no one, "And I get the feeling he really believes what he's doing."

Frank Sinatra didn't yet realize it, but his subconscious conscience, his deep down gut, was trying to tell him something.

He looked at the clock on the nightstand. It was midnight. He made a couple of calls to check on the script, trying to get all his ducks in a row, and then he called out for a little late night chicken chow mein.

Colonel Parker, after chartering a private plane to fly across the border for the Mexican premiere of Presley's latest film, *Fun In Acapulco*, hurriedly returned to Las Vegas. He owed the boys at The Flamingo big time, but he was broke, as usual. He needed some money as soon as possible. Like, yesterday. He asked if the casino would cover him until he could come up with the dough, if they could wait until December? [59]

"That'll be the day," he was told.

Then, after letting him sweat it out a little bit, the boys at The Flamingo promised to cover him, as a temporary, personal favor to Mr. Frank Sinatra.

"That'll be the day"
'That'll be the day' was Wayne's oft-repeated mantra from John Ford's classic 1956 Western quest film *The Searchers*. The line inspired Texan singer Buddy Holly to write and record the classic rock hit 'That'll Be The Day.'

---

[59] Not one scene of *Fun In Acapulco* was filmed on location. Elvis never travelled to nor was ever seen in Mexico City during his lifetime.

Sinatra once again found himself cast in a familiar nocturnal scene ...

The platoon was divided into teams of two for actual hand-to-hand training. Elvis wielded his rifle, bayonet fixed, in expert thrusts. The Sarge walked behind him and tripped him as he passed. Presley fell off balance. Elvis' opponent smashed his rifle against his and knocked it to the ground.

"Wide open, huh, Presley? Maybe seven laps will teach you to watch yourself ... "

Frank Sinatra, Elvis' newest buddy, wielding his M-1 rifle madly, yelled over in defense. "Hey, I saw that ... I saw what you pulled ... " Only now it wasn't a rifle. It was an Oscar.

Elvis and Sinatra then ran the track together, holding matching Oscars as if they were rifles, singing the mindlessly hypnotic lyrics to 1960's 'GI. Blues' ...

Frank Sinatra couldn't take it anymore. The nightmares were becoming worse and more frequent. For months he awoke absolutely covered in sweat, screaming away at one vivid image after another. Elvis singing 'Witchcraft' to him as he sang 'Love Me Tender' in return on Sinatra's 1960 *Timex Welcome Home Elvis* ABC-TV television special. Elvis in the Army. Elvis marching. But this time it was too real. Too close to home. It was a scene *From Here To Eternity*, the film for which Sinatra won his Academy Award for Best Supporting Actor, based on the novel of the same name by James Jones, except in this dreamy version Elvis is playing the Montgomery Clift role of Robert E. Lee Prewitt.

Every night, Elvis, fresh from the Army, singing 'Witchcraft,' now instead of Clift, it's Elvis getting 'The Treatment!'

Frank couldn't take it anymore. It was too much for one crooner to bear.

Something had to be done.

Come on, buddy boy, think ... think ...

Sinatra started to connect the dots and piece this koo-koo three-ring circus altogether.

In reading, researching, and making *The Manchurian Candidate*, Sinatra had become privy to some of the techniques and methods of mind control, or brainwashing, and now, after months and months of dream analysis and introspection, Sinatra became determined to get at the inner source of his demons.

And now he thought he finally had it all figured out.

Wayne at Nixon's office. Wayne and The Colonel at Nixon's birthday party. Elvis. The Army. Germany. Communists. Kennedy. Sinatra set out to make the nightmares finally go away. But he feared that unless he stopped Presley in his tracks, The Colonel's sinister, comic-book plot would end up using himself, Francis Albert Sinatra, the son of Italian-American immigrants, as an instrument to destroy America; The land that he loved. He couldn't let that happen. Switching party allegiance from Democrat to Republican and From Kennedy to Nixon was one thing, but this, well, this stuff was better left up to the other boy scouts in the business. He had to figure it out, whatever it was, and stop it, rewrite it, before it was too late. But how?

He sat up in bed with a bit of a hazy hangover, and a big belt of 'now it all makes sense, buster, now I get it' understanding. Big time, baby.

He punched his down pillow. And, as a result, punched his pillow down.

He remembered his first meeting with Nixon. *Big Casino in the Sky?! No no no, I just thought they was gonna work him over a little bit. Now, wait a minute now, Charlie ... I never said I wanna kill him, no no no ... I just wanted to rough him up a little bit you see ... set him straight on a few things here ... this guy was like my brother ...*[60]

He thought about his future, his career, his life and his country, and in doing so, was reminded of Albert Maltz, the man they all said was a 'commie,' and the song he wrote for Sinatra back in '45, the song that won Frank his first Academy Award, his honorary Oscar ... 'The House I Live In' ... and then before he even went to the bathroom or brushed his teeth, he sang his first spoken words of the day ... he didn't even warm up first ... no tea, no honey, nothing ... he sang the song that should have been the country's national anthem ...

O beautiful for spacious skies, for amber waves of grain,
For purple mountain majesties, above the fruited plain ...

America! America! God shed His grace on thee,
And crown thy good with brotherhood
From sea to shining sea ...

(Then the lyrics started to get a little hazy, he didn't do this number too often ...)

O beautiful dooby-doo, ba ba da dooby dee, whose dooby doo dab a
ba ba,
Across this wilderness ...

America! America! God get us through this kooky thing,
Confirm thy soul in self-control, ba da ba my binka-bing ...

O beautiful for heroes died, those binka-binka binks,
Who more than their own country loved, and freedom more than life ...

America! America! God shed His grace on thee,
That cat crowned his good with brotherhood
From sea to shining sea ...

(Well, close enough).

---

[60] Frank Sinatra was an only child (as was Elvis Presley).

253

Frank Sinatra sat down on the edge of the big bed and shook his head. *No no no no Buster Brown ... wait a second here now ... this ain't no movie buddy boy! This is my life!!*

"And I ain't doin' it from the slammer, baby!!"

Sinatra reached for the telephone.

Elvis sat up in bed in his hotel room in Vegas with Ann-Margret, his publicly randy, yet privately shy, redheaded girlfriend and co-star in *Viva Las Vegas*.

He had been on a steady diet of amphetamines, which he had been introduced to in the Army, without a day's break, for what seemed like weeks. The pills had helped him stay awake and focused on night watch in the Army, and to lose weight when he needed to, but that was years ago when he was stationed in Germany, and he was now in between films. The amphetamines, or 'bennies,' had now become a habit, one that caused his hands to tremor uncontrollably.

Seeking to calm himself, Elvis opened the nightstand drawer and reached for the other pills, the tranquilizers, and the *Gideon's Bible*. He thought he wanted to read some Psalms. Instead, he found a deck of cards, placed there by The Colonel. Face up was the Queen of Hearts.

The telephone rang. It was another redhead, Lucille Ball, the comic actress who had been Sinatra's first choice to play Lawrence Harvey's monstrous and overbearing mother in 1962's *The Manchurian Candidate*.

She was calling from the pay phone on the Paramount lot.

"Elvis, dear," she began in her smoky voice, "Hi, honey. The Colonel has asked me to call you. Listen, why don't you pass the time by playing a little solitaire."

"Pick a card, my boy, any card, okay, sweetie," she said.

And he began to play.

In the fixed deck, the red queen of hearts came up quickly, again and again. Elvis paused, staring at the line of cards.

"You will meet John Wayne in Arizona," Lucy explained, exhaling after taking a healthy tug off her Chesterfield cigarette. "You will bring with you a costume from one of your early movies, one of western attire. A new script will be waiting for you when you arrive. This is what you were meant to do. And then, once Richard Nixon regains power they will all be held in contempt for what they did to you. And you will rise again. And you, my son, will be a King. Is that absolutely clear, my dear!!?"

"Yes, mother," answered Elvis. He hung up the phone.

"And say 'hello' to Junior for me (Lucille Ball's nickname for Ann-Margret), okay, sweetheart? Bye, bye, kiddo."

Lucy's cameo was now complete.

Back at The Sands, Sinatra turned in bed toward an aspiring showgirl that he had met that afternoon in the entrance of a Vegas wedding chapel, where he had gone to light a cigarette out of the wind.

He squeezed the inside of her thigh, not at all sexually ... well, maybe a little sexually ... but mostly because he was in a good mood, he was thinking that he had figured it out after all. He thought he now knew how to stop Elvis from ruining his reputation and dragging down the country's with it.

"It's the heart card," Sinatra mumbled, leaving the bedroom. "It's the heart card!"

He just hoped Elvis wasn't too far gone under the spell.

Sinatra firmly closed the bathroom door tight and threw some cold water on his face, smiling at himself in the mirror. "Yeah ... it's the queen of hearts, baby ..."

Sinatra sat on the closed toilet's fluffy, orange terrycloth set cover and grabbed a deck of playing cards that he kept in a gold case on top of the toilet lid, next to the gold cigarette case. He started to fan them, looking for the heart cards.

The face cards!

He found the queen and snapped his fingers.

He snapped again. And agai ... he looked at his fingers in mid-snap.

"Well I'll be damned ..."

Hold on here chickie-baby.

Sinatra held the queen up to his face.

Now wait a second ...

"I remember it now, I remember what Elvis was doing with his hands when we did the duet ... he was snapping his fingers, like he was dealing, like he was dealing off the top of the deck!" Elvis had never snapped his fingers before then. He was always about the hips. The finger snap was a new move for the kid. But why?"

He put the cards away and soaked a warm facecloth, almost shrouding his face in it. Then Sinatra looked in the mirror.

"The kid's a mama's boy, right? It all makes sense now. Just like in the movie. I'll find the kid's room, have a little chat with him, play a little cards, talk about the old days, how they filmed him from the waist up, those shit movies he makes, the Army, then I'll make a few suggestions and crumple up their systems forever – remove the controls, rip out the wiring, and baby ... then it'll all be over and done with. Mission accomplished baby. And then maybe I'll get a little hey-hey and grab a fucking good night's sleep!"

He checked his teeth and made sure he was without nose hairs and gave his face a quick all-over look-see in the mirror and then he grabbed a peppermint, popping it in his mouth.

But he still needed a finished script, and he had to somehow get it to Wayne. He made a phone call, then one more. Then he went back into the bedroom, killed the light, and slid back into the feathers to cuddle with his little mouse, what's-her-name.

"C'mere, you ..."

The next day Elvis was in his room, playing solitaire. The cards were imprinted with the name and crest of the Flamingo hotel and casino and had gold edges. He dealt out the seven-card play. The queen of hearts didn't show.

Ann-Margret sat on the edge of the bed with her face in her hands, crying. Elvis was never able to be intimate with her when he was playing solitaire, and he had been playing for weeks now. She couldn't take it anymore. Then she heard him square away the deck. She looked up. The queen of hearts was on top.

"Elvis, I have to talk to you" she said. "Something's wrong, baby. You're not yourself. You haven't been in a while."

There was a knock at the door.

"Damn" she sighed. "Who is it?"

"It's me, baby. Frank. Lemme in kid. I'm here to help."

Ann-Margret turned the knob, letting Sinatra in.

Elvis stared at the red queen, oblivious that Sinatra had entered the room.

"Alright kid," Sinatra began, quietly motioning Ann-Margret to wait outside. When she protested lightly, Sinatra reached out to hold her elbow in his gentle grasp.

"He's sick, honey. Very sick."

"I know, Mr. Sinatra. I know." She was weeping now.

"No, you don't know. You don't wanna know. But I do. And I'm here to help. Let me help, baby. Why don't you go freshen up a

259

bit. I won't be here long." Ann sulked away, her thin, black mascara streaking, She knew she was losing him, and it killed her. She looked back once at Elvis over her shoulder, through her beautiful, red hair, and closed the door behind her.

Sinatra took a seat alongside Elvis on the hotel room bed.

"Alright pally, let's get to work. Let's unlock a few doors."

Sinatra reached into his sport coat for his own deck of cards.

"Let's play us a little solitaire."

Sinatra placed the deck down beside Elvis and directed his eyes and shaky hands to it. As Elvis worked to train his eyes on the new deck Sinatra slipped the old deck into his other pocket. For a few seconds, Elvis' eyes tried to focus on the grainy scene before him. Then he reached to play the top card. It was the queen of hearts.

"Alright, kiddo, here we go. It wasn't your fault Sullivan shot you from the waist up. It was the deadbeat censors! It was Sullivan! It was The Colonel! It wasn't you kid. You hear me! It wasn't you! You hear! It's not your fault!

Elvis nodded that he understood.

"Alright, next card."

Elvis turned over the card. Another queen of hearts.

"Alright Elvis, c'mon now babe, what happened on *The Steve Allen Show*? Tell me! What happened that night?!"

"They dressed me in a tuxedo and tails, Mr. Sinatra. I couldn't move. I couldn't be myself. The whole show was terrible. Mr. Allen thought it was funny. Yeah. Funny as a crutch. They made me sing to a dog! A hound! On live television! It was terrible!

"Then what? What else kid?"

"They made me go in the Army. My career was just takin' off. Things was really goin' good. Then they made me go in the Army, and to Germany. And then mama ... mama ..."

Another queen of hearts was drawn. This time by Sinatra.

"What Elvis?! What about your mother?!" Sinatra's voice grew hotter.

"Then mama died, and The Colonel made me sign new contracts 'cause he said he had to look out for my daddy now too, now that mama was gone."

"Why is it all being done, Elvis? What have they built you to do?" Sinatra was covered with sweat.

"It happened in Germany. The Method. Stanislavsky. Whatever it is, it's supposed to happen soon."

Stanislavsky? The Method? What the ... ?

Sinatra remembered the Timex TV Special. Song interpretation. Method acting. Method singing. Oh, no, Sinatra remembered, the kid knocked 'em dead that day. And then, he remembered ...

Stanislavsky. Method singers. No, I gave the kid a double dose!

Elvis methodically flipped over another queen of hearts.

"What's supposed to happen soon, kid? Tell me! Says who?" Sinatra implored.

"The Colonel," answered Elvis dutifully. "The Colonel."

"Well you listen here kid," yelled Sinatra. "You tell them it's over. Do you hear me?! Over!!"

"He can make me do anything, can't he Mr. Sinatra?"

Sinatra remembered what he hoped to be the truth, praying that it was a certainty beyond even a scintilla of a doubt

... no hypnotized subject may be programmed to perform an act that is abhorrent to their own moral duty ...

Sinatra picked up the deck and fanned the cards at Elvis, "Kid. Look here. Fifty-two queens. They're smashed! Because we just ripped out the wires, baby, and all the king's horses and all the king's men can never put Elvis back together again! He can't touch you anymore! No more contracts baby! You're free! From now on you just tell The Colonel 'sorry buster, the ballgame's over!!' And that's an order!"

The telephone rang. Elvis picked up the receiver.

"Yes, mother" he said.

It was Lucy again.

Sinatra smiled. *Lucy. What a pro. Right on time.*

She had a little more explaining to do.

The first week of September, 1963, JFK spent an extended Labor Day weekend with his entire family at the family's waterfront home in Hyannisport, Massachusetts. The sea and shores he loved like no other place on earth, except of course, Palm Beach, or Malibu, or the French Riviera.

For an entire week and a day he gathered with his parents, surviving brothers and sisters, his wife, children in-laws, nieces and nephews at the big house – his father's house - with its rear lawn facing the roaring Atlantic ocean.

But tonight would be extra special, cocktails and dinner and a bittersweet seventy-fifth birthday celebration for his disabled, mute, stroke-ridden father, Joe. The man who had made it all happen. Together, they had silently watched a private release of the Alfred Hitchcock movie *Charade*, starring Cary Grant and Audrey Hepburn, which JFK just loved.

Though the generations were between them and they were starkly different people, the one thing he had in common with his father was a love of movies, among other things, and JFK appreciated it. Over the weekend, most of their time was spent in eerie silence, as JFK wished his father would get better, or maybe pass away quietly, and be out of his misery.

Poor bahstahd (bastard). That bettuh (better) not be me. When my time comes, it bettuh (better) be quick.

After the big celebration dinner Teddy looked over at his motionless father, who although incapable of words, was not deaf, and suggested that his brother Jack sing *Hooray for Hollywood*.

"Yes! Jack!! Please!!" They all cheered. "Please!"

"Please Jack! Go ahead … sing …"

263

The President said that he would sing only if younger brother Teddy would do his number first.

Puffing out his barrel chest, and with his classically trained spouse accompanying him on piano, Teddy bellowed out a carbon copy of his old reliable stand-by, *Heart of My Heart*.

As Teddy crooned, Jack recalled a conversation he had with one of his Secret Service agents a few weeks before, after he had gone into a thick crowd somewhere to shake hands one day. When they were back inside the automobile, the agent had said him, "You know, Mr. President, I think that by going into these crowds you could be leaving yourself wide open to be assassinated or seriously injured." Kennedy's reply had been, "Well, I'll tell you. I couldn't get elected dogcatcher, and I don't think any other politician could, if they didn't get out and meet the people. People vote for us, and we have to go out and shake hands." He believed it to be true then, and he believed it to be true now. But he was tired. He looked at his brother Bobby, who had just announced that he was leaving his Attorney General post to run for the U.S. Senate in New York, and he suddenly felt very much alone.

In the past few months he had spoken at the Berlin Wall that separated Germany and visited his ancestral homeland of Ireland for the first time, promising them he would "be back in the Springtime." The reception had been tremendous. But now, since returning to the United States, Kennedy felt that something was in the air. He felt as though his life was in danger. That forces were conspiring against him. That something was brewing. He felt it in his gut. [61]

After little brother Teddy took his bows, everyone in the room looked to The President, Jack, their own son, brother, father, husband and uncle, and insisted that the he make good on his promise.

"Jack, go ahead, please …"

---

[61] Despite JFK's rousing "Ich bin ein Berliner" speech, privately, he was relieved about Germany's physical boundary, privately admitting that "A wall is a helluva lot better than a war."

At first, he had wanted to sing 'As Time Goes By,' or 'September Song,' but then decided that they were too melancholy for the occasion, and with everything else that he had on his mind, he didn't feel like dealing with the copyright infringement issue with all the goddamned lawyers and businessmen. So, without expression, he leaned down over the piano keys and quietly whispered to his sister-in-law, "Let's do, 'When Irish Eyes Are Smiling.'"[62]

She nodded and gently began to play the opening verse two or three times to find his key, as everyone else looked on, curiously. Then, to his entire family, the President began to speak the opening words ...

There's a tear in your eye and I'm wondering why,
For it never should be there at all.
With such power in your smile, sure a stone you'd beguile,
And there's never a teardrop should fall,
When your sweet lilting laughter's like some fairy song
And your eyes sparkle bright as can be.
You should laugh all the while and all other times smile,
So now smile a smile for me ...

The other number had been greeted with boisterous, friendly clapping, but now the entire family, the entire room and seemingly the world, was silent. As he went into the song's chorus, his family joined in gently, almost under their breath ...

When Irish Eyes Are Smiling, sure 'tis like a morn' in spring.
In the lilt of Irish laughter you can hear the angels sing,
When Irish hearts are happy all the world seems bright and gay,
And When Irish Eyes Are Smiling, sure, they steal your heart away ...

JFK uncharacteristically closed his eyes, bracing the piano as he spoke the next lines ...

---

[62] 'September Song,' was perhaps most famously sung by actor Walter Huston (father of famed director John Huston) in the 1938 Broadway musical *Knickerbocker Holiday,* in addition to entertainer Jimmy Durante (who also recorded 'As Time Goes By'), and by Frank Sinatra in 1946, 1961, and again in 1965 (on the album *Point Of No Return*).

For your smile is a part of the love in your heart,
And it makes even sunshine more bright.
Like the linnet's sweet song, crooning all the day long.
Comes your laughter so tender and light.
For the springtime of life is the best time of all,
With never a pain or regret.
While the springtime is ours, thru all of life's hours,
Let us smile each chance we get ...

His gray-green eyes now opened and wet, JFK turned to look at his entire family gathered around him, one by one, resting a second on each face. Closing his eyes once again, as if to concentrate and maybe even ease the tension he sensed, JFK playfully walked his two fingers across the top of the piano as he slowly spoke-sang the final chorus alone ...

When Irish Eyes Are Smiling, sure 'tis like a morn' in spring.
In the lilt of Irish laughter you can hear the angels sing,
When Irish hearts are happy all the world seems bright and gay,
And When Irish Eyes Are Smiling, sure, they steal your heart away ...

The Kennedy family, some with tears in their eyes, applauded.

"That's it," said the President. "That's all folks."

Then he thought about doing a quick, funny Bugs Bunny impression, or was it Porky Pig?

But thankfully, he didn't.

The yellow cab was waiting alongside the Vegas curb. In stepped Elvis Presley, fresh from wrapping up *Kissin' Cousins*. For the first time, an Elvis movie that came in over budget and with no time to spare. Waiting for him in the back seat was his stateside 'handler' and manager of almost a decade, Colonel Tom Parker, wearing his usual white ten-gallon cowboy hat. Always the 'good guy.'

Presley shook The Colonel's hand and grinned, "Good to see you Colonel, how's business?"

"Oh, nuthin' much son, just wanted to have a little talk with you, that's all," The Colonel answered warmly.

Elvis smiled, "Well, Lord knows you're a talker!"

The Colonel leaned forward and barked to the cabbie, "Take us to The Flamingo!"

"I thought we was goin' to the airport? Back to Memphis?! Said Elvis, a little out of joint.

I gotta place a bet at the casino first" replied The Colonel, "Besides, this'll give us time to talk." But Elvis knew there was more to it than that. He'd known The Colonel a long time.

The Colonel took out a fat cigar and wet it in his mouth before biting off the tip. Reaching into his breast pocket for matches he said, "Some of the fellas are sayin' you're startin' them actin' lessons again, you ain't studyin' that Method again, are ya boy?"

"I don't know Colonel" said Elvis, rubbing his forehead. "I ain't figured it all out just yet."

The Colonel knew his boy like a book and approached the topic accordingly, "C'mon now son, you know, you're pushin' thirty.

267

Time's come to start thinkin' bout getting' some smarts. You're Daddy's gonna live a long time son, he's gonna need you."

Elvis brushed it off. "Smarts? … man Colonel, I ain't goin' nowhere. Me and Daddy gonna be just fine." The Colonel searched out the cab window for answers, "I hope so son, I hope so."

Then The Colonel grew a little agitated. He should have had this matter wrapped up already. This conversation was starting to become a waste of his time. The Colonel put his hand on Elvis' shoulder, "Listen son, I'm in the middle of a big million dollar deal right now, one that will make you set up for life, your Daddy too. Three pitchas a year – Elvis Presley pitchas!! - for the next five years son. That's 1968. At a million dollars a shot, boy! That's fifteen million big ones, son, and that's not even countin' them RCA records!"

"Hell," The Colonel continued. "You won't even have to do a goddam thing neither, just walk right on through 'em, just like you've been doin'. Son … hell … you won't even have to act! Just sing …"

Elvis looked hurt. He'd been making movies for over five years now and he just knew he could do better. He knew he could be a top-notch actor. Just like Dean was, or Brando. "There's more to it Colonel" he said. "It ain't just money."

"You're talkin' bout Method again?! Goddamn, son, what aren't you understandin'? I have a plan! This is the next five years of your life! We can't afford to blow a deal like this! Not with you goin' out, buyin' gifts and cars for everyone in town the way you do. Son, where do you think the money's gonna come from?!"

"Aw, I dunno Colonel, I don't need much, as long as I got another gig, a few Cadillac's for the boys …" Elvis' voice was now barely audible, "… I don't know Colonel. I don't know …"

The Colonel grew more impatient, turning sideways in his seat to give his full attention to the matter, "Well, you better know soon. I gotta sign this deal in the next few weeks or there ain't gonna be no deal, you hear?!"

Elvis' eyes looked sadder than an old, tired hound dog. "I ain't set on it yet," he said.

The Colonel snapped back, "Well you better get 'set' on it before Thanksgiving!"

"Before when?" said Elvis like a lost child. "Before when?" Then, suddenly, The Colonel brandished a standard Film Actor's Guild (F.A.G.) motion picture contract and stuck it into Elvis' ribs, "Do these pictures son. Let's do the deal ..."

Elvis couldn't believe The Colonel had just pulled a binding contract on him.

Elvis dropped the binder into his lap and opened it.

"Roustabout? Harum Scarum? Tickle Me? ... oh Colonel, no, no, oh man, Colonel, no man, Colonel ..."

The old manager looked into the boy's wet eyes and remembered the early days, "How much you weigh son?" Elvis was known to pack on a few extra pounds when he wasn't performing live, and by 1963 Elvis hadn't performed live in over five years. "You was skinny as a rake back in '56 son, handsomer than ten of them movie stars, couldda been another Frank Sinatra. Maybe I rushed you along too fast. If I did, I'm sorry boy ..."

Elvis became filled with anger, clenching his fist. "You remember that night on the Ed Sullivan Show!? You came down to my dressing room and you said 'Boy, this ain't your night, they're gonna shoot ya from the waist up,' You remember that don't ya Colonel ... NOT MY NIGHT! Every satin-assed teenage girl in the country watched me that night! Their families too! Not my night?!! It was he biggest show Mr. Sullivan ever had! And what do I get for that?! I sure ain't singin' in no ballparks! I ain't tourin' Europe and China and Japan! No way man, not ol' Elvis here. What do I get? I get a one-way ticket to Burbank. You're my manager Colonel ... you should of taken care of me a little bit. You should of watched out for me a little so I wouldn't of had to do these silly singin' movies just to cover your ass at the poker table!!'"

The Colonel put up a quiet fight, "C'mon son, you made some money too, you know!"

Elvis shook his head wearily, "You don't understand man, I could've been an ACTOR! I could've been nominated ... I could've won an Academy Award ... instead of bein' typecast, which is what I am ... let's face it man."

Elvis' stared out the cab window at nothing as his eyes narrowed to slits, "No way, man ... it was you, Colonel. It was you."

The Colonel slumped back against the seat. "All right, do what you want." Then he handed Elvis the multi-picture contract, "Here, take this son. Take it with you to Arizona. In case you change your mind." The Colonel ordered the cabbie to pull over. Elvis' face was wrought with confusion, "Wha wha wha what's goin' on in Arizona, Colonel? I thought we was goin' back to The Flamingo?"

The Colonel attempted to light his cigar again, "I didn't figure on you goin' for the picture deal son, so I got you a cowboy pitcha with John Wayne, they shoot in November ... all on location ... lots of preparation involved, stunt-work and the such ... and don't worry son, there ain't no singin' in this one. It's all real gen-u-ine cowboy action!"

A minute later the cab pulled up to the TWA terminal. When it stopped, The Colonel said, "I got your bags all packed, they're in the trunk. New boots, too. Fresh shined. They tell me the script'll be there waitin' for you. You can thank me after the job when you get home."

Elvis looked at The Colonel plaintively. He was appreciative to be working with a big star like Wayne, but that didn't change the fact that he wanted to go home today. He'd planned to surprise his Daddy by getting back to Graceland ahead of schedule.

The Colonel said, "Don't worry son, I'll get word to your Daddy when I think the time is right."

Elvis let himself out of the cab and stepped to the rear to remove his luggage.

The Colonel tossed his cigar butt out the window and called back to Elvis, "Don't worry son. I know you'll just knock 'em dead. Just like y'always do ..." Then he tapped the cabbie on the shoulder, "Now take me to The Flamingo!"

The Colonel had conned him again.

The cab pulled away as Elvis stood there on the curb holding a big overstuffed suitcase with his mouth wide open.

ACT III
THE SHOOT
'OPERATION STAGECOACH'

Named for Wayne's 1939 breakout film about a group of stagecoach passengers who ultimately ride into an Indian ambush, 'Operation Stagecoach' was underway.

Over the next few weeks, through telephone conferences with Sinatra, each man's unique role in the plot unfolded. Financed with cash that had been laundered through Hughes' international accounts, Wayne would head up a team that would include Presley and a second gunman to be named later.

It was an unfortunate spot for Elvis to be in. But The Colonel had no choice. Nixon knew of his illegal immigrant status, and should The Colonel refuse to offer Elvis' services, Sullivan would surely blow the lid on Presley's sexual exploits and drug use, destroying the all-American image Presley and himself had worked so hard to construct. The unseen presence of Nixon would insure that The Colonel hold up his part of the bargain. The Colonel had no choice but to comply, but he couldn't help trying to use this unfortunate predicament to the boy's advantage.

Not at all satisfied that a project of such magnitude could be accomplished by the steady hand of only one man, John Wayne quickly requested that a search commence for a second gunman.

The Duke's expense account covered meals, costumes, makeup, and other props and assorted sundries which would be needed for the rehearsals and shoot. It would also provide some extra cash, which would allow Wayne to be well kept in whisky and cigarettes during training (Wayne smoked an estimated five to six packs of non-filtered Camel cigarettes a day).

Work on 'Stagecoach's' technical details began in late October.

JFK's life was now in John Wayne's hands.

At the plan's outset, during Nixon's birthday party, when Bebe Rebozo had asked Richard Nixon who their man was, Nixon had answered that day with an unequivocal "John Wayne," knowing that Wayne would embrace the chance to direct again while serving both Nixon and his country.

As director of the project, Wayne would be able to fulfill his professional need, avenge his liberal detractors, further Nixon's political career, and produce a work he could be proud of, all while promoting the national interests of American conservatism. And to instill even more confidence in the project, it could never be refuted that Wayne, with almost a hundred feature films under his leather belt, most of them being either war films or westerns, was one of the best mentors the squad could ever hope for – Wayne was conservative, professional, and he knew more about shooting a man than anyone.

And, most importantly, he was a Republican.

Wayne fondly remembered that his old friend and mentor, director John Ford, always liked to use two men in a crossfire. It was the only way to do it, Ford always said. That way, there were no exits at the pass. Everything would be covered. In order for the ambush to succeed, Wayne knew that a seasoned marksman of unparalleled skill was needed. He considered volunteering himself as the second man – largely because he had never gotten over the fact that he had been denied Navy service during the Second World War. While men fought and died overseas, Wayne's career had thrived. Still looming large in his mind was his long unfulfilled need to erase the deep guilt and do more for his country.

Even though he did his best for decades to further the American cause up on the big screen, Wayne never felt it was enough. After allowing himself a brief pause for thought, Wayne decided he didn't feel he was up to the task. He had acquired a deep, heavy cough that he couldn't seem to shake, and he felt that by involving himself in the actual shooting that he might put the ultimate outcome of the project at stake.[63] He decided he could do more for the team as director. So he deliberately forced himself to stay on the sidelines, deciding that by properly directing the team, he would actually be doing something 'hands-on' to defeat the communist threat, not just up there on the silver screen, but in real life.

Nevertheless, that personal decision didn't solve Wayne's problem of needing to acquire another hired hand, and thus, an industry-wide search for a second gunman began. First, he had to be an accurate shot. But not only that, he had to be able to get off a round within the allotted time period, ten seconds. And like Presley and Wayne, he had to be able to blend in with the mob of Texans expected to attend the parade.

Early on, Rebozo had privately yet enthusiastically proposed hiring a team of anti-Castro Cuban bandleaders, Desi Arnaz, Xaiver Cougat and Tito Puente, to do the job. However, this early, overly ambitious idea never developed beyond early discussion. [Desi Arnaz would later serve as President Richard Nixon's Ambassador to Latin America].

Nixon had also nominated a second actor, an unemployed actor named Ronald Reagan. From 1947 to 1954, during the height of the Cold War, Ronald Wilson Reagan, known to friends as 'Dutch,' served as President of the Film Actors Guild (F.A.G.). He had publicly supported the blacklisted 'Hollywood Ten' who were singled out during Senator Joe McCarthy's communist witch-hunts.

From 1954 to 1962, Reagan had hosted television's General Electric Theater and *Death Valley Days*, supplementing his income by acting as public relations spokesman for the home appliance giant. After losing a ratings war against *Bonanza* in 1962, General Electric quickly dropped Reagan from the show. He switched party loyalty from freethinking Democrat to ultra-conservative Republican soon

---

[63] Wayne later had a lung removed in 1964 after it was discovered he had lung cancer. Or as he called it, "The Big C."

afterwards. And by 1963, Ronald Reagan, Republican, was in between jobs and desperately in need of money. [64]

Wayne, however, still considered Reagan a liberal Democrat, and too closely tied to the Film Actor's Guild, so without even talking to him, they dismissed his name from the field of candidates.

The Political Evolution of Ronald Reagan

Ronald Reagan started out in politics as a registered Democrat and Roosevelt New Deal supporter. He campaigned against Nixon in his 1950 Senate race, and asked General Dwight D. Eisenhower to run for President as a Democrat in 1952. While he was working as a spokesman for General Electric, however, his views shifted right. "Under the tousled boyish haircut," he wrote Vice President Nixon of John F. Kennedy in 1960, "is still old Karl Marx." When Reagan decided to formerly become a Republican in 1962 he said, "I didn't leave the Democratic Party. The party left me."

Then they briefly considered *Bonanza's* young, cocky ladies man, Michael Landon. As 'Little Joe Cartwright,' Landon was talented, did his own stunts, and was handy with a trigger. He seemed perfect for the role, until Wayne found out he was a southpaw. Wayne didn't trust lefties. "They always muck things up," he said. Plus, *Bonanza* was a success and the show was in full gear. Scheduling would be a certain problem. Then Wayne heard that the young Landon also had an interest in directing and that was that. "There's only one director on this shoot," he said.

Next, *Rawhide's* Rowdy Yates. Clint Eastwood. He had always wanted to work with Wayne, even sent him a letter saying as much, but The Duke sensed that Eastwood would get too violent. Unnecessarily so. And rumor had it that he too fancied himself a director.

Next.

---

[64] In 1960, Joe Kennedy had met with Reagan to try to persuade him to change his mind and support JFK, but Reagan turned him down and stuck with Nixon.

276

Nixon nominated journeyman character actor and real life World War II hero Lee Marvin. On the surface, the idea made sense. Wayne and Marvin had already worked together, in *Donovan's Reef, The Man Who Shot Liberty Valance* and *The Comancheros*. He was now in between pictures and available. But Wayne knew Marvin was no good with a rifle and this was a rooftop job. Marvin was good with a handgun but couldn't fire a rifle if his life depended on it. War hero or not, a pistol was out of the question. He'd be shooting from clear across the park. He'd never hit his mark. The whole town would be full of buckshot before Marvin was through with it. As Wayne put it, he "couldn't hit a cow in the tit with a tin cup."

No, Wayne needed a seasoned sniper. One good enough to hit his mark in one take. Wayne had no use for a rookie on this job. He needed a veteran actor. A seasoned sniper. He needed 'the real McCoy.'

Wayne thought about his best friend and frequent co-star, Ward Bond, who had died in a Dallas hotel room of a massive heart attack just after *The Alamo* release. The *Wagon Train* star would've been perfect for this job, mused Wayne. And working together again would've been fun, too. But Bond was gone.

Was there a second gunman available anywhere?!

Chuck '*The Rifleman*' Connors was ready, and Wayne knew his career intimately. A former and versatile professional athlete for baseball's Brooklyn Dodgers and Chicago Cubs and basketball's Boston Celtics, Connors had begun playing bit parts and B-movie roles in the 1950's. But it was as star of TV's *The Rifleman* where Connors made his professional mark. As star of the grim western, from September 30, 1958 to July 1, 1963, he portrayed Lucas McCain, a widower trying to raise his young son on a ranch outside North Fork, New Mexico. Unfortunately, the character had little time to farm and parent, as he was constantly called on to use his prowess with a .44 Winchester rifle to rid North Fork of its assorted undesirables.

277

However, with his television series recently cancelled, Connors was now desperately in need of work. Admittedly, his career too was at a crossroads.

Wayne practically hired him on spec. He was perfect. Plus, Connors had already appeared alongside Wayne in the forgettable 1953 Warner Bros. film, *Trouble Along the Way*, and as Wayne remembered, he wasn't too bad an actor, either.

Held his own, as I recall.

And to boot, although he had friends on both sides, he was a Nixon supporter.

And so, with the addition of Connors, in an unholy and unprecedented alliance of television and the big screen, the casting was complete.

Mapping out the ambush, it was decided that Connor's sniper's lair would be atop one of the buildings. Elvis would be stationed behind the picket fence, above the lush embankment that later became known as the 'grassy knoll.' And Wayne would be on the green in the center of the plaza, on horseback, armed with two six shooters and a rifle, just in case things got out of hand.

That decided, Wayne called for a celebration and sent Presley to the liquor store for a carton of cigarettes and a jug.

It was ten p.m. and pitch black at the juncture of Broadway at State Street in Lower Manhattan. Jimmy Stewart stepped out of a New York City taxicab and paid the cabbie, tipping him conservatively. The taxi then did a U-turn and quickly disappeared around the corner. Stewart was visiting New York ostensibly for a brief vacation, he had told his wife, who knew better. To appease her doting husband, Mrs. Stewart agreed to spend the day shopping and possibly attending a Broadway musical on her own, while her husband attended to his 'business.'

Stewart squinted his eyes skyward against New York's concrete jungle, and then gave the street area around him a quick once-over. He began to walk through the downtown financial district and glanced down at the piece of paper he had taken from his pocket bearing the address of Richard Nixon's law offices. He was completely alone on the quiet street, so much so that his footsteps clicked on the pavement and created the sound and feeling of an echo. As he walked he listened to the echo and for a moment wondered if it was indeed an echo. He slowed up and came to a stop.

Other than the seldom, late evening traffic and noises that in part defined New York City, there was complete silence. A short, rotund gentleman holding a down-turned, closed umbrella as if it were a cane bumped into Stewart, accidentally, and stopped. "Good eeeeve-ning," the man said, in a strange English accent, hauntingly yet vaguely familiar to Stewart, before brusquely sidestepping Stewart, and proceeding on his way.

N-N-No. Couldn't be ...

The short rotund man disappeared around a corner. Jimmy Stewart resumed his walk. The echo started again. He slowed up again and stopped. But this time the echo continued. He became tense, and looked over his shoulder and all around him in alarm.

A slight paranoia had set in. Jimmy Stewart had information, or so he thought, that a secret and suspicious anti-American project was in the works. And he wanted to stop it. Fearing wiretaps, he had foregone a simple phone call and had flown cross-country from Los Angeles for this express purpose. Kennedy, like him or not, was a war hero. He'd seen battle, as had Stewart. But beyond that, he was a human being. He knew that deep down Wayne was gentle and loyal and decent, but he was far from perfect. But this! This here was just plain crazy, and he was dead set against it. Duke must be out of his mind, he thought. He must be off his nut?! Arguing over politics was fine, he and 'Hank' Fonda even had a fistfight over their political differences once. But never again. Politicians come and go. Democrats. Republicans. In the end, who cares? Wasn't worth ruining a friendship over. But this?!

Stewart looked all around him cautiously. There was no sign of anyone.

He resumed his walk. He stopped suddenly, and tried to trap the echo with his shoes. But the echo continued to follow him. He was slightly scared. He resumed his walk with a more hurried pace. The echo got louder. He glanced quickly over his shoulder again.

A man was following him, at about the same pace. He was rather well dressed, and appeared nonchalant and oblivious.

Stewart continued walking, and after another short time he cautiously looked behind him again.

The same man was still following behind.

Stewart looked down again at the paper in his hand, and looked up trying to locate the right building as he walked. The street was one steel gray high rise after another and another and another. Stewart remembered his architecture courses at Princeton, before he became an actor. He was unfamiliar with this part of New York City, or any part of New York City, as he hadn't been here in ages and not for any real length of time since he shared an apartment with Henry Fonda on the Upper East Side, when they were still stage actors back in the late thirties. Stewart's expression indicated that he would like to find his destination before the man following caught up with him. Then he changed his mind. He deliberately slowed up.

Stewart walked slowly along, listening to the pace of the man approaching behind him, listening with the back of his head, and with his whole body. The man walking behind was aware that Stewart was aware. He began staring at him.

Stewart instinctively clenched his right hand into a fist of preparedness. Though he was tall and lanky, disturbingly so, he was sure of himself and not afraid of a fight. As the man closed in on Stewart he saw that he was younger than himself, forty-five to fifty years old, perhaps. As the man reached Stewart, and passed him on Delancy Street, Stewart actively followed him and stayed close, to study him, softly whistling and humming the words to 'Manhattan' so that now he too would appear nonchalant and oblivious …

It's very hmmm-hmmm, on old hmm-hmm-hmm - mmm you *know*

Da dada da da da –

Mmm mm mm-mm mm – mmm mm mmm …

Jimmy Stewart watched the man go on ahead of him at a faster pace. Suddenly the man turned a sharp right into a doorway, and disappeared. Stewart glanced at the paper in his hand again. He stopped and looked up in astonishment.

At the little side doorway in which the old man turned, above was an inscribed granite sign with gold leaf lettering that read, 'Nixon & Associates.'

For the first time he noticed that the smell of salt water was about. I must be near the river, he thought.

Stewart noticed that the heavy glass revolving door was slowly turning on its own.

Stewart hesitated briefly in thought, put the piece of paper into his pocket, and made up his mind and went through the revolving door.

Stewart, rather cautiously, made his way across an elaborate and almost ostentatious lobby, and came to face a black lettering on silver plate backing glass encased wall directory. 'Nixon & Associates. Richard M. Nixon, Senior Partner.' His eyes slowly, carefully scanned over to the right to '13th Floor.' The elevator door of the building was just closing as he made his way across the marble floor. He thought he smelled cigar smoke and words entered his mind like 'stodgy' and 'ego.'

Stewart paused inside the door of the elevator, and looked down at the two vertical rows of pushbuttons. He pushed number '13.'

Twenty or twenty-five seconds passed. The doors opened. Startled, Jimmy Stewart recoiled instinctively. Then he crossed the elevator's thin metal thresh-hold, took a deep breath, braced himself, and pressed the office buzzer. The door was soon opened by a fortyish-looking, uniformed security guard of medium build, and armed.

"Yes?" asked the security guard, unsurprised.

"I ... I'd l-like to speak to M-M-Mr. Richard Nixon, please," said the kind, soft-spoken Stewart.

"Come in."

The security guard pulled open the door, and Stewart entered.

Stewart followed the security guard into the office. It was cluttered with stuffed animal heads of every size and shape imaginable. Lions and tigers and bears. Elephant heads, swordfish, crocodiles. Everything. And potted plants of all shapes and sizes. From cactuses to rubber trees to small, planted samplings of various herbs and spices. Near the window he saw three crates of full Pepsi bottles, with the odd empty bottle strewn about the room. Stewart stared all around at what he saw. A number of workmen were busy dismounting, un-stuffing, and methodically pulling apart the animals and plants. The security guard who let him in called to someone.

"A man to see you, sir," said the security guard, firmly, through the adjoining room's doorway.

Richard Nixon turned from inspecting the leaves of what looked like a maple sapling, and came forward to Stewart. He was gracious, and gentle upon seeing his longtime Republican ally and friend.

"Good morning, Jimmy."

Stewart studied Nixon briefly. His face showed disbelief that such a man could be part of any project or plan that was anti-American. Nixon stopped in front of him, and waited a brief moment.

"What [inaudible] can I do for you, friend?"

"Well you see, I uh ..." stammered Stewart.

There was a twinkle in Nixon's eye.

"Tell me, how was your [unintelligible] flight Jimmy? That might be a start."

"Oh, of course, Dick. Mr. Vice-President. I called you. I left a message with y-y-your assistant that I would be in t-town today." Though Stewart's military rank at the time was that of a Brigadier General, he remained deferential and respectful to his old poker buddy, especially since they shared a common former boss in General Eisenhower.

Nixon was unemotional, but mindful. Although he had intentionally called him 'Jimmy' earlier, he knew that Stewart preferred to be addressed by his proper name. "Yes. You requested to see me, James."

Stewart feared that his eyes were deceiving him.

Do I really know this man? Am I really here? Is this really happening? I am in New York City with Richard Nixon, right?

Stewart leaned forward, peering close, "You are Richard Nixon?"

Nixon smiled with cool detachment, all teeth. "I have been Richard Nixon for just over fifty [expletive deleted] years." Nixon winked faintly. "But I think I understand your problem."

"You do?" asked Stewart almost in disbelief. And right then he is fast reminded that a little knowledge can indeed be a dangerous thing.

Old lessons learned at the poker table had surely served Nixon well. During potentially tense moments such as this, Nixon operated with all the cunning of a card hustler. Poker had taught him to control the visual cues that come with a good hand or a necessary bluff. He instinctively knew how to modulate his breathing, keep his stomach muscles from visibly tightening and steady any physical signs that would telegraph information.

Stewart saw what he thought to be an autographed photo, framed, of actress Joan Crawford, on the wall behind Nixon.

"I-I-Is that who I-I think it is?" said Stewart, pointing.

"Yes," replied Nixon. "Joan's a client."

Nixon smiled at Stewart stoically as he gently turned and called out to Bebe.

From behind a doorway on the far side a man emerged in response to the call. He was somewhat younger than Nixon, but not by much. He was the gentleman who had been apparently following Stewart on the street. I should have known, Stewart thought. Have my career choices taught me nothing.

Stewart was rumored to have been an FBI informant in Hollywood and had starred (at J. Edgar Hoover's request) in Republican Hollywood producer Mervyn LeRoy's 1959 FBI propaganda film, *The FBI Story*, Richard Nixon's favorite movie - in which Stewart plays a retired FBI agent who recalls his battles against crime and communism. The film co-starred Nick Adams, who was a Hollywood friend of Elvis and also of James Dean, having appeared in *Rebel Without A Cause*.

"Bebe," Nixon said. "I think this gentleman wants to talk to us."

"Now, Dick. Now why don't you go and have a little rest ... I will handle things from here," said Bebe.

Plausible deniability, boss. Always plausible deniability.

"Humph!" Nixon chuckled. "But Bebe, I have centuries of rest ahead of me [unintelligible]."

Nixon nodded to Stewart. "Have a good day, Jimmy."

Stewart nodded in return, confused, and he watched Nixon refocus his attention back to the nearby plants and animal heads.

"Now what can we do for you?" Bebe Rebozo asked Jimmy Stewart.

Stewart turned his attention back to Bebe. He was now a little more in command of himself.

"I'm Jimmy Stewart." Stewart waited, to no reaction. "Does the name mean anything to you?"

Bebe thought for a moment. The name obviously didn't register.

"No, I don't think so."

Stewart named his two most recent films, both released in 1962.

"... *The Man Who Shot Liberty Valance* ... ? ... *How The West Was Won* ..? ..."

The workmen alongside Nixon paused their work to look in the direction of Stewart with some curiosity.

Bebe nodded his head downward and scratched the side of his nose, then waited with a deadpan expression for Stewart to continue. After a pause, Stewart did.

"You have no idea why I came here?"

"Mister, sir, I haven't the ... faintest idea!"

Stewart's expression showed that he felt Bebe is putting on a poker bluff, but he still went on.

"I overheard your boss's name uttered by someone I happened to overhear in Hollywood."

Bebe's expression didn't change, except for a slightly raised eyebrow.

"Oh, yes?"

Stewart now had more confidence in his idealistic mission. He'd thought and thought about this for months. Always the hesitant, reluctant hero, Stewart was.

Bebe seemed to be turning something over in his mind. Stewart turned to look at the workmen around them.

The workmen, half-listening, returned their attention to the various plants and animals. They were a bit self-conscious at being observed eavesdropping.

Stewart turned his attention back to Bebe. He moved in a little

286

closer, and dropped his voice somewhat. Bebe watched him warily.

"Let's stop jabbing with words, huh? I overheard a conversation. I heard that there's auditions. A secret project. Training exercises going on. A script in the works. People talk, you know. Seems like months ago now," Stewart scratched his head. Is my mind playing tricks on me, he wondered. '*Seems* like months anyway.'

Rebozo remained silent.

Stewart continued, "N-N-Now, I came to make a business proposition," Stewart said. "And to ask you, your boss, to help me stop this thing, before, before it's too late. And I don't see how you can turn it down." In addition to his income from films and his military pay and pension, Stewart had accumulated millions due to his sound business investments over the years.[65]

Bebe Rebozo looked over to a man who was un-stuffing animals heads, and untangling wires and various devices. "What did you have in mind?"

"You want to talk here?" asked Stewart.

"Certainly. We have no secrets from our employees."

Stewart looked over at the workers and then over their heads and beyond them, out the window. He saw the Brooklyn Bridge to the left, what he thought to be Staten Island ahead, and a ferry heading towards it in the river below. If memory served him, the Statue of Liberty and Ellis Island would be down the river to the right, just out of their view.

"Okay," began Jimmy Stewart. "First of all, I haven't uttered one word of what I heard. And I won't. Frankly I'm not interested in political intrigue, and I don't care who it is you're going to kill here in New York, or out West, or wherever. Duke is a grown man. And there's no talking to him anyway. He can take care of himself. All I

---

[65] Stewart, like Wayne, came from humble beginnings. Stewart's father ran a hardware store in Indiana, Pennsylvania.

want is that boy to be safe, and you know the boy I mean, and then I-I-I aim to get on the first plane back to California …"

When Stewart began mentioning a killing, Bebe's face took on a look of alarm, almost panic. He moved back from Stewart, watching him like a cobra. Stewart, however, now convinced that he has the right man in front of him, moved in on him to finish his proposition.

"Now that isn't all. If money will do anything …"

Bebe now seemed thoroughly frightened. He moved back from Stewart, almost stumbling. Then he turned, and went back to the door of a small office, in which was now standing Nixon.

Nixon leaned closer to the open door, as Bebe spoke urgently and almost silently to Nixon. "Boss. Phone security. Quick."

Bebe turned back toward Stewart, trying to assume a pleasant and casual manner.

"Now, sir, shall we go into this a little more carefully? You said something about money?"

Workmen paused their work to look at the pair, wondering about the mention of money.

"You told him to call the police," said Stewart. "Now don't try to bluff me like that!"

He reached out quickly, and grabbed Bebe by the lapel. Bebe gave an involuntary cry of fear.

Nixon was on the phone.

"This is Vice-President Nixon – 13th Floor - Will you send someone up at once?" He smiled cordially at Stewart. "There is a very important individual here, and we really can't accommodate him at this time."

Bebe struggled to get loose from Stewart's grasp.

288

"Let me go!"

"You don't know who I am?"

"I've never heard of you."

"And you don't have any idea about what's going on out West, about the auditions, or where the boy is?

"No, of course not! ... Help!"

Stewart let go of Bebe and turned in panic and confusion.

The workmen dropped their tools, and moved in on Stewart quickly and threateningly. Even Nixon came out of the office in alarm. Stewart backed away toward the door.

"N-Now j-j-just a minute," eased Stewart. "Take it easy. I obviously got the wrong place. Now stay away from me."

But they didn't. They came upon him. Stewart looked quickly around for a weapon, or an exit. He saw the door, and moved quickly toward it, but the workmen were faster than he was. Two of them barred the exit. Stewart tried to shove them out of the way and get through the door. The men grappled with him. Bebe and another workman rushed in, working to subdue Stewart. A silent, but furious struggle ensued. It was now a complete scrum among the four men and Stewart as they tried to hold him down.

"Hold him ... hold him ..." said Bebe.

Jimmy Stewart broke loose temporarily, trying to find another escape. He realized that the time for talking was past. But as fast as he was, the men were on him again. They twisted and struggled through the stuffed and mounted animals and potted plants. There was a mixture of lion heads, a broken swordfish, leaves and soil and wires and plugs and microphones all about. Stewart, in his struggle, came face to face with the angry head of a bared-tusk elephant. Bebe himself at one point found the branch of a very painful cactus somewhere

289

about his anatomy. Stewart eventually wrenched himself free.

Stewart shot toward the doorway. The confusion gave him a free moment. He made it to the door, twisted the glass knob open, and dashed out into the hall. Suddenly he turned back and dashed in again.

Bebe and the workmen retreated in fear.

Sprinting out of the elevator and the lobby, Stewart picked up his fallen hat and dashed out of the building, and out into the dark city streets. He raised his hand to his mouth as if to say something, maybe call the police, and then thought otherwise. *No, it wouldn't do any good.* He then hailed down a cab and ducked inside, checking over both his shoulders to see if he was being followed again. He saw no one.

As the cab pulled away, Stewart buried his face in his hands and prayed for divine intervention to help him. "God help us all, please …" he cried into his fists. He thought about who to call for help. Someone who had power in Hollywood. Someone who people feared. Someone who knew how to get things done. Someone who loved America and what she stood for.

He decided to call Frank Sinatra.

The Chairman of the Board.

Back inside the law offices, Rebozo and Nixon looked at each other.

"It's okay, Bebe," said Nixon confidently. "He was never here."

After having to shut down production and losing two weeks of valuable rehearsal time due to prior commitments, personal appearances, and various other scheduling conflicts, Wayne's team was finally ready to re-commence training in Utah. At Wayne's sentimental insistence, Presley, Connors and himself were again holed up amid the giant vista of Monument Valley, set upon the scenic Navaho lands on the southern Utah, Arizona border. It had been the shooting location of many John Ford-John Wayne collaborations.

As Wayne had succinctly put it, "A little inspiration never hurt no one."

After yet another grueling ten-hour day of absorbing Wayne's directorial wrath, Connors, frustrated with Wayne's omnipotent scorn, upset at the turn his career had taken, and perhaps a trifle nervous about working with two stars of such magnitude, threw his modified Winchester to the ground in disgust. He regretted taking the job now and was sorry that he had to for reasons of money.

"I don't want no gun," moaned Connors. "Shoot! Can't we just put him in jail?"

Wayne couldn't believe his ears and laughed sarcastically, tossing aside his worn copy of the old script in disgust. "And who are you, may I ask?! The goddamned sheriff?! Christ. We're here to solve a problem, not pass it off to somebody else."

"This is a democracy, isn't it?" pleaded Connors. "Then why can't we just vote him out?!"

"That'll be the day," drawled Wayne.

Connors looked at Wayne sideways. He wanted out of his contract. After all, he liked Kennedy. Even met him at The White

House, his brother too. He wanted no part of it anymore. But he knew Wayne would never void his contract. Never. Desperate, hands off his sides, ready to pick up his gun and fire, he hushed at Wayne, "I should take you out right now."

Wayne held his gaze. "You should try." He knew he had Connors beat long before the first bullet fired or punch thrown.

"Kennedy's a commie," stated Wayne, "And commie votes won't stand up against guns."

"You hear what you're saying?!" said Connors. "Now, Duke, listen to me for a minute. Just hold your horses and listen. I'm a Nixon man, just as you are, but Kennedy is our President. And he's not a bad man, Duke. Trust me, please. He 's not a bad guy. And you know, the devil you know is better than the devil you don't. Now, Christ, what kind of world is this? Listen to yourself! What the hell kind of man are you?"

"I know what kind of man I am, pilgrim," replied a somber Wayne, now facing Connors squarely under lidded eyes. "What kind of man are you?"

Connors stood silent, frozen.

Knowing he had him beat, a stern Wayne arched his brow and looked up under his hat at Connors.

"Go ahead … pick it up."

Connors stared down at his Winchester lying on the red, dusty ground, proud that he's taken a stand, but scared to death of confronting Wayne with a gun.

Wayne said it again, only slower. "Go ahead pilgrim. Pick it up." Connors glanced up at him for a split second but didn't budge. Elvis watched the scene in silence, looking about as frightened as a lost pup.

Wayne moved an inch closer and 'slow as molasses' and sarcastically drawled, "Go ahead … gunslinger … pick it up … I ain't gonna kill ya …"

"Isn't," said Connors without looking.

"What was that?" questioned Wayne.

"Ain't. You said Ain't."

"Isn't. Ain't what?" said Wayne.

"You said ain't" said Connors. "It ain't ain't,' it's isn't."

"What the …!!" screamed Wayne, "It ain't bad enough I got the boy callin' me 'Sir' every two seconds – now you're talkin' to me in goddam riddles?! What the hell's goin on around here!? What the hell is this? A cowboy shootout or a goddamn Keystone Cops -Marx Brothers matinee?!"

Connors shook his head in defeat, swept his thighs and brushed the dust from the seat of his pants, and walked off the set. He was mad as a hatter but too intimidated by Wayne to do anything about it. He was a big man, over six feet, but still no match for the seasoned veteran actor.

"Where the hell you goin'?!" barked Wayne. "We got work to do you know! Get back here!"

Connors answered him without looking back. "Back home, Duke. I'm goin' back to Television City, where I belong."

Wayne, not one for excuses, dismissed Connors out of hand. "What is it?" he dared. "Your conscience …?"

Connors froze, turned, and looked over Wayne from head to toe. "Isn't it enough to just to kill a man, without bein' proud of it?"

Wayne remained self-assured. "You're a tenderfoot. For this job we need someone tough as picket wire. On your way, pilgrim."

Then, as he stared him down, Wayne glanced over towards Presley and added, "Courage is being scared to death … and saddling up anyway."

Connors, his head down, opened the door of his Ford station wagon, pumped the gas twice, turned the key, and rode off for Television City, the land of the small screen and reruns, turning up a cloud of trail dust in his wake.

A **Rerun** or **Repeat** is a re-airing of an episode of a television broadcast. The invention of the rerun is generally credited to Desi Arnaz. In the early days of television, most production was done in New York, mainly because the Hollywood studios considered television to be a threat to their film empires. So, quite naturally, CBS expected Arnaz and Ball to move from Hollywood to New York. But the couple insisted on staying in Hollywood. CBS protested, claiming that live production in Los Angeles was impractical. Because of the time difference between the coasts, the network would be forced to air blurry kinescopes in the East, where most television-viewing homes were located. Arnaz and Ball offered a simple solution: produce the show on film and dispense with kinescopes altogether. CBS agreed, and in one fell swoop Arnaz and Ball invented reruns, paved the way for syndication, and pulled off what would become one of the most lucrative deals in television history. (Although some TV viewers find reruns annoying, many viewers appreciate the opportunity to re-watch a program they enjoyed or watch one they missed the first time around).

Wayne picked up his script. A few minutes and two cigarettes later, Wayne turned to Elvis. "Well thank the good Lord there was no back door at The Alamo, 'cause if there was, that yellow belly would've been lookin' for it."

Wayne walked around for a few more minutes, pacing, as he smoked the last in the pack. He was supposed to be directing this goddamn job and now one of his men had just walked off the set. His first thought was to call his old mentor, John Ford, for some advice, but he quickly thought better of it, deciding to make do with the cards he was dealt.

"Well, Memphis," said Wayne to Elvis. "That leaves you and me, and since I ain't up for no shootin'," Wayne poked Elvis three time in the chest, "That-leaves-you!"

"Are you up to it? Or are ya gonna get all righteous on me and bellyache like the television man that just run away?"

"Yes Sir," answered Presley, practically standing at upright attention.

"Mr. Wayne, uh, Sir. I never looked for no trouble, but I-I-I never ran ..."

Wayne arched his back and took a good measure of the young man before him. "Well alright then. Let's see if you can shoot that thing. Follow me."

Elvis followed Wayne fifty or so paces west, to where Wayne had set up a row of empty glass Pepsi bottles atop a row of cactus. Then, without warning, a suddenly limber Wayne turned, released his catch, drew and fired fast – one two three – piercing the three center bottles one after the other and smashing them backwards, spraying glass shards and slivers up to thirty feet from the stump. He moved quick for such a big man, and he knew Presley was watching intently behind him.

"You think I could learn to shoot like that Mr. Wayne?! said a wide-eyed, eager Elvis.

"Well I don't see why not!" replied Wayne, handing Elvis a friendly slap on the back.

Wayne walked a few steps away from Elvis and along the length of a long, wooden fence nearby, script in hand, stopping every now and then to repeat a line to himself, gesturing accordingly, and then walking a stretch more before stopping again, repeating his lines over and over. Trying to commit the script to memory. To make it second nature, but he couldn't.

Unbeknownst to Wayne, Elvis was already a pretty good shot. He'd been around guns all his life. He shot rabbits as a child growing up in Tupelo, Mississippi. He honed his firearms skills during his Army service in Germany. He held private target practice at the makeshift firing range he had set up on the grounds at Graceland. (In later years, he used Robert Goulet as target practice whenever he saw his face on his RCA television).

Elvis steadied his cherished German Mauser rifle and peered one eye down the length of its barrel. Then he turned his head over towards Wayne, squinting at him hard.

"You've killed lots of men, haven't you, Sir?" said Elvis in a hushed tone.

"Maybe," answered Wayne quietly, still studying.

"Hundreds I bet," said Elvis boyishly. "Maybe even thousands, huh? I bet they all had it comin' too, right Mr. Wayne."

"I'd say most of 'em did," he answered. "That is, if it was called for in the script."

"Oh, right," said Elvis to himself. "Yeah. I forgot. The script."

"It's funny son," said Wayne. "Sometimes movies make a man do things he don't wanna do. Right or wrong. I ain't sayin it's right. I'm just sayin' it is. Just the nature of the business, I guess."

"But how can you keep on killin' men over and over like that, for years and years, and it don't seem to bother you none."

"I didn't say it don't bother me none."

"Then why do you keep doin' it?"

Wayne put down the script and slowly turned and took a brief, hard look at Elvis. His eyes didn't blink once.

"I'm an actor," Wayne said. "It's my job."

President John F. Kennedy was spending his last night in Washington hosting a White House reception that was divided into three acts. The first, upstairs, was a formal affair. The second act would be afterwards, downstairs, where he could enjoy the other hundreds of White House worker bees who had been his most devoted and talented volunteers from way back long ago, in 1960. *His* hires. It was this second act which he most looked forward to, in addition to the evening's third act, which would hopefully be a private late night screening of *From Russia With Love* or maybe *The Great Escape* before retiring for the evening for a good night's sleep prior departing for Texas in the morning.

No, it would be *From Russia With Love*, he decided. He was sure of it. He had waited for it too long now.[66]

While 'hostess with the mostest' Jacqueline Kennedy detached herself from her husband to exchange light banter and sip a cocktail with the guests, her husband, the Chief Executive of the Free World, circled the room ceremoniously, smiling broadly, but he wasn't himself. He was nervous about going to Texas. It was something in his gut. It all seemed phony to him, like he had been sucked into it. But there were other things on his mind too. There was a call-girl scandal in Great Britain that he knew could be traced to Washington. Maybe even to *him*. Vice-President Johnson and his aides were secretly under investigation. And Bobby, the only person in town he could trust, was leaving to run for the Senate in New York.

Plus, JFK was scared. And rightfully so. His enemies were out to get him. He knew he was a marked man. Of that he was certain. But his '64 re-election was already underway, and Texas would be the first stop, there was no getting out of it now. The train had left the station. He tapped his teeth.

---

[66] The title track for 'From Russia With Love' was sung by Matt Monro.

He scanned the career public employees posturing and pontificating around him.

Many are called, few are chosen. Whether it be law, politics, paperhanging or theatre. Not everyone can be the best.

Kennedy looked around the room again.

Well, maybe a few. Bobby. JFK laughed to himself. Bobby. The ruthless sonofabitch. Heaven and Hell with no in-between. Black and White Bob, no gray area. Should be a movie. 'Atticus Finch Against The Mob - Part II.' Kennedy compared himself to his brother yet again, and again smiled when he decided that 'his' life had a LOT of gray area.

So little brother's running for the Senate. Well, good for him. It's about time he got a real job, JFK half-kidded himself.

The President forced himself to smile as he briefly studied a few more of the milling minions.

Maybe one, two others ...

Although it came out the year before, he hadn't seen *To Kill A Mockingbird* yet, Kennedy was familiar with the book and had always been a fan of Gregory Peck. He thought about *Roman Holiday*, with Audrey Hepburn, which JFK knew had been secretly written by exiled Hollywood Ten member Dalton Trumbo.

My God, Greg Peck is good in everything he's in. He thought about *The Snows of Kilimanjaro*. He thought about Hemingway. He thought about Audrey Hepburn again.

JFK glanced at a few of the staff lawyers, and their wives.

The study of law, my God look at them. Thank God I never went to law school it would have killed my desire to read, my love of it. Not that I get much pleasure reading in, not these days.

One of the white-jacketed White House waiters nodded to the President, motioning to the daiquiri he held as if on a pedestal atop his tray. Kennedy waved it away politely and repaired to a newly upholstered rocking chair under a huge, stately mantel clock.

The employees' star-struck wives swooped in and began to slowly and subtly surround him, one by one. After all, these receptions only came once a year, how often do they get to meet the President? JFK, the suave and charming and charismatic man of a thousand faces, perked up to greet them. *Showtime!* The women were nervous but the reserved Kennedy singlehandedly disarmed them with idle yet charming chat. It was his gift. He remembered minute details about their husbands, their families. About *them*. He was vibrant and aware, an aloof, perceptive aristocrat.

Kennedy. Jack Kennedy.

The President's wife watched him from across the room. She had first met him back in 1951 and they had just celebrated their fifth wedding anniversary. She knew him better than any other woman present, and she knew that these affairs bored him. She knew his mind was elsewhere, millions of miles away, for deep down he was a romantic, she knew, despite all the rest. She watched him lean back in his rocker, pretending to care about the small talk that he appeared so unbelievably interested in. She realized that there was something very serious on his mind. She felt it in her stomach. JFK held his chin under his thumb and forefinger, gazing absently out into and through the crowd. "Texas will be rough," someone said, out of the President's range, or so they thought, for he gave no reply. He had withdrawn into his own private world of thought, and no one else was invited to this party. Just him.

His brother Bobby looked at him from across the room and thought about today's latest death threat. *Or was it a warning?* "He will be assassinated," the message had said. "Tell him not to go to Texas."

Now Bobby, he remembered his older brother telling him early on. You can't worry about every goddamn bastard who hates me. If they get me, Christ, they'd be able to fill Fenway Pahk after they

299

round up the usual suspects. If they're going to get me they're going to get me. It'd just a question of who gets me first. So forget about it.[67]

Why is he so preoccupied, his wife Jackie wondered. She walked over to him and quietly said his name.

"Jack."

For the first time in over a decade she felt him look right through her. *My God, where is he?*

"Jack. Jack," she whispered.

Oh, Jack. Please stay with me, at least for tonight.

He is so deep, she thought.

And he was.

Deep in the heart of Texas.

Kennedy's head turned and he stared out past her and through the crowd at nothing, as his chair gently rocked in time.

---

[67] Fenway Park is home to the World Champion Boston Red Sox.

Wayne insisted that for reasons of team morale and cowboy authenticity that he and Presley should shut down production at Monument Valley and go to Texas a day early, setting up camp just outside the Dallas city limits on the eve of the shoot. Wayne didn't want any last minute traffic holdups or weather conditions dampening his long laid plan. They would stay on the Dallas perimeter and ride on into town in the morning. Nice and easy, just like the revised, sealed, 'For Duke's Eyes Only,' oversized envelope said, which had been delivered earlier that day just-in-time by the Paramount shoeshine boy, courtesy of Mr. Sinatra's personal pilot and plane, the 'El Dago.'

Elvis had been dropped off at camp earlier by the boys, As far as the boys were aware, on this November day, they were just dropping him off on yet another film set for yet another day of shooting.

But come ten o'clock that night Connors was still absent. Thursday, November 21, and Chuck 'The Rifleman' Connors was nowhere to be seen. The Duke knew there was a chance he wouldn't reconsider. That he wouldn't show. But he still held out hope. He knew the job could not be done properly without a crossfire. It could be done, yes, but not properly. Without a second gunman there was a good chance they'd never be able to head 'em off at the overpass.

No need to worry about Memphis, thought Wayne. The kid's as agreeable as an old dog. Too agreeable, almost. Well, at least he's *here*. "Now where in tarnation is that sonofabitch Connors?!"

Wayne found a stump and put the script down and sat. He motioned for Elvis to do the same. He drew a dark, glass bottle from beside the stump and pulled the cork with his teeth. He passed the bottle to Elvis.

"No thank you, Sir," said Elvis. Wayne, already a bit lubricated, frowned and put the booze to his own lips.

"Memphis," asked Wayne. "Son, I've been wonderin' … why don't you ever smile? Yer head's always hangin' like you haven't a friend in the whole world."

"Well, it's this way Mr. Wayne. You see, I've made a study of poor Jimmy Dean, and I've made a study of myself, and I know why girls, and least the young 'uns, go for us. We're sullen, we're broodin', we're something of a menace. I don't understand it exactly, but that's what girls like in men. I don't know much about Hollywood, but I know you can't be sexy if you smile. You can't be a rebel if you grin."

"Number One. That's bullshit. And Number Two," Wayne enunciated, "There-are-no-fe-males-out-here-on-the-range-to-night!" Wayne took a deep breath. "So try and smile a bit now and again. It's better that way."

Elvis grinned. "I knew by heart all the dialogue of Dean's films. I could watch *Rebel Without A Cause* a hundred times over."

Wayne sighed and paused a few seconds, amused. He had heard the kid was a quick study. He changed the subject, to keep the kid fresh.

"So you like girls, do you?"

"Yeah, man, yes, Sir, sure, sure I do," answered Elvis quickly.

"Good," said Wayne. "A boy oughtta let the badger loose now and again. It's healthy. Natural. Way God planned it." He paused to light up another. "And you know somethin', between you and me son, the good Lord loves a good woman." [68]

"I-I-I have a steady girl, now. Her name's Ann," said Elvis.

---

[68] Wayne later loaned Ann-Margret the use of his private plane to go to the Academy Awards in 1971 when she was nominated for *Carnal Knowledge*. The pair starred together two years later in 1973's *The Train Robbers*.

"Well, stick with her son. I hear she's a fine little gal. Talented, too. Gonna be in this business a long time, same as you. Mark my words." Wayne had heard recently that Presley's girlfriend was Ann-Margret, and without even knowing her, he had taken a sort of paternal liking to the girl. Same as he had to Presley.

But I'll say this much, boy, is she ever a looker! When I go, they should have that girl dance on my coffin. If they don't see me in five minutes, they'll know I'm dead for sure.

Wayne thought about Maureen O'Hara, his friend and red-headed co-star in *The Quiet Man*. He wheezed. *What is it about redheads? Boy, they sure have some kinda spark and fire to 'em!* He thought about Fitgerald, the Irish kid. He wheezed again. [69]

Damn these goddamned nails ...

Wayne took a long drag and rested his arm across his knee, looking up at Elvis under an arched brow. "You know, I never asked my country for a goddamn thing but a chance to earn a livin," began Wayne. "And I was lucky, luckier than most 'cause I got that chance. Got a good bit of it, too. Guess I been about as lucky as a cut cat. But things are a little different now, country's gone a little soft. And I'm gonna do my share to see she gets herself straightened out again. My country needs me now, and I ain't about to let her down."

Elvis had no idea where Wayne was going with all this, but it sounded awful good the way he said it.

"Hell. I prob'ly ran up the flag more than most. I admit that. But I never told no one what to do. Never told no one how to live their life. But I will tell you this, there's right and there's wrong, and you gotta do one or the other."

---

[69] John Ford's 1952 romantic-comedy-drama classic *The Quiet Man* takes plae in Innisfree, a town on Ireland's Sligo-Leitrim border. The film was mostly filmed on location in Ireland. Wayne and Maureen O'Hara made five films together between 1948 and 1972. *Rio Grande, The Wings of Eagles, The Quiet Man, McLintock!* and *Big Jake.*

Wayne paused, disgusted, before he continued, "This New Frontier, helpin' people help themselves crap ... where I come from, you best pick yourself up by the bootstraps and carry on. A man oughtta settle his own problems. Take care of his own house first. But now this country's tellin' it's people what to do and how to do it and it's wrong. And I don't like it much. You hear me son, I just plain don't agree with it."

"New Frontier ... what on God's green earth is this country comin' too?"

Elvis gently nodded his head that he understood even though he still had no idea what Wayne was getting at, "Yes, Sir," guessed Elvis. "It's like my mama used to say, she said 'son, you never let nobody push you around."

"That so Memphis?" said Wayne.

"Yes, Sir. Kids used to rib me sometimes 'cause I sang different music and dressed a little different."

"I bet them kids ain't makin' fun of you now," said Wayne, grinning.

"No, Sir" said Elvis, laughing out loud. "They ain't laughing now. No. I'm doin' alright now."

Elvis had a good, strong laugh and Wayne appreciated it.

"Course you are son," said Wayne. "You're on top now. And you deserve it. You earned it."

"Yessir, things is a little different now."

"Yes they are, son," whispered a sentimental Wayne. "Yes they are."

Wayne got up and walked a bit to stretch his legs. He found a spot he liked by some cactus blossoms and lit up again. The moon was bright and the horizon had a sort of reddish hue to it. Wayne liked the way it looked and called Elvis over to see it, "Now look out there yonder" said Wayne as he threw his arm towards the sky. "Ain't that just about the prettiest thing you ever did see?

Now that's what I call 'cin-em-a-tog-raph-y!' Looks like a damn movie scene, don't it son?"

"Like back in the old days, when you was at Republic Pictures?" ventured Elvis. He knew that Republic Pictures was Wayne's frequent employer back in the early days.[70]

Wayne waxed nostalgic, impressed at Elvis' knowledge of the industry. He chose his words carefully. "Republic. I like the sound of the word. Means people can live free. Talk free. Go or come … buy or sell … be drunk or sober. Some words give ya a feeling. Republic is one of those words that … makes me tight in the throat. The same tightness a man gets when his baby takes his first step, and his first baby shaves … makes his first sound like a man. Some words give ya a feeling that can make your heart warm. Republic was one of those words."

Wayne's horse, Liberty, a pace-horse on loan for the shoot from California's Santa Anita racetrack, let out a loud neigh, shaking her head violently. As scheduled, the horse had been unceremoniously driven to Texas by one of Wayne's trusted production company gofers earlier that week. [71]

Wayne turned back over his shoulder to check on the startled animal.

---

[70] The two parted company in the late fifties, however, when Republic failed to back *The Alamo*.

[71] Santa Anita racetrack was partly owned by staunchly anti-Castro Cuban bandleader Desi Arnaz, husband of comedienne Lucille Ball. They divorced in 1960.

"Coyote," said Wayne quietly, pronouncing it 'ky-ote,' and he scanned the night landscape.

Elvis hunched his shoulders.

"Aw, she's a good old gal," said Wayne. "Been with me a long time that old filly. Eighteen years, I'd say. Seen a lot of sundown's, me and her. She's like kin to me. You know, when I first started in pictures I didn't like horses much … guess they kinda grow on ya."

Wayne smiled and looked over at Presley. Elvis was shaking, his eyes darting back and forth like he was scared for his life.

"What in Sam Houston's gotten into you boy?! You look like a cockroach on a candlestick. Son, you alright!?" Wayne thought about asking the kid a question, but decided against it.

"Um, Yes, Sir" said Elvis, twitching his legs back and forth. "I-I-I can't help it none. Every now and then I get a little crazy for a stretch. I've always been nervous, ever since I was a kid. Mama says, said it's 'cause I was born with the nerves of two people."

"Well I'd say there's about four or five in there now" said Wayne. "Son, set yourself down. You sure you don't want a poke?"

Wayne extended the uncorked bottle once again.

"No, Sir. I'm alright Sir."

Wayne walked over to a pile of brush and broke a few twigs and tossed them into the campfire, except one, which he put to the fire and used to light his next cigarette. "Aw, you're prob'ly better off."

He broke another twig. Then another.

"Memphis, your ma sounds like a mighty smart woman son," said Wayne as he stood over the flames. "Hope you're good to her."

"She's uh, gone Sir. She went to heaven a short ways back. When I was in the army."

"That so." Wayne wanted to crawl under his saddlebag right then and there.

Shit. Now, why didn't I goddamn know that ...

"Yes, sir," said Elvis so softly you could hardly hear him.

"I'm sorry to hear that Memphis. You still have your pappy though, right?"

"Yessir. He's at Graceland now. I've got some family there that stays with me some."

"Graceland?" asked Wayne. "What? You live in a hotel or somethin'?"

"No sir. That's my house. It's what I call it."

Wayne broke into a big smile. The kid names his goddamn house. Jesus H. Christ it's a regular 'Pickfair.' ['Pickfair' was the legendary estate of early silent film stars Mary Pickford (an ardent Nixon supporter) and her husband Douglas Fairbanks].

Wayne thought to himself. "You ever meet the king?" he asked.

"Huh, what's that Mr. Wayne?" answered Elvis, thinking he missed part of the conversation already.

"The king," Wayne repeated. "Gable. You ever meet him"

"No, Sir."

"Made a lot of movies with a lot of that man, woman stuff. Talked too much too. Despite the looks of him, He was short on ears and long on mouth. Don't care for that sort of thing much. God gave us two ears and one mouth for a reason. I seen a lot of good men lose themselves by talkin' too much."

Wayne turned to face Elvis directly.

"Want some advice Memphis ... when you got somethin' to say ... say it low, say it slow ... and ..."

"And ..." Elvis quickly added with confidence, "Don't say too goddamn much ..."

Wayne smiled and then it came back to him.

The kid remembered. Well ain't that somethin' ...

"... Yessiree," finished Wayne out of habit. "In this business, you'll last a lot longer that way."

Elvis was so tired and confused his head hurt. "You know Mr. Wayne, sometimes I don't care if I last in this business at all. I like entertaining people. I really miss it. I miss my singing career very much. It's my favorite part of the business. But I see myself losing my musical direction in Hollywood. I mean, they're terrible, those movies I make. I hate most of 'em. Stupid scripts. Dumb-ass songs. Shoot, I just play myself. I just want a good role. One that ain't typecast."

Wayne listened quietly, patiently. He picked up the script and opened it to a page he had turned over.

Elvis continued, "When I was a boy, I always saw myself as a hero in comic books and in movies. I grew up believing this dream ..."

"Now stop right there!!" demanded Wayne.

"If there's one thing I can't stand it's a man who turns his back on the very thing that makes him famous. And if that means you gotta sing and dance in your movies you do it. 'Cause that's what your fans want, and it's up to you to make 'em happy. This business didn't choose you son, You-Chose-It! So don't knock what got you here! Christ Almighty! Doesn't anybody wanna work anymore?! Hell, I been playin' myself for the last thirty-five years. I play John Wayne in every part, regardless of character, and I've been doing okay, haven't

I? Ain't nothin' wrong with that. No Sir. Crissake, just show up on time, hit your marks and remember your goddamn lines!"

"What's gotten into you son," Wayne asked. "You're not studyin' that Method, are you?"

Wayne was extra impatient. He hooked his thumb into his britches. He wanted an answer now.

"No, Sir," said Elvis, weakly.

Wayne was exasperated. "And another thing. Memphis, you call me Sir one more goddamn time and you won't have to worry about pickin' your roles - 'cause you won't be able to get out of your goddamn cot!"

Elvis couldn't keep from smiling now. Wayne had gone way over the top with that one.

After Wayne settled down and seemed to relax a bit, Elvis finally felt like it was his turn to talk a little.

"Mr. Wayne, uh, I mean, Duke ..."

Wayne sucked on his upper lip and tried to calm himself down.

"You think Brando's any good? I mean, as an actor ..."

"Brando?!" Wayne dismissed the word, inhaling deeply. "Goddammit son he's Method. What'd I just tell you 'bout Methods?"

Elvis sunk down in his place, hiding his face behind pulled up knees.

"Brando" spat a disgusted Wayne, improvising. "Christ! You can't understand a goddamn word he says. And you know what else? He's part injun!" Wayne said it like it was the end of the discussion.

"You know that for a fact?" asked Elvis. "That Brando's part Indian. How do you know that?" Elvis was nervous that Wayne would now berate him for portraying a half-breed in his 1960 film *Flaming Star*, a film originally intended for Brando himself.[72]

"Never mind how I know," said Wayne defiantly, gesturing. "I just know. That's how."

"He can't help that," said Elvis, braving the worst, silently defending part of his own, mixed heritage.

"Man can't help the blood he's born with son," said Wayne. "That's true. It's what a man does with that blood once he becomes a man. And he's usin' it to study commie Method. I know that much and that much I know!"

Wayne drew another burning twig up to his cigarette and pulled on it hard. "People like Brando and Clift talk a lot about Method Acting. Preparation. Motivation. Hell, I'd been doing the same damn thing since my first job in pictures. I just don't make a point of explaining it to everyone. I don't brag on it. I don't give it a goddamn name. I just study my lines til I know 'em, say 'em out loud, and get on with it."

Wayne ground what was left of his cigarette into the dirt. He turned his head to Elvis and recited his lines verbatim.

"You're a singer boy," he said. "And you best keep at it. 'Cause if you go on studyin' Method, mark my words son, you may think you're livin', but you won't be. 'Cause even though you'll be walkin' around, it won't feel right, you'll be dead inside … dead as a beaver hat."

Elvis was now seriously afraid. He contemplated Wayne's mighty words. "You're right, Mr. Wayne, uh, Duke. You know, I've had intellectuals tell me that I've got to progress as an actor, explore

---

[72] Originally intended for Marlon Brando, many critics consider 1960's *Flaming Star* one of Elvis' best dramatic performances. The film was directed by Don Siegal, who later directed John Wayne's final film, *The Shootist*.

new horizons, take on new challenges, all that routine. I'd like to progress. But I'm smart enough to realize that you can't bite off more than you can chew in this racket. You can't go beyond your limitations. They want me to try an artistic picture. That's fine. Maybe I can pull it off someday. But not now. I've done thirteen pictures and they've all made money. Most of them. A certain type of audience likes me. I entertain them with what I'm doing. I'd be a fool to tamper with that kind of success."

Wayne was done talking business. He smiled and reached into his saddlebag for a blanket. He grabbed two and tossed one to Elvis. Wayne pulled the blanket over his shoulders and reached down beside him for the whiskey. All this talking had left him dry. Thank God there was still plenty left. He pointed the bottle towards Elvis.

"No, Sir. Thank you Sir, but my mama told me never to touch strong drink. It don't agree with me much."

"Bad stomach?" asked Wayne.

"Yessir," he said, sadly. "It's a family thing."

Elvis thought about his mother, and how he wished she never took a drink either.

"Son," said Wayne. "Your mama told you a lot of things, didn't she?"

"Yes she did Mr. Wayne. My mama was a fine woman."

Wayne fought a tear that was now trying to grow in his eye as he pulled on the neck of the bottle. Then he slumped backwards into his roll bag, punching in the blanket he'd tucked under his head, retiring for the night.

"Night, son," said John Wayne to Elvis Presley. "Now kick some sand on that fire and get yourself some shut eye. You'll be thankin' me come sun up."

"Elvis mumbled, "Yessir. Goodnight Mr. Wayne."

Wayne quickly turned his head around on his makeshift pillow. "I told you son. My name ain't Mr. Wayne. Call me Duke."

"Aw, alright sir. Goodnight Duke." Elvis remembered again that as a boy, he had a dog that his mother named 'Duke,' after her favorite movie star, John Wayne.

Wayne smiled when he heard that. Then he put his head back down, shut his eyes, and thought about the day ahead.

Elvis wanted to sing for Mr. Wayne, maybe sing one of his early recordings, 'Old Shep,' a sad, sad song about a young boy forced to shoot his dying dog. But copyright laws prevented him from doing so without express, written consent.

So, after a few minutes, roused by Wayne's passion and overcome with homespun sentiment, with a shining moon overhead and the amber glow of dying embers at his feet, Elvis put some other words in order in his head and then he slowly, softly, began to sing …

Oh Danny boy,

The pipes, the pipes are calling
From glen to glen, and down the mountain side
The summer's gone, and all the leaves are falling
T'is you, T'is you must go and I must bide …

But come ye back when summer's in the meadow
And when the valley's hushed and white with snow
T'is I'll be there in sunshine or in shadow
Oh Danny boy, oh Danny boy, I love you so …

And when ye come, and all the flow'rs are dying
And I am dead, as dead I well may be
You'll come and find the place where I am lying
And kneel and say an 'Ave' there for me …

And I shall hear, how soft you tread above me
And then my grave shall richer, sweeter be

For you will bend and tell me that you love me ...

And I shall rest in peace until you come to me ...

Wayne had his back to Elvis the whole time he lay listening to the heartfelt ballad. When the song was finished, Wayne's eyes were wet and resting heavy when he said proudly, "That's some mighty fine singin', son. Mighty fine singin'."

As sleep fast descended, Wayne settled on a notion, 'That boy sings one helluva nice 'Danny Boy.'[73]

The sounds that filled the Texas air never sounded better than they did that night.

Out on the moonlit prairie, as Elvis Presley and John Wayne lay sound asleep, a lonesome coyote howled longingly out into the Texas distance.

---

[73] Elvis recorded 'Danny Boy' twice, the first a homemade recording while in Germany in 1959. The second version was recorded in Graceland's 'Jungle Room' in 1976, the year before his death.

In a four-star hotel in Fort Worth, Texas, Chuck Connors sat propped upright against his hotel headboard, his feet crossed at the end of the bed. Stressed and nervous and exhausted, he had put aside the script and was watching his regular Thursday night CBS lineup, *Rawhide* and *Perry Mason* on a small black and white television, as he contemplated his next move.

Should he lay down his arms or go ahead with it? Pick up his gun and finish the job he signed on for or get the hell out of Dallas? It wasn't an easy decision to make. Television had been good to him, but still, Connors thought, 'Duke takes a liking to me, this could be my big break back into movies ...'

Personally, Connors doubted it would amount to much, but a paycheck was a paycheck after all, resentful as he was. To take his mind off things, Connors decided to clean his gun.

After carefully inspecting his firearm, as was his nature, Connors scooped a fistful of his own, homemade grease and lubricant mixture, grabbed hold of his trusty Winchester, and began to gently stroke his beloved weapon. Cleaning his gun was a nightly habit, one that gave Connors a great deal of personal satisfaction when under stress.

A light breeze entered the single window and gently tossed the white translucent drapes.

"Movie stars ..." cursed Connors. "Damn movie stars get all the glory."

He turned on his side and watched as the wind gently blew through the sliding glass door. It was dark and getting late. He wondered what Wayne and Presley were doing. If they were talking about him. He was sure they were.

"Movie stars," he repeated with angst, on the cusp of sleep.

"Damn movie stars …" Connors firmly held the now gleaming rifle close against the pit of his stomach.

Although it wasn't in the script, as a deep and heavy slumber began to fall upon The Rifleman, he began to dream. In his unscripted dream, a vision appeared. A buxom, voluptuous vision scantily dressed in a form-fitting gown made entirely of glittery, flesh-colored sequins. She was young, redheaded (Marilyn's natural hair color), and she was beautiful. She was Marilyn Monroe. Movie star. Method actress. And she was wearing the same dress she wore when she sang *Happy Birthday* to President Kennedy in Madison Square Garden in May of 1962. Three months before her mysterious, untimely death. The dress was holding up pretty good, too.[74]

Norma Jean-Marilyn Monroe
Born Norma Jean Mortensen in a Los Angeles charity ward, then Norma Jean Baker, the orphaned girl would remarkably go on to become Marilyn Monroe, whose luminescent beauty exuded a combination of innocence and sexuality that in photographs and on film was mesmerizing. Even though she was the biggest star in the world and a top rate comedienne, Hollywood continued time and time again to cast her as the 'dumb blonde.' But Marilyn yearned to be taken seriously as an actress, and she worked hard to study her craft, becoming an apt and devoted pupil at Lee Strasberg's 'Method' Acting Studio in New York City.

On that night in Texas, Marilyn appeared to Connors in full Technicolor. And, as was her custom, she was sans bra and panties. Though Connors didn't have a pistol in his pocket, it was plainly obvious that he was glad to see her.

The celluloid goddess cooed deep into the heart and mind of Connors' aroused subconscious, "Big old Chuckie wucky wucky baby waby need a hug?"

---

[74] Marilyn Monroe's dress was so tight when she sang 'Happy Birthday' to JFK she reportedly had to be stitched into it while standing up, sans panties.

As Connors grinned impishly in his sleep, holding his ripened Winchester between his outstretched legs, Marilyn began to sing ...

"Bayonets – in the hand

may   be

Quite Continental

But rifles are a girl's   best   friend

Small handguns – are   just   grand

but they

Won't kill our hero –

Mis-ter Pres-i-dent ...

(doodoo doo doo)

(whispering) ... *you'll be lucky if you make a dent*

.38's are too small!!

But Win-ches-ter's have balls!!

I-just-know   you'll-come-through   in-the-end ... (da dada da da da da)

(now, with feeling)

TO QUIT NOW'S A MIS-TAKE THE WHOLE COUN-TRY'S AAATT STAAKE!!!

(Marilyn gently brushes up against Connors and softly repeats the phrase)

.... Aaaatttt   staaaaaake ...

(Marlyn winked and licks her lips seductively, shaking both her cleavages in Connors face. Connors gulped in his sleep. Then, Marilyn went on to The Big Finish)

Cause Riiiflllleeesss ...

(burlesque-style rat tat tat drumbeat)

Riiiiflllleeesssss ...

(rat tat tat tat)

(Marilyn, in a high-pitched voice)

ARRRRE a girl's best

(climactic drumbeats "bah-bah bah-bah bah-bah bah-ha)

BEST FRIENNND!!!"

The song ended, and the unconscious Connors prematurely expelled his cartridge and sprung backward and to the left across the bed, slamming his head on the imitation oak headboard. In all the excitement he had forgot to fasten the safety. When he looked down into his greasy, dampened lap, he breathed a heavy sigh, and his trouser pony, predictably, had slowed from a gallop to a trot.

"I'll think about it ma'am" moaned the morally compromised Connors, now wide awake fully aware that he had just fired three rounds into the hotel ceiling and was talking to a dead woman.

Connors picked up his Timex watch off the nightstand and looked at it. It was 10:35 PM. *Shoot*, he thought, too weary to get up and change the channel. He was missing the *Sid Caesar Show*, which was already in progress.

So, weary from his premature rapid fire and subsequent recoil, and with his barrel now cleaned for another day, as the hotel television turned to static, The Rifleman and his .44 caliber, modified Winchester lay together, spent.

Connors then shut his eyes and again fell into a deep, deep sleep, while the dreamy Marilyn Monroe, her night not yet over, spiritually flew to San Francisco to once again haunt the florist of Joe DiMaggio. [The lovelorn DiMaggio had a half-dozen red roses delivered to Monroe's crypt three times a week for twenty years].

Richard Nixon was in Dallas and was already awake in his hotel room that morning, having arrived two days prior on Wednesday, November 20, ostensibly for a bottling convention with actress and Pepsi-Cola heiress and President Joan Crawford, and other Pepsi Board Members. The Presidential parade was scheduled to pass directly by the Pepsi convention site at 12:15 CST, and Nixon had intended to watch Kennedy's motorcade pass by, to silently wave and morbidly bid him a final farewell. But to avoid any unnecessary suspicion, to maintain plausible deniability, he decided otherwise, and departed for New York early, on the first available flight from Dallas' Love Field.

The Dallas-Fort Worth newspapers that morning were chock-full of anti-Kennedy headlines … "President's Visit Seen Widening State Democratic Split" … and "Storm of Political Controversy Swirls Around Kennedy's Visit," and "Kennedy To Drop Johnson in '64," to name but a few.

In his Fort-Worth hotel room that morning, President Kennedy cast the papers aside and finished eating his breakfast. Freshly squeezed orange juice to wash down his vitamins and medication, two four-and-a-half-minute boiled eggs, four strips of broiled bacon, toast and coffee. Except today. Today was Friday. On Fridays, per the inexplicable orders of the Catholic Church, the bacon was omitted.

The President picked up the Dallas morning paper again and turned it inside out. After a quick glance, he folded the newspaper, disgusted, and handed it to his aide, telling him to take it out of the room. "I don't want Jackie to see it now," he said.

It was a full-page advertisement headlined "Welcome Mr. Kennedy to Dallas." Surrounding the ad was a quarter-inch black mourning border. The ad listed twelve questions of the President, each slanted toward the ultraconservative and accusing him of, among other things, being praised and endorsed by the U.S. Communist Party as their candidate in 1964. Kennedy poured himself a little fresh coffee.

319

"How can people say such things?" Then he said with obvious disgust, "We're really heading into nut country today."

His wife entered the room and gave him a look.

Kennedy looked at his wife and it was like he could read her mind. He'd seen that look before. A thousand times. "But Jackie," he added, perhaps thoughtlessly, carelessly, answering as if she had indeed spoken out loud, "If somebody wants to shoot me from a window with a rifle, nobody can stop it, so why worry about it ...?"

On the outskirts of town, John Wayne whispered to himself as he lit his second cigarette of the morning amid the cactus blossoms that he and Elvis had stood by the night before.

"Prettiest Texas rose I ever did see," Wayne sighed. The Duke had been up and dressed before dawn, and had already fried three helpings of steak, eggs and bacon for the boys over a new morning fire. Fridays didn't matter much to Wayne.

But there was still no sign of Connors.

"He'll circle his wagons," said Wayne. "He'll be back."

As the morning vittles simmered, Wayne ground some fresh coffee and wondered what was keeping Presley. Wayne had been fore-warned by Nixon and others that the hardest part of the job would be getting Presley up before noon.

"That boy sleeps like a dead man," mused Wayne. "Well, I reckon he's gonna have to eat it crispy," he added. Then, as the high fat, high cholesterol meal still simmered, Wayne went to rouse a disturbingly groggy Presley.

Back at his hotel room, the President was asked by one of his Secret Service agents if he wanted the bubbletop put on the car. Kennedy's aide nodded 'no' - That The President did NOT want it on. "The people come to see the President," Kennedy had told his aide earlier, "Not the Secret Service." The bubbletop wasn't bulletproof, although it would certainly deflect a bullet to some extent. But it would offer some protection in the event of rain, or jeers. But even if it *was* fully bulletproof, Kennedy still would have rejected its use. His mind was made up.

Once stirred and stretched, Elvis dressed quickly. The German Mauser rifle was cleaned and ready, and on his hip he wore his favorite sidearm, a commemorative wooden-handled World War II-era Colt .45, just in case. As costume attire he'd chosen the fire engine red cowboy costume he'd saved from his 1957 Hal Wallis film, *Loving You.*

The finishing touch was a brown cowboy hat and a police badge he had chosen from his vast law enforcement collection, which he pinned onto the lapel of his worn suede jacket.

"Can't act like you're killin' a man, on an empty stomach, son," said Wayne, as he heaped out the mornings vittles. But Elvis didn't feel much like eating, he was nervous as all hell. And besides, he didn't like his bacon crispy, he liked it burnt.

With patriotic sentiment, Wayne had selected the fringed suede jacket and neckerchief he had worn as the ultimate freedom fighter, Davy Crockett, in *The Alamo*. Except without the coonskin cap. Instead, Wayne donned a Stetson. A big, tall, white Stetson. His lucky one. Despite his hard-talking, hard-drinking façade, the irony of the moment was never lost on Wayne. When the mood took him he was as soft as the next guy. On his hips hung a pair of matching .45's with antique ivory grips.

Poring over the day's plan as he ate and drank his morning coffee under a gray Texas sky, Wayne thought a bit about his getaway plan. He knew this moment would come. He was nervous. But he also knew the nervousness was good. When a man's scared it makes him think. So Wayne thought again about the plan. He was concerned about the crowd. On the plaza green, he would be right out there in the open. Once the hit was made he would have to move fast. He pondered again his chances of escaping on horseback. He had no choice, he decided. Traffic would be at a standstill. He just hoped the old girl was up to it.

As Wayne scraped off the morning's tin plates, a few of Elvis' friends pulled up to the campsite in Elvis' 1955 pink Cadillac.

Wayne barked out, "Now what in hell is goin' on here!! I thought we was ridin' into town together. That's how we planned it, ain't it!?"

Elvis never looked so embarrassed in his life. He had grown quite attached to Mr. Wayne in the past few weeks, just as Wayne had become fond of him, but Elvis' father Vernon was worried about Elvis being away from home for so long. With the boys within earshot, Elvis told Wayne that he wanted the boys to drive him straight home after the shoot, even though it wasn't mentioned in the script.

Wayne hung his head and thought for a moment. It had been decided earlier that Elvis would just drop his gun and walk away after the shooting. After all, he had the police badge. Who was going to question him? But after admitting that Elvis had a pretty big following, Wayne decided it probably was a good idea after all for the boys to scoot him out of there. He knew Elvis would have to get out of there fast. Wayne did, nevertheless, question their mode of transportation.

"Now what the hell is that?!" bellowed Wayne in the general direction of the pink Caddy. "Kinda flashy, ain't it boys?"

"Flashy?" said Elvis. "Naw, this ain't flashy. They left the flashy one back home. This here's mama's."

"Mama's what?" asked Wayne.

"Her Cadillac. I got this for mama. Back in '56. After my first hit record."

Wayne let go a big laugh and wished the boy luck, closing Elvis' passenger door before waving him and the boys off. "Remember now son!" Wayne repeated. "Balance it light in your hand, and don't jerk the trigger … squeeeeeeeze. Like I told ya, my weapon's gonna be empty. Not even blanks. I'm just gonna be watchin', you boys … you (Wayne jabbed a finger at Elvis) … are gonna be doin' all the work today."

With the Caddy still within earshot Wayne earnestly added, "And be careful son, 'cause if you go and get yourself hurt, or arrested, your Pappy'd never let me hear the end of it!"

And off Elvis went.

Wayne was confidant Elvis would get the job done. Presley was a good kid and a damn good shot too, "But goddammit! Where the hell was that blond beanpole Connors?! Goddamned if Connors doesn't jack up this whole thing. Prob'ly shacked up in one of them fancy hotels. Damn TV guys don't know nuthin' bout cowboy authenticity. Bout doin' a man's job."

After packing up and clearing out the site, Wayne sat down to finish his third mug of coffee and have a smoke. He went over the script again in his head. It would be a long ride into town, and Wayne had to get there early enough to rest and feed Liberty her oats before the ambush. He packed up his rifle and saddlebag and hooked his toe into the right stirrup. Once mounted, he pulled on his tall Stetson and checked his pouch for his carton of cigarettes. He figured he would need them all that day. Then he felt his hip to make sure his flask was secure. And then, after he bounced both heels off the horse's ribs, John Wayne rode off toward downtown Dallas. The deed was fast approaching, and the day was getting warmer.

Thanks to Marilyn's impromptu visit to the set and ad-libbed dialogue, Connors hadn't given up on the boys. After a light continental breakfast, Connors hailed a cab, and arrived in Dallas at 11 am, one hour before the President's motorcade was scheduled to drive into town. Casually slung over his left shoulder was a canvas satchel that contained his disbanded Winchester 44.

At the plaza, Connors called for the cabbie to pull over.

He walked purposefully towards his assigned building, keeping his steady gaze straight and narrow. Before entering the building he stopped to sign autographs for two men wearing cowboy hats, one of whom held Connors' satchel so as to free up The Rifleman's hands while he signed. Then Connors walked the stairs all the way to the

323

roof. After reaching his sniper's nest he was reminded of his recent television past.

"Here we go again," he mused. "Same old story. Lucas McCain has to come in and take care of everything ..."

Although the President had read the morning's papers, what he hadn't seen that morning were the handbills which spun across the clean sidewalks of Dallas over the past few days. They were not signed, nor was there any printer's signature, and they only featured a solemn view of the President, accompanied by three words, in large type ...

WANTED
FOR
TREASON

It looked like a typical Sheriff's poster in a cowboy western.

Arriving at Love Field in Dallas (from Ft. Worth) aboard Air Force One, JFK chuckled and remembered the John Wayne note he had scribbled when he had laryngitis in California. Kennedy looked at the cowboy hat on the seat next to him that someone had given to him, and he yearned for those easier days before he became President. [75]

... New Frontier. I must be out of my mind ... this job is no great joy to me – fuck it - Lyndon can have the goddamn job ... Christ, he can have it tomorrow ... and Nixon can have it after that ...

There were men with cowboy hats all over Dallas that day. As the crowds gathered to see the motorcade people were heard publicly criticizing Kennedy. People said he was un-American. People said he was soft on communism. But mostly, people said, "Hey, what time's the motorcade gonna pass by? It's almost lunch-time and I'm getting' kinda hungry."

---

[75] Some of John Wayne's 'Big Oil' Texas millionaire friends had fronted production money for *The Alamo* in 1960, after Republic Pictures had backed out of the project.

It was high noon.

The actors waited.

Everything was going according to plan. A two-man crossfire. John Ford would have been proud.

It would be a turkey shoot, and just in time for Thanksgiving.

It was 12:13 pm.

The actors waited some more.

The grassy plaza was the traffic funnel out of downtown Dallas. Three main streets, Elm, Main and Commerce, met in the plaza, carrying the bulk of traffic that headed south, southwest, west and northwest, out of town. Three buildings formed an inverted U at the top of the plaza, and traffic ran downhill for two hundred yards towards a railroad overpass before disappearing beneath it to reach any one of six adjoining speedways.

The final part of the Presidential motorcade was scheduled to come down the middle avenue, Main Street, turn right on Houston Street, and then make a left on Elm Street, in front of the buildings, and go downhill, while the President and Mrs. Kennedy waved to the last few hundred people scattered across the green and grassy knoll to the left and right of the parade route. Once at the underpass, the automobiles would speed up, make a right turn onto a freeway, and head for the event where the President would deliver a speech, less than three miles away.

Amidst the sidewalk crowd there were obvious signs of discontent, "Go Home Yankee" read one, "LBJ in '64" read another. "What About Cuba?" … "Commie" … and "Coca Cola – 5 cents."

The day had become hot and sunny as bystanders lined the Dallas streets. JFK felt the inside pocket of his Brooks Brothers jacket for his favorite pair of tortoise-shell sunglasses. They weren't there.

Dammit, he remembered, I left them in the hotel room, on the dresser. Goddammit!

The motorcade, flanked by several police motorcycle escorts, approached Dealey Plaza. JFK was tanned and smiling, squinting hard, waving to the crowd. Jackie Kennedy, although not usually accustomed to making political trips, was also smiling and waving to the crowd.

She was not tanned.

The lead car turned right onto Houston Street, slowing to a snail's pace in order to make the acute left turn onto Elm.

From behind the wooden picket fence atop the grassy knoll, Elvis watched the motorcade approach. Off in the shadows of the world stage, like some rogue Ed Sullivan show cameraman, waiting to shoot JFK from the waist up.

JFK brushed the hair from his eyes and looked at the sky.

My God, the sky looks just like the ocean. Like The Riviera ...

He squinted hard and thought again about his tortoise-shell, wayfarer-style sunglasses. He hoped he hadn't lost them. He stared toward the knoll off to the right. In the same area, the President thought he saw a man with a movie camera, standing up on a wall.

As JFK started to wave to a little boy up ahead, he glanced to his right and saw the man with a movie camera again. JFK quickly glanced down at his Lord Elgin watch. It was 12:30

He worried about his kids, picturing them.

Shots rang out.

Bang.

They will be okay, he thought. This will be tough on them but they have a good mother. Thank God they have a good mother.

Elvis fired, fumbling his German-made Mauser rifle, caught his suede cuff on the top of the picket fence, and fired, missing everything entirely.

Bang!

A quizzical expression momentarily flashed across Kennedy's face as he glanced in the direction of the gunfire. Kennedy knew that sound. He knew it from the war ... *Uh oh, here it comes* ... He thought he saw the man with a movie camera again to his right. *So this is it. Here we go.* He had imagined this very moment so many times, and now it was here.

Bang!

Seconds later, Elvis recovered, hitting the President in the throat, at the knot of his tie. Kennedy's chest grew warm.

Bang-Bang!

"My God, I'm hit," Kennedy strained to say. He quickly imagined himself in a cowboy western ... *Oh, they got me* ... he pictured himself saying. Then he got hit in the back and felt the wind knocked out of him.

Please, God, please - let's get out of here - Go   go   go ...

Atop one of the buildings, Connors had cocked his modified Winchester and fired, missing the entire Plaza.

Bang-bang-bang!

The Rifleman began fanning his gun almost as good as Michael Landon on *Bonanza*, missing him every time. But the other man in the car looked like he was hit. Connors eyes scanned the crowd and perimeter for armed extras. Whoever they were, wherever they were hiding, they were hitting the wrong man.

Elvis steadied his fire and put a slug into the nose of the blue convertible. Another shot sailed over the car and ricocheted off the front left hoof of Wayne's horse, Liberty.

Startled, Liberty jumped back on her hind legs and bucked, alerting a previously semi-conscious Wayne, who had dozed off after the long journey into town, bloated and groggy from consuming three servings of steak, eggs and bacon earlier that morning.

Immediately cognizant of the fact that his team was failing and that the shoot he had spent months orchestrating was about to be botched well beyond any hope of success, Wayne pulled hard on the old girl's reigns and kicked.

Holding steady, The Duke snarled ruthlessly, showed his yellow, nicotine-stained ivories, and squinted hard as he bit on the backs of his teeth.

"I lied to you, Memphis," he said to himself as he reached into his vest pocket. "I saved three bullets."

And with the horse in full stride, he loaded his rifle, pulled down the brim of his Stetson, and threw the bulk of his heavy frame forward, riding high and hard toward the knoll. And with the hot Dallas sun pounding against his sweat-soaked back, a vehement Wayne bellowed to Presley,

"Fill your hand, you sonofabitch!!!"

It was a line that Wayne, admittedly not much of a method actor, would never forget. The line later became famous in Wayne's only Oscar-winning role in *True Grit*, where he played Rooster Cogburn, the hard-drinking, one-eyed, ruthless U.S. Marshall with the heat of a giant. It was followed by a moderately successful, critically acclaimed but likely titled sequel *Rooster Cogburn*, which gave Wayne the opportunity to work alongside fellow film veteran and

Academy Award winning screen legend Katherine Hepburn, but I digress ...[76]

Atop the building's roof, Chuck 'The Rifleman' Connors luckily found himself out of ammunition. Leaning over the roof's ledge, the spent sniper intently watched the historic scene being played out beneath him. There he was, the legendary John Wayne in all his glory. He couldn't help but grin as Wayne charged the motorcade, still unrecognized by the scores of spectators, who by then had frozen, collectively hushed amid the onslaught of crackling gunfire. At that moment Connors knew what it must be like to be a movie star. Almost.

Despite the heated fury of his charge, Wayne rode ever tall in the saddle, his rifle cocked under his left arm while he fired simultaneously from the two classic, ivory-gripped .45 caliber replicas he wielded with both hands. He was nearly upon the President's car.

Elvis, still blinking in utter disbelief that Wayne had just inferred that his mama was a bitch, thought Wayne was about to kill him. He stood stunned against the fence as Wayne approached at a mighty clip.

Presley's life passed before him. His frightened mind saw baby pictures. Everything seemed in slow motion. He was apoplectic to the point of shock.

Instinctively, Elvis reached for his commemorative Colt .45, took aim at the screen legend, fired, and missed, accidentally hitting Kennedy squarely in the side of the head.

Bang! Bang!

A red mist exploded over the limousine and showered over Mrs. Kennedy and her beautiful pink suit, a Halston original.

---

[76] *True Grit* was produced by Hal Wallis. Katherine Hepburn was also once romantically linked to Howard Hughes.

Kennedy's body pitched forward and up and then down and then back and to the left, pivoting in mid air as he crashed headlong and face first to the car floor, his now raggedy body upside down, his left foot somehow left dangling over the convertible's side door.

'... *a cah (car) that saves the day* ...' JFK said, or thought he said, and then he felt the hot heat.

The President's Lincoln convertible accelerated.

Sure enough, the boys had the car running just feet away. Elvis bolted for the pink Cadillac, slamming the pistol into its holster and tossing the Mauser into the open trunk, before diving through the open passenger window as they stepped heavy on the gas out of the railroad parking lot and away from the scene, leaving behind the total pandemonium that had fast ensued.

Yes. Elvis had left the plaza.

Once out of sight, Elvis reached down behind the seat for a ready made fried peanut butter and banana sandwich on white, blaming his errant shots on a missed breakfast, and bemoaning the fact that he had damaged the front right quarter panel of the beautiful, custom-made Lincoln Continental with suicide doors and hand-stitched leather interior.

"Man, that was a fine car," said Elvis. "Boys, you see that Lincoln, man oh man. Looked like velvet inside, or suede, or leather ... I-I-I ... I think I killed it."

As they pulled out of the lot, Elvis shook his head in apparent disbelief, "All in one take too. Man, Mr. Wayne sure knows his stuff."

Connors, still morally tormented and struggling with the eventual outcome, but much obliged for his own, well-rehearsed misfires, broke down his weapon and dropped it piece by piece down the storm drainpipe before heading down the same stairwell he had ascended earlier. Then, exiting the building through the main lobby, he was passed by some men who rushed by him without asking for an autograph. Connors thought this odd but dismissed it, and walked two blocks before stopping to hail a cab to the airport, praying for his uncertain future, grateful that he had at least been lucky enough in life to fulfill his life dream to play for the Brooklyn Dodgers, and hoping that either a residual check from *The Rifleman*, a new script to read, or both, would be in his mailbox when he got home.

As for John Wayne, he felt he had fulfilled his role as director and succeeded in motivating Presley to shoot the President. And after the shooting he never stopped charging. The Duke stormed across Elm Street just behind the President's car, took the grassy knoll in stride, vaulted the picket fence like an equestrian half his age, crossed the railroad parking lot, and never looked back once, as the old girl carried him steady, sure and true, all the way to the airport, from where he would catch a flight to Mexico for some much needed rest and relaxation.

Que Sera Sera ...

At 1:36:50 PM Eastern Standard Time, the ABC Radio Network was feeding Doris Day's version of 'Hooray For Hollywood' to its affiliated stations across the United States when they interrupted the song to broadcast its first bulletin concerning the assassination.

Nearby, inside the Texas Theatre, a movie house originally built and owned by Howard Hughes, a young man was arrested, after having entered without buying a ticket. The two movies on the Texas Theatre marquee that day were *Cry of Battle* starring Van Heflin, and *War Is Hell* starring Audie Murphy.

Up in Hyannisport, just after being fed his lunch, seventy-five year-old Joseph P. Kennedy, former Hollywood producer-bootlegger-Ambassador and father of the President, speechless, paralyzed on his right side, and severely weakened from his stroke two years earlier, sat and quietly watched a private screening of a new Hollywood film release in his basement home theatre, as was his midday custom. Usually a patient viewer, not even the film's organized-crime plot and Irish backstory could hold Kennedy's interest that day. Halfway through the movie, the elder Kennedy became visibly restless, and he frantically motioned that he wanted the TV to be turned off. He later learned that his eldest surviving son was gone.

> The movie shown to Joe Kennedy at Hyannisport that day was *Kid Galahad* starring Elvis Presley, a story about a young, good, decent, sincere Army veteran who is taken advantage of by his shady, financially desperate employer who is under government pressure.

John Ford's final complete film *Cheyenne Autumn*, had begun production in Monument Valley that day. The film was a departure western for the patriotic director, perhaps to make amends for his less than sensitive portrayal of the American Indian throughout his career. Jimmy Stewart, although he had a cameo appearance in the film, was not on hand that day. On hearing the news of the President's death in Dallas, Ford joined cast and crew in a moment of prayer as a costumed Calvary officer played 'Taps' on his bugle.[77]

Although his story changed over the years, for fear that people may think that he was involved, at the time the events occurred, Richard Nixon had already returned from Dallas and was sitting in a taxicab in traffic in the heart of New York City's Times Square.

Nixon looked at his Timex. He wondered what had happened, if The Duke had got him in time. He wondered if he could make his comeback. If he would be President. If he ...

He looked at his Timex again, and shook it. It had stopped ticking.

When Frank Sinatra first got the news of the events, he was in a cemetery in Burbank, California, on location with Dean and Sammy (and Bing Crosby, but minus Peter Lawford) filming *Robin and the Seven Hoods*, a comedy about prohibition-era Chicago gangsters. There had been scattered laughter only minutes earlier when someone spotted a gravestone inscribed 'Kennedy.' But when the news from Dallas came, Frank walked off among the graves for a few minutes, alone in thought.

Then Sinatra made a phone call.

---

[77] *Cheyenne Autumn* starred Richard Widmark (who co-starred in *The Alamo* with John Wayne), and Dolores Del Rio (who co-starred in *Flaming Star* with Elvis).

As Air Force One, carrying the newly sworn in President of the United States Lyndon Baines Johnson, and JFK's closed casket, taxied the Love Field runway for takeoff to Washington, D.C., a small twin-engine DC-6 bearing a single orange stripe along it's sides and the name 'El Dago' by its door, sat out of sight at the furthest corner of the airport's tarmac. Brigadier General James Stewart, on standby, answered Sinatra's cockpit telephone.

"They get him?" Sinatra asked Stewart, quietly.

Stewart fastened his seatbelt with one hand as he turned his head around to look through the cabin door.

"T-T-Ten-four, Chairman. Ten-four … Mission accomplished. The El Dago is on its way home … Over."

"Atta boy, General …" said Sinatra softly, his voice trailing off, "… atta boy …" Sinatra hung up the phone and breathed a long, hard, well-deserved sigh of relief.

Stewart gave the instrument panel one last once-over …

All systems go.

Stewart called back to his passengers.

"Aw-aw-alright everybody. Prepare for takeoff … and W-W-Welcome aboard, Mr. President …"

Atop a stolen hospital stretcher, under a thick layer of sheets and blankets, a bruised and battered, but no less the worse for wear, former President and now extremely private citizen John F. Kennedy slowly pulled down the covers, carefully propped himself up to sit, and smiled.

Facing Kennedy, standing in formation, saluting him, were Chuck Connors, Elvis Presley and John Wayne.

Kennedy, wearing only a white towel around his waist, stood as straight as possible, and returned their salute.

"Never was one much for stuntmen, myself, Mr. President," said Wayne, handing JFK a damp cloth so he could start wiping off all the pig's blood and ketchup and chocolate syrup and gelatin-covered foam rubber facial prosthetics. "Here, you go."

Wayne hitched up his trousers and arched his back. "I'll say this much, Mr. President, that Hollywood makeup man does one helluva job!"

JFK swept his hand through his mussed hair. "You know, back there, I was, uh, really ... in the moment, wasn't I?" His voice was hoarse from being hit in the throat with a pellet full of pig's blood. He looked at the three actors. "You know, Brando's right, acting is all about, uh, reacting." They all roared. Wayne struck a match off his belt buckle as Elvis offered Kennedy one of his own miniature Cuban cigars. Connors handed a grateful Kennedy the pair of tortoise-shell sunglasses he had left at the hotel.

In the plane's small, galley kitchen, atop a complimentary case of Pepsi and a gift-wrapped, autographed, self-published, 1st edition of the 1951 historical novel *Spartacus* by Howard Fast, was a farewell note for the President, "Enjoy the Riviera, Stay as long as you like! Best Wishes, your colleague, R.N."

Nearby, atop a chair, was Wayne's dog-eared copy of the script. Beneath the chair was a freshly buffed and shined pair of old, size 10-D brown loafers, the left shoe bearing a custom hand-made ¾ inch built-in lift. A small note inside read, 'Cheers, your friend, Fitzy.'

Then Wayne barked out to Stewart up in the cockpit, "All right, Skipper ... let's move 'em out!"

And so, as Sinatra's swinging rendition of 'I Love Paris' came over the El Dago's stereophonic speakers, John Wayne, Elvis Presley,

Chuck Connors, JFK, and Brigadier General James Stewart flew up, up and away and off into the wild, blue yonder, west, to Hollywood ... the land where dreams come true ...

Hooray for Hollywood!!!

[The following day, three certified checks for $250,000 were sent anonymously to The Actors Retirement Home, the Motion Picture Relief Fund, and The Actors Studio. The remaining $250,000 cash was given to JFK, so he would be sure to have, as Sinatra put it, a little 'walkin' around' money).

THE COVER-UP

On the day of Kennedy's funeral, November 24, 1963, Ed Sullivan received a telephone call from England.

It was a promoter named Brian Epstein, who represented a rock and roll band consisting of four young and talented British lads, and suggested that Sullivan consider them for an appearance on his show. Epstein touted the group, only known as 'The Beatles' to Sullivan, as the Number One novelty act of all time, saying they were like 'four Elvis Presleys'. Sullivan had already heard of the group while vacationing in England that Fall, having encountered a Beatle's inspired mob scene firsthand at London's Heathrow Airport.

> The Beatle's second album, **With the Beatles**, was released in the United Kingdom on the exact same day that Kennedy was shot, November 22, 1963.

Immediately, Sullivan realized this was his opportunity to divert national attention from the recent tragedy and take advantage of the country's loss at the same time. He asked Epstein what was the earliest they could come to America, or "across the pond," as Sullivan put it, displaying his facile grasp of the British vernacular.

"Not until February, I'd say," said Epstein. "I've just signed on a new drummer."

"Good," said Sullivan. "February it is."

On February 7, 1964, just three months after the death of President John F. Kennedy, The Beatles landed at New York's newly dedicated JFK Airport and took the country by storm.

Two days later, the four talented lads from Liverpool made their American television debut on The Ed Sullivan Show. Colonel Parker wrote a congratulatory telegram and signed Elvis' name to it. After they sang their big hit, 'I Wanna Hold Your Hand' to 74 million television viewers, half of the population of the United States, Sullivan read Elvis' warm words on the air.

And, for a short while, America was young again.

The rest, as they say, is history.

AFTERWARD

On December 21, 1970, in a closely guarded, secret Oval Office meeting (one of the rare moments when Nixon had remembered to make sure that the tape recorder he had inherited was in the OFF position), Elvis Presley presented President Richard Nixon with a special gift, a commemorative World War II pistol. The weapon, and the famous photo of that meeting, are presently in the custody of the Richard M. Nixon Library, in Yorba Linda, California, and the National Archives in Washington D.C.

As for The Colonel, he continued to live what amounted to be the unenviable, life of a conman, 'a riverboat gambler.' In 1973, he got the idea (from Nixon's televised 1972 China summit) to beam Elvis, via satellite, around the world at the 'Aloha from Hawaii' concert, allowing Elvis to 'tour' the world, without himself or The Colonel ever leaving the United States.

It was perhaps his biggest con of all.

In 1964, Lyndon Johnson's campaign slogan was
"All The Way With LBJ."
The slogan was coined by none other than Colonel Tom Parker.
(In the wake of JFK's demise, LBJ won in a landslide).

POSTSCRIPT

Not so ironically, in 2006, I first met Fitzy in an Irish bar in Boston.

Five foot-eight and maybe one hundred and fifty pounds soaking wet with a cinder block under his arm, Fitzy's aged, yet boyish face was a wonderful combination of Peter O'Toole and Richard Harris, with the eyes of Clint Eastwood, but he most resembled Steve McQueen, had the actor lived longer, all rolled into one. Weathered by chain-smoked, home-rolled tobacco cigarettes ('roll-ups,' he called them), and beer, which Fitzy smirked was, 'the drink of moderation,' Fitzy was an ever-grinning, twinkle in his eye, sharp as a tack, yet dumb like a fox, white-haired warehouse of memories who recalled a simpler yet better time long gone.

As we sat and sipped over many Sunday, and Monday, and oftentimes Wednesday, sometimes Thursday, now and again the odd Friday, the occasional Saturday, but rarely on Tuesday, pints, Fitzy shared with me his memories. And it was through those memories, that I finally found my answer, that I was finally able to pull the pieces together, that I finally learned the answer to the question, *Who Killed JFK*?

Over a few short years and pints and pints, Fitzy shared with me his vast collection of interwoven memories, always a curious mixture of history and entertainment, most of which would always end up, somehow, related to the events of November 22, 1963.

Fitzy, he told me, had first met John Wayne back in Ireland, on the set of John Ford's classic film *The Quiet Man* in 1951, filmed in nearby County Mayo, when Fitzy was eight years old. John Ford and Wayne were looking for extras for the famous fight scene and Wayne had tapped the young boy gently on his then chestnut-red head, saying in his famous slow drawl, "You'll do." (Whether Fitzy can be seen or can't be seen in the film, I don't know for sure. He said his acting debut may have ended up on the editing room floor, or he may have been there in the background but not captured on film. But there was one thing Fitzy was sure of, he *was* there).

Fitzy had emigrated from County Sligo, Ireland to Boston in 1960. Then he went west to Hollywood, California, where he set up his stand in 1960 to become the shoeshine and newspaper boy to the stars. It was in 1960 when Fitzy met John Wayne the second time. Fitzy was then seventeen years old, and he wasn't in Ireland anymore. This time, Fitzy and John Wayne met in Hollywood, California.

During his not-so-brief stint as Hollywood's paperboy shoe-shiner to the stars (from 1960 to 1972, mostly on and around the old Paramount lot), Fitzy also worked as an on-call waiter-bartender for private events. But whatever his task, much of Fitzy's job, while he was buffing and shining shoes and hawking *Variety* and *The Saturday Evening Post* and pouring drinks and waiting tables, was to listen, and that he did. For he had learned very early in life, he often said, that God had given him 'two ears and only one mouth for a reason.' And he often heard more than he wanted to hear as he cleaned John Wayne's cowboy boots (Fitzy repeatedly told me The Duke had exceptionally tiny feet for such a large man), polished Frank Sinatra's jet-black stage wingtips (he said Sinatra called them 'Mary Jane's,' and that Sinatra was the best tipper he ever had, quietly slipping him a thrice-folded twenty dollar bill every time). Fitzy also repeatedly cleaned and repaired the soles and heels of Elvis Presley's size 11-D 's (he reckoned Elvis was very hard on his footwear from all the nervous shuffling and moving around that he did).

Much of what Fitzy heard he knew was better kept secret. So he did what he always did. He quietly went about his business, did his job, and he kept his mouth shut.

But then in 1972, after production work on Paramount Pictures *The Godfather* on was finally complete, and the Elvis-Nixon-White House meeting began to be rumored, and word got out in Tinseltown and beyond that maybe Fitzy knew a little about a lot more than he should, he thought it best to flee Hollywood, taking up residence in the Mid-West under an assumed name for over thirty years. Finally, in

341

2006, he returned to Boston, Massachusetts to, as he often said, "remember my memories," where he lived alone in a small, two-room apartment in a five-story brick building, where he acted as custodian in exchange for his rent and utilities.

Before Fitzy died by my side last year from lung cancer, he entrusted all of his belongings and sentimental treasures to me, most of which he kept in an old travel chest under lock and key (the same one he used when he came to America from Ireland in 1960). Among its contents were autographed photos from John Wayne and Frank Sinatra and Elvis Presley ("to Fitzy, the 'other' King Karate"), various record albums and singles, mostly Sinatra. And an old, oversized, severely worn, wooden shoeshine kit. Inside of which I found a gold tie clasp bearing the words "PT-109," along with a thick, oversized, and tattered (but still sealed) manila envelope. It was the script.

I opened it.

On its yellowed cover page was typed:

HOW HOLLYWOOD KILLED JFK

Written by Albert Maltz, Dalton Trumbo,
and Ian Fleming

November 1963

.

"This is the West, Sir.
When the legend becomes fact, print the legend."
-'The Man Who Shot Liberty Valance,' 1962

FIN [78]

---

[78] French for 'The End.'

About the Author

Joe Burke has been captivated by the characters and subject matter of HOW HOLLYWOOD KILLED JFK for a very, very, very, very, long, long, long, long time. He lives in the Boston area.

SPECIAL THANKS TO

M O'B, JB, RH, KB, BB, JS, FV, LG, Am, MQ, KD, NK, RG, JM, JB, MB, MB, JB & JK, JR, JS, MS, & RF.

17534577R00199

Made in the USA
Lexington, KY
05 October 2012